Praise for the novels of Paula Treick DeBoard

"In Paula Treick DeBoard's latest breathtaking thriller, she paints a stark and chillingly real portrayal of a family torn apart by teenage transgressions. Gritty and inauspicious from the start, *The Drowning Girls* left me awestruck, revealing DeBoard's true brilliance as an author. Spellbinding."

—Mary Kubica, *New York Times* bestselling author of *The Good Girl*

"Think *Fatal Attraction* meets *Desperate Housewives*, and you have DeBoard's latest thriller.... This is a gripping, tense suspense story with a good surprise ending."

—*Booklist*

"Give this tale of domestic suspense, with its pitch-perfect pacing, to Gillian Flynn and Mary Kubica devotees."

—*Library Journal*, starred review

"*The Drowning Girls* by Paula Treick DeBoard is cleverly plotted, full of twists and turns and so well-written that it pulls you in from page one. Genuinely suspenseful, DeBoard delivers a disturbing, multilayered, provocative novel that is impossible to put down."

—Heather Gudenkauf, *New York Times* bestselling author of *The Weight of Silence*

"A heart-pounding look at what lies behind the deceptively placid veneer of the well-to-do suburbs. The kaleidoscopic view of innocence, danger, and malice shifts and twists as it races to a shattering conclusion."

—Sophie Littlefield, bestselling author of *The Guilty One*

"This tale of a family in peril closes with a death that's tragic and unexpected."

—*Publishers Weekly*

"Fans of *The Good Girl* and *The Luckiest Girl Alive*, and really anyone who enjoys great suspense, have found their next must-read... I could not put it down."

—Catherine McKenzie, bestselling author of *Fractured* and *Hidden*

"A coming-of-age tale about a family in crisis expert̶l̶y̶ ̶ ̶ ̶ ̶ ̶ ̶ ̶ ̶ ̶ ̶ ̶ ̶ ̶ Board. *The Fragile World* examines how pr̶ ̶ ̶ ̶ ̶ ̶ ̶ ̶ ̶ ̶ ̶ ̶ ̶ ̶ ̶ ̶ced to come to terms with it. Touching an̶

—Lesley Kagen, *New York Times* ̶ ̶ ̶ ̶ ̶ ̶ ̶ ̶ *he Dark* ̶ ̶ ̶ ̶ *Blessing*

"*The Drowning Girls* casts a spell as̶ ̶ ̶ ̶ ̶ ̶ ̶ ̶ ̶ ̶ the gated community of its setting. Paula Treick DeBoard maps this world of privilege and secrets with a deft hand... A suspenseful and compelling page-turner."

—Karen Brown, author of *The Clairvoyants* and *The Longings of Wayward Girls*

Also by Paula Treick DeBoard

The Drowning Girls
The Fragile World
The Mourning Hours

PAULA TREICK DeBOARD

HERE

WE

LIE

PARK ROW BOOKS

PARK
ROW
BOOKS

Recycling programs
for this product may
not exist in your area.

ISBN-13: 978-0-7783-3026-4

Here We Lie

ParkRowBooks.com
BookClubbish.com

Printed in U.S.A.

For my sisters—the ones I was born with, and the ones I met along the way.

HERE

WE

LIE

OCTOBER 17, 2016

LAUREN

It was raining, and I was going to be late.

The press conference was scheduled for ten o'clock, and by the time I found a parking space in the cavernous garage, I had twenty minutes. I slipped once on the stairs, catching myself with a shocked hand on the sticky rail. Seventeen minutes.

I followed a cameraman toting a giant boom over his shoulder, navigating a path through the crowds of the capitol. Thank goodness I was wearing tennis shoes. I passed a group of schoolchildren on the steps, prim in their navy blazers and white button-down shirts. Their teacher's question echoed off the concrete. "Who can tell me what it means that we have a separation and balance of powers?"

Only one hand shot into the air.

Balance of power, I thought. A good lesson for today.

I glanced at the display on my cell phone and quickened my pace, taking the rest of the steps two at a time. Twelve minutes.

I set my shoulder bag on the conveyer belt at the security checkpoint and watched as a bored guard picked through it with a gloved hand—wallet, cell phone, tube of hand lotion I'd forgotten about, an envelope with twenty-five dollars for the giving tree that should have been turned in to Emma's teacher that morning. *Shit*. Annoyed, the guard removed a water bottle, waving the offending item in front of my face before tossing it into the trash container at his feet. His eyes flicked over me, already disinterested, already moving on to the next threat, which was apparently not a suburban mom in her stretchy pants.

I followed a directional sign for the press conference and hurried down hallways and around corners before arriving outside the door, where another line had formed. A woman at the front, officious in a burgundy blazer, was checking press credentials. My heart pounded. Each time one of the double doors swung open, I caught a glimpse of the people collected there, accompanied by their cameras and cords and laptops and phones.

Then I was at the front of the line, and the woman in the blazer was blocking my entry, shoulder pads increasing her bulk. "Show your credentials, please."

I reached in my purse for my wallet. "I don't have—"

"I can't let anyone in without appropriate credentials," the woman said, more loudly than necessary. She was a head shorter than me, but her voice carried enough authority to make up for it.

"I'm not a member of the press, but I have to get in there," I pleaded. I flipped my wallet open to a picture of my face— my name, address, vital statistics. Behind my Rhode Island license was my old one, a Connecticut ID with my younger face, my maiden name.

She frowned at me, waving two others past, identification badges hanging from their necks. "Ma'am, I have to ask you to step to the side. This conference isn't open to the general public."

I gestured again with my open wallet, pointing desperately to my name. "I'm family," I said finally, catching the attention of those waiting behind me. I could feel their ears perk up, the unsubtle uptick of their interest. *Did she say she was family?*

Finally, this got me her attention, in the form of slow blink and unabashed pity. "Go," she hissed, and I darted past before she could change her mind.

I stayed close to the back wall, trying to find a vantage point but at the same time be invisible. At the front of the room was a podium with a microphone, and off to the side was the Connecticut state flag, its baroque shield visible on a blue background. A woman was at the microphone, saying Megan's name.

And then she was on the stage, instantly recognizable despite the years between us. I gasped, catching the back of a folding chair for balance. She was more polished than I remembered, but then, she used to wear oversize sweatshirts and thrift store jeans, which either fit her waist or her inseam, but never both at once. She had been a teenager then, brash and funny and lovable and so different from me. The person at the microphone, of course, was thirty-five.

Still, I remembered her in our shoebox of a dorm room, drinking from my contraband bottle of schnapps.

I remembered her on our bike rides, the sun so bright on her hair that it looked like her head might, at any moment, burst into flame.

I remembered her that New Year's Eve, wearing a borrowed dress, her feet wedged into my too-tight shoes.

And I remembered her as she'd looked that last night, sitting on the edge of my bed, hugging her arms to her chest.

Her voice now was shaky at first, as if from underuse. "I'm here today to right an old wrong," she began. Camera shutters clicked, and she blinked away the flashes that momentarily blinded her. "I'm here today to tell you what happened to me fourteen years ago, and why, for far too long, I've kept silent."

It was too much all of a sudden, and I bent down, hands on my knees, struggling for breath like a kid beaned in the stomach with a playground ball. Fourteen years. That was a long time to live a lie.

1998–1999

MEGAN

For years, my parents kept the painting I made in kindergarten on our refrigerator, secured by a free magnet from a local insurance company. The painting featured three stick figures so out of proportion they dwarfed the house and the tree in the background, and so tall they almost bumped against the giant yellow orb of the sun. Dad, Mom and me. That was my world, and we were happy. Not that Dad never raised his voice, not that Mom never nitpicked, not that I never misbehaved, not that we ever had any money. But still—happy. We had dinner together most nights, went to a movie once a month and ate out of the same giant tub of buttered popcorn, licking our fingers between handfuls. It was the sort of happiness that was so uncomplicated, I figured it would last forever.

Dad's diagnosis came during my senior year in high school, and it stunned him, immediately, into submission. He seemed determined to live out his days in his recliner in front of TV Land and Nick at Nite, catching up on all the shows he'd missed during years of ten-hour workdays at one job site or another. That was when we still pronounced *mesothelioma* with hesitation, before we grew used to hearing it on television commercials, the symptoms filling the screen in a neat list of bullet points: *chest pain, coughing, shortness of breath, weight loss.* Dad had inhaled tiny asbestos fibers day after day and year after year, and those fibers had become trapped in his lungs like dust in a heating vent. *The poor man's cancer,* he called it sometimes, because mesothelioma affected people who worked construction, who served as merchant marines.

Maybe because we didn't know how to talk about what was happening, what would happen within twelve to eighteen months, according to the specialist in Kansas City, it was easier for Mom and me to join Dad in front of the television in our family room, listening to Sergeant Schultz claim he knew *nothink!* and laughing along as the POWs plotted their elaborate schemes, always a few steps ahead of the enemy. Our world had narrowed to this space with Dad's coughs hanging in the air between us.

Before his diagnosis, Dad had trapped a garter snake in the backyard, and we kept it inside a terrarium filled with sand and rocks and a fake hollowed-out log from the pet store. We named the snake Zeke, and he was more Dad's pet than mine, although once Dad became sick, it was my job to provide for Zeke's general well-being and happiness.

Once a week, I bought a mouse at the pet store on my way home from school and transported it across town in my third-hand Celica, the paper carton on the passenger seat jerking with sudden, frantic motions. At home, I dropped the mouse into the cage, and Dad and I watched until the poor thing was only a tumor-like hump in Zeke's gullet. "Look at him go!" Dad would wheeze in his new, strange voice, with all the solemnity of someone announcing a round of golf.

All I could think was that it was too bad it had to be that way, that something had to die so something else could live.

That was the lesson of biology textbooks and visits to the Kansas City Zoo, but it wasn't so easy to watch it play out in our living room.

In high school, I had been one of the girls who was going somewhere. I'd ignored the boys in my class, sidestepping their advances at parties, letting the nerdy boys take me to prom. I was smart enough, one of the kids who always had the correct answer, even if I wasn't the first to raise my hand. With my curly blondish hair and D-cup breasts, physical traits I'd inherited from my mom, I was pretty enough, too—and this was a near-lethal combination in Woodstock.

No matter what, I'd always promised myself, I wasn't going to get trapped here.

Up until Dad's diagnosis, I'd been planning to start Kansas State in the fall. But that spring and into the summer, I threw away the envelopes unopened—housing information, scholarship notifications. "Maybe next year," Mom would say, her fingernails raking over the knots in my spine. We didn't stop to talk about what that meant or what it would look like when the three-pronged family on the refrigerator was reduced to only two. After graduation, I got a job at the Woodstock Diner, a twenty-four-hour joint off I-70 that catered to truckers and the occasional harried families that spilled out of minivans, everyone passing through on their way to somewhere else. Always, they thought they were funny and clever, that they were better than this town and better than me. But in my black stretchy pants and white button-down, I was different from the Megan Mazeros I'd been before—honor student, soccer halfback, Daddy's girl. Here I was witty and hardened as one of the veterans, old before my time.

"Where's the concert?" one guy or another would invariably ask, making a peace sign or playing a few bars on an air guitar. "Different Woodstock," I said over my shoulder, leading the way to a booth in the corner and presenting him with a sticky, laminated menu. "Although for a quarter, you can start up the jukebox."

Inevitably, the guy grinned. Usually, the grin was accompanied by a tip.

Sometimes Dad was still awake when I came home from work, propped in his recliner. In the near dark of the family room, he wanted to talk in a way he wouldn't during the daytime. "Just sit," he urged. "Stay up with me a bit."

I yawned, my legs tired and my feet aching, but I usually complied.

He always asked about work, and I would tell him about bumping into our old neighbor or receiving a twenty-dollar tip on an eight-dollar order. I didn't mention that the neighbor hadn't made eye contact, or that the twenty dollars had come with a phone number and the name of a local motel scrawled on the back. I didn't tell him that I hated every second of it, the tedium of wiping down the same tables, of watching the minute hand slowly creep around the clock hour after hour. I didn't tell him, as summer turned to fall, how I spent my time wondering what my friends were doing at KSU, how they liked the dorms, how they were doing in their classes.

"Look," he said one night, pointing at the terrarium. Zeke was shedding his old skin, as he did every month or so, emerging new and shiny from a long, cylindrical husk that was so fragile, in a day it would crumble away to nothing. Dad made a funny choking sound, and when I turned, his face was shiny with tears.

"What's wrong?"

"I can't do this," he wheezed.

Zeke must have been something for him to root for, the only thing that was thriving while the rest of us were in a horrible holding pattern, like a slow walk on a treadmill through purgatory. Dad couldn't shed his lungs. He couldn't grow a new pair, pink and shiny and tumor-free. Even if he'd been healthy enough for a transplant, I didn't have an extra pair to give. Every morning as I spooned his breakfast into him, he said, "Well, maybe today's the day, kiddo," as if he were looking forward to it, as if death might arrive on our doorstep carrying balloons and an oversize check, payable immediately.

"Don't be so morbid," I told him, and even though it hurt him to talk, and there was nothing in the world to smile about, he managed his old Dad grin and said, "What morbid? I'm being practical."

I swatted in his direction, and he said in his strange wheezy voice, "You could do all of us a favor. Put a pillow over my face. Done and done."

"Is that supposed to be funny?"

He looked at me for a long time before he shook his head.

Mom and I took care of Dad in shifts, delivering reports to each other like nurses—noting intake and output, commenting on Dad's general well-being and happiness. Mom had been young before all of this, but now her face sagged, puffy sacs hanging beneath her eyes. We didn't even try to tell each other that it would all be okay, that it would work out. Our days were punctuated by the arrival of home health aides in cotton scrubs with cheerful, juvenile patterns—hearts and smiley faces, polka dots and rainbows. Their optimism was insulting. Who did they think they were kidding? Acting cheerful wasn't going to change anything.

One night at the diner that September, I seated Kurt Haschke in a booth by himself, settling him with a menu and a glass of water. We'd gone to school together from kindergarten through our senior year and barely exchanged so much as an *excuse me* when we bumped into each other in the halls. He'd seemed as inoffensive and inconsequential as wallpaper. I asked, "Can I interest you in our dinner specials?" and he smiled at me, his face open and plain.

I thought, *This is what you get, then*.

Kurt came every night that week, waiting in the parking lot for the end of my shift. We kissed there, long and deep, my back to his truck, pinned between his erection and a half-ton of steel. That weekend and every other weekend when Dad was dying, I met Kurt at the ridge overlooking the Sands River and we had sex, sometimes in the bed of his lifted Dodge pickup, sometimes in the back seat of my falling-apart Celica, with a piece of the ceiling fabric dangling over our heads, sometimes on a blanket on the ground, never fully undressed.

Kurt wanted me to be his girlfriend, and I guess in a way, I was. There certainly wasn't anyone else for me—between waiting tables and changing Dad's soiled sheets, I couldn't even consider the possibility. Kurt talked about us going places—not exotic ones, but just far enough away to be interesting—amusement parks and county fairs and festivals dedicated to things I wasn't particularly interested in, cars and trains and beer.

"Mmm," I said, neither a yes or no.

"I want you to meet my parents," Kurt would say each time, practically while he was still zipping up. I had a vague memory of Mr. and Mrs. Haschke from various science fairs and class field trips, and while I always said, sure, eventually, I couldn't imagine myself in their house, at their dinner table, as a part of their lives. It went without saying that Kurt wasn't going to meet my parents, not now, when Mom's face was etched with grief, when Dad was less and less lucid, his breath coming in ragged gasps.

★ ★ ★

Dad made it to Christmas, and we celebrated by putting on brave faces, as if this were any holiday and not our last one together. Mom picked out a spindly tree by herself, and we decorated it with Dad watching from his recliner, *Mannheim Steamroller Christmas* drowning out the sounds of his raspy breathing. He made it to New Year's Eve, which we spent together, Mom drinking too much brandy and passing out on the couch, leaving me to get Dad into his bed.

Dad made it to February, which came with a snowstorm that clogged the roads and kept us homebound for days. He watched through the window as Mom and I took turns shoveling out the driveway, our limbs numb from the cold.

"I can't take this anymore," Dad told me that night, when I'd rolled him on his side to change his sheets, as efficient as a candy striper. "Look what it's doing to you and your mom."

"Don't worry about us," I said. "We want you as long as we can have you."

"Not like this," he said, tears leaking onto his pillow. "You don't want me like this."

Dad made it to March, and by that time, his speech was so distorted by pain, so breathy and thin, that it was hard to understand him at all. He was under hospice care, his pain managed by kindly nurses who talked about timing and dosages and offered gentle reassurances that left us numb. The doctor had told us that in the advanced stages of mesothelioma, Dad's body would be racked with tumors, the cancer spreading to his lymph nodes, the lining of his heart, even his brain. Still, sometimes he rallied for brief moments, as if he were reminding us that he was still alive.

One afternoon, he tried to get my attention when Zeke once again shed his skin, a shiny new body separating from the old. I followed his limp gesture, but this time, I couldn't summon enthusiasm for the process. I couldn't make myself believe in new life and regeneration and second chances. We'd moved the terrarium closer, so Dad could see it from his hospital bed. Still, the effort of raising and lowering his arm had exhausted him, and his breaths were patchy.

"Maybe you should get some sleep now," I suggested, tugging a blanket up to his chest.

His eyes were squeezed shut, blocking out the pain. The syllables came slowly, a breath between each one. "Please... help...me."

"What do you need? More medicine?" That wasn't the exact word for it, since nothing could make him better. *Palliative care*, the nurses had explained, another new word for our horrible vocabulary.

"Megan..." There was a sheen of sweat on his forehead, brought on by the effort of speaking.

One of Dad's pillows had fallen into the crack between the mattress and the plastic headboard, and I lifted his head to adjust the bedding. "Tell me what you need. Are you hot? Or cold? I could bring in another blanket."

His breath came sour against my ear, reeking of rot and medicine and the trickle of chicken broth he'd allowed through his lips. "Do it with the pillow," he breathed. "Please, Megan."

The pillow was in my hands, slippery in its hypoallergenic case that was changed daily in our constant rotation of linens. It would be easy to do—fast, almost painless. "No," I protested, stopping my thoughts. "Dad, come on."

"Please," he whispered. "I can't— You have to—"

Tears dribbled down my cheeks, and I wiped them away with the sleeve of my sweatshirt. "Don't ask me that."

His hand was on mine, the skin papery thin, a hand I didn't

recognize anymore. He was crying, too, his eyes strangely dry, too dehydrated for tears. "Megan…please."

"I can't," I sobbed. But it was all just too much—for him, for Mom, for me. The part of me that could still reason was working through it like a complicated question on an exam. What was the right thing to do, the moral thing? To let him suffer, to let all of us suffer? It was cancer that was immoral; it was this horrible life, this horrible room, this horrible disease that was immoral. The pillow was heavy in my hands, and I considered its weight, its power to change our lives.

"Do it," Dad said. A tear fell from my cheek and landed on his, sliding in a glistening trail to his neck. We held each other's eyes until I placed the pillow ever so gently, over his face.

Afterward, I lifted the entire terrarium off its stand and lugged it through the house, down the back porch steps and across our overgrown yard to the invisible line where our property ended and the neighbor's began. The snow was thawing and patchy brown grass peeked through, a reminder that spring was around the corner. I had to tip the terrarium on its side, and even then, Zeke was slow to grasp what was happening. "Go, go," I urged, nudging my foot against the glass. "This is your chance."

Snot dripped into my mouth, and I smeared it away. Finally, Zeke slithered out, hesitating as if he were waiting for me to reconsider. Then he inched forward and in another minute, he was gone.

Mom's car came around the corner, tires squealing, the gravel in the driveway scattering. For a long moment she stared at me through her dirty windshield. I hadn't been able to make sense on the phone. When I'd opened my mouth, all that came out was a wail.

Inside, I'd draped one of the clean blankets from our laundry rotation over Dad, and beneath it he seemed smaller than he'd been that morning, as if he were already decomposing, the flesh going, only the essential bones of his skeleton holding him together. Without him, no one in the world knew the truth of what I'd done.

A few of my high school friends came to the funeral, and afterward they stood around our kitchen with plastic cups full of red punch. Kurt was there, solemn in a pair of khaki pants and a new shirt straight from its package, boxy with creases. The hospital bed had been removed, and our house seemed larger now, smelling sharply of the Lysol that had been used to chase away the lingering odor of a slow death. My friend Becky Babcock cried on my shoulder for a full ten minutes, and when she was done, she wiped her nose and asked, "Maybe you'll come to KSU this fall?"

"Maybe," I said.

After our family members had cried their tears and hugged their hugs and scattered back to the four corners of the state, I met Kurt one last time out by the river, and he asked me to marry him. He had a ring and everything—a tiny diamond, a thin gold band. For all I knew, he'd had it for months and was just waiting for my dad to die. When I didn't answer right away, he laid out his argument—he'd be finishing his auto tech program in another year, and that gave us time to figure out where we would live. I didn't say anything.

"It doesn't need to be a big wedding," he continued, a desperate note creeping into his voice. "Or it could be big, whatever you want."

I stared at him, wondering how he didn't see that there was no possibility of me marrying him, that now that my dad was gone, I didn't need to be tied here anymore. Until that mo-

ment, it hadn't occurred to me that Kurt wasn't just biding his
time, that I wasn't a substitute for something or someone else.

When I finally told him no—just that single word, that
lone syllable—he'd snapped the velvet case shut, and a moment later he'd slammed the door of his pickup and gunned
the engine, spinning an arc of mud into the air.

A week later, Mom told me about Dad's life insurance
policy—two hundred thousand dollars, which he'd wanted
us to split down the middle. The paperwork had been neatly
arranged in a fat manila folder, pages clipped together, nota-
rized along with Dad's careful signature: *Mitchell E. Mazeros.*

I looked at the date beside his name—January 7, 1998—
and met Mom's eyes. He'd taken out the policy, and then a
month later, he'd visited the doctor about the lingering pain
in his chest, his shortness of breath.

"He must have known a long time ago," Mom said with a
sad shrug. "Or at least he suspected. He never told me about
this—" a gesture indicating the money that would change
everything "—until a few months ago. He asked me not to
tell you until he was gone."

My throat was tight. All that time when Dad had been in
his recliner growing weaker and weaker, he had figured out
a way to take care of us. He'd known, when he asked me to
end it for him, that this gift was waiting.

Mom rocked back in her chair, looking at me. "That's a lot
of money, Megan. It's enough for me to pay off the house. It's
enough for you to go away to college—any college, wherever
you want to go. Doesn't have to be in Kansas."

"But you would be..."

"I'm staying here, in Woodstock."

"I can't leave you," I said. "At least, I could come home
on weekends..."

She lit a cigarette, not meeting my eyes. It was a habit she'd put on hold after Dad's diagnosis, but one she'd picked up again with grim purpose, lighting the next one off the first. I thought about the man she'd been referencing from time to time—Gerry, her boss at the tax office. Gerry who was not dead, was not dying, was very much alive. A puff of smoke trickled out the side of her mouth. "Listen." She patted the back of my hand. "I'll take care of myself. But you're going to have to take care of yourself, too."

That night, I dug in the back of my desk drawer for the admissions brochures I'd collected before Dad's diagnosis, their finishes bright and glossy, offering rose-colored glimpses of college life. Of course, I'd been planning to attend KSU—it was close and convenient, it was where all my friends were going, and between in-state tuition and scholarships, it was affordable, too.

But now, I could go anywhere.

I sorted the brochures into piles—Harvard and Yale and Princeton, places that were out of my reach, thanks to the grades I'd pulled after Dad's diagnosis; Bates and Brown and Bowdoin, schools that seemed too snooty now that I was truly considering them; the Southern California schools that featured tank-top clad students on beaches, where I would be forced to put my pale and flabby body on display; schools that were in big cities, where I might feel like a Midwestern hick; schools that were quirky and artsy, where I would stand out for not being quirky or artsy enough; schools that boasted NCAA rankings, schools that looked too institutional.

At the bottom of my stack was a brochure from Keale College in Scofield, Connecticut, a private, girls-only school. On the front of the brochure, before a backdrop of towering brick, two girls stood with their arms around each other's shoulders in what seemed to be a spontaneous display of happiness and camaraderie. An inset picture showed a scene of ivy-covered buildings and open expanses of green lawn, complete with girls lounging on the grass, girls sitting cross-legged with books thrown open in front of them, girls chatting, laughing, girls with futures I couldn't even imagine.

I ran my thumb down the fine print and found the fees. Tuition, housing and other costs totaled $23,000 annually. Dad's life insurance would buy me four years, free and clear.

"Keale College," I said into the silence of my bedroom, trying out the words.

It was about as far away from Kansas as I could get, which meant it was about as far as I could get from everything—from the whistles of the truckers at the diner, from Kurt Haschke, from the memory of myself standing over Dad's bedside, tears running into my mouth, promising myself that it was the right thing to do, that I shouldn't feel guilty for doing it.

Maybe somewhere else, it would be possible to believe that those lies were true.

LAUREN

If you live in Connecticut, you know my family—or you think you do. You've seen us on the news, in the *Hartford Register*, on campaign posters. We're the all-American family—the dad, the mom, the three kids, the golden retrievers. We have an estate on eleven acres in Connecticut, a townhouse in Washington, DC, and our very own private island off the coast of Maine.

We're the all-American family on steroids.

A brief history:

My mother, Elizabeth Holmes, was born into a family that had made its fortune on steel, although by the time I came along the mines were long sold, and the refineries no longer bore any trace of the family name. Being a Holmes meant property and trust funds and serving on the board of various charities and foundations. She graduated from Vassar with a degree in history that she never intended to use, and later that year at a party in Manhattan, she met Charles Mabrey, who was in his third year of law school at Princeton. The Mabreys didn't have the immense wealth of the Holmeses, but they had their own kind of pedigree; Dad's father, George Mabrey, was a West Point grad, a general in the US Army and an overall badass. His wife and son had followed him around the world—Germany and Cuba and Kuwait and Italy and Germany again—and by the time my dad met my mom, the Mabreys and the Holmeses were like interlocking puzzle pieces. My parents spoke the same language of private tutors and elite schools, of dinners with ambassadors and troubles with housekeeping staff. I figured Dad was a lawyer for about fifteen minutes before Mom started planning his political career, but I might be wrong. She might have sniffed that out from their first dinner party in 1962. With her old money pedigree and his military connections, they were practically a golden ticket.

Sometimes, I wondered if it had all happened exactly the way Mom had planned it—if she'd been able to foresee each move, like our lives were pieces on a giant chessboard. Because planning was needed, and that wasn't Dad's forte—he was best at making one-on-one connections. He could remember every name and face; I used to joke that it took us more than an hour to pass through the dining room at the

Wampanoag Country Club, because Dad had to stop to say hello to each person we passed.

There were certain expectations for the Mabrey kids, too—things that were planned in utero, that were written somewhere in Mom's long-range planner, cousin to her well-worn daily planner. I was the third dark-haired, blue-eyed Mabrey kid, eight years younger than Katherine and six years younger than Michael, who to me were always Kat and MK. There should have been one in between MK and me, another Kennedy-esque boy, another future politician, but that baby was stillborn, the cord wrapped tightly around his neck during delivery. I figured that three was always the goal, and if that baby had lived, there wouldn't have been a need for me.

Sometimes, I wondered if my parents blamed each other for how I turned out, how I didn't fit the Mabrey mold. Maybe they worried about how much time I spent with nannies, since Dad and Mom had both been busy with his career. Maybe they questioned whether they'd sent me to boarding school too young—not every kid could hack it as well as Kat and MK had. Maybe they'd been too indulgent, giving in because it was easier than arguing. Maybe I should have been disciplined more or disciplined less, talked to more like an adult, talked to more like a child.

Maybe I was just the bad seed.

It probably started when I was in kindergarten, at the fancy Brillhart School where I didn't sit the right way, didn't follow directions and sometimes wandered off in the middle of a lesson. I remember my teacher showing me the proper way to sit at my desk—hands at my sides, thighs parallel to the floor beneath me. Everything was like that, it seemed—there was one exact way to do everything, and a million wrong ways that I tried instead.

Kat and MK had been straight-A students. They were the

captains of their teams, honors students and debate winners—
the sort of achievers who could be held up as models to everyone else. At Reardon Preparatory School, where I boarded
from seventh to twelfth grade, there were reminders of Kat
and MK everywhere, in trophies for academic decathlon and
essay-writing and long jump and water polo. My most dis-
tinguishing characteristic was that I was not at the top of my
class; there was a huge pack composed of future doctors and
lawyers and Fortune 500 executives, then a large gap and
then me—Lauren Mabrey, the senator's daughter, content
with her 2.5 average.

"You'll never get anywhere in life like this," Mom had
seethed to me more than once, driving me back to our house
in Simsbury at the end of the school term.

But I knew that wasn't true. For one thing, she was determined to get me there, and where I hadn't succeeded or
hadn't been particularly concerned with succeeding, Mom
was going to be victorious—that I never doubted. She'd gotten me into Reardon, after all, no doubt greasing a few palms
along the way.

I was eleven when Dad became a state senator, and I was
thirteen when a kid at camp passed me my first joint behind the counselor's cabin. The smoke stung my nose, but
I laughed it away. A year later, a girl from Manhattan dem-
onstrated for me on a zucchini how to give the perfect blow
job, which I tried out the first chance I could on a skinny
boy from Syracuse.

By that time, I was used to seeing my dad in the papers—
his graying hair, his dark suits, his demeanor that was serious and affable at once. There was a growing divide between
the picture-perfect Mabreys and me. Dad was instrumental
in passing legislation that regulated the purchase of pseudo-
ephedrine, an ingredient used in methamphetamine produc-

tion, and I once snorted a line of coke in someone's bathroom and danced the rest of the night on top of his kitchen table.

"Our wild child," Mom would say without a hint of affection when she saw my report card, when she chatted with Reardon's dean of students, when she saw me slouching next to Kat and MK.

She didn't mean this as a compliment, but I wore it like a badge of honor.

When I was seventeen, Dad ran for a US Senate seat, a campaign that consumed our lives all summer with photo ops and media blitzes, the Mabrey name plastered on posters and lawn signs and headlines in the *Hartford Register*. Since I was officially too old for another summer away at Camp Watachwa, I was forced to present myself with a smile at family outings and lunches around town. Tired of dragging me along with her, Mom found a volunteer position for me at the Hartford Arts Cooperative, half an hour from our house in Simsbury. The Coop, as it was known, was a politician's dream, bustling with five- to twelve-year-olds who arrived with dirty hands and growling stomachs to produce cheerful portraits of their future lives as pro football players, astronauts, doctors and teachers. Even though I knew my position there was more or less an extension of the campaign, a footnote on the larger résumé of what the Holmes-Mabreys had done for Connecticut, I loved it anyway. Four afternoons a week, I stocked supplies and rinsed brushes and posted artwork on the walls, while as many as thirty kids ran circles around me. By the end of the day I was exhausted and satisfied, convinced that for once I was doing something that actually mattered.

During my first week on the job, I fell hard for Marcus, a sophomore art major at Capitol Community College and one of the few paid staff at The Coop. That summer he was working on a giant mural going up on the south side of the building, where previously there had been only the initials of taggers and a giant F YOU in five-foot letters. Marcus had a broad chest and ropy arm muscles, and his fingers were permanently paint stained with a crusty layer of blues and yellows and greens. The first time he touched me, brushing a piece of hair out of my face as I stood over the sink washing brushes, I felt a thrumming all the way to my toes. The next night he stood behind me at the sink, his thumbs pressing into the knots of my shoulders as the water ran from blue-purple to clear. When I turned off the faucet, he wrapped his arms around me in a giant backward bear hug, rocking me from side to side in a goofy, loose way, as if to tell me I shouldn't take it or him too seriously.

Another girl might have left it at that, but not Lauren Mabrey. Marcus was the exact opposite of everything that had been planned for me from day one. He had never known his father, had three half siblings, lived off student loans and a stipend from The Coop. He didn't own any button-down shirts, and he hadn't recognized my father until I pointed out a campaign advertisement with the five Mabreys all lined up, Dad's arm around Mom's shoulders. "That's cool," Marcus had said. "So your family is famous or something?"

I laughed, not denying this, although *famous* was the wrong word. *Powerful* was more accurate. *Influential*.

At any rate, I knew Marcus was the exact wrong pick for me, but when the bear hug ended, I turned around, pressed my wet hands to his T-shirt and kissed him full on the lips.

Twenty minutes later, I'd lost the rest of my virginity on the sagging couch in the break room, and soon enough sex became an everyday thing, part of our closing ritual after the paint caps were tightened and the brushes laid out to dry. Marcus locked the outside door and flipped off the light switches, and we undressed each other in the semidarkness, laughing at our more adult version of blind man's bluff. Afterward, staring up at the bulbous tubes of exposed piping near the ceiling, I felt for the first time that I could have been anyone in the world, not Lauren Mabrey, not part of a political family, not a prep school kid, not wealthy.

I was just happy.

Marcus always had a baggie of pot in one pocket or another, and sometimes we went up to the roof of The Coop to smoke, the sky darkening in lazy purple drifts, and listened to the sounds of the city: horns and sirens and barks and scraps of conversation that floated upward from street level. That summer, more and more, I was flirting with disaster, arriving home long after The Coop closed, sometimes after my parents had returned from one fund-raiser or another, picking a fight with them the moment I walked through the door. I was lazy, I was irresponsible, I had a bad attitude and I didn't care.

I'd smoked here and there at Reardon, whenever one of my classmates went home for vacation and connected with a local hookup, returning with a few buds. The most I could handle was a hit or two before I felt sleepy and weak-kneed, but I didn't want Marcus to see that I was a lightweight. When he passed me the joint, I always took my turn.

"I can get you more, if you ever need any," Marcus said into my ear, a sweet trail of smoke wafting past my nose.

I laughed. "Pretty sure my parents bought into the whole Just Say No thing." My words came out slurry—*sure* as *soor*, *bought* as *brought*.

"I mean like a side business, for when you go back to school. I bet those Reardon kids have deep pockets."

I shifted, leaning back against his chest, hoping he would drop the idea if I didn't offer encouragement. This time when he passed me the joint, I only pretended to inhale. My body felt heavy, and I still had the drive back to Holmes House.

"Or bennies or 'shrooms. Whatever you want, I could probably get it."

"What are you, my dealer?"

He pinched out the end of the joint and dropped it in a plastic baggie, which he returned to his pocket. "Hey, some of us have rent to pay, you know."

I'd been to a pharm party last January at Reardon, where everyone was required to contribute a few tablets filched from their parents' medicine cabinets to enter, and then got to take from the bowl whatever they wanted to try. I'd added three muscle relaxers, my dad's drug of choice for his occasional back spasms, and fished out two pastel pink pills for myself. On a beanbag in the corner, I'd waited for the pills to do something, to make me feel anything, but it never happened. The only thrill had been from the idea of getting busted, of my parents driving up from Hartford, the blue veins in their foreheads pulsing with rage as they helped me pack my suitcases and then led me in disgrace from the dorm. But nothing so exciting happened. A staff member came in, took one look at the pill potpourri and unceremoniously flushed the remains down the toilet, before ordering us back to our rooms.

This fall, if everything in the campaign went as planned, I would be *Lauren, the senator's daughter*. It gave me a perverse thrill that I might also—or instead—be known as *Lauren, the girl with the pot*. I stood up, brushing my palms on my jeans, trying to sound casual, like this was the sort of deal I negotiated every day. "Maybe," I said. "Let's see what you've got."

A week later, at the beginning of my shift, he showed me a quart-sized baggie fat with green clumps of pot, then shoved it deep into the zippered interior pocket of my backpack. "It's good stuff," he said. "Two hundred should do it."

My stomach turned, a weird, queasy flip-flop. I'd pictured myself at a party this fall, casually producing enough to roll a joint. I couldn't possibly hide this much at Holmes House, where Mom would sniff it out with her razor-sharp sense for whatever I was doing wrong. I thought about telling Marcus that I'd made a mistake, that I couldn't do it—but that would mean losing whatever reputation I had with him. It would mean, most likely, losing him. Maybe I could ditch it somewhere on my way out of Hartford, make some homeless person's day when he found it in a Dumpster.

"I know you're good for it," Marcus said, giving me a quick kiss on the cheek, and I said, "Course I am."

That afternoon, I was replenishing paint palettes from giant tubs of tempera when the police officer came in, a radio crackling at his hip, a drug-sniffing German shepherd at his side. It was like watching an after-school special, some cautionary tale about what happened when a good girl met a bad boy from the wrong side of the tracks. I watched as the officer and my supervisor chatted with their heads bent close together before they disappeared into the break room. Later, the rumor would be that someone had smelled marijuana and called the police. More likely my supervisor had been watching Marcus and me all along.

A minute later, she reappeared in the doorway of the break room, scanning the studio until her gaze settled on me, frozen in place, a blob of yellow paint running down my arm.

It was one thing to flirt with disaster, to tiptoe up to the edge of the canyon and peek over the side. It was another thing entirely to jump.

I said, *That's my backpack, but I don't know what that stuff is.*

I said, *Someone must have put that there.*

I said, *I need to make a phone call.*

A lawyer met me at the police station, demanding that I

be released immediately. Marcus, it turned out, had a previous misdemeanor; he was cuffed and led away, and he passed me without making eye contact.

I never knew what my parents did, what strings they pulled or how they'd known to pull them in the first place. That night, I was cited for a misdemeanor and released, and my name never made it into the papers. At home, Dad paced while Mom did the talking, her voice losing its customary coolness. Did I understand the damage I had caused? Did I know what something like this might do to Dad's career, to his reputation, to our family? Was I aware of his stance on drugs, the hypocrisy of his daughter being involved with a drug dealer, being found with an amount that constituted a felony? And just what did I have to say for myself?

I asked what would happen to Marcus, whether he would have to spend the night in jail.

"Wake up!" Mom hissed. "What do you think will happen to him?"

A few weeks later Mom wrote a check, I pled to a lesser charge and my record was sealed. My only punishment was the type of community service that would eventually work its way onto my résumé.

More pot had been found at Marcus's loft, a place I'd tried to imagine over the six weeks we'd been together, when I'd fantasized about the two of us in an actual bed, on an actual mattress, with actual sheets. For bringing drugs into a place whose official mission was to serve children, Marcus was charged with a felony. That fall, I served a Mabrey-imposed house arrest, only leaving my bedroom on Tuesdays and Thursdays when Mom brought me to a local senior center to serve out my sentence.

One day that October, she slapped the *Hartford Register* in front of me, open to an article about an inmate that had been killed in a brawl. He was identified as Marcus Rodriguez, twenty, of Hartford, awaiting trial for felony drug sales. The article didn't mention that he'd been a student at Capitol Community College, that he'd coordinated the new mural at the Hartford Arts Cooperative, that he'd had a kind smile, that he liked to talk after sex, that his girlfriend had sold him out.

In November, Dad won the senate race by a landslide.

I spent most of that fall on my childhood bed in Holmes House, shifting from hysterical to catatonic like they were the only settings that had been programmed into me. Marcus was dead, and I was going to come out unscathed. Marcus was dead, and his death was directly related to me, set in motion by the kiss I'd given him that night at the slop sink, my hands soapy with water, as if a line could be drawn between the two, a simple dot to dot.

Mom had spread the word that I was suffering from a bad case of mono, and from time to time get-well cards arrived from my classmates at Reardon. I completed my coursework that semester through independent study, moving zombie-like through worksheets and take-home tests.

Once Mom found me on my bed, sobbing into a pillow. "What now?" she asked, as if I'd done some new horrible thing.

I wiped away my tears, but my voice came out weak and blubbery. "He was so young."

Mom leaned close, and for a moment I thought she might do something to comfort me, like pat me on the shoulder or tell me it would be okay. Instead, she slapped me across the face. "You will snap out of this," she ordered. "You'll get on with your life and we will never speak of this again, do you understand?"

She was true to her word; if Kat or MK knew anything

about what I'd done, they never mentioned it me. Dad had already leased an apartment in Washington; after the election, that became his permanent residence, his stays at Holmes House brief and rare. Up until then, Dad had been a buffer between Mom and me, a mild-mannered negotiator. Now that he was gone, the silence stretched between us, too large to be breeched with a phone call.

Once I wandered downstairs while Mom was hosting a meeting for the local branch of the League of Women Voters, pausing in the hallway as the women chatted and sipped tea from china that had been in the Holmes family for a hundred years. Hildy, our live-in domestic help, passed me with the tea service rattling faintly on a silver tray.

"How *is* poor Lauren?" one of the women asked, and I started, hearing my name.

Mom didn't miss a beat. "We were so worried about her, but she's been growing stronger every day. This virus just hit her hard, poor thing."

I leaned against the wall, listening to the women's sympathetic murmurs as Mom reinvented my troubles—fevers and listlessness, loss of appetite, how devastated I'd been not to participate in more of the campaigning. "Lauren's a strong girl, though," Mom said. "She'll be back to her old self in no time."

It was an amazing performance, award-worthy. Somehow, Mom had managed to erase the drugs in my backpack, the hours I'd spent in the police station, Marcus bleeding to death in the Hartford Correctional Center, the months I'd spent crying into my pillow. She'd reinvented me as a brave warrior, a dutiful daughter.

She was so convincing, I almost believed it myself.

OCTOBER 10, 2016

MEGAN

The alarm on my cell phone went off at 6:25, then again at 6:30 and, as a last call, at 6:35. Marimba—the world's most hateful sound. Bobby's side of the bed was empty, and when I entered the kitchen five minutes later, he was already draining his first cup of coffee and filling his thermos with the thirty-two ounces that would get him through the day.

I stood in the doorway, yawning.

"Well, if it isn't the woman of my dreams," Bobby said, grinning at my disheveled state. I was wearing one of his old UMass shirts, the decaying hem hanging to my knees.

I pulled a face. "Save any for me?"

Bobby gestured to a steaming cup on the end of the kitchen peninsula. The coffee was the exact murky shade of brown I liked, tempered with a bit of cream. He was dressed in everything but his shoes and his pants, which were draped over a bar stool, and I gave him a thumbs-up at the effect: a blue-and-white striped shirt, a tie with the tiny floating heads of the Beatles, plaid boxers, tan dress socks. Bobby was one of the cool teachers. Every high school had one—the teacher who donned the giant tiger mascot for pep rallies, who somehow managed to make class so interesting that his students forgot all about their smartphones for fifty minutes. If he had to, he would stand on his desk to get their attention, à la *Dead Poets Society* or challenge a student to a lunchtime dance-off as a form of motivational bribery. Once, I accused him of having literally no shame, and he seemed surprised by the idea. Why in the world should he have shame?

I took a few fast sips, willing the caffeine to head directly to my brain. "What's on the agenda for today?"

He screwed the lid on his thermos, tightening it and holding it upside down, just to make sure, before setting it next to his briefcase. "Still slogging through the American Revolution."

"At least you're finally done with those Puritans," I commented.

"Those prudes." He grinned, giving me a slap on my decidedly round ass. I looked more and more like my mother each year, despite eating salads for lunch and pounding out the miles on a treadmill at Planet Fitness.

The movement sent my coffee sloshing, and I cupped my hands around the rim to stop it from spilling. "It's far too early to be so frisky."

"No such thing as too early." Bobby was stepping into his pants, creased sharp from ironing the night before. "What's your day like?"

I grimaced. "Meetings from eight-thirty to noon, drop-ins after that."

"Do we have any plans for tonight? Because if we don't—" he tucked and zipped and reached for his belt "—a few of my buddies are playing at this bar in Ballardville."

I shrugged. "Okay."

Bobby worked his feet into his shoes, bending to tie the

laces. "They aren't very good, or at least they weren't the last time I heard them."

I smiled. "I'll adjust my expectations accordingly." Bobby was the exact opposite of me—he made friends easily and collected them everywhere he went: work, fast-pitch softball, hockey games. Two minutes after leaving a party, Bobby's phone would *ping* with the notification of a friend request from someone he'd just met. Me—I kept things cooler, played my hand close to my chest. For the most part, other than those times I snooped from Bobby's account, I avoided social media altogether, and my work friends were just that—friends at work.

I met Bobby's goodbye kiss head-on, cringing at my own blend of sleep and coffee breath. Bobby didn't seem to mind.

He grabbed his thermos and laptop bag, patted around for his wallet and keys. "Maybe we can leave around seven?"

"Sounds good."

I emptied the rest of the coffee from the pot, swirled it with cream and sugar and reached for the remote. These were my private moments each morning—coffee, the *Boston Globe* and whatever dishy gossip was happening on the *Today* show. At work, I would be slammed—first our weekly departmental meeting, with its twenty-bullet-point agenda, then the dozens of students I would see, some in two-minute bursts while I helped them find the right form or directed them to the right staff member, and others for long, tear-streaked discussions that began with a question about registering for fall classes and ended with a general unburdening about the difficulties of balancing work and school, the impossibilities of child care, the unreliableness of their transportation.

I flipped from NBC to MSNBC to CNN, dodging commercials. Like the rest of America, I was on election overload, but it was an itch I couldn't resist scratching. What had happened overnight? Who had said what on Twitter? Bobby and I rarely talked politics—not because we weren't interested in elections or invested in their outcome, but because there were sticking points, touchy subjects that led us from reason to argument in about sixty seconds flat. "I thought people from the Midwest were supposed to be conservative," Bobby would tease.

"That's a stereotype," I would remind him, and besides, it was a long time since I'd been in the Midwest.

I heard news of a suicide bombing at a market in Pakistan, then the financial report. The Dow was up, and that was a good thing. Thirty-five years old and I still had only a basic grasp of the stock market, although for the first time in my life, I actually had money there, in the form of a direct transfer from my monthly paycheck. I stretched and stood, making my way back to the sink. Behind me the news had switched back to the national scene, to politics. That's when I heard the name *Mabrey* and wheeled around. It was as if I could face him head-on, as if he were in the room with me, that slow grin on his face. My head went fuzzy with the white noise of memory—rushing and pulsing, things that were long buried threatening to rise to the surface.

The caption on the screen read Senatorial Sex Scandal.

I didn't even know that I'd dropped the mug until I heard it shatter, the last inch of lukewarm coffee splattering on the tile and a small shard of ceramic nicking me in the shin.

And just like that, it all came back.

FRESHMAN YEAR
1999–2000

MEGAN

From the window seat on the bus, America was a blur of fields and forests, the brick fronts of small-town buildings, the jutting skylines of cities. Every bit of it was unfamiliar and terrifying. *Maybe this was a mistake.* Maybe Woodstock, Kansas, was my destiny, and I was only fighting it by heading all the way to the East Coast with my worldly possessions crammed into two army-green duffel bags and my old JanSport backpack. Maybe Woodstock was what I deserved after everything I'd done.

Enough. I tried to sleep, but besides the occasional jolting was the fear that I might close my eyes and wake up in Canada or Texas, or all alone. Each time the bus stopped, I hooked my backpack over my shoulder and lined up for the exit, then rushed to the bathroom and back, afraid to be left behind. Once a man about my dad's age tried to chat with me, but outside the bounds of Woodstock and the diner, I seemed to have forgotten how to have a polite conversation. Did I look like a typical college student or an overgrown runaway?

"I'm not going to kill you, you know," he huffed, and when I slid back into my seat, my cheeks were flaming.

We were delayed fifty miles outside of Wilkes-Barre, Pennsylvania, with an overheating engine, and it took a few hours for a replacement bus and luggage transfer, then for new tickets to be issued. It didn't occur to me until we were on the road again that I would be arriving at the bus station in Scofield much later than originally planned. Keale's shuttle system ran on the half hour, but it stopped each night at nine. Using my wristwatch and the illuminated road signs, I calculated the distance and realized I was officially screwed. The bus wouldn't be arriving until ten at the earliest. In the beam from the overhead light, I consulted the map supplied by a travel agent at AAA and learned that the Scofield station was five miles from campus—an impossible distance to walk with my bulging duffel bags.

Three hours later, I pressed my forehead to the glass when I saw signs for Scofield. *You live here now*, I told myself— something that seemed both impossible and incredibly surreal, as if I were trying to convince myself that I'd grown a third foot. Two miles south of town, the bus rumbled past a good-sized lake, the surface shimmering with boats and Jet Skis docked for the night. Everything felt sleepy, winding down from too much summer. I squinted out the window at the license plates on the Audis and Peugeots, trying to determine if they belonged to locals or vacationers.

Either way, I thought, *wealth* lives here. *Privilege*. People different from me.

The main drag was settling down for the night—lights off at most of the stores. Everything had a cutesy name—*To Dye For* and *Slice of Heaven* and *Scoops & Swirls*, which had a giant ice cream cone protruding from its striped awning. A few families were still clustered around sidewalk tables, wearing flip-flops and suntans, catching the drips on their ice cream cones.

There were four passengers left aboard the bus, and only two of us—myself and a man with a pronounced limp—stood to disembark at the Scofield station. The porter handed down our luggage, and the other man left immediately with his pull-along bag, dragging his bad leg behind him, aiming for the lone car in the parking lot.

I stood with the duffel bags that contained everything I owned in the world, my gaze following the porter's gesture to the pay phone at the end of the platform.

"Maybe you can call a taxi, if you don't have someone meeting you," he said, although his voice was hesitant, rising in a question. We hadn't passed any taxis in town.

"I'll be fine," I said, not wanting to concede helplessness already. As the bus pulled away, I hauled my bags one at a time up to the platform, plopping them beneath the closed ticket window. Fishing a few quarters from my wallet, I set out to investigate the payphone. If there was no taxi service in Scofield, I'd try the college. And if no one answered there, what would I do? I could call Mom back in Kansas, where she and Gerry Tallant were probably sitting down to dinner, thrilled that I was out of the picture and that they had the place to themselves. It was a horrible idea, one that belonged to my life as a teenager, not an independent college student. How could my mom help from fifteen hundred miles away?

Twenty yards out, I saw that the payphone was broken, its coiled metal cord dangling without a receiver.

Well, shit.

The night had quickly descended into late-summer darkness, the air humid and thick with insects that dive-bombed my face. I circled the station, weighing my options. In Woodstock, I would have hailed a passing car, because I was likely to know the person who stopped—someone whose kids I'd gone to school with, someone who had worked with Dad or managed a booth at the fair with Mom.

The phrase *You're not in Kansas anymore* burned in my brain. Hah, a bad joke.

An older-model Honda passed on the road, tailpipe rattling. I wondered if the driver had seen me, or if I should have tried to flag down the car. Too late now.

Suddenly, the urge to pee, which I'd been battling since we crossed into Connecticut, became insistent. With the bus station closed, my only option appeared to be a secluded space behind a commercial-sized trash container. I heard the Honda's clunky tailpipe again while I was zipping up and cursed myself. Someone could be rooting through my bags right now, making off with my clothes and books and my beloved afghan with the red, white and blue Chevron stripes, not to mention my wallet and driver's license and the painting I'd taken off the refrigerator, the oversize stick figures of Dad and Mom and me. I zipped and broke into a run.

A man in jeans and a black T-shirt was leaning against the Honda, smoking a cigarette and not looking in my direction, as if he'd been there forever and his being there was in no way connected with me. I stopped next to the platform, catching my breath. It startled me when he spoke, as if he might be addressing a third, unseen person.

"You know, any one of the local creeps could have come by and made off with your stuff."

"Are you one of the local creeps?" I asked.

He dropped his cigarette, grinding it beneath the toe of a scuffed Doc Marten. "I am *the* local creep."

I laughed despite myself.

"Actually, the city of Scofield has hired me to enforce its public urination laws, which is a common problem with our—" he hesitated, looking at me pointedly "—vagrant population."

Conscious of my unwashed hands, I jammed them into the pockets of my jeans. "Guilty," I confessed, blushing bright red.

He grinned. "So. Not from around here?"

I shook my head. "Kansas."

"That's what I thought. Well, not Kansas, specifically, but I knew you were from somewhere in the Midwest."

"I have that Midwest look about me, do I?"

He gave me an appreciative up-and-down glance, taking in the greasy blond hair I'd pulled into a ponytail, the teeth I hadn't brushed since that morning, somewhere in Ohio. I was wearing a baggy T-shirt—I always wore baggy T-shirts—but I felt his gaze linger for a moment on my chest. "Yep. Corn-fed goodness," he said.

I looked past him, out toward the road, trying to figure out what came next.

He cleared his throat. "Isn't there anything you want to ask me?"

"Like what? Your name?"

He dipped at the waist in a mock bow. "Joseph P. Natolo, at your service. Actually—I thought you might need a ride."

"Well, yeah. I'm a—"

"A student at Keale," he finished. "That's not exactly rocket science. Come on, let me load you up." He grabbed one of my duffel bags, mock wincing at its weight. "What did you do, pack your library?"

I hesitated, watching him cram the bag into his trunk, already cluttered with loose shoes and clothes and fast food bags spotty with grease. "Do you work at the college?"

He took the other bag from my grasp, his hand brushing mine. "Would you believe I teach cultural anthropology?"

"No," I said.

He laughed. "Good for you, Midwest. Being gullible is never a good thing. No, I'm just Scofield's one-man welcoming committee."

The trunk was so full, he had to lean his weight against it before we heard the telltale click. He looked at me. "Well? Come on."

Joe's car smelled faintly of pot, although an evergreen air freshener dangled from the rearview mirror. I belted myself in, heart hammering beneath my rib cage to warn me this was not my brightest idea. Outside my window, the scenery was a dark blur of open meadows divided by wooded areas, dense with trees. I rested my fingers on the door handle, planning an emergency exit—stop, drop and roll.

Joe glanced at my hand. "Seriously, I'm not a psycho. I was driving by and I spotted you there, and I figured you needed some help."

I gave him a weak smile. "Thanks."

He pointed at a rectangular green sign that appeared in front of us and receded in the side mirror: Keale College, 3 Miles. "See? We're heading in the right direction."

"I wasn't worried."

The corners of his eyes crinkled as he laughed. "Could have fooled me. So let me ask you this. What's so horrible about men, anyway?"

I half turned in my seat. "When did I say men were horrible?"

Joe rolled his eyes. "Please. You come all the way from Timbuktu or wherever just to go to a school where there are no men, except the odd janitor or history professor. What's that all about?"

"It's not about hating men," I said, my mind searching for

one of the phrases from Keale's brochures. "It's about empowering women."

Joe shook his head. "Why would anyone want to deprive themselves of this?" He raised a hand from the steering wheel and made a circle in the air, meant to encompass the two of us.

I snuck a sideways glance, trying to determine Joe's age. At least as old as me, maybe a few years older. Still, there was a confidence to him—the way he'd tossed my bags into his trunk without getting my explicit permission, his easy, flirtatious jokes. He seemed decades more sophisticated than the boys (men, really, although they didn't seem to have earned the title) I'd known in Woodstock. I cleared my throat. "So, do you go to school around here, too?"

He shrugged. "It's been a few years now."

It wasn't clear if he was referring to high school or college. "Here in Scofield?" I pressed.

"Sure. You're looking at a proud graduate of Scofield-Winton High School, class of 1995. Well, I was proud to graduate. I'm not sure the powers that be at SWHS are thrilled to claim me. But beyond that—no. I'm not what you'd call scholar material."

He didn't seem embarrassed to tell me this, but I was embarrassed that I'd asked. Without taking a single college class, I was already a snob. Joe's car slowed, and I spotted twin brick walls, formed like parentheses around either side of a wide entryway. Giant steel letters spelling *Keale College* rose out of a manicured lawn. "The school was established in 1880," Joe boomed suddenly, adopting the inflections of a tour guide. "If you look straight ahead, you'll see the place that has been home for more than a hundred years to privileged girls from Connecticut, the larger New England area and, apparently—" this was said pointedly to me, with a raised eyebrow "—regions beyond."

"Ha ha," I said.

We passed acres of gently rolling lawn before coming to the buildings themselves—towering brick structures bathed in golden lights. Footpaths crisscrossed the campus, cutting around and between buildings. Joe stopped to let a girl pass with her rolling suitcase and then cleared his throat, preparing to launch into the next stage of our tour. "Keale was founded by prominent members of the Episcopalian Church, presumably as a way to keep young ladies away from the horrors of intermingling with the opposite sex. I hear that the school isn't particularly religious today, although they have maintained a fine tradition of refusing young eligible bachelors entry into the sacred dormitories of said young women."

"Really?"

"Really," Joe said, dropping the tour-guide impression. "And believe me, I've tried. Men aren't allowed to step foot in the dorms unless they're family. So up here we have the Commons—that's the dining hall. Classroom buildings, the science center, fine arts auditorium, a gym complete with indoor track and racquetball courts…"

I followed his gestures, trying to take it all in. Keale looked like its own small town, separate and distinct from Scofield, operating on its own purpose and pace. I knew from the brochures that there were just under two thousand students at Keale, but only a few were visible that night, including a girl lying on a blanket, looking up at the stars, and a trio running past in gym shorts and tennis shoes, ponytails swinging, their steps perfectly synchronized.

"What's your dorm?" Joe asked.

"Stanton." I'd read the housing form so many times that I'd memorized the details by heart. Stanton Hall, room 323 South. Roommate, Ariana Kramer.

Joe circled a row of buildings and pulled into a parking

lot that was mostly empty. He nodded his head in the direction of a brick monolith, patches of ivy creeping up its sides. "That's it, then."

I unbuckled my seat belt and it zipped back to its holster. "Thanks for the ride. I really appreciate it."

"Hold on," he said, shifting the car into Park. He popped the trunk and met me there, hoisting both of my bags over his shoulders with an exaggerated groan.

"I can at least carry one," I protested.

"You ordered the deluxe service, right? This is the deluxe service." He staggered next to me like a pack mule. At the door to Stanton, he set the bags on the ground and held out a hand, palm up. "So. Five dollars."

"Oh." I blinked and felt around in my pocket.

He laughed, shaking his head. "Just kidding. The first ride is free. Maybe someday we'll run into each other in town and you'll buy me a cup of coffee or something."

"Absolutely."

He turned, waving over his shoulder.

"Hey," I called. "You ended up not being a creep after all."

He put a hand to his heart. "I'm flattered, Midwest. A bit disappointed in myself, but flattered."

I'd only managed to drag one bag inside the dorm when I heard his car start, followed by the rattle of his tailpipe, which grew fainter and fainter until it became part of the night.

Five minutes later, I'd retrieved a key from the resident advisor on duty and wrestled my bags into the elevator and down a long hall, past dozens of closed doors. My roommate hadn't checked in yet, and two neatly arranged sets of furniture greeted me—beds, dressers and desks, industrial and plain. I was too exhausted to change clothes or find my bedding, so I collapsed onto one of the bare mattresses still wearing my tennis shoes.

You did it, I thought, grinning in the dark. *You made it. You're here.*

For the first time in hours, I thought about my dad. I didn't know if I believed in angels that could look down from heaven or karma or anything beyond this very moment. But right then, I thought he would be happy for me.

LAUREN

The summer after I graduated from Reardon, I spent ten lazy weeks on The Island, our five acres in the Atlantic, not far from Yarmouth. The land had been in the Holmes family for generations, passed down to Mom as the last standard-bearer of the name. With nothing expected of me, I slept in until eleven, dozed in the hammock in the afternoons, avoided my mother except at mealtimes, and took late-night smoke breaks with MK in the old gazebo, perched on the east cliff of The Island.

"I wish I could just disappear," I told MK, staring out at the water, the cigarette turning to ash in my hand.

He narrowed his eyes, giving me a faux push, as if it might send me not only toppling over the edge of the gazebo but out to the Atlantic itself, to the blue-green forever that waited beyond the rocky edge of The Island.

"Very funny," I told him.

He stubbed out his cigarette and flicked the butt, which bounced on the railing and disappeared into the vegetation below. There were thousands of cigarette butts there by now, the accumulation of our idle summers. "Poor kid, condemned to a life of luxury."

I tapped off an inch of ash, watching it crumble before it hit the ground. "Easy for you to say. You're doing what you want to do."

MK shrugged. He was starting law school at Princeton in the fall, following in Dad's footsteps. The only difference was that he didn't seem to mind that his life had been planned out for him, the way I did. "Well, what do you want to do?"

I shrugged.

"There must be *some*thing you're half-good at," he said, knocking his shoulder into mine in a way that suggested he was joking.

"Nope."

He was quiet for a minute, as if he were trying to dredge up some hidden skill I didn't know I possessed. Eventually, he said, "You used to draw people's faces all the time. Remember? It made Mom furious. Instead of taking notes in class, you would basically just doodle."

I laughed. "I could be a professional doodler."

"Artist, dummy." He patted me on the shoulder. "Don't worry. You'll get the lingo down."

Except I knew that the little faces I drew really weren't more than doodles, and certainly not the sign of artistic talent. I'd taken a drawing class at Reardon, and the instructor had been less than enthusiastic about my work. The proportions were all wrong, she said—the necks too skinny, the shoulders too broad. At The Coop, I'd watched Marcus capture the essence of a person with a few brushstrokes, not needing to pencil in first or leave room for erasure. I might have liked doodling, but it clearly wasn't a skill that was going to get me anywhere.

Every day on The Island, I'd read the classifieds in the

Boston Globe, scanning for options: education, engineering, medicine, social work—anything to get me away from the predicted Mabrey track. I didn't even meet the qualifications to be a night clerk at the 7-Eleven, which required previous cashier experience. I'd entertained briefly the idea of the Peace Corps—a lifestyle that would have suited me for about five seconds—but there was a surprisingly long list of requirements, none of which I met. It turned out no one was looking for a spoiled eighteen-year-old with an unimpressive GPA.

Finally, I gave in.

It was easier to accept that I was nothing more than a cog in a machine that had been set in motion long before I was born.

Keale College in northwest Connecticut was the perfect choice from my mother's viewpoint—far enough away that we wouldn't bump into each other, but close enough to keep me under her thumb. Since it was an all-girls school, she must have figured I was less likely to become romantically involved with the resident pot dealer. She filled out my application, requested housing, registered me for classes and signed my name to everything: *Lauren E. Mabrey*. It amazed me to think of the strings she must have pulled to get me into Keale with my dismal grades and my spotty list of extracurricular activities. Had she begged administrators, promised to endow a scholarship or fund a new wing at the library? Or had the Mabrey name—as in Charles Mabrey, freshman senator from the great state of Connecticut and already something of a dynamo on Capitol Hill—done all the talking?

Mom drove me to campus at the end of August, the trunk of her Mercedes stuffed with the accoutrements for my dorm room: a new duvet, two sets of Egyptian cotton sheets, down pillows, thick blankets in zippered plastic bags. We were silent for most of the trip, the two hours stretching painfully between us. Mom's face was stony behind her Jackie-O getup, the dark glasses and headscarf she wore whenever she was at the wheel of her car, as if to announce that she was *some*one, even if she wasn't instantly recognizable. In the passenger seat, I closed my eyes against a pulsing headache and waited for the inevitable lecture, the Mabrey rite of passage, delivered on momentous occasions, like when I'd first gone away to summer camp, and every fall when I left for Reardon. Since my disaster at The Coop, her warnings were no longer vague but specific, centered on staying away from "certain kinds of people" and promising to yank me out of school if she caught so much as a whiff of pot. She wouldn't have believed me if I told her I'd sworn off all that, that I wasn't planning to get into any kind of trouble she would need to rescue me from, that I'd learned my lesson.

It wasn't until we were in Scofield itself, just a few miles from Keale, that Mom cleared her throat. I waited, steeling myself.

"Your father and I disagree on certain things," she began. "He's willing to give you more chances, Lauren. He's willing to excuse what you've done, saying you're young and you're still learning. He thinks we might have made some mistakes ourselves, taken our eye off the ball." Her eyes were dark shadows behind her lenses. "But not me. I don't agree with him, not for a second."

I looked from her face with its slightly raised jaw to her white-knuckled hands on the wheel, a two-carat diamond winking in the sunlight.

"As far as I can tell, we've given you plenty of opportunities, and you've squandered all of them. You've had chance after chance to do anything, one single thing, to make us proud. But even when you were under our noses, you were involved in unspeakable things—"

Speak them, I thought, like a dare. *Say his name, the one we promised never to say.*

"—and we had to scramble to cover for you, in the midst of all the stress of the campaign. But I won't do that again. I'm ready to cut you loose. The first time you get in any kind of trouble at Keale, I'm going to say, 'Too bad, so sad,' and let you figure it out on your own. What happens if you burn through all the money in your bank account? Too bad! What if you get caught for drinking and doing drugs because you haven't learned your lesson? So sad! I'll tell the officer to let you sit in jail until you figure it out on your own."

I closed my eyes, as if I could ward off her words. I wondered if she really believed them, or if she had already come to accept that Dad's career would always be paramount, the mountain that would bury all our sins.

"Can you at least nod to let me know you understand?"

"Mom," I said, "I'm not going to—"

She waved a hand, like she was swatting away a fly. "Or you could choose to see this as a fresh start, a chance to fall in line. And if you do that, of course, there will be rewards. There are benefits to being in a family like ours."

The laugh escaped my mouth before I could stop it. If MK had been here, we would have quoted lines from *The Godfather* to each other and talked about family with a capital *F*.

Mom's voice was icy. "You'll make your bed, Lauren, and you'll lie in it. And maybe then you'll see what it's like to be cut off from all of this."

We were heading out of Scofield by this time, in stop-and-go traffic on the tiny main street. I made eye contact with a little girl on the sidewalk holding a balloon in her chubby fist. *Don't let go*, I thought.

"Lauren!" Mom snapped. "Are you listening to me?"

Behind us a car honked, and Mom pressed on the gas. The

Mercedes jerked forward, only to come to a halting stop again a few feet later. I focused on what was outside the car—the hair salons and antique stores, a building with a giant tacky ice cream cone pointing toward the sky.

I already hated Scofield.

By the time we arrived on campus, Mom was back in loving mom/senator's wife mode, schmoozing with the other incoming freshmen and their parents, shaking hands and commiserating about "our babies going off to school," like she hadn't rushed to ship me off to Reardon each fall and to sleepaway camp each summer. A few Keale upperclassmen were on hand to help lug things from the parking lot to the elevator bank, and Mom asked them polite questions about their hometowns and majors. "Oh, let me help you," she said, holding the elevator for a harried-looking woman carrying a giant plastic bed in a bag. And then she held out her hand, introducing herself in her full, hyphenated glory.

"Elizabeth Holmes-Mabrey," one of the upperclassmen repeated as we stepped out of the elevator. "Isn't that—" The question was cut off by the doors closing, and by the time I caught up with her, Mom was already halfway down the hall, pushing open the door of room 207.

There were already two women in the room, wrestling with the corners of a fitted sheet. From the doorway, it was difficult to determine which was my roommate and which was her mother—they were both tall and slim in jeans and saltwater sandals, blond hair spilling to the middle of their backs.

I dropped my bags on the other twin bed and said, "Hi, I'm Lauren."

One of the women stepped forward, holding out a hand with a perfect French manicure. Up close she was clearly the younger of the two, wearing only slightly less makeup than her mother. "I'm Erin."

"Oh, goodness," Erin's mom gushed, clasping her hands together nervously. "I know who you are. I voted for your husband in the last election. Carole Nicholson."

Mom beamed. "Oh, that's wonderful. It's so nice to meet you, Carole."

The four of us bustled around each other, unpacking boxes and trying to navigate a space designed for two. Then Carole Nicholson let out a squeal and clapped her hands. "Oh, look, you two have the same sheets! Those are from Garnet Hill, aren't they? The flannel ones?"

Mom looked back and forth between Erin and me, as if we'd pulled off a noteworthy accomplishment. "Well, this couldn't have worked out better."

"We're practically twins," I said drily.

When Mom stepped around me to begin organizing my toiletries, the heel of her sandal ground into my instep as a warning.

That night Erin chattered away in her bed about her boyfriend back home and how amazing it was to meet all these other girls, and my thoughts drifted to Marcus, who had been dead for almost a year. If he had lived, we would have broken up at the end of that summer and gone on to the rest of our lives. If he'd lived, he would have finished the mural and gone on to other projects, other dreams. Instead, I was here, and I had no dreams at all.

Erin's questions interrupted my thoughts. "Were you a good student in high school? Did you have straight A's and everything?"

"I did okay."

She laughed. "I bet you're just being modest, and you were like class valedictorian or something."

"I wasn't a valedictorian," I assured her. It occurred to me that the Keale girls had probably all been at the tops of their classes, the sort of motivated girls who took seven classes a semester, played two sports and one musical instrument and spoke conversational French. Basically, they were just younger versions of my sister, Kat.

"Don't you think it's exciting?" Erin gushed, and I realized that I had no idea what she was asking, or what was supposed to be so exciting.

"I guess," I said. From her silence, I knew it was the wrong answer.

"Maybe it's not so exciting for someone like you," Erin said, and she snapped out the light.

The day before the semester was scheduled to begin, I made an appointment with the registrar. Mom had scheduled me for five general education classes, and there wasn't a single one that interested me.

"My parents are concerned about my class load," I told Dr. Hansen, who had a severe white bob and owlish eyes behind her oversize frames. I leaned close to her desk, keeping my voice conspiratorial. "I was hospitalized for stress last fall."

Dr. Hansen raised an untrimmed eyebrow, frowning at her computer screen. "There was no mention of a hospitalization due to stress," she murmured, tapping keys.

"No, there wouldn't be. My parents were trying to protect me, I think. They probably said it was mono or something."

"Ah," Dr. Hansen said, nodding. "Well, of course it's best for you to talk with your academic advisor, but—"

"Oh, I'll absolutely do that. But for now, with classes starting tomorrow..."

Dr. Hansen said, "Right. Well, let me pull up your schedule and see what we can do."

After a bit of searching and waiting for the appropriate screens to load, she agreed that with my medical history, it might be best to drop Biology for now, and switch my math class for Introduction to the Arts. Half an hour later, I left her office feeling decidedly better about life.

Intro to the Arts was taught by a team of professors, each quirkier than the last: a visual artist, a theater director and a musician. The goal was to spend five weeks studying in each discipline and finish the semester with a portfolio of critical and creative work. I completed a shaky landscape sketch and a self-portrait that looked more like the face of a distant cousin before attending a presentation on basic photography skills. *Fill the frame. Align by the rule of thirds. Look for symmetry.* I watched pictures flash by on the giant screen at the front of the room, subjects so close that I could see the crackly texture of leaves, the blood vessels in a woman's eyes. Afterward, on a whim, I wandered up to the front of the lecture hall where Dr. Mittel was packing up his equipment.

"Hi, I'm Lauren. I'm in this lecture," I began.

"Dr. Mittel," he said, his lower lip almost lost in an enormous beard. "But I imagine you know that."

I looked down at the table, where a binder was open to a page of detailed notes. I wasn't used to chatting with instructors eye-to-eye; I had never been the kind of student who was distinguished for academics, admirable work ethic or even, for that matter, decent attendance. "I was just wondering. You mentioned there was a darkroom on campus."

"Ah," he said. "Are you a photographer?"

"No. I mean—I'm interested, though."

He gave me a quick glance before closing the binder and zipping up his bag. "Do you have a camera?"

"Not a very good one," I acknowledged. Most summers, when I'd gone off to camp, Mom had sent me along with a cheap point-and-click camera and several rolls of film with the understanding that neither might survive the summer. Somewhere, in my jumble of unpacked belongings, I had a 35mm Kodak.

"Tell you what," Dr. Mittel said. "Why don't you shoot a roll or two and bring it by my office? I'd be happy to develop your film and look at it with you."

"Is there something…" I hesitated, afraid the question would be stupid. Knowing it was. "I mean, in terms of a subject, is there something I should focus on?"

Dr. Mittel's smile was kind, and behind it I read a sort of mitigated pity. *Poor little rich girl, trying hard for that A.* "Shoot what speaks to you," he said. "People, scenery, whatever."

That weekend, I rode the shuttle into town and bartered with the owner of an electronics repair store over a forty-year-old Leica, all but draining my bank account.

Erin whistled later, finding the receipt I'd placed on my desk. "You spent nine *hundred* dollars on that thing?"

"The owner said it was the best," I told her. The camera and its accessories were spread out on the bed, and I was figuring out the lenses and attachments from the store owner's scribbled notes. The Leica came with a somewhat battered case that I instantly loved, thinking of all the places it must have gone with its previous owner.

"But this is just for one assignment, right?" she asked. I could see her mind clicking like a cash register. She would tell her friends, all the other Keale girls who were just like her, and I would be an anecdote to their stories, an inside joke. The girl who tried to buy her way to an A.

"For now, but I might take a photography class next semester," I said, the idea just occurring to me.

Erin frowned. "Isn't everything supposed to be switching to digital?"

I raised the camera to my eye, locating Erin's perfect, pouty face in the viewfinder. She raised a hand in protest, and I snapped a picture, relishing the smart click of the shutter, the dark curtain spilling over the lens.

"Lauren! I don't even have my hair done."

"Relax," I said. "It's not loaded."

I spent the next week shooting rolls of film all over campus, looking for interesting angles and tricks of light. I lugged my camera bag to the chapel to shoot the sunrise streaming through stained glass, and onto the roof of Stanton Hall at sunset to catch the last wink of sun as it disappeared over a row of elms, the branches backlit. I stopped some girls on the way to class, and photographed them with their arms around each other's shoulders. "Is this for the yearbook?" one of them wanted to know, and I told her it just might be. What I liked most was the feeling of authority that came with the camera hanging from my neck, and the way I could instantly disappear when I looked through the viewfinder.

Dr. Mittel developed two rolls for me and we met in his office to look at the contact sheet through his loupe, a cylindrical magnifying lens that he kept on his desk. He passed over the smiling girls in their stiff poses, the sunrises and sunsets. "This is good for a first attempt," he said finally. "You're looking for all the right things—angles, lighting. And you must have a good lens on that camera of yours."

I told him about the Leica, my splurge, and he frowned,

either at the expense or at the thought of some no-talent hack having access to such nice equipment.

"I assume you're serious about this, then," he said, passing me the contact sheet. "The best thing for you, I think, would be to take a class this spring. I teach an intro course—very hands-on, lots of time in the darkroom, some developing techniques—"

"I'll look into it," I said, my heart hammering. Suddenly it was imperative that I take that class.

"As far as your portfolio is concerned, I think you probably already have a few prints here you could work with. But we've got some time, and you could certainly keep going. I feel like you've shot the things you think I wanted you to shoot—maybe the things you thought you should shoot. I'd like to see what you're interested in. What does Lauren find fascinating?"

Over the next two weeks, I shot a half dozen rolls of film, trying to let Dr. Mittel's words sink in. What did I find fascinating? I shot the empty girls' bathroom, with its rows of gleaming sinks, the jumble of shoes in the bottom of my closet, the third floor of the library, the shadows of the shelves creeping across the carpet. I shot tree branches and leaves, a lone red-breasted bird perched on a fence. *Shoot what you want to shoot, not what you want me to see.*

And then one morning, I looked over at Erin, sleeping, lovely Erin, who was just like all the girls I'd ever known. She had a boyfriend at Boston University, and during her nightly chatter, I learned that she had planned their lives down to the most specific detail—engagement after their junior year, the wedding after graduation, kids two years apart. During the daytime, she looked too calculated, too poised, her face hidden behind foundation and powder, blush and mascara, the pinkish lipstick she reapplied even when it was only the two of us and her grand plans for the evening included sending an email to her boyfriend.

But at that moment, with the sunlight filtered through our Venetian blinds, creating light and dark panes on her face, she was a different Erin entirely. Pale wisps of hair covered one cheek, and her mouth was slightly, sweetly slack, with the tiniest bulge of fat beneath her chin. Beneath her pale yellow pajama top, the hard knot of one nipple was visible.

Before I knew what I was doing, I was freeing my camera from its safe spot at the top of my closet. I snapped one picture, and then, moving closer, another. In this moment, Erin was lovely in a way she'd never been before—relaxed, vulnerable. A small red blemish on her chin was visible; her lashes were pale and fragile against her eye socket. I knelt next to the bed, snapping away, entranced.

"What are you doing?" she murmured, drawing a hand over her face.

"Sorry. Just checking something on my camera," I said, letting it hang loose from the strap around my neck. "I was going to head out to take some pictures…"

"It's so early," she moaned, rolling over, pulling her Garnet Hill sheets and the matching comforter into a heap over her head.

I was aware that it was creepy, that photographing a person without her knowledge was crossing a definite line. But I'd captured something good in that fleeting minute, which made me understand something else: none of the pictures I'd taken before—the landscapes and sunsets and reflections off buildings, the stained glass in the chapel—were any good. These ones were.

By this point, after a few weeks of tailing Dr. Mittel, I'd picked up the basics in the darkroom and he usually let me operate more or less on my own, only popping in occasionally to look at my negatives. It was a thrill to see Erin's face appear during the developing process, the sunlight catching the fine strands of hair, the wet corner of her mouth. I stared at her face in the stop bath, warmth spreading through my body. I'd created this. No—that wasn't quite right. It was simply there, but I was the one who found it. Afterward, I held my breath while I waited for Dr. Mittel's regular verbal cues—the *harrumph* and *hmmm*, the tapping of his finger against an image. Instead, he was silent.

Maybe they weren't good, I thought. Maybe they were horrible. Maybe I didn't have an eye for this kind of thing at all. Maybe, like the faces I used to draw in the margins of my notebooks, photography was something that couldn't be taught beyond the technical processes.

"What're these?" he asked finally.

"My roommate," I said, wiping my suddenly sweaty hands against my jeans.

He nodded. "Tell me about them."

My words came out in a rush, stumbling over each other. I told him about seeing the sun on her face, how it was like I'd never seen her before until she was framed in the viewfinder.

"They're good," he said. "Obviously, there are some techniques you need to learn, some tricks of lighting and shadow, and then there's a whole host of printing options…"

I waited, leaning back against the counter.

"But there's something here, Lauren. Something raw and intimate. You let the camera speak. It's almost like a lover's gaze, seeing everything."

"She doesn't know—" I stammered, my gaze flickering to the outline of Erin's nipple, which somehow looked innocent and obscene at the same time. "She was asleep."

He frowned. "Obviously, that's an issue. You'll need to get her permission if you're going to display these or use them in your portfolio. But maybe this is your thing. Portraiture, but not posed. Candid. Catching these unaware moments. This is something to pursue."

I nodded, trying not to burst through my skin with happiness. *This is something to pursue.*

"You're taking my class in the spring, I know. Maybe we'll see about getting you on the *Courier*, too. Have you considered that? They're always looking for photographers, and I could write a recommendation."

I grinned. The *Courier* was Keale's weekly newspaper, something I'd only glanced at occasionally in the Commons, thumbing through pages while I twirled my spaghetti with a fork. "That sounds great," I admitted.

I left his office feeling the most alive, the most *right*, I'd ever felt. The closest I'd come otherwise was with Marcus, when everything was thrilling and dangerous, thrilling *because* it was dangerous. This was something *I'd* done, something I'd created, not dependent on anyone else. Dr. Mittel didn't give a damn that I was a Mabrey, and I didn't, either.

MEGAN

Mom wanted to know everything about Keale, but even after the initial newness wore off, I had trouble putting it into words.

Keale was its own little world—sprawling green lawns and clusters of Victorian-era buildings, bordered on two sides by horse pastures and on another by a seventeen-acre forest that backed onto a tributary of the Housatonic. The buildings were named after female suffragettes and abolitionists and artists—the Susan B. Anthony Auditorium, the Alice Stone Blackwell Hall of Arts & Letters, the Rebecca Harding Davis and Elizabeth Cady Stanton residential halls. "Who?" Mom asked, but I could hardly keep them straight myself. The school seemed torn between its past—earnest and vaguely religious—and its present, where couples openly held hands and as a form of protest art, girls hung their bloody tampons on a display in the student center.

I'd expected a campus built in the 1800s to be showing its age, imagining a dusty reference library, cracks in foundations, crumbling facades. Instead, every outward inch of Keale was maintained to perfection. The brickwork gleamed; the sidewalks were pressure-washed to sparkling silver. Leaves and food wrappers were whisked away by a small army of maintenance workers in green jumpsuits. Inside, the buildings were light and modern, housing computer labs and rows of microscopes.

That first night, alone in my room, I had the impression that Keale was a sort of sacred space, a feeling enhanced by a quaint bell from the original chapel marking otherwise silent hours. But then the dorms filled, and this vision was shattered with feet pounding in the hallway, music pulsing through walls, female voices echoing up and down the stairwells. In the common kitchen on each floor of Stanton Hall, someone was forever burning popcorn in the microwave or losing the remote control right before *Friends* was scheduled to start or bitching about who had used the one-percent milk, despite the fact that it had been labeled in permanent marker as Hailey's Milk.

By contrast, my room was a tomb. Someone in Housing must have thought that Ariana Kramer and I made a perfect match, based solely on the fact that we were both from the Midwest. But Ariana was quiet and studious and serious, charged with living up to the expectations of her pediatrician father and her law professor mother. She lined the bookshelf above her desk with ribbons and plaques and trophies—First Place Academic Decathlon. National Honor Society Lifetime Member. Soroptimists International Achievement Winner.

"I didn't think to bring my Pinewood Derby participation ribbon," I told her that first day, after her parents had left for the airport and she was carefully arranging her clothes, grouping the hangers by color. I expected at least a courtesy laugh, but Ariana didn't crack a smile.

She had already started her course reading during the summer, something I'd never even considered, and her thick copies of *Organic Chemistry* and *Human Biology* and *World Cultures* looked worldly and sophisticated next to the yellow spines of my Nancy Drews, packed for sentimental rather than practical value. From the critical glance Ariana gave my side of the room, I might have brought my stuffed animals and pink plastic ponies.

"I'm an English major," I said, as if this might explain it. "I mean, at least, that's what I've declared for now..." I trailed off, not wanting to explain about my unplanned "gap" year and the feeling of comfort I'd felt when I stumbled on Keale's list of English courses. American Literature I and II, Writing Between the Wars, Post-Colonial Voices... Reading, I'd thought. Writing. I could do that. "What about you? Did you declare a major?"

"Oh, I'm a bio girl. Premed," she clarified, fiddling with her hair. I watched as a French braid emerged from her deft fingers, the strands of hair pulled too tight, giving her eyes a squinty look. If it were someone else, I might have suggested a different hairstyle, volunteered to do a loose fishbone braid like I used to do with my girlfriends in junior high. But somewhere, Ariana probably had proof that this was the best kind of braid—a ribbon from the county fair with her name embossed in tiny gold letters, maybe. "I'm leaning toward the heart," she said.

"The heart," I repeated, distracted by the efficient rotating motions of her wrists.

"You know, cardiology?" The last syllable rose to a question mark, as if to ask if I'd heard of it.

We didn't have the chumminess that other girls had, but we didn't have the volatile ups and downs, either. Ariana spent most of her time in the library, and during the day I caught rare glimpses of her crossing campus, bent forward beneath the weight of her backpack. Most days she couldn't be bothered to go to the Commons for dinner, and crinkly foil Pop-Tart wrappers glimmered in our trashcan.

The other girls—women, I supposed—seemed to move in packs, united by shared characteristics. At first, I assumed that they all knew each other somehow, like they'd been fed into Keale from the same high school, and the same middle schools before that, all the way to the preschools where they'd first finger-painted their names. It took me a while to realize that their familiarity was based on loosely shared experiences from communities up and down the East Coast—prep schools and summer camps and tennis lessons, summers on the Cape. They didn't need to know each other; they understood each other. They spoke the same language. In class, they raised their hands confidently, referencing books I'd never heard of, historical events that hadn't been mentioned in my history classes at Woodstock High. I might have been one of the best and brightest of my graduating class, but the bar was much higher at Keale, the work more rigorous, the competition fierce. In high school, skimming the reading and turning in completed worksheets had earned me A's and the occasional B, but at Keale the quizzes focused on obscure passages in the reading, and my papers were returned full of red ink.

On my weekly phone calls home, I told my mom that everything was fine, that Ariana and I were getting along well, that I was learning a lot in my classes. It was only to myself that I wondered if I'd made a huge mistake, if KSU wouldn't have been a better choice after all.

At the end of September, sick of riding the Keale Kargo shuttle into town, I bought a bike from an upperclassman for ten dollars. Even though the green paint was chipped and the banana seat was in need of repair, it was a steal, with a giant wicker basket perfect for transporting the toiletries and snacks and other things that cost a fortune on campus. One afternoon, I was locking the bike outside the Common Ground, Scofield's artsy coffee shop, when Joe Natolo walked up with his hands slouched into his pockets.

"A granny bike. Nice," he said, running his hand over the seat I'd repaired with a few strips of duct tape.

"A *cruiser*," I corrected. "It gets me around."

Joe laughed. "Tell the truth. Too many female hormones on campus. You just had to get out of there."

I rolled my eyes. "You know it's nothing but constant talk about our periods."

He gave me a grin that was already identifiable as his alone, a mismatched alignment of teeth, a dimple that appeared in the hollow of his cheek. "You headed in here?" He jerked his head in the direction of the coffeehouse, and I nodded. It had become my own little oasis on the lazy afternoons when I didn't have class.

I didn't tell Joe that part of the reason for wanting a bike was wanting *this*, the chance to bump into him again. In the weeks since I'd arrived in Scofield, he had begun to seem like a conjuring of my travel-addled brain, but here he was—floppy dark bangs, the long eyelashes that my mom would have said were wasted on a man. Joe Natolo, in the flesh.

Remembering the promise I'd made when he'd dropped me at Stanton Hall, I paid for his coffee. Joe took one sip and grimaced, reaching for a canister of sugar. He asked about Keale, and I told him about my classes, my work-study job at the switchboard, life with Ariana.

He stirred his coffee elaborately with a tiny spoon and sipped, testing its sweetness. "Have you been to any good parties?"

I laughed. "Um, no. I basically study all the time, and still, I'm hardly keeping up." As proof, I unzipped my backpack and took out my notebook and dog-eared copy of *The Awakening*. My paper wasn't due for four days, but I was already starting to panic about my thesis, and my ideas weren't coming together. On my last essay, the professor had written "Remember, there are tutors available in the writing center."

Joe reached for my notebook, spinning it around so that my scribbles were facing him. "'In fact,'" he read, loud enough to get the attention of a frowning woman at the next table, "'through penile penetration, she both finds and loses her identity.' Writing an autobiography?"

"Very funny." I slapped the notebook closed before he could read any of my other observations, such as the one about Edna Pontellier confusing orgasm with independence.

He sat back, arms folded across his chest. "Tell the truth, Midwest. The lack of men is killing you."

I rolled my eyes. "I'm managing. Besides—" I took a careful sip of coffee and leaned forward "—you do know that everyone at Keale is a lesbian, right?"

The smile he gave me sent a rush down to my toes. "Not *every*one, surely."

No, not everyone. Just sitting across the table from Joe was enough to confirm my own sexuality, not that I'd ever been in doubt. I hadn't come to Keale to find a boyfriend, but I had a sixth sense dedicated to Joe alone, marked by hairs that stood up on the back of my neck when he entered a room and sweat glands that seemed to sprout from nowhere. Through Joe, I could easily find and lose my own identity.

We started bumping into each other more regularly—at Common Ground, at the Stop & Shop, where I loaded up on off-brand crackers and jars of peanut butter, and once when he pulled up next to my bike at a stoplight, revving his engine. "Race you," he'd called through the open window.

It was impossible not to laugh when he was around, impossible not to feel a thrill when his knees bumped against mine under a café table.

"We should get dinner sometime," he said, and I didn't overthink it.

"We should," I agreed.

We made plans to meet during Parents' Weekend, to get me away from campus while it was overrun with families. I hadn't mentioned the event to my mom—it seemed too far to come for two days of scheduled activities that wouldn't have interested her. Ariana's parents had flown out, and I'd unsuccessfully dodged their presence on Friday, surprised when they burst into our room after sharing a meal in the Commons. I kept my nose in a book as Mrs. Kramer worried over Ariana's chemistry grade—an A overall, although she'd received a B on a recent quiz—and turned a page noisily when Mr. Kramer wondered whether it would be beneficial for her to find a tutor.

By now I knew Ariana well enough to recognize her controlled fury, like a toy that had been wound too tight and was ready to spring loose. "I do not need a tutor," she said, each word bearing staccato weight.

This was easily verified—several times Ariana had tutored *me*, making precise notations in the margins of my work—but I decided to stay out of it.

"Maybe this isn't a conversation we should be having right now in front of Ariana's friend," her dad interjected, and I looked up from where I was sitting on my bed, as if I'd been summoned. Were we friends? I felt closer to the girls I saw twice a week in my American lit seminar.

Ariana's mom looked at her watch. "Well, we can talk on the way to the lecture, I suppose." She cast me the same pitying smile she'd given me in August, when she learned I'd taken the bus all the way from Kansas, alone. "Maybe you'd like to join us for dinner afterward?"

I noticed the spark in Ariana's eye, a silent pleading. She didn't want to be alone with her parents any more than I did. I mouthed a *sorry* in Ariana's direction and explained that I'd made other plans.

"Maybe you could meet us for ice cream, then," Ariana's mom pressed. "We're going to go to that cute place in town, the one with the giant cone on the marquee? Maybe around nine?"

I smiled. By nine o'clock, I hoped to be in Joe's Honda, the windows fogging from the heat of our kisses. "I'll definitely try."

I changed clothes five times before meeting Joe, deciding on my most flattering jeans and a shirt that was tight across the chest and too sexy to wear around Keale. We'd planned to meet at Slice of Heaven, and Joe was already there when I arrived, breathless from my bike ride into town.

He whistled, spotting me through the window. We hugged,

same as we'd done the last few times we'd seen each other, but this one lasted a few beats longer, and our bodies were pressed just a bit closer.

"I hope you don't mind. I got here a bit early and ordered for us," Joe said, gesturing to the glass of soda in front of him, the empty glass in front of my spot. "Just regular pepperoni and breadsticks."

"Just regular pepperoni and breadsticks sounds great," I said.

"I was trying to beat the rush," Joe said, nodding to the line that had formed at the register, snaking halfway to the door. Most of the booths were already full. "I mean, this town is typically overrun with WASPs, but during Parents' Weekend, the BMW-to-human ratio is especially skewed, if you know what I mean."

I laughed at his description.

"Well, what about you? Don't you have parents, Midwest?" When I hesitated, he covered quickly. "Did I put my foot in my mouth? Sorry. It's none of my business."

"No, it's fine. It was just too far for my mom to come."

"What about your dad?"

I shook my head, my throat suddenly clogged. Since coming to Keale, I'd managed to avoid any mention of my dad. It was easier that way, although the omission implied that he'd never existed at all.

"I am an ass," Joe said. "Remember?"

I stood up quickly, grabbing my frosted red cup. "Be right back."

By the time our pizza came, we'd already refilled our bottomless sodas twice. Joe laughed as I blotted the top layer of grease from the pizza with a handful of napkins. *It's not a real date*, I told myself. *It's pizza and Coke.* Beneath the table, his leg brushed against mine, but instead of pulling away like a reflex, it lingered there. *Or maybe it is.*

While the restaurant filled up, we talked about our jobs. I mentioned the woman who called the switchboard fifteen times in one night, insisting that there must be a problem with the phone lines since her daughter hadn't picked up. Joe said that a former coworker at the body shop had opened a place in Michigan, and he'd offered Joe a job.

He shrugged. "But, I don't know. Michigan. It's pretty far away."

"Right," I said, picking off a pepperoni. I felt his loss as keenly as if he'd already packed up the Honda and left. So far, Joe was the only good thing about Scofield. "And you'd have to leave all this."

"Some things would be harder to leave than others," he said, and although he wasn't looking at me when he said it, my cheeks burned. "Anyway—it might not pan out. There are a lot of things to figure."

"Right," I said again. Someone at the next table stood, jostling my elbow. The restaurant was crowded now, the line out the door. I recognized some girls from Keale with their families and felt a stab of longing for my own family, back when it had been intact and perfectly imperfect. We would never again order a pizza, bicker over our choice of three toppings, then load up our leftovers to eat later that night in front of the TV.

"Whoa," Joe said, tapping me on the arm. He gave a subtle head tilt in the direction of a family standing by the door.

I half turned, pretending to casually glance at the line. "Who are we looking at?"

"The guy in the button-down shirt."

"You'll have to be more specific."

Joe laughed. "With the lady in the sweater."

"Again, you'll have to—"

"And the dark-haired girl with legs up to her neck."

"Ah," I said, glancing again toward the door. The man was tall with a full head of salt-and-pepper hair, a striped shirt with sleeves rolled up to his elbows. The woman wore a patterned sweater set, a giant diamond glinting from her finger. They didn't look familiar, but I recognized the tall girl from Stanton Hall. I associated her with the summer camp crowd, as I'd come to think of them, girls who played lacrosse and rode horses and moved around campus in tight cliques. "That's Lauren somebody. She lives in my dorm, but not on my floor."

Joe leaned forward, conspiratorially. It was hard to hear him over the general noise of happy families. "Her last name is Mabrey."

I raised an eyebrow. "And?"

"Her father is Senator Charles Mabrey of Connecticut."

"Seriously? A senator?" I craned around, getting another look.

"Be cool," Joe said, his thumb and forefinger reaching for my chin, steering me to face him. "People will think you've never seen a senator before."

I burned under his touch. "I haven't."

"Well, I suspect they're just like you and me, only they live in a nicer home—or more likely *homes*, plural—and they drive better cars if they drive themselves at all, and they're on a first-name basis with the president of our freaking country, but other than that, no reason to stare."

"Got it," I said. We were close enough for me to see a tiny red fleck caught between Joe's front teeth. "Did you learn all this in your civics class?"

Joe released my chin and reached for his tumbler, taking a

long swig. "They're probably all douchebags, but Mabrey at least seems to be a douchebag of the people."

I snorted, choking on a bite of cold pizza. "You should volunteer to write his campaign slogans."

"You know what?" Joe said, wadding his napkin into a ball. "Want to get out of here? There's a better place down the road, one that won't be overrun with all these hoity-toity types."

"Do me a favor," I grinned. "Say that again. *Hoity-toity.*"

Instead, he stood up and pulled me to my feet, threading his fingers through mine. I shot a last glance over my shoulder and saw Lauren's father, the *senator*, bantering with a cashier. It was the same way married men had talked to me at the Woodstock Diner, as if he were saying, *Look how young and virile I still am.* In that split second, Lauren turned and our eyes met. She smiled in a faint, pleasant way, as if she didn't recognize me at all. And why would she? Girls like that moved in their own circles, existed in their own worlds.

We ended up at a place called Moe's, too shady for the Keale crowd with its dim, low-ceilinged interior and the haze of smoke that hovered just above our heads. Joe navigated the rowdy crowd at the bar and returned to our table with a pitcher of beer. I thought briefly about pointing out that I was nineteen, and then let it go. It seemed like an incongruous fact, unrelated to this experience. I *felt* older and wiser, like a more mature version of Megan Mazeros, one who didn't have to worry about basic rules and regulations.

For a while we drank and watched a vigorous game of darts unfolding between a tiny, dark-haired woman with dead aim and her towering, tattooed companion; with each throw, they razzed and taunted each other. It was like watching an elaborate mating ritual, one based on catcalls and innuendos. When she won, he pulled her onto his lap and whispered into her ear. She stood, tugging him toward the door.

Joe drained his glass. "Do you play?"

"Do I ever." I slid off my stool, feeding off the charge in the air. We were an extension of the couple who had just left, playing off their energy, becoming more sexualized versions of ourselves. Between throws, Joe's hand lingered on my elbow, my waist, my hip.

I hadn't played darts since before Dad got sick, but we used to have a dartboard in the garage, our throw lines taped to the cement. Once I got good enough to be competitive, I'd lost the handicap and he'd eliminated my line once and for all. After a few warm-up shots, Joe and I were evenly matched, going head-to-head, throw for throw. We brushed against each other deliberately, laughing, when we retrieved our darts. When he beat me by three points, I conceded the loss with a mock bow.

"An honor, sir," I said.

He hooked an arm around my neck, pulling me into him. Our kiss felt effortless, a natural progression of the evening. He trailed one finger down my spine, coiling it in my belt loop. "Want to play another round?"

"Not particularly," I said.

Our faces were so tight together that I saw his beautiful, crooked grin up close. It was like looking at him through a magnifying glass, all his good parts becoming even better.

According to the clock on Joe's dashboard, it was just after nine. He agreed to drive me back to campus, so I could leave a note for Ariana. I didn't know what I would say, just *Sorry I didn't make it to ice cream* or *Don't wait up*. I planned to stuff my backpack with toiletries and a change of clothes, just in case. The night was ripe with possibility. At each stoplight on our way out of town, Joe and I kissed like we were perfecting what we'd started earlier. In the parking lot of my dorm, we reached for each other again, his hands inching beneath my sweater, palms hot on the small of my back.

"You know what I like about you, Midwest?"

I murmured, "No."

"What I like the most is—"

"I meant no, don't talk," I said.

"You see? That's it."

The car windows began to fog, and Joe's hand was on my bra, my nipple hard beneath his thumb. It was so close to what I'd imagined that it hardly felt real. Nearby, a car started, headlights springing to life.

"Hold on, cowboy," I said, pulling back. "Give me five minutes."

He groaned. "Five minutes is eternity."

I gave him a teasing kiss and grabbed my backpack from the floorboard. "Five minutes."

The night was cool, but I felt warm and reckless and happy. I took the side stairs and was breathless by the time I reached the third floor, where I paused to look down at the parking lot. Joe's car was there, idling with its headlights on. I spotted my reflection at the same time—blond curls wild, cheeks flushed. *I'm doing this*, I thought. *I'm doing it.*

In the hallway, I waited for a group of parents to pass. They were chatting loudly about how college had changed since they were in it, how the cafeteria food was better, the exercise facilities first-rate. After I passed, I heard one of the men say, "And the girls are prettier, too."

Our door was unlocked, although the lights were off. Ariana and her parents must have come and gone, forgetting to lock it behind them. I flicked on the light switch, moving fast. Fresh underwear, a tank top to sleep in, a clean shirt for the morning—if that was how it played out. I hesitated, momentarily frozen by the practicalities. Would he have condoms? Of course. This experience wasn't the novelty for him that it was for me. Still, I cursed myself for not refilling my birth control. It had seemed a silly, extravagant expense to pay thirty dollars a month for pills I wouldn't need at an all-girls school.

I was zipping up my backpack when I caught the movement from Ariana's side of the room and jumped a foot. She was in bed, her body a slight hump beneath the covers. Maybe she'd skipped out on ice cream and come back early, exhausted by her parents' constant nagging.

Then she moaned, a ragged and gasping sound that made me look closer. Her head was turned to one side, hair plastered against her face and half-covering her mouth. Across her pillowcase was a trail of vomit.

Fuck. Not now.

"Ariana?" I asked, then repeated her name louder. When she didn't respond, I dropped to my knees, shaking her shoulder. "Are you okay? Should I call someone?"

Her head flopped backward, mouth open. Flakes of white powder stuck to the corner of her mouth.

"Did you take something?"

I had to put my ear almost to her face, wincing from the stench of her breath, to understand what she was saying. *Your pulse. Yourpilse. Your pills.*

My pills.

Later I told the paramedics about the generic bottle of ibuprofen I kept in my desk drawer, taking a pill here and there for a headache. There had been a hundred pills initially, and I wasn't sure how many had been there earlier that night. Seventy? Eighty? Ariana had taken whatever was left, as evidenced by the empty bottle on her nightstand. I tried to imagine her swallowing the pills, one by one or two by two, washing them down with water from her Peanuts mug, the one that read The Doctor Is In, 5 cents.

After the lecture, Ariana had told her parents that she needed to study, and they'd gone out for dinner without her. She'd already taken the first pills by the time I met Joe at Slice of Heaven, and she'd finished them by the time we'd begun our game of darts at Moe's, when her parents were having ice cream sundaes without her. She must have been unconscious by the time Joe and I kissed; she'd vomited later, when Joe and I were in his car, when I was being reinvented by his touch, inch by inch. And I'd found her in time, *so lucky*, everyone noted. Only I wasn't sure if Ariana meant for me to find her earlier, or hoped I would only find her after it was too late.

Viv, our resident advisor, kicked into supervisory mode and took charge of the situation—which meant contacting Ariana's parents and taking care of me. "You cannot blame yourself for this," she said, taking hold of my shocked shoulders. Until that point, it hadn't occurred to me that I was responsible. Then guilt kicked in hard: I'd been planning a night of reckless abandon, and Ariana had been trying to end it all.

Worse, I felt just as bad for myself, for the lost possibilities of that night. By the time I'd alerted Viv and the paramedics had arrived, twenty minutes had passed, maybe more. When I finally wormed my way through the cluster of girls and their parents in the hallway to look down into the parking lot below, Joe's car was gone.

LAUREN

Although I hadn't mentioned it once, somehow everyone at Keale knew my father was a senator. It had started out with a little joke: my resident advisor, Katy, mentioned during our first floor meeting that we all had to follow the rules—whether our fathers were elected officials or not. She said this with a wink in my direction, and I heard the general buzz around me. *Who?* And he's an actual *senator*? Later that week, a mousy blonde girl sat next to me in the Commons and over eggs on toast mentioned that her grandfather had been an ambassador to Ghana, as if that made us related somehow, like second cousins.

"Do you have like, diplomatic immunity or something?" another girl at the table asked.

"No," I assured her, to general laughter.

Later I thought about it and realized that a more accurate answer would have been *yes*.

My parents had more or less ignored me since I left for Keale, but they came for Parents' Weekend, bustling into my dorm room with a towering gift basket from Harry & David, as if I were a client and not a daughter. It didn't occur to me until I was giving them an abbreviated tour of campus that this was an opportunity to see and be seen. For Dad, it was an unpaid advertisement, a chance to shake hands and trade college stories with other dads, homing in on the ones from Connecticut, his constituents. More than once when we were walking across campus, I was aware of camera flashes, of people catching the three of us in motion—Mom with an arm linked through Dad's, each of us holding bags from the Keale College bookstore, full of the sweatshirts and visors and coffee mugs that proclaimed them the proud parents of a Keale College student.

I was sure we would show up in future brochures advertising the college, with some kind of pretentious caption: Senator Mabrey, His Wife, Elizabeth Holmes-Mabrey, and Their Daughter Lauren Enjoy Family Time during a Visit to the Fine Arts Auditorium. It wasn't so much a visit as it was a campaign stop.

We went into town for pizza, but the line at Slice of Heaven was out the door.

"We could bring it back to my dorm," I suggested. "There's a little kitchen down the hall."

"It'll be like old times, Liz," Dad said, draping his arms around Mom's shoulders. She smiled up at him, and I wondered how much of this was genuine, and how much was for show, another chance to impress Scofield's voting public. Photographic evidence of my parents in their twenties did exist, but I'd never seen snapshots of them eating pizza out of a cardboard box, sitting cross-legged on the floor. In the photos I remembered, they were at important dinners, separated by centerpieces and goblets and place settings with three different forks, Dad in a suit, Mom's hair in a complicated updo held together by a million bobby pins.

I recognized a few other people in the pizzeria, including Cindy Hardwick, a girl from my dorm. We'd only exchanged the occasional hello as we passed in the hall, but she bounded over to shake Dad's hand and then, for good measure, Mom's. She lingered for longer than necessary, beaming up at them. "You must be proud. Lauren is so talented," she said. I tried to steer her away with an arm on her elbow, but it was too late. "I love her work."

Worse than the explanations that I would have to provide were the subtle frowns on my parents' faces, their hesitant glances between Cindy and me, as if to confirm she was in fact referring to their daughter.

"Lauren hasn't told us much about her classes, actually," Mom said, the question mark buried in her words.

"It was going to be a surprise," I said.

Cindy's perky face fell, her cheeks literally deflating. "I'm so sorry. I didn't know."

Mom touched her reassuringly on the shoulder. "You couldn't have known. Lauren's so modest. Why don't you tell us, honey, so we can all be on the same page?"

Dad's smile was nervous, his focus drifting around the room. This conversation wasn't part of the scheduled event, not even a bullet point on his agenda.

"I'm putting together a photography portfolio for one of my classes," I said.

"It's so brilliant," Cindy gushed. "She takes the best pictures—she really does. I can barely hold a camera steady..."

One of the pizzeria employees called a number, and Dad stepped forward to collect our order.

"Maybe you can show us some of those photos before we head back," Mom suggested. "It was wonderful to meet you, Cindy."

We gathered plates and napkins and little packets of Parmesan cheese and smiled our way stiffly out the door and down the street to Mom's Mercedes. The street was clogged with cars, and it took Dad a while to find an opening.

I popped the lid of the pizza box and put a slice of pepperoni on my tongue, relishing its salt and heat.

"I don't remember signing you up for a photography class," Mom said.

I chewed the pepperoni slowly, deliberately.

Dad's eyes met mine in the rearview mirror. "Well? Your mother asked you a question."

I shrugged. "It's for a class called Introduction to the Arts. We study visual art, music—"

"You're taking that in addition to your other classes?"

"No, I dropped the biology class." I'd also switched out of math, but this didn't seem like the best moment to mention it.

In the front seat, Mom's mouth was set in a tight line. "You need to be taking your general education requirements, Lauren. You're not just here to try a little of this and a little of that. There's an educational plan—"

"It's one class," I repeated. "And I'm thinking of studying fine arts, so it'll be part of the requirements for my major." This much was true, although I had been planning to wait as long as possible—at least another semester or two—before announcing it to my parents. Before their visit, I'd carefully packed away my Leica and slid my burgeoning portfolio underneath my bed.

Dad sighed, adjusting the visor so the setting sun didn't blind him. "At least your friend seems excited about your work. She said you were very talented."

Mom couldn't let it go. "Everything's always a lie with you. It's always about sneaking around behind our backs."

I leaned forward, my head between their bucket seats. "It's my education, Mom. You can't control the classes I take, like you did at Reardon."

"If I hadn't intervened there, you never would have graduated," Mom snapped.

I rolled my eyes. I'd earned mostly B's at Reardon, with the odd A and a few C's, yet the arrival of my report card in the mail had always felt like doomsday, as if I'd brought shame upon the family for not being as brilliant as my siblings.

A car slowed in front of us, and Dad braked suddenly, the motion shooting us all forward against our seat belts. The pizza box slid from the back seat onto the floor, but thankfully the pizza in all its greasy gooeyness remained inside the box, folded over on itself. I lifted the lid to inspect the damage and said, "Still edible."

Dad smiled, meeting my eyes quickly in the rearview mirror before returning to the road. I felt sorrier for him than I did for myself. He didn't seem to understand all the intricacies of being a Mabrey, although all of our lives revolved around him. He was the one who would have to drive back to Simsbury with Mom, after all, listening to her complaints about my thoughtlessness.

In the parking lot outside Stanton Hall, I unclipped my seat belt and Dad did the same. Mom sat stony, staring ahead.

I gestured to the pizza. "Aren't you coming inside?"

"Now that I think about it, we probably have to get on the road," Mom said.

"Liz, we have food to eat. We might as well—"

"I don't think I'm particularly hungry."

Dad sighed, drumming his fingers on the steering wheel.

I scooped up the pizza box. No point in letting perfectly good food go to waste. "It's a class," I repeated. "A stupid fucking class. That's all."

Mom said, "You will not talk to us that way—" And I knew there was more, but I wasn't going to stick around to hear it. I'd already slammed the door behind me and was walking fast across the parking lot, pizza box in hand. I waited for them to do something—for Mom to come after me or for Dad to pull even with me in the Mercedes, but none of that happened.

In my room, I moved some papers out of the way and set the box on my desk. Erin was still out with her parents, probably having the sort of happy family meal that regular people had, laughing and reminiscing and making plans for the next time they would see each other. But maybe there was no such thing as a normal family, a happy family meal. Maybe everyone was secretly, deep down miserable and they only put on brave faces for the rest of us.

More out of spite than hunger, I ate half the pizza and lay down on the bed, still dressed in my jeans and sweater in case Erin and her parents came back. I must have fallen asleep with the overhead fluorescent light still beaming down because the next thing I knew there were people running past my door, their footsteps echoing down the hallway.

"What's going on?" I called to a girl who stood near the elevators, a hand over her mouth.

"Someone on the second floor took a bunch of pills," she said. "It's horrible."

"Is she…" I faltered. "Is she going to be…"

"I don't know!"

No one seemed to know anything, but after a few minutes the paramedics rushed past, a girl on the stretcher. She was struggling against her restraints, and there was an audible sigh of relief. At least she was alive.

"Her name's Ariana Kramer," another girl called. "She's in my organic chem class."

"Oh, my God, really? She's so smart. She's always in the library—"

I went back to my room, changed into my pajamas, turned off the light and crawled under the covers. Maybe my theory was right after all.

The week before Thanksgiving and a return visit to Holmes House, I came back to my room to find Erin sitting on her bed and Theresa, a girl from across the hall, sitting on mine. They both turned stony faces to me.

"Hey," I said, placing my camera bag gingerly on my desk. "What's going on?"

In her hands, Erin was holding a stack of prints, and she thrust them in my direction like they were evidence. I spotted an old Kodak paper box, where I stored most of my eight-by-eleven prints, open on the floor and instantly I knew what she'd found. I'd promised Dr. Mittel that I would get Erin's permission to use her photos in my portfolio, but in all the weeks since, I hadn't managed to ask her. No matter how I approached her, she would have been horrified—the same way she looked right now.

"Those are private," I said, my voice thin, the objection weak.

"They're pictures of me, you weirdo," Erin spat. "So yes, they are *private*."

"How could you even—" Theresa said, shaking her head in disgust. "And why would you…"

"Theresa," I said. "Could I talk to Erin for a minute? I want to explain."

"She doesn't want to talk to you, you nutcase. She found the photos, and she called me over. How long have you been stalking her?" Theresa's voice rose dangerously, threatening to get the attention of other girls on our floor. Living in such close proximity to each other, we were always alert for a catfight, ready to take sides.

I snorted. "*Stalking* her? We live in the same room. I took some photos—okay. Erin—" her arms were folded across her chest, her eyes narrowed, lips trembling "—I'm sorry. I shouldn't have done that, especially not without your permission. But it just— I was trying to capture this beautiful moment. That's all."

Theresa threw up her hands. "What are you, obsessed with her or something? You're a lesbian, aren't you? I knew it. I said it from the first time I saw you, there's something *up* with that girl!"

If the situation wasn't so fragile, I would have burst out laughing. Theresa was just another Keale clone, blindly defending her friend's honor. "I let you borrow my shoes last week!" I reminded her. "I came in here to find you looking through my closet, and I still let you borrow my shoes! Now you're digging through the rest of my stuff—"

"Because we knew you were hiding something," Theresa said.

I swore, turning back to Erin. She was looking down at an image of herself—her mouth slightly open, her face relaxed. "I'm sorry I took the pictures. And I'm sorry I didn't tell you about them afterward. But my professor—he thinks they're really beautiful—"

Erin gasped. "You showed these to people? Look at me! You can see—"

Theresa's laugh cut her off. "What else is he going to say? Your dad is a fucking United States senator! Oh, yes, they're brilliant, because you're a Mabrey. Do you think that gives you permission to do whatever you want?"

I don't think I'd ever hit anyone before, except MK sometimes when we were fighting, which he always started. But I was mad enough to do it this time. I could almost feel my fist connecting with Theresa's nose, could almost see the resulting dribble of blood.

Erin was trembling with anger, shaking all the way down to her fingertips. The prints in her hands were crumpled beyond repair. "I know who you are, you know."

I had a brief, horrible flashback to Marcus, the drugs, my court-ordered community service and fake bout of mono. Did Erin know somehow?

She made a fist around the photo, her sleeping face disappearing into a crumpled ball. "You think you're so privileged, you think you can do whatever you want. You don't give a shit about anyone else."

"That is not true," I insisted, although it was true enough that I felt like I'd been punched in the stomach.

"You violated her!" Theresa yelled, eager to draw herself back into the fight. "You're some weird sicko stalker and you just need to admit it!"

A cluster of girls had gathered openmouthed in the doorway. Maybe she was playing for the audience, or maybe she'd been planning to do this all along, but Erin looked down at the stack of prints in her hands, at all the lovely, sleeping reflections of herself, and began to rip through them. Theresa grabbed a stack of other prints from my photo box—prints that weren't even of Erin—and began shredding them, too, the pieces falling down in the air around us like confetti. Then she went for the negatives, pulling them out of their plastic holder, the film fluttering to the ground.

"Stop it," I yelled. "You bitch!"

By the time our resident advisor arrived, I had Theresa in a full headlock and Erin was on her hands and knees, ripping the pictures into ever smaller pieces. Katy banished us to the corners of the room like overaggressive boxers, as if we were each champing at the bit to get back in the ring. She looked around the room in horror—a lamp had been overturned, its shade punctured. Clothes and books and shoes, whatever we could get our hands on, littered the floor. One of my fancy flannel sheets had been ripped, and the potted plant Erin's parents had brought her had tipped over on her desk, soil spilling on top of her homework.

"Holy fuck," Katy said, her eyes wide. "And I thought this would be a quiet night."

Later, Katy moved Erin's belongings into the spare bunk in Theresa's room, while I gathered the ruined scraps of my photography, my heart still pounding. Katy had heard the story by then, and she wasn't showing me any pity.

"What's going to happen?" I asked, imagining some kind of suspension or expulsion from Keale. What was the punishment for taking pictures of someone without their permission, even artsy and mostly innocent ones? I imagined myself getting booked on a misdemeanor at the tiny jail in Scofield, using my one phone call to contact Mom, who would either come to pick me up or refuse to help. Either way, I had earned another notch in my belt as the family fuckup.

Katy's eyes slid coolly over me. "If it were up to me," she said, and I knew the rest of the answer before she said it. Nothing would happen, effectively: it was the Mabrey get-out-of-jail-free card. Erin and Theresa and I would be officially or unofficially warned about fighting, but that would be the end of it. The dean would encourage Erin not to pursue her complaint any further on the unstated grounds that I was a Mabrey and that was important here.

"Wait," I tried again. "Just tell me. Housing-wise, what happens to me? Do I just stay here?"

Katy's arms were loaded with the last of Erin's shoes, and she didn't meet my eye. "What happens," she said, "is that we'll find you another roommate."

And that was how I met Megan Mazeros.

MEGAN

The phone call from the housing department came over Christmas break, when I was staying at Gerry Tallant's house in Woodstock and trying not to feel like a third wheel in the relationship between my mother and her boyfriend. I'd been jumping at the phone every time it rang, convinced that Joe was trying to track me down, to apologize for that night and all the nights that had come after, when I had missed him like a phantom limb. This was illogical, of course; I wasn't sure Joe even knew my last name, let alone how he would have traced me to Gerry Tallant. If he'd wanted to talk to me, I was easier to find in Scofield.

Still, I felt myself deflate when I heard the voice of the woman from Housing and then had to ask her to repeat herself twice. "Lauren *Mabrey*?" I squeaked. "Are you sure?"

"I don't understand," my mom said when I hung up the phone. "You're going to live with this girl? And her dad is a senator?"

Back at Keale, everything about Lauren fascinated me. It was as if her life was a movie, and I was eager to pay the admission just to escape into it for a few hours. There was the famous family, of course, smiling from a silver frame on her desk—her father and brother in dark jackets, Lauren and her mother and sister in red sweaters, all so perfectly coordinated and softly lit, they might have been the model family that came with the frame, a prepackaged version of what a family should look like. And they were practically celebrities—they were American royalty, the people who had it all figured out, who had achieved what the rest of us could only dream. Even Lauren thought of her family this way. Once I got to know her, she sometimes referred to her parents as The Senator and The Countess.

Everything Lauren owned was beautiful—her floral sheets and satin-edged blankets, the thick down pillows that I carefully laid my head against when she was out of the room, testing them out. Her bed was heaped with throw pillows and something called a *bolster* that seemed uncomfortable in any position. I wondered what she thought of my pink-and-black reversible bed-in-a-bag from Walmart, the stained pillow I'd had for years, not realizing it was something that could and should be replaced, and the mismatched bath towels I'd bought from the sale rack, trying to stretch Dad's insurance money as far as it could go. After only a few months, the ends of my towels were frayed and the sheets were faded to a paler pink.

Lauren wore what I came to consider her uniform: cashmere sweaters that she casually balled up and tossed to the side when she was undressing for the night, slim dark jeans, tall boots with zippers snaking up the inside of her calves, the leather so soft it made me realize that there was leather and then there was *leather*, and the kind I owned was nothing like the kind she did. Her wardrobe held several fancy dresses that never came out of their dry cleaning plastic, and rather than one functional winter coat, she had a half dozen, black and gray and winter white, long and short, fancy and casual. And always, always, there was her camera bag, slung over one shoulder, rattling with film canisters. It was the only thing she seemed to truly care about, and I often found her cross-legged on her bed, blowing dust from crevices and wiping the lenses gently with a soft cloth.

She was beyond messy, tossing things on the ground as if she expected someone else to come along and pick up after her—an actual maid, as opposed to how my mom used to say, "What am I, your maid?" when I left a pair of shoes by the front door. She hoarded the handouts she received in class at the bottom of her backpack, which had to be periodically up-ended in order for her to find anything. When I got to know her better, I sometimes pinched the silky fabric of yesterday's underwear between a thumb and forefinger, flinging it from the floor in her direction, or piled her dirty socks on the foot of her bed or took a few bucks from her wallet and went downstairs to do her laundry myself. But in the beginning, I just watched the growing pile, mesmerized even by her dirt.

Lauren was beautiful—there was hardly any other word for someone tall and slender with glossy hair and straight teeth and clothes that fit like gloves—but she didn't bother with makeup and her hair regimen was a casual, twisting bun that was always in a slow process of falling apart. She seemed amazed by my tubes of Cover Girl and Maybelline, the fourteen different eye shadows that left powdery dust over the inside of my makeup bag. These were staples of existence in Woodstock, but Lauren would ask, "*Why* do you need that?" as if she couldn't spot the zit on my chin or the dark circles under my eyes, an inheritance from the Mazeros side of the family.

That first week, though, we hardly talked, other than polite exchanges about where we were from, what classes we were taking, when we liked to eat and sleep and shower. She stayed busy with her photography, and I was determined to read ahead for my British lit class. I'd heard about the fight with her roommate—all of Stanton Hall had heard about the fight with her roommate, if not all of Keale itself—but she never mentioned it, even when I deliberately asked, "Didn't you have a roommate last semester?"

She only shrugged. "Didn't work out."

I watched her, waiting for more.

Lauren gave me a quick, curious look. "And your roommate was the one who—"

"Yeah," I said, relieved that we were finally going to address it. "She took a bottle of pills."

But Lauren only nodded, unimpressed. "It was just Advil, wasn't it? She must not have been serious."

"Right," I agreed, although this was not the kind of thing that would ever occur to me. I realized this about Lauren: we might have been about the same age, but she'd lived about a million times more life than I had, and most of it she was able to dismiss with a shrug.

At the end of January, a snowstorm caused the electricity in our dorm to go out, and we huddled in the common room with dozens of other girls in their flannel pajamas, wrapped in blankets, eating peanut butter and crackers like the world had ended and we'd decided to dip into our stock of nonperishables to survive. Someone had contraband whiskey, and we passed the bottle, taking throat-burning shots, giggling like twelve-year-olds at a sleepover. Eventually, the lights came on and everyone drifted back to their rooms. Lauren and I weren't tired anymore, and after a few minutes of trying to sleep, she said, "That reminds me" and rummaged through a dresser drawer, coming up with a bottle of peppermint schnapps.

"For emergencies," she explained, winking.

It was hard to imagine someone like Lauren ever having an emergency at all.

We ended up getting sloppy drunk and laughing so hard that occasionally one of the girls next door banged a shoe against the wall to get us to be quiet. Most of the comedy came from our differences—the blue blood/prep school/summer camp/senator's kid and me, who'd spent eighteen months asking, "Would you like to hear today's special?" We sat on our own beds, backs pressed against the bumpy plaster, and passed the bottle back and forth. Peppermint schnapps was truly disgusting, even compared to some of the concoctions I'd tried at parties in Woodstock.

"So," I asked Lauren, the alcohol making me brave, "is everyone at prep school as snooty as I imagine them to be?"

She pretended to consider this very seriously, before saying, "Yes."

I laughed. My head felt light, like it had been pumped full of helium. "What was it like? I mean, I only have my overcrowded public school classrooms as a reference point."

"Let's see." She took a sip, nearly missing her mouth, and a clear trickle of alcohol, like drool, ran down her chin. She swabbed at it with the heel of her hand. "Navy-and-white uniforms. Pushy parents, including my own. Kids with fancy cars. It was all about routine, really, so we looked forward to anything that broke the routine. Parties. Gossip. The sex so-and-so was rumored to be having. Days away."

"What are days away? Like field trips or something?"

Lauren wiped her mouth more vigorously, this time on her sleeve. "They were these planned trips where the school chartered a bus and took us to museums or monuments or plays, and then afterward dropped us off to go shopping for a few hours."

"We had those, too," I commented. "Only they were called field trips, and we had to pack our own lunches to eat on the school bus, and at the end we spent a few bucks on overpriced magnets and key chains and crap because clearly the one thing missing from our lives was a souvenir of every place where a president had spent the night."

Lauren nodded sagely, the effect somewhat lessened by a soft belch, followed by a louder one. On my bed, I contorted with laughter.

"Confession," she said. "All I know about Kansas is from *The Wizard of Oz*. You know—fields and barns and tornados."

On the other side of the room I froze in position, hands wrapped around my shoulders like a self-imposed straitjacket. I had to wait a full minute for Lauren to notice.

"What?" she asked. "Is that offensive?"

I said, "Actually, I've never watched that movie."

She opened her mouth and another burp fell out. "You're kidding me! Isn't it like, an official state movie or something?"

"Confession," I said, tucking my chin into the shelf I'd made with my arms. "My grandparents were killed by a tornado. It caught them while they were driving, swept their car up into the funnel and spit it out in about a million pieces a few miles away. So I guess we never found the movie too cute."

"Oh, my God." Lauren lurched forward, stumbling from her bed to mine. Suddenly she was holding me, her peppermint breath rank against my cheek. "I'm so, so sorry," she said, petting me awkwardly until she realized I was shaking from silent laughter.

"Seriously?" She pulled back, studying me in the glow of my bedside lamp. "Were they killed by a tornado?"

I shook my head. "Cancer and a heart attack."

We stared at each other for a long moment, and then Lauren let out a shriek that was somewhere between outrage and admiration. "I can't believe you said that! You had me feeling so horrible."

I wiped my eyes with the corner of my blanket. "You should have seen your face. I almost told you the house came down on them, and all we found were their legs."

She reached past me and smacked me with my own lumpy pillow. I stumbled to my feet and armed myself with her fancy bolster, finally figuring out an appropriate use for the thing.

This time the pounding came from both sides, two sets of girls telling us to shut the hell up, it was nearly 3:00 a.m., and they had classes in the morning.

"We'd better stop," Lauren said, capping the schnapps and returning the bottle to her drawer, only an inch of liquid still sloshing about. She flicked out the light and stumbled back to her bed, tripping over one of her textbooks, still splayed open on the floor. "I might have blown any free passes I have with the housing department."

We retreated to our separate beds and snuggled down, quiet under the covers. In the dark, I couldn't stop grinning. Partly, this was from the alcohol, the general warmth that I felt all the way down to my toes. But the rest of my happiness was from Lauren. This was the female camaraderie that had been promised by the Keale brochures but which had been, up until now, elusive. Wasn't this better than how I'd spent my nights since October, pining away after Joe Natolo and wondering what might have been? For the first time, that hurt seemed distant, like a bullet that had grazed me but moved on, leaving me mostly intact.

Lauren's breathing had evened out, but just when I thought she was asleep, her voice came from the other side of the room, blanket-muffled.

"Tornado," she whispered, and we started all over again.

It was surprising what came out of my mouth when I was talking to Lauren. Not lies, exactly, but more like shreds of truth held together by exaggerations. There was no one to contradict me when I told Lauren that I'd grown up in a trailer park, that my family's prized possession was a giant satellite dish, that I had a pit bull named Killer who snarled at the world from behind the chain-link fence. I was at Keale as part of a scholarship program, I told her, one designed to keep me from a lifetime of unplanned pregnancies and meth addiction. The words somehow felt true, coming out of my mouth; I could have been describing someone's life, after all—there had been enough general poverty and discontent in Woodstock to go around.

"Wow," she breathed. "That's so—wow."

My lies, at first, seemed harmless. I let her believe my relatives were toothless and inbred, that I'd grown up in the
"hood" rather than our modest Craftsman on a tree-lined
street. I hinted at drug-fueled nights—things which probably existed in Woodstock but were beyond the realm of my
experience. I told myself that it was simply the opposite of
seeing the world through rose-colored glasses; I was showing
her my life through unwashed, finger-smudged lenses. And
the lies came more easily than the truth, which lingered like
a tough bruise, going green and yellow and staying tender to
the touch. It was easier to imply that my dad wasn't around—
a partial truth, easier than telling about his months of dying
and what I'd done to help him along at the end. It was easier
to be flippant about my mom and her disgusting boyfriend,
when the alternative was to admit that he was a decent guy,
different from my dad, but not disgusting. After all, he'd offered to let me stay with them in his new beige house in his
new beige subdivision for as long as I wanted. But I told Lauren that Gerry had at least a dozen pastel-colored polo shirts,
like the colors in a baby nursery. ("Gross," she said.) And that
when he went out in public, he kept a hand cupped low on
my mom's ass. ("Nasty," she said.) And that sometimes I saw
him looking at me in the same way, and it was all I could do
to hide my body behind my oversize sweatshirts. (Lauren's
eyes had gone wide. "Whoa," she said.)

And then there were the nights when we split a bag of microwave popcorn and talked about guys and sex. In reality,
all I could contribute was from my time with Kurt Haschke,
but it was easy enough to elaborate here and there, to invent
names and places, things the fictional me might have done—
behind the bleachers after the football game, in the Fun House
at the carnival, on the couch when my mom was down in the
basement, doing laundry. I liked this Megan, the one who saw

sex as casual and meaningless, rather than what it had been
for me: an act of desperation, a way to remind myself that I
was capable of feeling *some*thing.

"You didn't," Lauren would gasp with each story, her eyes
wide with admiration.

And I would shrug, having grown comfortable with the
lie. "Why not?"

"I'm so pedestrian," she lamented, flopping onto her back.

Lauren's experiences, I imagined, had involved fancy sheets,
slinky lingerie, chocolate and strawberries and a housekeeping
staff to take care of the mess. She mentioned someone named
Marcus, and I pictured him tall and dark and handsome, arriving on her doorstep with a bouquet of flowers, plying her
with the name of a wine I couldn't pronounce, feeding her
expensive delicacies. Basically, I imagined for her all the things
that I could never dream of for myself.

I rationalized my lies like this: Lauren and I knew each
other only in the context of Keale, and it seemed unlikely that
our lives would intersect in other ways. We weren't going to
bump into each other at Shady's Hardware on Main Street
in Woodstock. Our vacations weren't likely to overlap, with
the two of us staying in the same all-inclusive island resort
with our families. And weirdly, the story of my fake miserable childhood gave me a bit of status with Lauren, a sort of
fabricated self-confidence that started to feel genuine. It allowed me to be the foul-mouthed heroine of my own life, the
fearless friend, a more adventurous version of myself.

Once the snow began to melt, Lauren bought a bike, too—
hers an expensive, sturdy one from a shop in town—and
we spent our Saturday afternoons cruising the country roads
around Keale, scouting locations for her photo shoots, then
heading into town for dinner. We liked the all-you-can-eat

pizza buffet at Slice of Heaven, where I always hoped to run into Joe, but never did.

Lauren inevitably produced her wallet at the register, pushing away the handful of crumpled bills left over from my work-study paycheck.

"It doesn't matter," she said, and I knew that it didn't—I'd seen the receipts from her bank account, the generous monthly deposits and the casual, here-and-there withdrawals.

"You think you can buy me off so easily?" I asked, and she laughed.

"Yes. Yes, I do."

Our favorite booth, tucked in the corner, had vinyl seats sticky to the touch and a Formica tabletop that we slowly, determinedly, picked at with our fingernails as we talked, often for hours. On the Saturday that cemented things, that made our friendship an official thing, not an accident of the housing department but more like a contract signed in blood—we'd arrived at Slice of Heaven later than normal. It had been Lauren's idea to bike along an offshoot of the Housatonic, and she'd shot three rolls, including one of me, shivering in my gray Keale T-shirt. By the time our pizza arrived, it was fully dark, and we had to hurry if I was going to get back in time for my evening shift at the switchboard.

Lauren was complaining about the upcoming summer—if she couldn't find something to do, she would end up interning for her dad in DC. I'd heard threads of this argument a dozen times, but I still couldn't understand what made interning for her father such a bad option. I was trying to decide whether I should beg for my job back at the Woodstock Diner or accept Gerry Tallant's offer of a temp job in the tax office. I would have jumped at the chance to intern for a senator.

While Lauren talked in circles, I picked the pepperonis off the uneaten slices and popped them in my mouth, one by one. Licking the grease from my fingers, I caught the glance of a guy across the restaurant, wedged into a booth with two companions, their bulk spilling over the end of the bench seat. One of them smiled at me, raising a glass. The others turned toward us, following his gaze.

"Hey," I said, interrupting Lauren's monologue. "Don't look now, but those guys are checking us out. I said *don't* look now," I repeated as she swiveled her head.

Chastened, Lauren allowed an appropriate amount of time to pass before sweeping the restaurant with a casual glance. She wrinkled her nose. "They look like townies. Are you interested?"

I raised an eyebrow. "Loserville, population three."

"What should we do? Keep being our charming selves?"

"Want me to burp the alphabet?" I offered.

She laughed and glanced over at them again. "Shit. I made eye contact. One of them is coming over here."

"Is it too late to hide under the table?"

We were both laughing now, too loudly, and in a moment the guy was standing there, a shadow falling over the remaining scraps of our pizza. He was our age or a bit older, light brown hair peeking out like a fringe around the edges of his baseball cap. His moustache was untrained, leaving wispy hairs to spill onto his upper lip. Lauren looked down at her plate.

"Are you two from around here?" he asked.

I rolled my eyes. "Really? That's the best you've got?"

When he smiled, his lip disappeared beneath the fledgling moustache. "All right. I could ask if you'd let me buy you a drink."

"We have drinks," I pointed out, gesturing to our sodas in their red tempered plastic cups.

"Not that kind of drink. There's a bar a couple blocks down, if you want to see where the locals hang out." His gaze moved from me to Lauren, whose eyes were fixed on me. It was clear she was going to be useless in this situation. I was sure she'd been hit on by dozens of guys, but they'd probably had hyphenated last names and cars that cost more than their private school tuition. The last thing we needed was to end up doing shots at a dive bar with these guys just because she was too polite to say no.

I reached across the table for Lauren's hand, lacing her fingers through mine. Her eyes widened, but then I felt the warm return pressure of her grip, the creaminess of her skin from the lemon-scented lotion she applied every morning. I smiled at her, then up at the poor guy, whose cheeks flamed with embarrassment.

"So," I said. "Do you often hit on lesbians?"

Lauren cleared her throat. "Seriously. Do you mind? We're trying to have a private moment here."

"My apologies," the guy said, giving us a mock bow. To his friends he called, "They're a bunch of dykes!" A few heads turned—the openmouthed shock of high school girls, the raised eyebrows of a man old enough to be my father.

I was angry about the slur, even if it didn't apply to us. "Hey, you know what? Why don't you back the fuck away and save yourself years of reconstructive dental work?" More heads turned; there was open staring now, and one of the pizza employees who had been wiping down the buffet took an uncertain step toward us, a bar towel in her hand.

He glared at me, muttering "Bitch" as he turned around. His friends were on their feet now, balling up their greasy napkins, teasing him.

I settled back, shaking, embarrassed to be the center of attention, but when I looked at Lauren, she was beaming. Before I could register what was happening, she had leaned across the table to give me a generous kiss, one that landed half on my mouth. I heard the guys hoot with laughter, and when I looked up again they were gone, their table littered with napkins and plates.

"I can't believe you did that," I said. "Seriously—well played."

Lauren grinned. "I can see the headlines now. Senator's Daughter Involved in Torrid Lesbian Affair."

"Ooh," I said, taking the last slug of my soda. "*Torrid.* I've always wanted to make the papers, you know."

Lauren shook her head, almost sadly. "Unfortunately, it would never go that far. My mom would get to everyone first. She'd threaten the pizza employees with their jobs if they talked. She'd dig up the dirt on those fine, upstanding gentlemen. And she'd pay you off, of course. Within a week, you'd be back in Kansas, living like a queen."

I laughed at her seriousness, as if any of this were an actual possibility. "Your mom would pay me off? Really? What's the going rate for despoiling a senator's daughter?"

There was something strange about the look Lauren gave me, a smile that curved slowly upward, so slowly it didn't seem like a smile at all. "You'd be an idiot if you took anything less than two million."

I blinked.

"Come on," she said. "Let's get out of here."

Our ride back to campus was eerie and quiet, the road clear and the sky dark, stars hidden behind a sudden low cover of clouds. I took the lead, pumping hard to set a pace that would allow me to make it back to campus before my shift.

Behind me, Lauren called out, "Someone's coming," and I scooted as far as possible to the right. Headlights washed over us, and I glanced over my shoulder. Instead of moving into the oncoming lane to give us a wide berth, the way cars usually did, this one pulled up close and hung even.

"Shit," Lauren said, and even before I dared a glance, I knew who it would be. There were three guys in the cab of the truck, and the one who leaned out the passenger window was the one with the moustache, his mouth pressed now into a flat line.

"Hey, ladies," he called, his voice cutting through the night. "Remember us?"

"Go faster," I told Lauren, sweat blooming beneath my shirt.

"Looks like you're in a hurry," he called. "Want a ride?"

"Fuck off," I snapped. "Leave us alone."

The truck stayed even with us, dangerously close, the warmth of the engine a palpable thing. Lauren let out a sound behind me, a half whimper, and I imagined that headline: Senator's Daughter and Friend Attacked on Rural Connecticut Road. The guy in the middle leaned toward the window, the brim of his hat shading most of his face, only the humorless line of his mouth visible. "Why so nasty?" he called. "We're just being polite."

The truck edged closer, pushing us toward loose gravel and a sloping decline into the ditch that lined the side of the road, a repository of graying snow and slush. We were about a mile from Keale, the lights of campus not yet visible, the town several miles behind us. There would be no witnesses, I thought, my heart thudding, fury building.

"Megs," Lauren breathed. "What are we going to—"

I held one hand aloft, flipping a mighty bird in the direction of the truck. "Get out of here, assholes! Go screw your pet cows or something!"

Behind me, Lauren whined, "Megan, don't. Let's just keep going."

As if moved by her plea, the truck pulled ahead, belching a cloud of exhaust as it accelerated.

"We're fine," I called over my shoulder, trying to sound like I believed it. "They're a bunch of idiots. Let's go."

Up ahead, near the slight sloping crest before the Keale campus came into view, the pickup braked suddenly and executed a wild U-turn, kicking up gravel on the side of the road.

Shit. Sweat crawled down my neck, tangling my hair. They were coming back for us.

I yelled, "We have to keep going! We can't stop now."

It was like a scene from a movie, surreal but fascinating, the sort of thing you watched through spread fingers. Engine roaring, the truck started for us, headlights bleaching out the rest of the world. Lauren pulled even with me, and we stood, feet on the ground, frozen. *They're going to force us off the road,* I thought, and I could see it, could feel it—the two of us sliding into the ditch, legs tangled in our bikes. The next frame belonged to a horror movie, our mouths gagged with our own shirts, our wrists held down.

Lauren clutched my sleeve with one hand, her mouth a gaping hollow. I wanted to tell her that they were only trying to scare us, but I couldn't keep up the facade any longer. They were three shadowy figures in the front seat of a pickup truck on a quiet road at the tail end of spring, and they were going to do more than scare us.

This is what you get, I told myself. *This is the punishment you've been waiting for.* It was always coming, all along. I'd known it since that moment I'd held the pillow over Dad's face, feeling the tug-of-war between life and death.

"Lauren," I said, wanting to apologize because it was my fault, it was always all my fault.

Headlights approached from behind us then, and a car slowed, navigating the narrow space between the truck and our bikes. Someone in the back seat waved—a girl I recognized from our dorm, and I raised my hand in return, the gesture halfway between a wave and a cry for help. On the other side of the road, the pickup roared past, its taillights disappearing until the truck was only a speck in the distance, benign as a child's toy.

"Holy crap," Lauren breathed, but I couldn't even form words. When we started again, my legs wobbled on the pedals. I nearly sobbed with relief when we crested the hill and the campus came into view a minute later, the dorms lit like candles on a tiered birthday cake. We biked, wordless, to the green space in the center of campus, in front of the building that housed the switchboard.

I retied my ponytail with shaking hands. "Well, that was interesting."

Lauren's cheeks were flushed, her chest heaving. "I thought I was going to wet myself. Seriously—I almost lost control of all bodily functions. But you! You were so cool. I was almost afraid for those guys."

"Ha," I said weakly. "I was a mess all the way through."

Lauren shook her head. "No, you were great. You went all Kansas on them."

"Is that what it's called?" I swung one leg over the bike, dismounting. "I'd better go. Try to stay out of trouble, okay?"

She pushed off, heading for the dorms. When she reached the edge of the path that veered toward Stanton, she stopped and looked back at me. It took a moment for me to understand what she was saying since her words were bouncing off the buildings, the sound echoing back to me. "You're a freaking hero! You're my hero!"

All that night, the words echoed inside me, too.

A hero.

Me, a freaking hero.

OCTOBER 10, 2016

LAUREN

We were running late; we were always, always running late, no matter how early we started. My alarm had gone off at 5:45, when the day was still dark, and everyone else was asleep. Schnauzer, our unfortunately named golden retriever, was already doing frantic circles by the back door when I made it downstairs in my yoga pants and tennis shoes. I pulled on one of Brady's old college sweatshirts, leashed Schnauzer, and we were out the door, stopping first at the birch tree in the front yard for a long, relieved pee, and then heading out for a quick sprint around the block that left both of us panting. It would be the only meaningful exercise either of us got all day, and it was over in ten minutes.

Back at home, it took longer than normal to wake up Emma, and Stella had a minor meltdown about her hair, which still looked puffy despite her attempts to straighten it. "All the girls in the eighth grade have straight hair," she whined as I ran a comb through the frizziest parts and attacked them with the flatiron she'd begged for last Christmas.

In the middle of this, Brady had kissed me goodbye, mouthing *I'm sorry* in my direction. He did more than his share at night, but in the parental division of labor, mornings were mine.

Now Stella seethed next to me in the front seat of the Pathfinder, her jaw set against whatever obstacles the day would bring. I thought about telling her how I had hated school when I was her age, too, but that was a world away, fancy prep school versus perfectly good public school, old school snobbery versus SnapChat and Instagram. In the back seat, Emma was wondering aloud about moths, and why they wanted to fly so close to the light, and why when you saw a moth up close, it looked like it was a hundred years old. Our childhoods, truthfully, were nothing alike.

I dropped Stella off at the edge of the middle school property and watched her go as I waited through the chain of minivans and SUVs. She was a thin silhouette in skinny jeans and a tunic that hung halfway to her knees, and she was in an incomprehensible hurry to grow up, to get her period and fill out her bra, to enter the complicated world of adults.

Someone behind me honked, and I raised my hand reflexively in apology.

Emma's school was less than a mile away, but it was a clogged mile, full of parents like me making the morning run, their back seats crammed with car seats and soccer cleats. It was already 8:05, and the warning bell would ring in five minutes. I put on my blinker at the last moment, spotting a place on the side of the road.

"What are we doing?"

I put the Pathfinder into Park and killed the engine, tucking the keys into the pocket of my jacket. "I'll go ahead and walk you from here, okay? It'll be faster."

Emma held my hand as we made our way down the sidewalk and around the bus lane to the second-grade wing. She took her lunch pail from my hand, angling her head upward to meet my lips for a goodbye kiss. When she ran off, the lights on the bottoms of her shoes blinked against the pavement.

The sound of the first bell sent a throng of second graders rushing past. Someone jostled my elbow—it was Emma's teacher, Ms. Marris, young and golden haired. "Oh, I'm sorry. You're Emma's mom, right? How are you?"

"Oh, fine. Just dropping her off." I was acutely aware of my yoga pants, the same ones I'd been wearing yesterday when I picked Emma up from school. That was the problem with working from home; certain standards were necessarily relaxed.

"She's such a sweet girl," Ms. Marris said. I tried to remember her first name from the parent-teacher conference where she'd shown me a stack of Emma's drawings of salmon at various stages of their life cycles. Rachel, maybe? Rachelle?

I smiled. "She gets that from her father."

She hesitated, and I began to sense that something was strange about this conversation, about the way Emma's teacher was just standing there, not moving along to her twenty-five students who were lined up according to a mysterious, prearranged pattern. Her eyes held mine for just a beat longer than friendliness required. Was there something she wanted to say to me? Something about Emma, her grades or her behavior? That didn't seem likely. But instead she touched me quickly on the arm. "You take care."

"Thank you—I will," I answered, puzzled. "You take care, too."

The tardy bell rang, and I stood on the sidewalk as the chaos of a few minutes earlier became a sort of order and lines of students traipsed past on their way to class.

My pocket vibrated, and I pulled out my cell phone. Probably Stella, telling me she'd forgotten something at home—her PE shorts, maybe, or ten dollars for one fund-raiser or another. But this message was from my mother, who contacted me so rarely that it was always a shock to see her name on the screen. It was in all caps, either because the message was important or because to my mother texting was still an elusive technological function.

DON'T TURN ON THE TELEVISION. CALL ME FIRST.

SUMMER 2000

LAUREN

As my mother would have said, Megan Mazeros wasn't someone we *knew*. She wasn't from an important family, she wasn't one of Dad's constituents and there were no obvious extrinsic benefits to our friendship.

I hadn't told Mom anything about my fight with Erin, so she was surprised the first time Megan answered the phone in our dorm room at Keale, and she was still grilling me about her when I came home for two weeks before starting my summer job. After the relative freedom of Keale, Holmes House felt like a form of house arrest, as if I were wearing an ankle bracelet that would alert my mother whenever I left the grounds. When I took my camera out in the mornings, with the light glinting through gaps in the trees, she inevitably followed me, picking her way carefully behind me in a pair of gardening shoes that had never once been worn for gardening.

"Mazeros," she said for the millionth time, turning over the name in her mouth, placing the accent on a new syllable, as if there was something untrustworthy about the letters themselves. "Where is she from, exactly? Poland? Hungary?"

"*Mom*, I told you. She's from Kansas." The ghost of Marcus

Rodriguez hovered between us for a moment, and I knew that she was seeing Megan the same way, another person with a foreign-sounding name, another person who couldn't be trusted. That was her default position, despite any evidence to the contrary.

Mom hesitated, as if she were running through a mental Rolodex of people she knew from Kansas and coming up empty. "And where did she go to school?"

"In Kansas, Mom. A public school." I enunciated the words for her carefully, in case she'd never heard them.

"I'm only asking! We don't know anything about her. It's just surprising, when you and Erin seemed like such a perfect match. I don't understand why you girls didn't want to stay together."

I turned to her, holding the camera at eye level. She put up a hand, ducking my shot. When I developed it later, her delicate ringed fingers would seem large as a catcher's mitt.

Out behind Holmes House, the lake reflected ripples of sunlight. It was so quiet out here, a change from the constant female chatter at Keale. But then, it had always been quiet out here, since the lake was within our property line, and the property was hemmed in by one of those rambling Connecticut forests, the trees muzzling the rest of the world. Mom followed me down the steps and onto the path that led across the lawn. "Well, I suppose I'll meet her this fall, then. Maybe for Parents' Weekend."

I wasn't eager to repeat that particular experience. Megan had the right idea, keeping her mother securely stowed away in Kansas.

"It'll be nice," Mom continued, forcing the smile into her voice. "We'll have dinner, maybe take the two of you to a movie or something, whatever you'd like to do."

I laughed, imagining The Senator and The Countess and

Megan and me, all lined up in Scofield's falling-apart theater. "Actually," I said, the idea coming to me suddenly, brilliantly, "maybe I could invite her here sometime, for Thanksgiving or Christmas break." Now that the words were out, I was sure it was the best idea I'd ever had. Megan never seemed to be in any hurry to return to Kansas, and I was already dreading the thought of an uninterrupted month of the Mabreys.

Behind me, Mom stopped short. "I don't know if that's such a good idea."

A duck flapped into the water, ducking its head beneath the surface. I shot its tailfeathers and webbed feet, then the quick, bewildered expression as its head reappeared. "Why not? It was never a problem when I brought my Reardon friends here."

"But we knew..." Her voice trailed off, and I finished the sentence for myself. *We knew their families. We knew where they were from. We knew what their fathers did.*

We knew who they were.

I bent down, rolling the hems of my jeans into thick cuffs. "Don't worry. I'll have her brush up her résumé and letters of reference. Maybe Dad can get someone from the FBI to run a background check. It'll all work out." I kicked off my flip-flops and left her on the grassy bank, glaring at me, while I wandered a few steps into the water, bending low to shoot the pale skin of my feet and the meandering ripples that widened outward.

Since arriving at Holmes House, I'd emailed Megan every day from the computer in Mom's office. Sometimes it was just a quick How are you? I'm dying here. She always replied immediately. Hey! I'm good. Bored as hell. Or maybe I just got a papercut from an envelope, so I've had my excitement for the day. I could almost imagine her at the county tax office, sandwiched in a cubicle, surrounded by filing cabinets and washed out beneath fluorescent lights. She'd only laughed when I invited her to apply to Camp Watachwa with me.

"I've never been to summer camp," she'd pointed out, thumbing through the application materials. "I don't even have a frame of reference for being a counselor. And this other stuff—watersports specialist, equestrian coach? Please."

"You could apply, though. I mean, you have good grades. They'd find something for you."

She'd continued reading from the packet in her faux-snooty voice. "*Our staff hails from more than sixteen countries.* Is that new, or did you have staff from sixteen countries when you went there?"

I frowned, trying to remember. There had been a counselor once from Sweden, Lars. But he'd attended a prep school in Manhattan and despite an accent that made every girl older than eleven drool, he hadn't seemed particularly exotic. "I think there were people from other countries who worked in the kitchen."

Megan raised an eyebrow. "Are you aware of how that sounds?"

"I mean, no. That's not what I meant." But when I thought about it, it was true. When I'd passed behind the kitchen after mealtimes, I'd heard them laughing and teasing and singing, breaking into phrases of their native language, almost as if they inhabited an entirely different world from the rest of us.

Megan tossed the packet back to me. "Seriously? This place would never hire me. And I'm trying not to work in a kitchen for a change."

I hadn't been sure that Camp Watachwa would hire me, although I'd spent six summers there as a camper, mostly managing to stay out of trouble and once being a captain on Color Days. I wasn't sure it was what I wanted to do, either, but I hadn't left myself with too many options. Megan had helped me craft a personal essay about the impact of Camp Watachwa on my life, how the counselors had inspired me, what I'd learned about bonding and friendship—none of which was exactly true, but by the third draft, it *felt* true. Dr. Mittel wrote a letter of recommendation for me, and Megan proofread the whole thing with her ferocious red pen before I sent it off.

It had been Megan's idea to tell Camp Watachwa about my passion for photography—by that time, I joked, I knew my way around a darkroom blindfolded. There hadn't been a photography option at Camp Watachwa when I attended it, but I wrote that I would be willing to set up a darkroom, run mini craft camps for the kids and coordinate an art show at the end of the summer.

Some combination of personal essay or letter of recommendation or grand promises had done the trick, and I would be spending the summer in the humid paradise of Camp Watachwa, but I did feel bad about Megan, stuck in the Woodstock County Tax Office, licking envelopes and getting paper cuts on her tongue.

Being back at camp as an adult was a surreal experience. Not much had changed in the basic structure of the place, but now that I was on the other side, it all looked too contrived—the cheery cabin signs, the stacks of red canoes, the "rules" spelled out in giant letters across the dining hall. 1. Have Fun. 2. Respect Others. 3. Respect Yourself. 4. Don't Forget to Have Fun! It seemed like a scam, a sort of forced march toward merriment, and I was amazed that I'd bought into it for so long, from eight to fourteen years old.

It had been a surprise to recognize some of the same staff members from my time as a camper—as if they'd been here all along, year-round, day in and out, for the last five years. One of them was the camp manager, Camden Pierce. When

I was younger, he'd seemed so effortlessly, naturally *cool*—enthusiastic and supportive and authoritative, all at once. Now I saw that this was a veneer for his real persona, the wannabe frat boy who had never grown up, who hit on all the female counselors, farted openly when we stood in line together for breakfast, and turned into a child when things didn't go his way. Megan would have put up with him for all of five seconds. If he'd patted her casually on the ass, the way he did to me each morning, she would have snapped, "Hands off, bitch." I only smiled when he stood behind me in line and tried to maneuver myself out of arm's reach.

Despite his morning overtures and the odd suggestive remark, Camden was okay, though. He let me take charge of the new darkroom, formerly a janitor's storage room, equipped with a sink and countertop. I spent the first week in it by myself, completely absorbed in arranging equipment and getting ready for the first campers to visit. When it became clear that the supply of developing fluid and photo paper wouldn't last more than a few weeks, I ordered more out of my own meager check.

The darkroom wasn't as big of a hit with the campers as I'd hoped—most of them had come equipped with digital cameras, and although their shots lacked artistry, they were content with the instant gratification of the medium. Still, my Monday-Wednesday-Friday photography lessons gained a following, and I ended up with a small troop that hiked with me through the forest and down to the water, trying to capture the extraordinary in the ordinary—light and color and feeling. On Saturdays and Sundays I held darkroom sessions, taking students into the tiny space two at a time to watch the images emerge before our eyes—deep blacks and silvery grays and alabaster whites, faces and places and things preserved now, more permanent than memory.

I emailed Megan from one of the rickety computers in the staff lounge, nearly drifting off while I waited for the dial-up connection. Maybe I should take some education classes, I wrote. What if I'm even the tiniest bit good at this? It was a question I wouldn't have asked anyone in my family, where their disbelief would have been difficult to hide, their sneering too obvious.

I could hear Megan's voice in her reply: Of course you'd be good at it, you moron. You'd be good at anything.

If only she knew me—really knew me, she would never have believed that. But I rode that compliment for days, trying it out. *Lauren Mabrey, good at anything.*

One Saturday I was in the darkroom after the last trio of girls had left, their prints still hanging from tiny clips around the room, fluttering in the slight current from an overhead vent. There were supplies to put away and tools to rinse, and I was puttering around, thinking that I needed to write Megan back and take a stack of dirty camp polo shirts down to the staff laundry when I heard voices outside the door. I'd locked it behind me—my usual habit whenever something could be exposed accidentally, a very real threat in a place teeming with eight- to fourteen-year-olds.

It didn't take much to recognize Camden's voice, bursting with confidence. The other voice belonged to Julia, the counselor he had been flirting with for the last few weeks, his admiration for her lanky volleyball-playing physique obvious. She was saying something about her classes at Brown—it had been *Brown this* and *Brown that* all summer from her, and I stood motionless, a bottle of developing fluid in one hand, waiting for them to wander in another direction. It wasn't until the door handle jiggled that I realized what they wanted—a private room, the most precious commodity in the camp.

Camden swore, and the doorknob continued to rattle aggressively.

"Isn't there a key?" Julia asked.

It sounded like Camden was jumping, taking sweeping stabs at my hiding place on the ledge above the door. Not such a great hiding place, I realized now. How long had he been using my darkroom for his rendezvous?

"Dammit," he said. "It's supposed to be right here."

I reached down with one hand and felt the reassuring outline of the key in my pocket.

"Lauren must have it," Julia said. "Want me to go look for her?"

"Hold on," Camden said. "Let me just try—"

This time it seemed like he was jamming something in the lock. Another key? A toothpick? If the lock broke, would I be trapped here, at the mercy of one of the girls in my cabin to notice that I was missing? It was too late to announce my presence now, to call casually through the door for them to hold on, or suggest they find a different room.

"I don't like her," Julia was saying. "She's so snooty."

"Who, Lauren?"

"Yeah. The senator's daughter." I could hear the way she was rolling her eyes.

Bitch. I'd never done anything to her.

The doorknob seemed to be moving more loosely now, Camden's jerking motions sending it backward and forward. What would happen if the door popped open and we came face-to-face with each other?

Julia was still talking. "She's a complete snob. You know she never does anything with the rest of the counselors?"

I held my breath, shaking. Up until this point, I'd never given Julia, or any of the other counselors, much thought. I'd been focused on doing my job, making the darkroom work. But apparently by not being chummy, I was aloof—no, *snooty*. It explained why conversations paused when I entered the dining hall, then adjusted themselves around me, as if I'd displaced the air by entering the room.

Camden laughed. "You want me to fire her or something?"

"You can do that?"

"Actually, no. Probably not. But if I'd had a choice, I wouldn't even have hired her."

"What do you mean?" Julia asked. "I thought you were in charge of hiring the staff."

Yes, I thought, my heart thudding. *What do you mean?*

Another laugh. "I got a phone call from her mother. It was basically a threat—if I hired Lauren, she would donate money to the camp, and if I didn't, we could count on never seeing a cent of their money."

"Fucking A," Julia said.

My insides twisted like a sheet in the laundry.

"Yeah, some people think they can just buy their way into anything." Camden laughed. "Of course, it worked, didn't it? Lauren's here and I got a raise. The Mabreys can take credit for sending three underprivileged kids to camp, and we got a darkroom out of the deal, which I happen to believe is useful in many ways."

"Hold on—" Julia squawked, apparently rebuffing his advances. "They paid for three kids? Are you saying her mom donated thirty thousand dollars just so you would hire her?"

Thirty thousand dollars. I turned the number over in my mind. Probably Camden had settled for too little. Mom might have gone higher—fifty thousand, maybe. Thrown in a resurfacing of the pool, a new diving board, a commercial oven.

"Julia, hold on. You can't say anything to anyone. I mean it."

She laughed. "Why not? You've got the money. Oh, I see. You want to see if you can squeeze out a few more drops down the road."

"I'm a businessman second," Camden said, and then, in a husky voice that made me gag, "but I'm a lover first."

Whatever he did next must have been convincing, because Julia moaned and asked, "What about the storage room behind the pool?"

I stayed in the darkroom for another twenty minutes, leaning against the counter, not trusting my feet to hold me up. I was both the senator's daughter and the charity case. If Camden knew, others knew—Julia now, but later her friends, other staffers and counselors. So much for the hours I'd put into that application, the careful proofreading from Megan, the recommendations that had made me seem like an ideal applicant rather than an average or questionable or shitty one.

Apparently, none of that had mattered.

Mom had paid Camp Watachwa to hire me for the summer. It made sense, the more I considered it. The camp got a pile of Mabrey money, with the caveat that they had to hire the Mabrey with the least potential. And since I was only going to earn two thousand dollars for eight weeks of round-the-clock labor, plus room and board—it was a good deal for them. All things considered, it was a fucking bargain.

Over the next few weeks, I tried to write this to Megan. She would have reassured me somehow, either by calling my mom a bitch or reminding me that she was essentially in the same position—a temp employee at the tax office because her mother was dating (*schtupping*, Megan would have said) the county tax assessor. She would have told me that those things happened all the time—it was all about knowing the right person, having the best connections. But in the end I was too humiliated—it was better to lie and say that Camp Watachwa was amazing, the summer was amazing, everything was amazing.

During the final week of camp, one wall of the cafeteria was dedicated to the art show. I had the campers help me choose their best work to put on display, the artists and titles of the work identified on three-by-five cards. There was "Sunset on Lake Watachwa" and "Spirit of Watachwa" and "Best Friends at Watachwa" and then, after they left, there were a few I'd added myself, "Camden and Julia"—a picture I'd taken of the two of them behind the pool shed, "Camden and Monique" behind the counselor's bathroom, "Camden and Carly" down by the lake.

My pictures of Camden and his conquests were gone by the time the campers streamed in the next morning, leaving gaping holes in the display. When I sat down to breakfast, some of the girls at the table stood up with their trays and moved to the far end of the room. But some of them stayed, and one of them said, "It's about time."

In the end, though, it wasn't really about Camden. My own mother had set me up for humiliation. I thought about throwing it in her face the moment I met up with my family again on The Island. *You pretend to care about reputation, but you were pretty quick to ruin mine.* How many girls had Camden told about my mother's generous checkbook, her charity-case daughter? The only thing that stopped me was the knowledge that she wouldn't have denied it. She would have said, in the calm voice of a senator's wife, that she was only looking out for my best interests.

Maybe it was time, then, that I started doing that for myself.

MEGAN

I spent most of the summer missing Keale like a phantom pain, half expecting to wake in the dorm room I shared with Lauren, to see her sleeping face buried beneath a dark swatch of hair. Instead, I'd opened my eyes to the beige walls of the spare bedroom in Gerry Tallant's house, unpacked clothes spilling out of my duffel bag, a novel spine-down on the floor next to the bed. The few boxes stacked in the corner were all that remained from my childhood.

From eight to five, Monday through Friday, I sat at a desk tucked into the back of the tax assessor's office, inserting numbers into templates, then printing and posting the letters for mailing. "A payment in the amount of $841.62 is due by the 15th. For every day after this date, a charge of $76.00 will accrue. After ninety days of delinquency..." It was depressing as hell to think of people opening these letters and scrambling to find the money for their payments, or living in fear of the moment that Uncle Sam would become the official owner of their property.

Sometimes, I borrowed Mom's car to drive past our old house. New people lived there, now, and they'd spray-painted the rusting screen door and repaved the driveway—things Dad had always meant to do. There were yellow curtains hanging in the kitchen window and rose bushes along the south side of the house. Everything was familiar but different, changing and moving on.

I wondered what Dad would think of me, a college student with one year under my belt. Thinking about him never ceased to fill me with an aching emptiness. He'd never get to ask about my classes, never see me in a cap and gown, even though he'd made it all possible. For her part, Mom was interested in my life only insofar as it intersected with Lauren's. *How rich are they, really? Is her father as handsome as he looks on CNN?*

After a week, I wrote to Lauren: I changed my mind. Maybe I want to work at Camp Fancy Pants after all.

She wrote back: Camp Fancy Pants wants you, too.

I asked for the last week of the summer, the week before I headed back to Scofield, off from work. I'd envisioned going to the community pool but spent my mornings in front of the TV and my afternoons driving around aimlessly, remembering things Dad and Mom and I had done together. At the end of the week, I visited the mall in Junction City with two hundred dollars from my temp earnings, wishing Lauren were there to advise me, fashion-wise. Of course, her advice would have been to go to nicer stores, to buy "higher quality" than what was available in the mall. I was coming out of the dressing room at Maurice's with two pairs of jeans and an armful of shirts when I ran into Becky Babcock, holding a purple sheath dress on a hanger.

We hugged tightly, and Becky invited me to her end-of-summer party. "For everyone heading back to college. The whole gang. You should totally come," she said, giving my arm a chummy squeeze.

"Thanks. That's so nice, but..." *Idiot*, I cursed myself. I couldn't even come up with a plausible excuse. Still, I'd stopped myself before saying, *I'd rather stay at home and read a book or watch old movies with my mom and her boyfriend.*

Becky's eyes narrowed. "We're probably not as exciting as your new friends, from what I hear."

"Hey, no. It's not like that," I assured her, although it might have been exactly like that. "I'll try to come."

And so I'd gone to Becky's party, and I'd refilled my red plastic cup more than once at the punch bowl, and I'd laughed with the girls I'd known in high school, most of whom hadn't come to my dad's funeral, and I'd listened to the gossip about who was dating whom and who was engaged or getting engaged, and who was knocked up or who wanted to get knocked up. I forced a smile until it felt real. What was the harm, being here? Soon enough I could be back at Gerry's house, eating ice cream directly from the container, and in a week I'd be back in Connecticut with Lauren, back in the life that felt more like mine than this one did.

I was standing with Becky and her friends Shelly and Yvette, girls from neighboring towns who attended KSU, when Kurt Haschke stepped onto the patio. We locked eyes, and he came over.

"Hey," I said.

"Hey."

"Oh, that's right," Becky trilled, her voice rising dramatically. "I forgot that you two know each other." She looked between the two of us, like she expected either sparks to fly or a fight to erupt, Jerry Springer–style, maybe with thrown chairs or pulled hair. *Okay.* If Becky Babcock knew about Kurt and me and last summer, everyone knew. Growing up in Woodstock should have taught me that nothing was private, that secrets only stayed intact if the other person died.

"How's Massachusetts?" Kurt asked.

"Connecticut." I smiled. "It's fine."

We stood a few feet apart, as if we were mere acquaintances, high school classmates who hadn't seen each other since graduation day. He looked the same as the last time I'd seen him—a summertime tan, hair shorter on the sides, but otherwise the same guy who'd once drawn a heart on the riverbank and written our names inside.

"How's here?" I asked.

"It's fine." He smiled. "It's good."

There was nothing else to say. We turned to look at the pool, where Becky and I used to float on giant rafts, holding cans of Diet Coke. Now it was swarming with bodies and beach balls. A guy wearing jeans and tennis shoes was pushed into the water, and then someone else in only a pair of striped boxers cannonballed in, to wild cheers.

"That idiot," Becky said with affection.

"Becks, come here," someone called, and she wandered away.

Kurt and I stood side by side, not looking at each other. I wanted to ask about his auto tech program, but decided against it. If I'd said yes to his proposal, we might have been married already, living in someone's basement apartment, scoping out furniture at garage sales and eating Pasta Roni for dinner. The truth was that we'd barely known each other then, and we knew nothing about each other now.

I crinkled my empty cup until the plastic snapped, the sides shattering. Since alcohol was officially forbidden in the dorms at Keale and high school barn parties were long behind me, I was out of the habit of serious drinking. My head felt heavy, and I thought longingly about Mom's car, parked a block away.

Another guy ran past, jostling my elbow as he headed for the pool.

Kurt turned to me. "Do you want to get out of here?"

And I knew—of course I did—exactly what he meant.

Later, I would try to explain it to myself, offering up rationalizations. I was drunk, I was lonely and maybe I didn't care.

We were quiet as we navigated our way back through Becky's house, out onto her front porch. My hair, damp with sweat, stuck to the back of my neck. Kurt still had his same truck, the lifted Dodge I'd been in so many times before. I grabbed the handle and hoisted myself upward, surprised at how the motion came back to me, like muscle memory. The engine sputtered and caught, and I knew where we were heading: the river, our old spot.

In that moment, it was as if there were two Megan Mazeroses—one who had gone to the party and left early, changed into pajamas and settled in front of the television. I could see her on the corduroy couch, could imagine her listless boredom as she flipped through channels on the remote, finding nothing. The other Megan, the one whose body I was trapped inside, sat motionless as Kurt reached for her waistband, tugging so hard that the metal button sprang off and clanged against the dashboard. He kept the A/C blasting while he rolled her jeans down her hips, while his hand unhooked her bra.

Sex with Kurt had always been pleasant, if not earth shattering. There had been a routine, a predictable order of events that brought an undeniable comfort. My life might have been a mess otherwise—the shitty tips at the diner, my father slowly dying in his recliner—but I'd been able to forget that when I was with Kurt.

This time, it wasn't so much sex as it was punishment, making a point. Kurt's hands were rough, his stubble like a Brillo pad on my skin. His eyes bored into mine, as if he were delivering a message. *Look what could have been yours. Look what you're missing.* Or maybe it was something else, more sinister—*Look what you deserve.*

I gasped when he entered me, my body resisting although my mind had already agreed. He took this as a form of encouragement and pushed harder. With each thrust, his T-shirt fluttered over my face. I turned my gaze to the side, unable to look at him, focusing instead on the floor mat where an inch of green liquid sloshed in a lonely bottle of Mountain Dew.

I didn't protest, didn't refuse, didn't say no, didn't stop him. *It's just one time*, I promised myself. *One last time.*

He pulled up his shorts when he finished, and I reached behind my back, trying to bring the stubborn halves of my bra together.

"What now?" he asked, and I stared at him. We hadn't spoken the entire time, and now it didn't seem that there was anything to say. There was something hopeful in his question, as if we could go back to Becky Babcock's party, his arm around my shoulder, my hand tucked into his back pocket.

"Now you take me back to my car," I said.

He pounded the steering wheel once with his fist before hitting the gas. The tires spun, kicking up a cloud of dust outside the window.

It wasn't until later, when I'd retrieved Mom's car and was driving back to Gerry's house that I glanced in the mirror and saw that my cheeks were tear-stained. I pulled over at a gas station and went into the bathroom, wiping my face with a scratchy paper towel and mopping up the shame between my legs. When I got home, Mom and Gerry were already in bed, the lights off except for a lamp in the foyer. I logged onto Gerry's computer in his office and saw an email from Lauren.

Hello from paradise, she wrote. Can you believe we'll see each other in a week?

There was an attachment, and it was slow to load, starting as a pixelated blue that ended up being the sky. It was a picture of a boat out on the water, taken from The Island, as the Mabreys called it—their own private paradise. *The whole family was there*, she said. *You should be here, too*, she said. *Wouldn't that be fun?*

I went to bed knowing I wouldn't ever see Kurt Haschke again, and for that matter, vowing that I would never return, in any significant way, to Woodstock.

By morning, I'd reframed the story, Megan-from-Kansas-style, planning how I would tell it to Lauren in one of our late-night dorm room chats. I'd tell her that I ran into my old boyfriend, that we'd had some wild times down at the river, that we'd hooked up at a few parties. I'd shrug the whole thing off like it was nothing serious, like it didn't mean anything at all.

OCTOBER 10, 2016

MEGAN

I cleaned up the ceramic shards, my hands fumbling with the broom and dustpan, and then I watched the press conference again, using the rewind and fast forward buttons on the overly complicated remote. A young blonde woman, identified on the bottom of the screen as Anna Kovics, read from a statement as cameras clicked and flashed around her. "He came up behind me and forced me into his office, where he held me down…" There was a slight waver to her voice, a sheen of sweat on her face under the studio lights, the purplish stain of dark circles under her eyes.

"He tore my skirt," she said.

She looked directly into the camera when she said, "He raped me."

I watched it again and again, a dozen times, unable to look away. All the while, the minutes were racing; I'd used up the morning's extra time. Still, I watched it again. The girl on the screen looked a whole lot like me, down to the purple circles under her eyes. Or at least, she looked like me when I was in college.

Fourteen years was a long time. It was long enough to forget, forgive, move on.

And yet when I finally got to my feet, nausea surged inside me, threatening to bring up the morning's coffee and whatever was undigested from last night's dinner. I heard Anna Kovics's words, filtered through my long-ago self:

He came up behind me.

He held me down.

He raped me.

At 8:20, I logged onto my email and sent an apology using the vaguest of terms. An upset stomach, a sudden onset. This much was true, although the real story was a dozen layers deep, buried with the person I'd been then, so different from the person I was now. Calling up the memories was like watching an old home movie and not recognizing myself on the screen.

I spent the day surfing headlines on the *Hartford Register*, *the Boston Globe*, CNN and MSNBC. There was a blurb in *the Washington Post* and later, a short mention in *the New York Times*. I read every single comment on every article, cringing. Some were supportive of Anna, some were against men in general and politicians specifically, many were inflammatory and a few were horrific—a regular verbal vomit stew.

Just another money-grabbing whore.

These men think they can get away with anything. It's time to hold them accountable!

This is what happens when you get a little bit of power.

I'd do her, lol.

What else are interns for?

I pressed on, grimly determined not to look away. Not this time.

It was a smaller story than it might have been under different circumstances, without the craziness of the presidential election or the backdrop of police shootings and drilling on sacred land in North Dakota. This was one woman, one senatorial candidate, one accusation. But the story came in the midst of a condemnation of "locker room talk," the pushback against a swell of misogynistic behavior, an anti-*boys-will-be-boys* movement.

In the middle of the day, I summoned the energy to climb the stairs, strip off my pajamas and stand in a cloud of steam in the shower, my forehead pressed against the cool tile, hot water stinging my back. That night was there, the memories waiting—*he came up behind me, he ripped my clothes, he held me down*. And then I grabbed a loofah and scrubbed my skin raw, trying to wash away fourteen years of shame.

By the time I returned to my laptop, the story had turned: Anna Kovics went to nightclubs. She drank. Her Instagram account had a selfie of Anna in a tight red dress, her lips pouting at the camera. An ex-boyfriend from UConn described her to a conservative news site as "wild." She wasn't virginal and unspoiled, the way we like our victims to be.

By one-thirty, the Mabreys had released a statement expressing shock over the allegations, and it was there, on all the cable news stations. It wasn't hard to imagine Mrs. Mabrey in her tidy home office, under her daughter's framed *New York Times* wedding announcement, dictating the official wording: "Senator Mabrey was sadly deceived by the character of Ms. Kovics, who worked closely with our family during the last campaign. We are confident that these charges will be exposed as false, and Senator Mabrey will continue to work on behalf of the people of the great state of Connecticut." There were various shots of the senator—dark-suited and poised behind a microphone at a congressional hearing, at a ribbon-cutting ceremony earlier that month in Hartford, in a navy sweater with his arm around his wife.

Anna Kovics was nothing more than a crumb to be brushed from his lapel.

Bobby always teased that I was the least connected person in the world. A *Luddite*, he claimed, although this wasn't exactly true. I had a cell phone, although it was only sporadically charged; I had a single email address, used only for work. Bobby loved social media, especially since it allowed him to follow his sports on a half-dozen platforms—Retweeting baseball scores and Instagramming snaps from his slow-pitch softball league, posting status updates about trades and injuries for his Fantasy Football league. He had more than seven hundred friends, including colleagues and former students and just about everyone he'd ever met socially. Sometimes, he posted a picture of the two of us—at a birthday dinner or a New Year's party, some occasion where we were both dressed up and smiling—but I insisted that he identify me only as *Megan*.

Megan no-last-name, Megan the social-media-phobe, Megan who shall not be tagged.

I knew his Facebook log-in, though, and occasionally I went onto the site—not so much to snoop on Bobby, who was transparent to a fault—but to peek at Lauren's account. I'd found her first years ago, after clicking on the page for Keale alumni. Unlike women from a generation ago whose trails were lost by marriage and name changes, the Keale page listed everyone's maiden name. Once I clicked on the name Lauren (Mabrey) Leavitt, her life had spilled open like a sack of rice.

Facebook told me that Lauren was married to Braden Leavitt, a Georgetown graduate and immigration attorney. They lived in Tiverton, Rhode Island, a place I'd Googled, bringing up the map and street views, trying to imagine Lauren walking there, living there, being Lauren there. I tried to pick out her neighborhood, based on what I knew of the Mabreys. A single-family home, a large yard, a European sedan in the driveway. The postings on her actual page were sparse—no doubt she had enabled some privacy settings to keep people like me from finding her—but a few were viewable in an album of profile pictures. It was a shock, always, to encounter this more recent version of Lauren, to reconcile her with the reel-to-reel Lauren of my Keale memories, the girl who was always behind a camera, the shutter blinking like a giant third eye.

In her new life, Lauren had two daughters and a husband with a kind smile. Her hair was still dark and thick and long, spilling over her shoulders like she was posing for a shampoo advertisement. Tiny lines were etched around her eyes, and there was a crease at the corner of her mouth when she smiled. She looked happy. Why not? Why shouldn't life work out for her, the way it worked out for all the Mabreys?

There was no mention on her Facebook page of today's scandal—the allegation or its aftermath. Not that there would be—the Mabreys as I had known them were unfailingly insular; they were probably hunkered down in their Connecticut estate, coming up with plans and strategies and counterattacks. Maybe Lauren was in the thick of their discussion, or maybe she was down in the basement dungeon, her feet up on the coffee table, flipping idly through channels.

What would she think of today's allegations?

Would she dismiss Anna Kovics instantly—*we were sadly deceived by the character of Ms. Kovics*—or would there be a flickering moment of doubt, one that wormed its way deep inside her, one that reminded her of me?

Not for the first time, I wondered if she ever searched Facebook for Megan Mazeros, if she ever thought about that summer, if she regretted that night.

Not for the first time, I wondered if she ever thought about me at all.

By the time Bobby came home, I was propped up in bed, the television muted in front of me, the misspelled comments of the announcers appearing in short bursts of closed captioning. He kissed me on the forehead, as if feeling for a fever. "Doing any better?"

I shook my head.

"Forget about tonight, then," he said, loosening his tie and pulling it over his head like a noose. He went through his end-of-the-day routine: hanging up his tie and belt, placing his shirt, pants and dress socks in the hamper, reaching for the jeans and T-shirt that were draped over a chair in the corner of the room. "Do you think it was something you ate this weekend? I thought the chow mein smelled a bit funny when I looked at it this morning."

"I don't think it was anything I ate," I said.

He sat on the bed next to me, a sympathetic hand reaching for mine.

On the television, the news cycle returned to Senator Mabrey. The pictures cycled, lingering on the one of him with his wife, the two of them as poised as a pair of Kennedys. I pointed the remote in the direction of his face, the female announcer's voice filling the room. "...in the wake of an accusation from a former intern. We'll continue to update you if there are further developments in this story."

I hit the mute button again, plunging the room into silence.

Bobby sighed, gesturing at the television. "What gets me is the women, you know what I mean?"

I tensed. "No."

"I don't mean the victims. I'm talking about the wives, the ones who just stand there with these fixed smiles on their faces while their husbands claim to be family men. How do they do it?" He stacked two throw pillows for cushioning and leaned back against the headboard.

"It's disgusting," I said.

"Yeah, it is." After a moment, he put his arm around my shoulders, his hand gently massaging through my curls. I thought I'd cried myself empty in the shower, but it turned out there was more—all the things I'd kept hidden, things I should have said years ago. I'd been too ashamed; it had been easier to be the person to whom horrible things hadn't happened. Not a victim, but not a survivor, either. A blank slate, unspoiled, undamaged.

"Hey—you'll be okay," Bobby said.

It was funny how love worked. The longer I was with Bobby, the fuzzier some of the specifics became, until it took moments like these to bring them back into focus.

Bobby was kind—to his friends and family, to our neighbors, to his students and coworkers, to the people he met in line at the grocery store.

Bobby understood things. He could talk to anyone—teenagers, their parents, cashiers at the 7-Eleven, random people we met in the airport who were wearing Red Sox paraphernalia. He could cry unabashedly—he'd done so when the Sox won the Series in 2013, and again at his aunt's funeral last spring.

He was loyal to his teams, to his school, to his friends, to me.

"Bobby, I have to tell you something," I said, and he turned to me, a question in his eyes.

★ ★ ★

It wasn't an easy story to tell, but then, it hadn't been an easy thing to live. I tried to begin at the beginning—but where was the beginning? All the way back when my dad died, or when I'd left Woodstock for the first time, excited and terrified all at once? It came out a bit muddled, but I got there: to the Mabreys and to that summer and everything that came after.

Bobby had gone very still, his arm balanced like a heavy weight on my shoulders.

It's okay, I promised myself. *Whatever he says or does, you're going to be okay.*

"Will you say something?" I asked finally. "Anything—whatever you're thinking."

"I don't know how—" He moved his arm, and when he brought it to his face, I realized he was crying, too. "First, I'm so sorry that this happened to you, and I'm sorry you didn't think you could tell me. And second, I hope you'll get some help. You know, really talk to someone who knows the right things to say, unlike me. And third—" he bunched his hands into fists "—I wish that guy was standing in front of me right now, because I'd kill him. I'd fucking kill him with my bare hands if I could."

I turned off the television, placing the remote on the nightstand and Bobby and I held each other until it grew dark outside. I felt a bit lighter, but guilty, too. I'd transferred some of my pain onto his shoulders.

Fourteen years, I thought.

It was a long time to keep a secret.

It was too long.

SOPHOMORE YEAR
2000–2001
LAUREN

Everything felt different that fall. We were sophomores now, no longer new to the campus and its rituals. Megan and I were in a different dorm, sharing a suite with two other girls. The word *suite* was somewhat generous, considering the cramped bathroom and kitchenette shared between the four of us. "I think my bedroom at home is bigger than our entire place," I complained without thinking one afternoon when it rained and the four of us were cooped up with our musty-smelling coats and boots. Megan only shrugged and said, "Feels like home to me."

I had a car that fall, too—MK's hand-me-down Saab that was pushing a hundred thousand miles. The car had been Dad's idea and Mom's concession; MK didn't need it anymore, and Mom must have been tired of ferrying me between campus and Holmes House for holidays and long weekends. Maybe she was too busy, or maybe she was simply loosening the reins a bit, a reward for keeping my head down and staying out of trouble. Megan and I took fewer bike rides and longer drives, winding our way past Connecticut's woods and lakes, singing along with Blues Traveler at the top of our lungs.

Once we saw a red fox down by the river, so brave it darted directly between the two of us. Another time we took off our shirts and lounged in our bras under an Indian summer sun. Only a week later, we got caught in a freak thunderstorm, the clouds rolling in low and black before we made it back to campus. I pulled over to the side of the road and we waited out the rain, buckets of water washing over the windows.

"Do you ever think about getting married?" Megan asked. She had told me about getting together with her old boyfriend over the summer, but her question caught me off guard.

I shrugged. "I guess, a million years from now."

"Not me. I'm never getting married."

"What? Sure you will. We all will, eventually."

"Not me," she said, rolling down the window a quarter inch to catch raindrops on her tongue. Then, after a beat, she threw open the door and ran into the rain, her jeans and sweatshirt immediately waterlogged. *Come on*, she gestured through the windshield. I shook my head, laughing, but after another minute I gave in. We danced in the rain until even our underwear was soaked, and dark streaks of mascara ran down Megan's face. We dried ourselves in the bathroom of a gas station, angling for a spot beneath the hand dryer, and we were still laughing an hour later when we walked into our dorm, shoes squishing.

I was busy that fall with my classes, including the biology class that had finally caught up with me, complete with its lab requirement and a weekly study group. I was freelancing for the *Courier,* too, taking the odd shot of visiting speakers and students being recognized for one achievement or another. Megan worked Tuesday nights at the switchboard in the student union building as well as alternating Friday and Saturday night shifts. I usually joined her there on Tuesdays when I got out of my bio lab, sitting cross-legged on the floor directly beneath the counter, so I wouldn't be visible in case her supervisor passed by. She helped me make vocabulary flashcards and quizzed me relentlessly; it was the only way I passed the random quizzes my instructor loved to hit us with at the beginning of class.

"This is something I will seriously never use in my life," I whined.

"But we're becoming well-rounded," Megan said, parroting one of Keale's basic tenets. "We know about history, philosophy, political science…"

"Oh, yes," I yawned. "We'll be able to talk about anything at dinner parties."

The phone rang, and I listened as she gave directions to an out-of-town visitor, then some recommendations for places to eat on and off campus.

When she hung up, I said, "That was impressive, Ms. Mazeros."

She rolled her eyes. "Do me a favor. Tell my supervisor I deserve a raise."

"You at least deserve an employee of the month plaque," I said. "It's outrageous that you haven't earned wild accolades for the work you do here."

The phone rang again, and Megan connected the incoming caller to a student's room.

I secured my flashcards with a rubber band, tossed them into my backpack and retrieved from its depths a half-eaten bag of potato chips. "What are we going to do after we graduate?"

"That's three years away," Megan pointed out. "And first you have to pass bio."

I ignored her. "No, seriously. We'll travel the world. We'll get one of those campers and live out in the middle of Arizona or something. We'll be some kind of fearsome duo, like in *Thelma & Louise*."

"You mean we'll drive off a cliff?"

I reached into my backpack for a water bottle and took a long swig. "It doesn't have to end that way."

She fielded two more phone calls and took a sip from my bottle. "I seriously have no idea what I'll do with myself."

"You're not going back to Woodstock?"

"Hell, no."

I laughed. "Well, I've got it all figured out, you know. I'm just biding my time here before I run off to join the circus."

Megan rolled her eyes. "You could be a special exhibit. The senator's daughter on a flying trapeze."

"You laugh, but that's about the best idea I have."

Megan said, "We should make a pact. We'll move somewhere together after we graduate."

"New York," I said. "Or London or Paris."

"You'd have to teach me French."

"Please. I'd have to teach myself. I took four years of French and can barely read a menu."

"Pinky swear," Megan said, hooking her finger toward me.

I laughed. "Is that really a thing?"

"It was all the rage at Woodstock High School. We pinky swore on anything important—not to get the same prom dress, not to sleep with each other's ex-boyfriends, not to go to the fair without each other."

"Serious stuff, then," I confirmed.

"Only the most serious." She waggled her finger significantly, and I hooked mine through it, and we made it official.

Holly, one of our suitemates, was dating someone from Yale that fall—a guy named Matt that she'd met at a party over the summer and talked to most weeknights, lying on her bed, staring up at the ceiling. It was driving our other suitemate, Bethany, crazy. "You should hear the two of them. It's 'I miss you' and 'I miss you more' and 'When can we see each other?' It's disgusting," Bethany said, plunking herself down on Megan's bed.

We commiserated; that was the nice thing about Keale, after all. It was perfectly acceptable to spend a Friday night dyeing each other's hair in the sink or watching an old Disney movie, or blasting one of Megan's Nirvana CDs and head-banging until we gave ourselves whiplash. We didn't have dates to plan, and we got along just fine without men.

Eventually, during one of their nightly conversations, Holly and Matt realized that they each had three single suitemates and began planning a quadruple date—dinner, a movie and then, Holly winked significantly, "We'll see where it leads."

"I thought one of the perks of being here was the absence of shit like this," Megan protested, and I had to agree. It sounded like a bad idea.

Eventually Holly and Bethany (who was apparently less disgusted by the idea of a boyfriend once one was suggested for her) wore us down. Megan swapped weekend work schedules, and the guys drove up from New Haven. They were all current economics majors and future MBAs, interchangeable, as far as I was concerned. "Any preferences?" Holly asked, giving us the rundown before they arrived.

"No one shorter than me," I said.

"No one more of an asshole than me," Megan said.

We paired off, and at first it was friendly and casual—Holly and Matt and Bethany and Nate in Matt's car; I offered to drive Megan and Jason and my date, Nicholas. Jason asked if we could listen to rap, which he claimed to love. In the rear-view mirror, I glimpsed the whites of Megan's eyes, midroll. Dinner in Litchfield was a somewhat formal and awkward affair that felt like going out with my parents—a nice Italian restaurant, fussy table linens, a giant round table with a towering centerpiece. Holly and Matt sat snuggled close, and the rest of us made awkward conversations about our majors and hometowns. We were all from the East Coast except for Megan, and after a few jokes about *The Wizard of Oz* and country music, Bethany chirped, "You know Lauren's dad's a senator, right?"

"Seriously?" Nicholas asked. He turned to Matt. "Why didn't you tell me?"

Matt shrugged. "I didn't know."

I glared at Bethany. Earlier, when we were jostling for position in front of our dinky bathroom mirror, I'd specifically asked if no one could mention my family.

"That's not a joke? He's a real senator?" Jason wanted to know. Previously, he'd been staring at Megan's boobs—everyone everywhere stared at Megan's boobs, so this was expected—but now he half turned toward me, his shoulder blocking my view of Megan.

"He's real all right," I said.

Jason leaned closer to me, peering at my face. He snapped his fingers. "Mabrey. I thought you looked familiar."

With Nicholas closing in on one side and Jason on the other, I was beginning to feel claustrophobic. I reached for my napkin, fluffing it out in my lap. "You thought I looked like a fifty-four-year-old man? Thanks."

"Nah, it's the pedigree. The…carriage. You know. You looked like someone important."

"She's not a fucking racehorse," Megan said.

"Relax," said Jason, not looking at her. "I'm allowed to call it as I see it."

Bethany darted nervous glances between us. "Hey, what do you think about—" she began, but the question was interrupted by the arrival of our food, the servers hovering over our left shoulders. For a few moments, the tension abated as we picked up our utensils and started in on our plates.

Nate asked, "So we're going to see a movie after this, right? Did we decide what we're seeing?"

Bethany smiled at him gratefully. "There are three different movies all starting around nine."

We went through the selections, none of which sounded familiar to me. Nicholas put his arm on the back of my chair. "Did you want to see a movie?"

I shrugged, picking at my ravioli. "I thought that was the plan."

Jason asked if there was anything else to do around here.

"Not particularly," I said.

"Well, what do you normally do on the weekends?" He directed the question to me, but Megan answered.

"Sometimes we go cow tipping," she said. "We sneak out into a field, come up right behind a cow and *wham*." She made a gesture with her fork, and a bit of red sauce fell onto the white tablecloth, spreading out like a bloodstain.

I laughed. "She's kidding."

Megan shook her head. "I'm not. We'll take you, if you want."

Bethany said, "I want to see a movie. I thought that was the plan. But I guess we could split up. You guys could always go back with Lauren."

Jason and Nicholas glanced at each other, and I wondered if they were considering it. I tried to catch Megan's eye, to get a read on her. There was something dangerous in her face, a warning sign. She reached for her water glass, the stem clanging loudly against her plate.

The conversation circled back to my dad—if he knew the president, if I knew the president, what we thought about Bill

Clinton, whether we thought it was odd that Monica Lewinsky had saved her navy dress. Nate made a joke about oral sex and Bethany laughed, slapping him on the arm.

"These guys in Washington, they have all the perks," Jason laughed. "Not your dad, I mean. Obviously."

"Thanks. Obviously."

Jason seemed to realize he'd offended me. "My dad's a corporate attorney. He handles all these big clients, like Enron and Exxon."

Megan said brightly, "You must be so proud of him."

He half turned back to her, lip curled. "What does your dad do?"

"My dad? I believe currently he's fertilizing a cemetery."

It went quiet. Even Holly and Matt noticed the silence and looked up.

"Megan," I said, reaching around behind Jason's back to touch her shoulder. She shook off my hand, not looking at me.

"What does that mean?" Nicholas asked.

"It means he's dead, asshole." Megan pushed back her chair. "Excuse me. I think I'm going to visit the powder room."

From the exaggerated way she swayed her hips, I knew she knew that we were watching her walk away.

Bethany looked at me. "I didn't know her dad was dead. Did you?"

I bit my lip, glancing in the direction of the restrooms. There was a lattice wall dividing the restaurant in half, and I couldn't see where Megan had gone.

"Does she have a chip on her shoulder or what?" Jason turned to Matt. "Why did you pair me with her, anyway? Nico gets a freaking senator's daughter, and I get—well, I don't know what I get."

"You're not getting anything," I told him.

Everyone but Jason laughed, somewhat nervously.

He put his fist down heavily on the table. "I told you this was a mistake. There are plenty of girls at Yale. These ones are just freaks."

Bethany and Holly jumped on him, their voices loud enough to attract our server, who was suddenly there, asking coolly if he could get anyone anything. Matt jumped in to defend Holly, and I pushed back my chair.

"It's all right," Nicholas said, reaching out a hand to stop me. "She probably just needs to calm down for a minute."

I snatched my purse from the back of the chair. "I'm going to check on her."

Megan was at the sink, washing her hands. Her cheeks were flushed. "Sorry," she said. "Look—I'm no good in situations like this. Is there any way you could drop me back in Scofield before the movie? I'll call someone from there."

"No way," I said. "You are not leaving me with those idiots."

She smiled weakly. "I can't go back out there."

I laughed. "You know what? Why don't we just split? They don't want us there, anyway."

"They want *you* there."

"Well, I don't want to be there."

We grinned at each other.

Megan went first, slipping out the bathroom door, keeping behind the latticework and disappearing out the front door. I followed a minute later, and we raced to the Saab like we were skipping out on the bill. Maybe we were; we'd never worked out in advance who was going to pay for what. I gunned the engine in Reverse, and we peeled out of the parking lot.

A mile down the road, Megan asked, "Where are we going?"

"Feel like seeing a movie?"

She shrieked with laughter. "God, no."

★ ★ ★

We ended up at a restaurant somewhere between Litch-field and Scofield—a burger joint with a definite smell of grease in the air.

"This is more like it," Megan said, sliding into a booth and reaching for a sticky menu.

I grinned. "My kind of date."

"Like hell it is."

We ordered Diet Cokes and a giant basket of fries. Megan squirted piles of mustard and ketchup on her plate and swirled the fries through them, one by one, before they disappeared into her mouth.

"Did I ruin everything?" she asked finally.

"Not for me. Holly and Bethany are probably going to kill us, though."

She tilted her glass and fished out an ice cube, crunching it between her teeth. "I should never have agreed to it. It's not my scene. Preppy guys, fancy restaurants, everyone's pedi-gree on display. It's so dull and—" She fished for the word.

"Pretentious," I supplied.

"Right. Give me the Burger Barn every time."

I understood what she was saying, but I understood, too, that our lives were very different. The Yale guys were an-noying, but I'd slipped seamlessly into their conversation. It was familiar and expected, Mabrey-esque.

Megan crunched another piece of ice. "Well?"

"Well, what?"

"Aren't you going to ask me?"

I took a deep breath. "Is your dad really dead?"

She nodded.

"Why didn't you tell me? I thought you said he was just—gone. I figured he'd moved to a different part of the state. I mean, I didn't realize that was a euphemism."

She fiddled with her straw in her glass, bending it backward and forward, stabbing it against frozen chunks of ice at the bottom of her glass. "I haven't told anyone here. He died the year after I graduated. He had cancer—mesothelioma. It's from asbestos. It gets into the lining of the lungs." Her words caught in her throat.

"I'm so sorry. That must have been awful." I did some mental math, some of the pieces of Megan's life snapping into place. The "gap year" she'd taken after high school, not at all like the gap years my friends and I had discussed at Reardon, wondering if our parents might fund six months on a catamaran, a winter of being a ski bum in the Alps. Her dad had died, and her mom had started dating someone else, and she'd moved out here.

"That's not the worst part of it," she said. "He was dying for so long. He got this diagnosis of eighteen months, but he could hardly breathe at the end. He was going to die no matter what. There wasn't any help for him, for what he had. There weren't any treatments, only morphine. It was going to happen anyway."

"What do you mean?"

A single tear dripped from Megan's right eye and trailed down her cheek to the corner of her mouth, where it quivered on her lip. She did nothing to brush it away. "I helped him along. He asked me to, and I did."

I realized I was holding my breath, trying to understand if I was hearing what I thought I was hearing. I had about a million questions, but I didn't know how to ask any of them, or whether I really wanted to know the answers. Finally, I said, "But he was going to die, on his own?" The last syllable rose into a question, and Megan nodded.

"That's what I tell myself. That's about the only way I can handle what I did." She reached for the metal dispenser and plucked several single-ply napkins out, one after another, and blew her nose.

"Why are you telling me?" I asked finally.

"I don't know. I was sick of not telling you the truth. And also I thought maybe you should know that about me, in case you wanted to—I don't know. Rethink things."

I raised an eyebrow. "Rethink things?"

"Like, find another roommate. Or start hanging around with Holly and Bethany. I won't be offended."

"What are you saying? And why would you say it? This doesn't change anything between us. I don't think less of you. I feel—I don't know. Sympathetic. Kind of horrified, but not because I think you're a monster. Just because you were in that situation, and that's horrifying."

She gave me a nervous smile—and I had another flash of understanding, one that told me I was seeing the real Megan, stripped of bravado and pretense. It was how I'd felt seeing my old roommate Erin that morning when she was still asleep, when she was unaware and unselfconscious.

"Okay," I said, rushing before I could stop what I was about to do. "We're telling secrets? I have one, too."

Megan laughed. "What—once you slipped a hundred-dollar bill from your mom's purse and didn't tell her? Somehow I don't think you're going to top mine."

"Listen," I said, and I let the story come, even though some of the details had gone fuzzy. I told her about the summer I'd volunteered at The Coop, about having sex with Marcus on the sagging couch in the employee break room. Megan was still, her eyes wide. I told her how I'd pretended not to know anything about the quart-sized bag of pot in my backpack, how Marcus had gone to jail, what had happened to him there.

"You couldn't have known that would happen," Megan

breathed. "It's not like you forced him to sell you the pot. It's not like you stabbed him in the chest."

I nodded, my throat tight. "That's what I have to tell myself."

We stayed out late, driving the grids of rural Connecticut, not wanting to return to Keale to face Holly and Bethany. Finally, I parked outside our dorm, looking up at our dark window on the second floor.

Megan cleared her throat. "Just for the record," she told me, "I don't think you're a monster, either."

I smiled. And then, although I thought I knew the answer, I asked, "You won't tell anyone...?"

She shook her head. "You?"

"Of course not."

It was dark inside the car, and at first I thought Megan was handing me something—there was the pale flash of her hand, her pinky finger crooked in front of me. We shook with all the solemnity of a blood oath.

MEGAN

I wasn't kidding about not being Mabrey material—a fact that was obvious the farther we got from Keale and the closer to her family's house, the two-hour trip made slower by a wet snowfall and slick country roads. At one point, Lauren overcorrected and the Saab spun out in the middle of an empty intersection, surrounded by nothing but trees. "Well, then," she said after a moment, and we drove on. The landscape wasn't that different from the outskirts of Scofield, but the homes we passed were set farther back from the road, the driveways longer and wider.

This is a mistake, I told myself. I didn't belong here, in Lauren's other life, where the contrasts between the Mabreys and the Mazeroses would be so obvious. I should have gone back to Woodstock and lived like a hermit in Gerry Tallant's house, where my secondhand jeans and falling-apart boots wouldn't be out of place.

We came around a bend and I was startled by a horse standing at a fence, its giant unblinking eyes studying us as we passed.

"Does your family have horses?" I asked as we passed acre after acre of fenced pastureland.

Lauren sighed. "Not anymore. When I was younger, we each had our own horse, but there's no one there to ride them now, especially with Dad in Washington. The stables are still there, though, if you want to see them."

We each had our own horse. Of course they did. "Are you kidding? I want to see everything."

Eventually, Lauren slowed, put on her blinker, and we crept down one of those long driveways, the snow smartly cleared to the sides. In front of us, available only in small glimpses at first, was the Mabreys' house. *Lauren grew up here*, I thought, taking in the three stories, the crisp black shutters against the white paint, the four towering columns that framed the front porch. On either side of the house, in perfect symmetry, were the type of balconies that seemed straight out of fairy tales, where women would wave their handkerchiefs or let down their hair or simply wait to be rescued. I pointed to a smaller building off to one side, still three or four times the size of the house where I'd grown up. "Is that another house?"

Lauren followed my gesture. "Oh, no. That's mostly storage, although I guess Hildy does live out there."

"Is Hildy a horse?"

Lauren laughed, killing the engine. "No, the housekeeper. You'll meet her."

In front of the house, the driveway looped into a circle around a towering stone fountain, stilled for winter. "Behind the house is the lake," Lauren said. "If the snow lets up, we can walk out there later."

I gaped. "You have a freaking lake? Of your own?"

Lauren said, "It's Connecticut. There are lakes everywhere."

I glanced around. There were no neighbors visible in any direction. Everything I could see belonged to the Mabreys. "Oh, sure. Everyone has one." I unbuckled my seat belt and hopped out, my boots sinking into an inch of snow that seemed somehow softer and more lovely than any snow I'd ever seen in Kansas. Lauren followed, less enthusiastic. Why not? She was used to all of this.

I paused on the porch in front of glossy red doors hung with matching wreaths and framed with massive topiaries. A bronze plaque near the front door read Holmes House, 1852. I turned to Lauren, who was coming up behind me. "The next time you're in Kansas, remind me to show you my favorite farmhouse turned meth lab."

The front door swung open before we could knock, and I recognized Lauren's sister from the framed family picture on her desk at Keale. She had the same dark hair and blue eyes, although hers were pinched closer together, her lips settling naturally into a frown. I remembered what Lauren had told me: *Kat's the good one, the responsible one.* And then, in the next breath: *you're so lucky you're an only child.* Balanced on Kat's hip was a toddler, her mouth rimmed with a purple juice stain. "Do you realize how late you are? Mom held dinner for you, and she's probably alerted the highway patrol to keep an eye out for your car."

"Hello to you, too, Kat," Lauren said, stepping past her and shrugging out of her coat. "There's a bit of snow on the roads, in case you didn't notice."

I followed Lauren's lead, stepping out of my boots and regretting the crenellated chunks of snow that fell onto the rug in the entryway. I also regretted the socks I'd chosen that morning, feeling festive—red with a jolly Santa on top of each foot, a yawning hole in one of the toes. Lauren hadn't mentioned that we were in any rush. We'd even stopped for coffee, killing an extra half-hour along the way. When Lauren didn't introduce me and her sister didn't acknowledge my presence, I held out a hand. "Hi. I'm Megan."

"I'm Katherine." Her skin was cool, the diamond of her wedding ring winking under the light of the overhead chandelier. "This monster is Lizzie."

"Nice to meet you. Hey, sweetie." I reached out a finger, and Lizzie hooked it with her stubby baby fingers, showing surprising baby strength.

"Watch out," Katherine warned. "Once she latches on, she never lets go." She adjusted Lizzie on her hip and the two of them wandered off, Lizzie's hand reaching forlornly over her mom's shoulder.

I looked up, breath caught in my throat. Mom would never believe this. The chandelier was like a tiered wedding cake, a thousand tiny prisms catching the light. Two curved staircases led to the next floor, their banisters dripping with green branches. It was like stepping into a Christmas carol—the "boughs of holly" and all that. In front of us was a tree that was easily fifteen feet tall, glistening with gold lights, its branches tied with gold bows—large on the bottom and tiny on the top. I tried to imagine someone standing on a fifteen-foot ladder, tying the bows with such precision.

"That tree is amazing," I said, which was every kind of understatement.

"My mom tends to go a bit overboard with Christmas," Lauren said. "There's probably a tree in every room."

I laughed, thinking it was some kind of joke. Only later, when Mrs. Mabrey gave me the grand tour, did I realize it wasn't an exaggeration. Every room of the house had a tree, each decorated with its own theme—tartan ribbons in one, pink and white hearts in another. Even the guest bathroom on the second floor had a three-foot tree next to the vanity, with the faces of dozens of owl ornaments watching me as I peed.

"Ready?" Lauren asked. "It's time to run the gauntlet."

"Your sister seems nice," I said, my voice echoing off the marble floor.

Lauren grabbed my arm, the suddenness of her movement nearly knocking me off balance. "Don't fall for it," she whispered. "We all seem nice at first."

Lauren's mom appeared in winter-white pants and a matching sweater with tiny pink pearls sewn into the collar. Her handshake was businesslike. "I've heard so much about you," she said.

I glanced at Lauren, wondering which of my stories were appropriate for someone who looked like a queen. And if this were a fairy tale, I understood my role—the poor urchin in from the cold, who had to sing for her supper. "Your house is beautiful," I said.

Mrs. Mabrey nodded. "Would you like to see the rest?"

I followed her carefully, placing my feet exactly where hers had been, in order not to intrude any more than necessary. Mrs. Mabrey had no doubt given this tour dozens of times before, and I was one of the least important people to be on its receiving end. Lauren trailed behind us, inserting comments that vaguely contradicted whatever her mother said. There were multiple living areas on the first floor, although I couldn't tell what they were for, exactly, or when they were used—rooms with white couches, rooms with stiff chairs angled toward each other for conversation, a room with a grand piano, another with a few love seats facing a bay window. It reminded me of touring a mansion on my fifth-grade field trip, where my class had traipsed obediently through the rooms, careful to stay behind the rope boundary. Everything in the Mabreys' house had the same sterile quality—there were no shoes kicked off by the couch, no stacks of unopened mail, no mugs of coffee growing cold. We passed the kitchen and an informal dining room, then a formal dining room, then separate offices for Mr. and Mrs. Mabrey. A woman wearing black pants and a black sweater came out of one of the offices carrying a wastepaper basket that held a single crumpled sheet of paper.

"Thank you, Hildy," Mrs. Mabrey said, not missing a beat. "I did also notice a handprint on the door about knee height. I suppose that's what life's like with a toddler."

"I'll take care of that," Hildy said, and disappeared down a hallway. I had a feeling—maybe not irrational at all—that I should be following Hildy.

There were five bedrooms on the second floor, and Mrs. Mabrey pointed to their closed doors one by one—Lauren's room, Michael's room, Katherine and Peter's room, the guest room that had been commandeered by Lizzie and the double-door suite at the end of the hall leading to the Mabreys' bedroom.

"There are more guest rooms on the third floor. Hildy has

made up one of them for you," Mrs. Mabrey said, starting for
the next staircase.

"It's okay," Lauren said, and to me, "You can sleep on my
daybed."

"Are you sure? I mean, you probably get sick enough of
me at school."

"If you get annoying, I'll kick you out," Lauren assured me.
I grinned. "Thanks."

Later, when some unseen hand had brought our bags from
Lauren's car, I flopped onto the daybed with its floral comforter and tried to imagine Lauren growing up here, in a
house where a speck of dirt must have been cause for alarm.
Even her room didn't look like her—the bedspreads too child-
ish, the dresser and vanity too fussy. On the wall, there was
a framed cross-stitched monogram of Lauren's initials, and
one shelf held a few tiny knickknacks, relics from family
vacations—snow globes, tiny models of the Eiffel Tower and
the Leaning Tower of Pisa. They might have belonged to a
stranger. Where was Lauren the teenager girl, with her posters of boy bands and snapshots of friends? I remembered what
she told me about Marcus dying, and how her parents had
kept her at home that semester. I couldn't think of anything
more depressing than spending months alone in this room.

Lauren was digging around in one of her bags for a hairbrush, and I watched her swipe the brush in even strokes until
the ends of her hair fluttered with static.

"I don't get it," I said. "Where do you hang out?"

She gestured with the hairbrush around the room. "You're
looking at it."

"No, no, no. I mean, where do you hang out? Where
do you lie around in your underwear eating out of a box of
Wheat Thins? I can't picture anyone actually sitting on all
those white couches."

Lauren tossed the brush on top of her bedspread. "Well, there is one place that my mother consistently leaves off the official tour. Come on, we're going down to The Dungeon."

I grinned. "Is that where your father tortures his political rivals?"

"Something like that."

Lauren led me down a flight of stairs, across the house to the kitchen, then down another flight of stairs off the pantry. I was going to need a map to find my way back.

"MK and I used to call this The Dungeon," she said, flipping on a light switch. Fluorescent bulbs hummed overhead, illuminating a cavernous space made gloomy with a lower ceiling and about an acre of dark wood paneling. I blinked, taking in a dated kitchenette with a polished wooden bar, large seating area and a pool table. The carpet beneath my feet was inch-and-a-half shag, much like the carpet I'd grown up with in Woodstock. There were two windows at the back of the house, but you had to be seven feet tall to see out of them. Light from a fading winter sunset filtered through.

"Whoa," I said, taking in the three mounted deer heads, their antlers polished and menacing. Then I stooped to pet the rug on the floor, which appeared to be a massive bear pelt. "Is this thing real?"

Lauren shrugged. "I guess. My mom is always threatening to get rid of it. Actually, she's been talking about remodeling this whole space as a guest suite. Can you imagine what this would look like covered in a million yards of white beadboard?"

I ran my hand over the green felt on the pool table, then stopped curiously in front of some built-in shelves that held not books but every board game imaginable—Clue and Risk and Monopoly and dozens of puzzles, some of the boxes never opened. Then I returned to the plaid couches, plopping down in front of the only modern touch in the entire space—a giant television. "This'll do," I announced. Lauren laughed, reaching for the remote.

Senator Mabrey and Michael arrived the following night just as we were sitting down to dinner at a massive table set for eight. I tried not to stare at Senator Mabrey, although he was as close as I'd come to royalty, dressed in a navy suit and striped tie, which he was unknotting as he came through the door. Michael was a younger version, sleeves rolled to his elbows, a swagger to his walk.

"Traffic," Senator Mabrey apologized, planting a kiss on his wife's temple. "What did we miss?"

"Dinner, almost," Mrs. Mabrey said stiffly. Lauren had warned me about her mother's sense of punctuality—five minutes early was still considered late; five minutes late was unconscionable.

He bent to kiss Lauren's head, then Katherine's, and shook hands with Peter. He took in the empty seat that would have been Lizzie's. "Where's my girl?"

Katherine sighed. "I had to put her to bed. She was exhausted. And she was exhausting me, too." But Lizzie was still there in the form of a gray plastic receiver, which occasionally emitted a baby-sized gurgle or sigh transmitted from the upstairs monitor.

"And you must be Megan," Senator Mabrey said, patting me on the shoulder. "I hear you've come along to keep Lauren in line. Welcome, welcome."

"Well, it's a tough job." I winked at Lauren across the table.

Michael pulled out the chair next to me, finishing my thought. "…and it takes a team to do it."

"Ha-ha," Lauren said. "And this is my hysterical brother, MK."

"Or you can call me Michael like everyone else in the

world does," he said, taking his seat and unfolding his napkin in one singular motion. I followed his lead, smoothing my napkin over my lap.

"What's MK from?" I asked. "Are those initials?"

He grinned, revealing the same straight white teeth as Lauren's. No money had been spared on dental hygiene in this family, that was for sure. "No—it's just what Lauren called me when she was about two years old. She used to call herself Lolo. Did you know that?"

I raised an eyebrow in Lauren's direction. "Lolo?"

At the end of the table, Mrs. Mabrey shifted, her impatience palpable. "Let's get started, shall we?" I was already learning that her questions were never really questions, since she had already determined all the answers.

Senator Mabrey said, "Let's say the blessing." On cue, everyone joined hands, until we were a wide, connected circle, with my hands clasped by Michael on one side and the senator on the other. It was a brief, nonspecific prayer about food and family and country, but it was hard to follow, nonetheless, since I was actually touching a senator. He ended the prayer with an emphatic "Amen!" which was echoed less enthusiastically by two or three other voices. Across the table, the baby monitor emitted a sharp cry, and Peter adjusted the volume downward, so that Lizzie's voice was only a thin wail.

Michael was still holding my hand, which he brought to his lips in a formal, courtly gesture. "Charmed, I'm sure."

I laughed, disentangling myself.

"Could you please be less disgusting?" Lauren asked. "Some of us don't want our appetites ruined."

I watched them carefully as the meal progressed, looking for cues about what silverware to use, and when to reach for seconds. Michael's left arm bumped against my right arm one or two times too many to be considered accidental. On my other side, Senator Mabrey was asking about my classes, my time at Keale.

I couldn't imagine that my literary theory classes would sound that interesting, so I told him about the poli sci course I would be taking with a new professor, Dr. Miriam Stenholz.

He nodded. "I've heard that name. She's an advocate for women in politics."

Michael gave a little snort next to me.

"So you're a political science major?" Senator Mabrey asked, turning a more interested face in my direction.

"No," I corrected quickly. "English, actually. That's just one of my required—"

"God, not another English major," Michael groaned.

"Michael," his mother said sharply.

"Well, what are you going to do with an English degree? Teach?" His eyebrows were raised, forming two points in the middle.

My cheeks felt hot. "Maybe." I hadn't fully answered the question for myself yet, but I'd romanticized the profession, admiring my professors in their tweed jackets with leather elbow patches, their shoebox-sized offices filled with stacks of student papers and books with yellow sticky notes curling over the edges.

"It's a noble profession," Senator Mabrey said, silencing Michael. "Without teachers, where would any of us be?"

I smiled, although it seemed like a soundbite, a line from a speech delivered to the teachers' union. It was hard to imagine a world where the Mabreys wouldn't be successful, education or not.

"Katherine taught for a few years," Mrs. Mabrey said, and the pendulum swung to her end of the table. "It was at one of the best preschools in the area. Mothers were registering their babies before they were even born."

Peter said, "Lizzie's going there next fall, when she's three."

There was some talk about teacher-student ratios and rising tuition, and I had the distinct feeling that we weren't talking about the same kind of teaching, at all. Under the table, Lauren kicked me, and I kicked her back.

"Hey," Michael said, indignant. "Are you playing footsie with me?"

"No—I'm sorry."

Lauren stifled a laugh. "Watch yourself, Megs."

At the other end of the table, there was a distinct squawk from the baby monitor, and a brief argument between Katherine and Peter about whether to let Lizzie cry it out or go check on her. Eventually, Katherine excused herself and disappeared. A minute later we heard her voice on the monitor, cooing, "What's wrong with my baby girl now? What's wrong, hmm? What's wrong with little Liz—" Peter turned the volume dial again, and her question disappeared.

"Yeah, *Megs*," Michael said. "Watch yourself."

The days before Christmas were a blur of errands that needed to be run, cards opened and cataloged. Every time the Mabreys' doorbell rang, it was a harried-looking delivery person with a cellophane-wrapped gift basket from one constituent or another. In between trips to town, Lauren and I escaped to The Dungeon, watching cheesy holiday movies on the big-screen TV and helping ourselves to the liquor cabinet.

"See, this isn't so different from Mazeros holidays," I said, gesturing to our shot glasses of Bombay Sapphire. "Except our liquor of choice is Bud or Coors."

Lauren grimaced. "I've never understood the allure myself. I mostly fake drank at Reardon."

"The allure is that it's cheap, and you can get hammered pretty easily," I explained.

"Well, yeah. That part I get."

I wandered over to the bookshelf lined with board games and pulled down a puzzle. The picture on the front of the box was of a quaint little cottage, surrounded by snow, lit by a few cheery lamps. It was the sort of thing I would have found romantic and idyllic before visiting the Mabreys. Now I wondered if the people in the cottage were poor, and if the gas lamps were a sign that they couldn't pay their electricity bill. I held up the box for Lauren. "What do you think? Feel like a puzzle?"

"Knock yourself out," she said.

At some point in the afternoon, Michael would join us, fresh from a kickboxing session at the gym or lunch in town with his dad—a "schmooze session," he called it.

"Who are you schmoozing?" I asked, imagining men in an oak-paneled room, smoking cigars and drinking from brandy snifters.

He grinned. "Anyone with money and an interest in politics."

"What kind of law are you studying?" I asked him one afternoon, when the puzzle was about half-completed. I'd spent half an hour trying to find a missing edge piece before turning my attention to a clump of fir trees.

"Criminal," he said, opening a bottle of Corona. "Want one?"

I shook my head. Lauren said, "Sure, hit me."

I was trying one odd-shaped piece in a dozen different places. "So you'd be what? A prosecutor or a defense attorney?"

Michael snorted, passing an open bottle to Lauren.

"Oh, please," she said. "He's trying to follow in Dad's footsteps. The law degree is just a stepping stone."

"You mean politics?"

Michael forced a lime down the neck of his beer and watched the resulting fizz. "It's the family business, after all."

"Check your soul at the door," Lauren said. She took a slug of beer and set the bottle by her foot, where it balanced unevenly on the shag carpet.

"Are you kidding? It's called making a difference in people's lives." He announced the words like they were a newspaper headline, or the title of a research paper.

Lauren rolled her eyes at me. "My brother, the humanitarian."

"Well, it's true. The economy, national security, balancing the budget…" Michael reached down for a piece of the puzzle, tried it unsuccessfully in two different places and abandoned it on the edge of the table.

"I suppose it has nothing to do with fame and fortune," Lauren said.

Somehow Michael had drained half the beer already, and he sat back, as relaxed as a guy vacationing on a beach. "Those are the fringe benefits."

I shifted positions on the carpet, my knees protesting.

Michael nudged me with his foot. "What are you—Republican or Democrat?"

"Independent," I said automatically—which was true. I'd gone so far as to register before losing interest in the process, and I hadn't voted before leaving Woodstock. As far as I knew, sample ballots had been arriving at Gerry Tallant's house in my name, and my mother had been throwing them away.

Michael scoffed. "Being independent is a waste of time. This country will never go for a three-party system. We're too ingrained in our beliefs."

"Eighteen months of law school, and he's already a cynic," Lauren commented. A commercial came on television and she reached for the remote, flipping between channels, settling on something just long enough for me to register what we were watching before flipping onward.

"Hey," Michael said, nudging me again, the ball of his foot rolling over my thigh. "I'm in charge of the summer internship program at my dad's office. You should apply. We have at least a dozen spots to fill. We'll even take an Independent."

I looked up. "In Washington, DC?"

Michael laughed. "That's where his office is, so yeah."

"What does an intern do?"

"Grunt work," Lauren said, at the same time Michael said, "You get to learn how the whole political process works, see some legislation in action, show student groups around Capitol Hill, that kind of thing."

"It sounds interesting," I said.

Lauren laughed. "No, it doesn't."

Michael's foot was still on my leg. I shifted to another position, and his foot dropped to the floor. "I'll send you a link to the application, then."

"What about you?" I asked Lauren. "We could apply together."

"I'd rather eat glass," Lauren said, getting to her feet. She'd forgotten about the beer, which toppled onto its side, liquid spilling in a golden stream. She swore, hurrying to the bar for a roll of paper towels.

"It's settled, then," Michael said. He reached over my head as if he were a giant and I were a child, and somehow, he spotted the missing edge piece that had eluded me.

Christmas came and went—big dinners that left us gorged and listless, followed by mindless hours of watching TV and playing Chinese checkers in the basement, our limbs draped over the ends of the plaid couches. I watched Lizzie when Kat and Peter were busy, taking her outside to make snow angels on a crisp afternoon and playing hide-and-seek with her in the living room, behind the white couches where no one ever sat. On Christmas morning, I joined the Mabreys when they opened their presents, smiling as embarrassing mounds of gift wrap and tissue paper were discarded and missing my Christmases with Dad and Mom, our ritual of hot chocolate and cinnamon bread. I'd always felt spoiled by them, the only child of loving parents. Now, watching the Mabreys open gift after gift, an impressive stack of sweaters and scarfs and boots and electronics piling up next to each of them, I realized that "spoiled" was relative. Lauren's big gift was a laptop, which she immediately freed from its packaging with a tool from Michael's keychain.

"Megan," Mrs. Mabrey said, passing a wrapped box over Lizzie's head.

"Really? For me?" I slid a finger carefully beneath the ribbon, working it around the edge of the box, then under the tape.

"Open it already!" Michael called, and I remembered how my mom had always exclaimed over the waste of using wrapping paper only once. She would save the tissue, flattening it out and refolding it, then tucking it away in a giant Tupperware container in the garage. I worked the tie free and opened the box.

It was a raspberry-colored sweater, the wool soft between my fingers. I draped it over my body like the clothes for a paper doll. "Thank you—this is so generous. Everything has been so wonderful, and this—"

"You're very welcome," Senator Mabrey said, at the same time Mrs. Mabrey said, "It's nothing." But it wasn't nothing to me. It was probably the most expensive thing I'd ever owned, including my old Celica.

"Okay, okay, enough of this," Lauren said, abandoning her

laptop for the moment. "Everyone open their gifts from me at the same time." I already knew what they were—black-and-white portraits, matted and framed back at Keale. Earlier this week, we'd wrapped them together in the Mabreys' basement, scraps of wrapping paper and ribbon collecting at our feet.

Lauren had captured them when they weren't looking—Katherine out on the boat at their summer house, her parents sitting side by side on a porch swing, Michael leaning against the railing of a gazebo, Peter in the boat, a fishing rod aimed over the side. Only Lizzie had been caught head-on, her mouth open in a goofy smile, her hair a dandelion tuft around her head. There were *ooh*s and *aah*s and general murmurs of appreciation. Lizzie said, "That's me!" and ran to each of us, shoving her picture in our faces.

"There's one for you, too," Lauren said, handing me a horribly wrapped package, this one clearly her own handiwork.

It was a picture of the two of us, taken in our dorm room, the corner of my class schedule visible where I'd taped it on the wall. I remembered that fall afternoon, rain cooping us up indoors. Lauren had held the camera at arm's length, and we'd alternated poses from serious to smiling to tongues out, as if we were in a photo booth at a carnival. She'd framed one of us smiling, our heads tilted together, one of my curls brushing her cheek. Only now did I notice that we were mismatched—Lauren had the blue eyes that matched my blond hair, and I had the dark eyes that matched hers.

"Don't you two see enough of each other already?" Michael said, snatching the frame from my grasp.

But I leaned over and gave Lauren a one-armed hug. "I love it," I told her.

She beamed.

On New Year's Eve, we went to a party just down the road at the home of one of Senator Mabrey's major donors. I borrowed a black dress from the back of Lauren's closet, one she'd worn to see a play on Broadway. The only fancy dress I'd ever owned was for the winter formal my junior year of high school—teal green and covered with about a million sequins that kept falling off when I danced. Lauren's dress was more sophisticated than anything I'd ever seen in the Junction City mall, one-shouldered and silky, the hem riding up on my thigh.

"Do you think it's too obscene?" I asked, gesturing across my chest, where the fabric stretched tight.

"Yes," Lauren laughed. "And it's perfect."

We drank too much champagne and danced together in a gigantic ballroom, twirling and dipping while Lauren's parents and their friends looked on, amused. Kat and Peter left early, carrying a sleeping Lizzie wrapped in a soft blanket. Michael, Lauren and I left at eleven, claiming we wanted to watch *Dick Clark's New Year's Rockin' Eve*. In his car, Michael cranked up the heat and said, "Let the drinking begin."

We ended up in The Dungeon, where Michael lined up tequila shots on the bar and we threw them back, laughing and sputtering. On television, musicians I didn't know danced on a soundstage, and the camera panned over a shrieking, shivering crowd.

"Dick Clark looks like someone's dirty old grandpa," I observed. Maybe because of the tequila, this struck Michael and Lauren as hysterical. We drank to that observation too, and then Lauren collapsed onto one of the plaid couches with a belch.

Michael took a pool stick off the rack on the wall and rubbed the tip with a cube of chalk. "Anyone up for a game?"

Lauren groaned. "I can't even stand up."

I kicked off my borrowed heels, the toes stuffed with tissue. "I'm game. I haven't played pool in forever, though."

"Billiards," Michael and Lauren corrected.

Lauren flopped onto her side, stretching out her long legs. "The Mabreys don't play *pool*, Megan. That's way too conventional."

"Provincial," Michael agreed, gathering the balls from their netted pockets.

Lauren yawned. "Cheap."

"Please," I said, rising to the occasion. "I'll tell you what, Michael. You play billiards and I'll play pool, and winner gets default bragging rights."

"You're on. But first—" He turned in the direction of the bar and returned a minute later with two long-necked Coronas.

"Ah," I said. "Good idea."

"Of course, I'm leaving in the morning, so I'll have to do all my bragging tonight," he said, handing me a bottle. I accepted, draining a couple inches in a long slug. I already felt loopy, and I wondered if it would be easier to sleep in The Dungeon tonight or crawl up two flights of stairs in Lauren's dress.

"Where's mine?" Lauren whined from the couch.

With one hand, Michael untucked his dress shirt from his waistband. "Please. You're going to be asleep in five minutes."

Lauren yawned, not denying it. "Be careful, MK. Megs will go all Kansas on you."

We played a warm-up round, taking sloppy shots. I hadn't played since the summer when I was fourteen, too young to have a job or friends with cars. That summer, Dad's cousin CJ had been evicted from his rental, and our garage had provided temporary storage for his pool table, golf clubs and hunting rifles. Dad had taken the opportunity to teach me every shot he knew from a lifetime of pickup games in bars. I had loved the satisfying *smack!* as the cue ball whacked a striped or solid, sending it flying into other balls, other pockets.

Maybe it was because of the nostalgia that I let my guard down. Or more likely, it was because of the tequila, plus the three Coronas I drank while Michael beat me handily in the first game, and by less of a margin in our second game, when it was clear the alcohol was getting to him, too. He weaved his way unsteadily around the table, leaning against the wood-paneled wall for balance, brushing against me in a way that might have been deliberate or accidental.

When he beat me the second time, he set down his stick and came up behind me, his breath suddenly on my cheek. "Bragging rights," he reminded me. I felt his erection bulging against my hip and half turned, glancing over my shoulder at Lauren. She was asleep on the couch, the dark mass of her hair blocking her face. She would have been horrified if she were awake, throwing a cushion at Michael, demanding he keep his hands off me.

"Hey now," I said, trying unsuccessfully to sidestep him. Michael's mouth loomed close, his breath as beery and unwelcome as my own. I braced myself for the kiss before it came, meeting it with pursed lips. My hands on his chest were a preventive measure, a barrier to keep him from coming closer. "We're drunk," I laughed, scooting out of the way before it could go further. And then, not knowing what else to do, I'd dodged his outstretched arms and headed for the stairs. It was a relief to find myself alone on the main floor, away from the stale, overheated air of The Dungeon. By the time I was in my pajamas and under the covers in Lauren's room, I was congratulating myself for avoiding a disaster, the kind of bad decision that ended up with the two of us in Michael's room, whispering drunkenly, my nylons rolled down, Lauren's silk dress pushed up to my hips. And then what? In the morning, would I have had to do the walk of shame down the long hallway past the closed doors of Lauren's sleeping family members? Would I have had to sit across the breakfast table from Mrs. Mabrey's disapproving glance? It was unthinkable.

If it had been anyone else, any other boy after any other party, I would have told Lauren everything about it, dissecting the kiss, analyzing it from every angle. I was aware—keenly, even in my drunken, spinning-ceiling state—that Michael Mabrey was a good catch. He was attractive in a Kennedy-esque way, with dark hair and a lanky body made for noncontact sports like golf and downhill skiing. Plus, he was smart. If he hadn't been her brother, Lauren and I would have analyzed that, too, ranking him for sexiness and future prospects.

But because it was Lauren, and because it was Michael, I never said a word. By the time Lauren and I stumbled downstairs in the early afternoon, searching for coffee, Michael was already gone.

That spring when I was trying to find a summer job that would keep me away from Woodstock, I thought about contacting Michael, reminding him that he was going to send me an application for the internship position in his father's office. But I was smart enough to realize that the offer hadn't been a serious one, the way his drunken kiss hadn't been serious, either.

OCTOBER 10, 2016

LAUREN

Brady came in when I was making dinner, a stir-fry recipe that allowed me to stab furiously at chunks of chicken and broccoli with a wooden spoon. The girls were in the den—Stella texting madly on her pink iPhone, Emma in the tutu from her last Halloween costume, watching Animal Planet.

He leaned against the door frame, working the tie free from its knot. "There are fifteen messages from your mother on our answering machine."

"See? I told you we should get rid of that thing."

He wrapped his arms around my shoulders, creating a little cocoon in which I relaxed, supported by his frame. The broccoli sizzled and popped, and Brady took the spoon from my hands, giving the meat and vegetables a few expert flips. The chicken was beginning to look dry and overdone.

"She's been texting me all day, too. I haven't been able to call her. What am I supposed to say?"

"I'm sorry," Brady said, fiddling with the knob to turn off the heat. "Would you rather talk in person? I could come with you."

I looked up at him. "In the middle of your hearing?"

"We may get a ruling before noon." His voice didn't ring with optimism.

"No—thanks, though. I have some thinking to do first."

"We've got this," he said, his chin resting on my head. "We can figure it out."

We stood that way for a long time, the distant sounds of Animal Planet filtering into the room.

"It could be nothing," Brady said into my ear. "This could all blow over tomorrow."

I nodded, but it felt like a tornado was brewing inside me, gaining power, sweeping each new thought into its path.

It could be nothing, like Brady said.

Or it could be everything.

After dinner, I sat on our bed upstairs, my cell phone in my hand. The texts from my mother had come all day, most of them repetitions of the original text.

CALL ME, DON'T TALK TO ANYONE.

DON'T LISTEN TO THAT WOMAN.

Of course, I hadn't obeyed her orders; I'd gone right to CNN, and I'd watched Anna Kovics's allegation a dozen times, until I'd memorized the set of her jaw, the tremble of her lips. I couldn't stop trying to understand why someone would invent a story like that, one that was sure to bring pain and humiliation. It was a twisted way to get fame, and there were easier ways to get money from the Mabreys. I suppose it might have been wounded pride from a crush gone wrong, or a case of mental illness with its paranoia and delusions of grandeur. But I didn't see any of this in Anna Kovics. She looked young and scared, but behind that trembling lower lip was a fierce sort of determination, one I certainly didn't have at her age. Or now.

I looked at my phone again, hovering over the green icon that would initiate the phone call, that would drag me back into that world.

Over the years, Brady and I had found reasons to visit my side of the family less and less. Dad and Mom had been too busy, for one thing, their calendar dotted with speeches and fund-raisers and important dinners, and it was difficult to remember when they were in DC and when they were back at Holmes House. Kat and I kept in touch via Skype every week or so, but our talk was inevitably of what was going on with our kids and who wanted what for her birthday. I talked to MK less frequently, mainly because his own career had skyrocketed, and as Brady said, he now regarded us as the "little people" he had promised not to forget on his climb to the top.

"Come over to the dark side," MK joked to Brady on the rare occasions when we were together, as if he were the older and wiser of the two, taking a young man under his wing. "There's never going to be money in that kind of law."

"Immigration law is not about the money," Brady would say, deaf to the way his voice came across, wounded and defensive in a way that probably tickled MK to no end. "It's about helping people, reuniting families—"

MK would inevitably laugh, clapping him on the shoulder. "Just teasing you, buddy. Course you do an important job. If I had a better sense of ethics, I'd be doing it myself."

"Your brother," Brady complained on our drive home from Thanksgivings and Christmases and Fourths of July, the girls asleep in the back seat, their heads leaning toward each other, mouths slack. "Does he hear how he comes across?"

"Ignore him," I advised. "He's always been an ass."

Then one year for Christmas, we vacationed with Brady's

family in the Florida Keys, happy to escape the New England chill for weather so humid, it made the girls' hair frizz and curl. The following year, Brady had a conference in Savannah in late June, and we rented a house on Hilton Head for two weeks, just the four of us. I'd forgotten how peaceful life could be without the constant forced chumminess of the Mabreys, the increasingly close quarters of summers on The Island. Instead, Brady and the girls and I took boat rides and rode horses and watched old movies. Brady and I made love every single night, something that rarely happened when we were with my family, where we ended up going to sleep annoyed and exhausted, nursing a dozen small slights. After that summer, we made Hilton Head our annual trip, and then it seemed that the rope that tethered us to the Mabreys had gone slack, as if the knot had come loose and we were being allowed to drift peacefully away.

I felt pangs of guilt from time to time when Mom called, reminding me that it had been months since she'd seen the girls, or when I dashed off a birthday card instead of making the two-hour drive to Simsbury. And then last year Mom's cancer had come back, unrecognized in the immediate aftermath of the funeral, as if we could only grieve for one thing at a time. It had spread to her lungs and then her liver, and the treatment was aggressive. Since then, Kat and Rebekah and I had alternated our visits, and I'd begun calling more frequently.

Even after all these years, Mom and I had nothing in common, and it was a stretch to find good topics for conversation. She wasn't a good source for parenting information, and I could hardly go to her with my concerns when Stella had a low quiz score. And anything relating to the past, especially that last summer on The Island, was off-limits, topics we tiptoed around as carefully as landmines. Mostly I shared recipes with her—kale smoothies and roasted squash salad, things she wrote down for Hildy to try. The rest of the time I tried not to reference the date she'd been given by her doctor—twelve to eighteen months, if the chemo didn't work.

I looked at the display on my phone. It was 8:17. Outside the bedroom door, I heard Emma's voice raised in a question—probably something about the toucans she'd been watching on television—and Brady's lower-pitched voice, answering. Straining, I heard the water running in the hallway bathroom. Brady would be standing in the doorway, reminding her to brush her back teeth, too, to rinse with the fluoride and floss.

This was my life now, and it was more precious to me than anything.

I pictured Mom in one of her velvet lounge suits, a scarf tied expertly around her bare scalp, sitting in her office, planning away. If anyone could save this family from the allegations of Anna Kovics, it was Mom. She had no doubt been behind the statement that was released earlier today, the one that denied the charges and subtly shifted the focus to Anna's loyalty, her motives.

If I called, she would insist on my cooperation, providing me with the approved narrative, the things I could do to show my support.

Instead, I picked up the phone again and tapped out a message: I'm sorry, but I have to think about my own family right now. I'm sure everything will work out the way it's supposed to work out.

I stared at the words before hitting Send, wondering exactly what I meant by that last sentence, and wondering, too, how Mom would interpret it.

But rather than waiting around to find out, I powered off my phone and went downstairs.

SUMMER 2001

LAUREN

We spent that spring trying to coordinate our summers. Megan wasn't going back to Woodstock—*no way, no how,* she said whenever the topic came up—and Camp Watachwa was out of the question for me, as was a summer spent solely in the company of my mother. It was our favorite topic of conversation, one we circled back to every few days with one unlikely suggestion or another.

"I read online that you can make a year's salary working on an Alaskan fishing boat for the summer," Megan would say.

"Or we could find some rich families who need nannies," I would suggest, and we would laugh at each other.

We would both be horrible fishermen.

I would be a horrible nanny.

Megan went so far as to bike down to a vacation rental office in Scofield, offering to clean properties between guests. Later, she plopped onto her bed, announcing her defeat. "They have someone already, and she's worked there for thirty-five years. It's the same everywhere."

"We'll figure it out," I said.

"Yeah," Megan sighed, staring up at the ceiling. "Someone is bound to need a pair of dishwashers."

"Or dog walkers."

"Or Sandwich Artists."

A week later, she presented me with a ripped page from the *Scofield Sentinel*, triumphant. "Here," she said, thrusting the scrap of paper in front of me. "I found yours."

"What am I supposed to be looking at? Lawnmower repair services?"

She jabbed one corner of the newspaper. "The *Sentinel* is hiring a photographer. See? Problem solved."

I read the advertisement slowly. *Freelance photographer needed. Experienced only. Pay per assignment.* There was a name and phone number listed below the article. I fingered the feathered edge of the paper doubtfully.

"You have experience," Megan pointed out. "All you have to do is pull out your portfolio and say, 'Here's the proof that I'm a genius.'"

I doubted that *genius* was one of the job requirements; the photographs in the *Sentinel* tended to be of championship teams in a semicircle around the three-point line, or the weekly "Good Neighbor" features, which were basically snapshots of women in their gardens.

But the first week of March, I found myself sitting in front of Phil Guerini, a portly, balding man my dad's age who had greeted me with a grunt and a frown. He was a retired firefighter who ran the paper more like a hobby than a business, as was clear from his cluttered second-floor office. He glanced briefly at the album Megan had helped me assemble, a portfolio of my collected works—the best shots from my photography classes, a few of the assignments I'd had with the *Keale Courier*, mostly profiles on students or visiting lecturers.

Toward the back, I'd added some of the photos I'd taken at Holmes House—snow falling and Lizzie laughing and one of Megan walking ahead of me into the sunlight, her body taking the form of a blurred silhouette.

He looked up at me, then down again at the book. "I don't think this job is the right fit for you."

I flipped to another page, drawing his attention to a photograph of my father, a newspaper open in front of him. He wasn't recognizable as Charles Mabrey, US Senator, but it was an interesting angle, a line of text reflected in the mirror of his glasses. "Here's another," I said before he could object, flipping to one of Megan in a tank top in front of a white sheet, Richard-Avedon style. "I've been studying portrait photography."

Phil tapped a finger against his chin. "The pictures are good. That's not the problem."

I shifted in the wobbly chair, the only seat in the room that wasn't covered with stacks of old *Sentinel*s. "What is the problem, then?"

"Look, Laurie—"

"Lauren."

He bobbed his head slightly. "Lauren. This is your basic hack operation here. It's not an art studio. There's no glory in it. One week I might need a picture taken of a big rig overturned on the highway. The next week someone's recipe wins a national contest. It's not—" He gestured to the album, which I closed. "It's not all of that."

"The ad said that experience was needed," I reminded him, feeling warm beneath my sweater. "I was showing you my experience. But I can shoot anything." My voice caught in my throat, and I realized how desperately I wanted this—the first time I was earning something without the interference of my mother, or the influence of my father. Phil Guerini seemed to have no idea who I was, and that was fine with me.

He was quiet for a long time, paging through the album. "Anything?" he asked finally.

I smiled. "Anything."

He grunted, which wasn't a yes or a no. "There's a science fair this week," he said finally. "Winners announced Friday."

I grinned. "I'll be there. I'll do it."

"I only pay twenty-five dollars per assignment. That's hardly enough to..." He waved his hand vaguely in my direction, as if to encompass the cost of my general upkeep and maintenance. He was right—it was nothing, comparatively speaking. The *Sentinel* was a weekly paper, appearing on front porches and café tables on Wednesday mornings, and each edition held only a handful of original photos, beyond the submitted artwork of second graders and the oversize real-estate ads. It wasn't going to pay my rent for the summer, not even for one of the basement apartments listed in the *Sentinel* classifieds.

Still, I *wanted* this. I held out my hand before Phil could change his mind, and he clasped it, surprised.

"We'll see," he said, gruff again as he removed his hand from my grasp. "We'll see what you can do."

The best part of the *Sentinel* was its darkroom, old and barely functional, a relic from the previous editor, who'd mostly used it to develop pictures of his grandchildren. I spent a week putting it back into shape, despite Phil's insistence that the trend was to use digital photography. It was faster, yes, and easier to see if one of my subjects had blinked, but I hadn't warmed to the digital medium. There was no mystery there, no grand reveal when the paper hit the developing fluid and a composition magically appeared. Phil was happy with my work, giving general grunts of approval to my pictures. He was right—the job didn't require a lot of artistry, although it gave me a thrill each time I saw my name in the fine print of the caption. *Photo by Lauren Mabrey.* Not bad at all.

On nights she wasn't working at the switchboard, Megan came with me to the *Sentinel*, sitting quietly on a stool in the corner, her face glowing red in the safelight. She was taking her final general education course, a massive political science lecture, and she'd made friends with some of the girls in her class, a ragtag group she referred to as *the Sisters*, as in, "The Sisters are grabbing pizza. Do you want in?" or "Some of the Sisters are going to that film festival at Smith this weekend..."

I always said no; it wasn't my thing, although it did give me a perverse pleasure to imagine myself being photographed with the girls in their Down with the Patriarchy! shirts. It was good that Megan and I had our own interests, wasn't it? It was natural, and probably healthy. I didn't have a lot of experience with female friendships, not the kind that spanned beyond months into years. The summer camp chumminess I'd experienced as a preteen had typically worn off by October, when our newsy letters became postcards and then nothing at all. Reardon had been full of cliques, a constant tightrope walk between praising one person and offending another, and I'd considered myself a free agent, beholden to no one. Sometimes it amazed me when I looked at Megan, thinking how improbable it was that we knew each other in the first place, and how amazing it would be if we were still friends in twenty years.

She'd even survived my family—the snootiness of my mother, the whininess of Kat, the general disgusting fratboy behavior of MK. I'd been half-asleep on the couch in The Dungeon when MK made his move on her on New Year's Eve, and I'd held my breath, praying that nothing more would happen. Good for Megs—she'd brushed him off and never even mentioned it to me. Now when she answered our phone and it was my mother on the other end, they chatted for a few minutes about her classes, and I listened, marveling at how much better she was at tolerating my family than I was.

Even though we needed summer jobs, I ignored the emails that came from MK all spring. He was persistent; each email had a link to the internship application for Dad's office, and I deleted them, one by one. Finally, he sent a read receipt, and I replied.

Do me a favor and pass it on to your girlfriend, too, he wrote.

Very funny, I wrote back.

He emailed again a few days later, asking where our applications were. I hadn't mentioned it to Megan, even though every morning when she combed through her wet curls, she told her reflection in our mirror, "I am not going back to Woodstock," like a mantra. But she would have hated DC, same as I knew I would: the social climbing, the political alliances, the law and public policy majors.

I wrote, Sorry, dude. Looks like Megan has other plans.

Are you kidding? This would be a great opportunity. Tell her to reconsider.

Face it. She'd just not that interested in you.

Impossible.

Quite possible, I shot back.

It took him a few days to write, Well, what about you? Mom seems to think you're going to do it.

That's because she's delusional, I countered. Washington wasn't plan A or B or C as far as I was concerned. Case closed.

★ ★ ★

Megan stayed at Keale for spring break, picking up some extra hours at the switchboard, and I went home to plead the case for staying in Scofield. I put off the question until the end of my stay, a Saturday morning when she was sitting in her office in Holmes House, organizing her calendar. It seemed an appropriate setting for a business arrangement. I was asking for a thousand dollars a month, but was prepared to settle for five hundred. That would barely pay our rent and keep us in ramen noodles and peanut butter sandwiches, but it was still a bargain compared to what Mom had paid to Camp Watachwa. I laid it out, step-by-step, but Mom only stared at me, her lips pressed in a half smile, half frown.

"Your father is offering you a job, and you could stay with your brother," she pointed out. "Or you could stay here, which would cost us nothing."

I protested that I was trying to build my résumé, not to mention my professional portfolio—

She sighed. "So bring your camera with you to DC."

"And take pictures of what? Men in suits?"

Mom's jaw was set. "You could take pictures of cracks in the sidewalks for all I care."

My cheeks flamed, and I held back a dozen retorts, all of which were guaranteed to get me exactly nowhere. I had a desperate idea, one that wasn't the least bit appealing even as I said it. "What if I took a summer class, and I got ahead on some of my coursework for the fall—"

Mom's laugh was brittle. "So you'd need money for tuition, too? Don't you think you're asking a lot?" She turned back to her calendar, to the rows of neat black lettering, the color-coded Post-it notes, blue for business and yellow for family. Blue for fund-raisers and speeches, yellow for birthdays and anniversaries. The blue notes far outnumbered the yellow ones.

After a minute, she turned to me again. "You're an adult, Lauren, so you can make your own choices. If you choose to stay in Scofield, that's your decision. But if you want me to pay for it—sorry. Not this time."

Megan was folding her laundry when I arrived back at Keale, a complicated operation that involved sorting and folding and unpacking half of her dresser to repack it with the clean clothes. She started babbling the moment I came through the door. "I got a job doing summer tours for Admissions. Part-time, minimum wage, but I'll take it. A bunch of the Sisters are sticking around, too. We found a place where they'll take six of us—two bedrooms, but we can do bunkbeds or a loft or something." She caught my expression. "What? There's room for you, of course."

I moved a stack of her T-shirts and lowered myself to the foot of her bed. "It looks like I'm going to DC after all."

She paused, holding up two mismatched socks that were missing their mates. "Are you serious?"

"Yeah—it's the only way. Well, it's complicated." I picked one of the missing socks from the floor and tossed it to her, like an offering.

"But you weren't interested. You said you'd rather eat glass."

Had I really said that? "Well, it's not like I'm thrilled. But my mom made all the arrangements..." I trailed off, watching the stiff set of Megan's shoulders as she paired her socks, rolling them into tight, angry balls. She was angry, I realized. "It'll be miserable without you," I said, trying to ease the tension. "Alone with my brother in the city for eight weeks? Wouldn't wish that on anyone."

Megan yanked open her top dresser drawer, tossing hand-fuls of socks inside without her usual care. "You do realize I was looking for a job all spring," she said. "For you, too. I found you the job at the *Sentinel*."

"Right, but it doesn't pay any—"

Megan slammed the drawer, stopping my thought in mid-air. "And you never even mentioned this. I didn't even think it was a real possibility."

"Maybe it's not too late to see if they need another intern," I suggested, knowing this was the wrong move as I was say-ing it. "I could email my brother—"

"Conveniently, I suspect it is too late," Megan snapped. I'd never seen her angry like this—not at *me*. "I just signed the forms for the Admissions job, and I put down four hun-dred dollars for a deposit. It's too late on my end, anyway."

"I don't see why you're so upset," I said. "You wanted to stay here, and it's all going to work out."

"With you," she said, nudging a dresser drawer shut with her knee. "I wanted to stay here with you."

"You'll be with the Sisters," I pointed out. "I'm the one who's going to be all alone with my jerk brother."

"You'll have to remind me later to feel sorry for you," she said. And then, leaving her laundry in piles, she grabbed her backpack from her desk and was out the door.

DC was humid and bustling with politics and scandal and busyness, not to mention the tourists who streamed from the metro stations each morning to begin their queues at muse-ums and national monuments. It would have been fun with Megan there, I realized—she would have wanted to go to the museums and monuments, too; she would have wanted to explore the Capitol and snap pictures of the Watergate Hotel and do all the things MK refused to do with me. As it was, he and I shared a two-bedroom apartment off Dupont Circle, and for the first sticky weeks of summer, we were in each other's faces constantly. In the office, MK was my boss, in charge of my bathroom breaks and lunch hours. At night, we bickered over where to pick up takeout and who controlled the remote. He preferred baseball; I wanted something that could make me laugh.

After three weeks, he brought home Gabby, one of my fellow interns, and I finally had the television to myself, although I had to turn the volume up high to avoid hearing the bedsprings and moans.

I went into his room the next morning while Gabby was in the shower and smacked him on the shoulder to wake him up. "This isn't a frat house, you know."

"Oh, I'm sorry," he murmured, smiling into his pillow. "Did we keep you up?"

"I'm telling Mom," I said.

He laughed. "Really? I'm twenty-six. I'm pretty sure she'll think this is normal behavior."

"Gabby's an intern, you idiot. You're supposed to be her boss."

"Hey," he said, leaning on one elbow. "I'll tell you what. There's a smoking hot lesbian who works for the EPA. I could totally set you up."

"Very funny." I whacked him with one of his pillows, and he rolled over, laughing. "You could at least be considerate. These walls are thin."

He yawned. "What happened with you and Megan, anyway? You've been such a nag since you broke up."

"Asshole," I muttered.

After Gabby there was Deena, an intern for the Republican senator from Nebraska who spent three loud nights in our apartment, and after Deena there was Sophie, the daughter of one of Dad's donors and a sophomore at NYU who was interning for the justice department. Sophie had the luxury of her own place, a fact she dropped casually into the conversation over dinner at a pizzeria near the Capitol. MK volunteered to see Sophie home afterward, giving me a thumbs-up over her shoulder. Fine—I was eager to be alone for a change, to play my music and watch my TV shows and slip into my most comfortable pajamas within five minutes of entering the apartment.

After that night, MK packed a small bag to bring over to Sophie's.

"Is this serious or something?" I asked, watching him sort through our plastic-sheeted dry cleaning.

MK winked. "Serious for now."

My main job in Dad's office was to run envelopes through the printer and then stuff those envelopes with letters addressed to each of his donors. As I tri-folded each paper, over and over, I caught snatches of carefully worded language. "At the close of a productive session in Congress, I remain grateful for your support." Dad was in the middle of the election cycle, which meant the next two years would be marked by stump speeches and endorsements and ribbon cuttings in every corner of the state. Mom would be at his side, and I was sure that whether I wanted to or not, I would be drafted into these appearances with MK and Kat.

I sent Megan the occasional email, but her responses were short, her voice cool. She didn't react when I told her about the sexy foreign diplomats I'd met (exactly none), and she seemed bored when she told me about the bratty high schoolers she was chauffeuring around Keale as part of her work for the admissions office. Her messages were perfunctory, and she always signed off with a note that she had to be somewhere or other—on campus, out to dinner, off to a movie. I couldn't tell if she was hurt, or if she wanted me to be.

It had been a mistake not to tell her about MK's internship offer, I saw now, or to raise the issue with my mother when I'd been busy pleading for other things. If Megan were here, we could have hung out at night, using our congressional IDs to get us into live music clubs. Or we could have eaten our way through a bag of microwave popcorn in front of reruns and old movies, and made fun of MK and his conquests together. Instead, I was alone and bored, scuttling from the metro station to the apartment at night and back again in the morning.

Eventually, I grew bolder, heading out by myself at night, ignoring catcalls from the drunken congressional assistants and lobbyists wandering from bar to bar. I always took my camera, the case tucked into my backpack, and shot surreptitiously the lines of partygoers, the raised glasses and, yes, over and over, the men in suits. Once I allowed myself to experience it, the nightlife in DC was intoxicating—a dangerous mix of youth and aggression and people letting off steam. On one of my last nights, when the apartment was stuffy and lonely, I snuck into a twenty-one-and-older jazz club near Logan Circle, making it past the bouncer by blending in with a chatty group of women. The bartender didn't bat an eye when I stepped up to order a beer.

The club was crowded, but I found a spot on the side and sipped my drink slowly, letting the music flow through me. For a while I watched a couple dance, back to front, his arms around her waist, and I wondered if that would ever happen to me.

More people packed into the club, and I felt someone at my elbow, too close for comfort. A man leaned close to me, his breath against my cheek. "Lolo? Lolo Mabrey?"

I reared back to study the vaguely familiar face—straight

teeth, a mole by the eyebrow, dark curly hair. He wore jeans and a dress shirt, the sleeves rolled up to the elbows. It was the dress shirt, more than anything else, that brought the memory back. "You're from Reardon?"

"Yeah, a long time ago. Braden Leavitt." He held out a hand, and I maneuvered my drink to shake it. "I was in your brother's class."

The song came to an end, and the crowd clapped. Someone yelled out the name of a new song, and after a beat, the band started again.

Braden leaned forward to be heard over the noise. "What's a nice girl like you doing in a place like this?"

"Ha."

"No, seriously," he said, tapping the side of my beer. "If I'm doing my math right, you're not quite twenty-one yet."

I took a deliberate gulp, locking eyes with him. "Age is a social construct."

He laughed. "I remember that about you. You were always funny."

I smiled. "And what else?"

"Well, I think the last time I saw you, it was during a field hockey match against Sheldon. You were being ejected for using excessive force."

I groaned, remembering that particular afternoon. "Better watch out. I've still got mad defense skills."

He held up both hands, like he was surrendering. "Anyway, what are you doing here? Do you go to school in DC?"

"Just interning for my dad for the summer. I try to stay as far away from this city as I can. What about you?"

He grinned. "Law school. Georgetown."

"Doesn't the world have enough lawyers?"

His smile wavered.

I took a final gulp of beer, leaving a half inch of frothy

foam at the bottom of the glass. "Sorry. I'm an ass. Did you remember that part, too?"

The band was back, the lead singer at the microphone.

"It's hard to talk in here. You want to go for a walk or something?" Braden asked into my ear.

I shrugged.

"I'm here with a few guys. Let me just tell them—" He made his way through the crowd to the bar, tapped someone on the back, and began a conversation that was mostly gestures. A few of the guys turned to look at me, grinning. *Not likely*, I thought, rolling my eyes. But then Braden was back with a smile so genuine, I couldn't help but relax.

Outside, it was still muggy, the air heavy with the relentless humidity that had settled in to stay. The night was permeated with the hum of air conditioners wedged into apartment windows, churning away above street level and dripping condensation steadily onto the sidewalks.

"Okay, let me ask you. How can you not love this place? There's all this energy and passion…" Braden opened his arms, a gesture meant to encompass the entire city. He almost smacked into a man in a suit moving at a near run, briefcase slapping against his leg. Braden looked at his watch. "You see? Exhibit A. It's after ten, and that guy's still hustling."

I shook my head. "He's probably late for dinner or his kid's birthday party or something."

"So cynical," Braden said.

"So practical," I corrected.

I wasn't sure where we were walking or if we had any destination at all, but I didn't complain. I hadn't seen Braden since he graduated from Reardon years ago, but it was easy to fall in step beside him, matching his legs stride for stride. He asked what I was up to, and I told him about Keale, about the pictures I'd been taking for the *Sentinel*.

"A photographer, huh? That's cool."

I glanced at him, trying to read his face. Did photography seem "cool" to someone in law school, someone with a defined future ahead of him?

Our forearms bumped against each other as I sidestepped a raised portion of the sidewalk. Braden put his arm around me for a brief moment, steadying me, and then dropped his hand back to his side. It was like walking with an older brother, or at least, an older brother who wasn't such a pain in the ass as MK.

We reached the edge of a tiny, unofficial-looking park, a forgotten wooded area with a few picnic benches. Toward the back of the lot, only faintly visible in the darkness, I made out a rusty-looking swing set.

"Race you," I said to Braden, bolting before he could react.

My only advantage was the element of surprise; after twenty yards, I heard Braden's breath over my right shoulder, and then he passed me, sliding precariously in the damp grass when he reached the swing set. I came to a stop, panting, beside him. Warm as it was, it had felt good to run, to get out some of the pent-up energy of the last few weeks.

I flopped onto one of the swings and caught my breath. "I'm glad you didn't let me win. I would have lost all respect for you if you did."

Braden swung beside me, kicking his legs out, pumping them back. "I'm surprised I could beat you. I haven't run like that since college. Or maybe even before."

We swung side by side, and I was aware of him slowing to keep my pace, speeding when I increased my speed. The dull noise of city traffic was occasionally perforated by specific sounds—a dog barking, a car honking. We'd been quiet for so long that I wondered who would be the first to break the silence. As it was, we both spoke at the same time.

"So—"

"You aren't—"

"Sorry," he said. "Go ahead."

"I just wanted to make sure you weren't going to tell on me, or anything."

Braden laughed. "Tell on you for what? Sneaking into a nightclub? Underage drinking?"

I laughed. "Sure, that or sneaking off with some creep my brother's age."

He put a hand over his heart, as if to staunch the bleeding. "*Moi?* I'm offended. And I haven't seen your brother since I graduated from Reardon, so...slim chance I'm going to bump into him anytime soon."

"Yeah, probably not. He's got a girlfriend. Well, a girl of the minute."

"Some things never change, then."

We slowed, our legs dangling loosely.

"What were you going to ask me? Earlier, when I cut you off."

"Oh." He turned in his seat so that his body arced sideways and our knees crashed gently together. "I was just wondering how long you're in town. If you like jazz, there's a festival in—"

"Only until Friday," I interrupted. "Well, I mean, I'm leaving Saturday morning. But I think there's some kind of party for the interns on Friday night."

Our knees knocked together once, then again as we came to a stop.

"That's too bad," Braden said. "Because I know an older, creepy guy who happens to love jazz."

We were quiet for a minute, and then I burst out laughing.

"That sounded better in my head," he admitted.

"It couldn't sound worse," I agreed.

Fat drops of rain started falling without warning, the water warm and stinging.

"I'll take you to the metro," Braden said. "Least I can do."

We walked with our heads down, shoulders hunched forward, as the drizzle turned into full-on rain. Our shirts were soaked by the time we reached the station, and we stood under the overhang, shaking off our clothes.

I smiled at him. "I can take it from here."

"No way," he said. "I'm going to make sure there aren't any creeps lurking down here. Real creeps, I mean. Do you have enough money to get back?"

I rolled my eyes. "Yes, Dad. Thanks for checking."

He grimaced. "Sorry."

"Well, then." I fished the metro card from my back pocket. "I believe my carriage awaits."

Braden didn't move, and in order to avoid the awkwardness of the hug that was surely coming, I took a step forward and gave him a quick peck on the cheek, no friendlier than what I would give to one of Dad's donors at a fund-raiser.

He smiled, caught off guard. "So, I guess I'll see you around."

But I knew he wouldn't see me. On Saturday MK and I would be taking the earliest train out of the city to Boston, and from there the Downeaster to Portland, followed by a water taxi to The Island. I only had a couple weeks there before I had to be back at Keale. Tonight would be an anecdote for my future life—the night I met up with my brother's prep school friend, walked through a sticky stew of humidity and ended up on a rusty swing set.

Just past the turnstile, I looked over my shoulder and Braden was still there, waiting to make sure I was through. "Hold on," I called, fumbling through my backpack for my camera, unzipping it from the case. A second later I was framing him in the viewfinder, noting the way that the rain had turned his curls into ringlets.

"What's that for?" he called, his voice echoing in the tunnel.

I yelled, "Documentation," and waved goodbye over my shoulder.

MK came in the next morning as I was getting ready, throwing his keys onto the floor and collapsing onto the couch. I stood over him, toweling my damp hair.

"Um, hello? Are you playing hooky today or something?"

He groaned into the couch cushion. He was in the clothes he'd worn yesterday—navy pants, a wrinkled Oxford with a stain that looked like ketchup near his pocket.

"Seriously. It's almost time to leave."

Another groan.

"Did something happen with Sophie?"

He rolled over, his face coming into view—a raspberry-colored bruise high on his left cheek and a deep gouge beneath his eye, the width of a fingernail. That wasn't ketchup on his shirt after all.

"Whoa. What happened? Did you get mugged or something?" I reached out to get a better look, but he turned away, face into the cushion. Whatever he mumbled had the word *Sophie* in it.

"Sophie did that to you? Sophie the socialite?" I whistled. "Why, did you break up with her?"

He laughed, then winced, bringing a hand to the left side of his face. "What did she think was going to happen? The summer's almost over. She's heading back to NYU. I'm finishing up at Princeton."

"You're right. Those sound like insurmountable odds."

I laughed despite myself, remembering what I knew of Sophie—blonde and lithe, one of those girls who looked like a sudden breeze could knock her off her feet. "So she hit you?"

"I'm glad one of us is enjoying this. But yeah, she did. Hell of a right hook."

"Looks like she took some of your skin as a memento."

He swore. "She just went crazy. I was lucky to get out of there."

I glanced at my watch. If I didn't leave now, I would definitely be late. "What are you going to tell Dad?"

"Could you take care of it for me?"

"Seriously? After the way you treated me all summer?"

"Hey, I left you alone. I thought you would like that."

I ignored this, remembering the handfuls of cereal I'd eaten straight from the box in front of the television night after night, until I finally worked up the courage to go out by myself. "How am I supposed to take care of it?"

"Tell Dad that I ate something funny, and I was up all night vomiting."

I laughed. "That doesn't explain why you look like a punching bag."

"And then tomorrow I'll say that when I was wandering around the apartment dizzy and dehydrated, I fell and hit my head on the coffee table."

I had to hand it to him—MK always had a story. Had it come to him just now, or had he figured it out on the way back from Sophie's apartment? He could, of course, just tell the truth—but that wasn't how things worked in our family, not when the truth cast shade on the Mabrey name. I remembered Marcus, and the truth that no one, especially me, had told.

No, this was what the Mabreys did. We assessed and reframed and came out with a better story, a better version of ourselves. And then we held the line.

I grabbed my shoulder bag, giving MK a goodbye pat on the shoulder. "Put some ice on that," I advised.

In a day or two, he would be fine, and no one would ever know.

OCTOBER 12, 2016

MEGAN

I'd been counting on Anna Kovics. She was intelligent, well-spoken, sympathetic. Her attack had been less than a year ago, and because it was within the statute of limitations, the district attorney could take her case seriously. I entertained, in between moments of shock and heartache, the fantasy of a dramatic arrest on the steps of the Capitol.

But by Wednesday, less than forty-eight hours into my rekindled nightmare, Anna Kovics had withdrawn her complaint and dropped out of sight. An attorney for Senator Mabrey said that she was seeking counseling, and that while they "were shattered by the grave and inflammatory nature of her false charges," the family "wished her well on the road to healing."

In other words—she'd taken the money, and the Mabreys had won.

All day Wednesday, my tears threatened to come in the middle of the most mundane activities—filling out a purchase order for office supplies, processing a request for a grade change. I was crying just as much for Anna Kovics as for myself, not to mention all the other women, victims who had fallen prey to the charm, the money, the inherent power that came with being a Mabrey.

I wondered what stories Anna had told herself, and if they were anything like the lies I'd been living with for fourteen years.

I'd told myself the I-must-have-led-him-on story, one that offered as evidence the black one-piece I'd bought that spring at Target, admiring my rear view in the dressing room mirror, not to mention all the times he and I brushed against each other at the dinner table, reaching for a pitcher of water or a pat of butter.

I'd told myself that *I'd sent the wrong signals*, that maybe it had been natural or understandable or at least not monstrous for him to see my friendliness as flirtation, to take a smile as a suggestion.

I'd tried to tell myself that *it was only sex*, that I wasn't a victim. I'd tried to place it alongside my last night with Kurt Haschke, the night of Becky Babcock's party.

And mostly, the only thing that could help me get back to sleep when I'd woken from the nightmares of footsteps on the path behind me and a hand on the back of my neck, was the story that *I was the only one*—a fluke, an aberration in an otherwise normal and law-abiding sex life, a one-off, a mistake he wouldn't ever repeat.

Anna Kovics had blown that theory to bits, and the fragments ricocheted in my brain. I'd been attacked fourteen years ago; Anna Kovics had been attacked last year. In between us, and maybe before and after, must be a trail of other women. And all of us, collectively, were too ashamed to do anything other than keep quiet and try to move on with our lives.

Bobby held me that night, smelling faintly of sweat from his after-dinner run, his body a reassuring weight. In his arms,

I was wooden. "What can I do?" he asked over and over. If I'd needed a cup of tea or a new box of Kleenex, he would have jumped into action, ready to solve anything that was solvable. But I shook my head each time, staring ahead into the yawning cavern of our open closet door, seeing nothing.

Anna Kovics had dropped her complaint, and he would get away with it all over again.

If I had come forward all those years ago, Anna Kovics would never have been attacked.

That was true, wasn't it? It was like that Ray Bradbury time-travel story: if you stepped on a butterfly in the past, you could significantly alter the course of human history. If I'd squashed him back then—if he'd been squashable, un-protected by the Mabreys—he might have done jail time, registered as a sex offender, been shunned by politics, forced to live out his days on one of the white couches in Holmes House. Or maybe not—I still believed that coming forward would have affected me more than him.

I shuddered, and Bobby held me tighter.

Back then, I'd made the best choice I could make at the moment. But I was no longer a twenty-one-year-old girl, crying on questionable sheets in a cheap hotel. I was no lon-ger the girl whose entire world had been disrupted, who was scrambling for a foothold in a life that wouldn't intersect, ever, with Lauren Mabrey or anyone in her family.

I wasn't that girl anymore.

I hadn't been her for a long time.

I sat up, and Bobby shifted next to me, head propped on the palm of his hand. "It's time for me to tell someone," I announced, even the words sending me into a cold sweat.

"That's good," Bobby said. "That's really good, isn't it? I was looking into our health plan, and I saw that we have be-havioral counseling, ten visits free."

"I'm not talking about a behavioral counselor," I said. "I'm talking about coming forward, period."

Bobby sat up, too. "You mean—"

"It's time," I told him, holding his gaze until he nodded back at me. "It's long overdue."

I reached for my cell phone, knowing where I should start. In my list of contacts was a number I'd called only rarely over the years, first in desperation, later to arrange the logistics of transport for my Keale belongings, and eventually just to check in with the major moments of our lives.

She answered on the third ring, her voice coming through so clear, she might have been standing in the next room.

"Miriam? It's—"

"Megan," she breathed. "Thank God. I've been waiting for your call."

JUNIOR YEAR
2001–2002
MEGAN

On a normal Tuesday morning, the world erupted. I was toasting an English muffin when someone screamed in the hallway, the words *terrorist* and *attack* sending us running to the television in the communal room. A group of us in our pajamas and sweatpants watched as one of the twin towers leaked a horrible gray puff of smoke, and then a plane flew, as smoothly as if on autopilot, into the other tower. We clutched hands as the buildings crumbled, one by one, into giant balls of dust onto the streets below.

We couldn't find the words for it. It was horrifying, it was a nightmare, it was, unbelievably, happening.

Keale canceled classes, and we spent Tuesday and Wednesday huddled in student union buildings and common rooms, hugging and crying, watching the TV screens with grim determination. Everyone had checked in with their families, needing the reassurance that we were okay, that they were okay, that our personal worlds were okay. Mom and Gerry had been scheduled to fly to Chicago at the end of the week to visit his brother, and now they were planning to drive. "It's horrible, it's horrible," she kept repeating, and then, although somewhat illogically, "I wish you were here, where you would be safe."

But it no longer seemed that simple.

Over the next few days, more news trickled in. One Keale girl, Anya Friedman, lost her oldest brother, who had worked for a financial firm in the North Tower. Other connections were more tenuous—a friend of a friend, the brother-in-law of a sister-in-law. Yet everyone was shaken, everyone was horrified.

It was a shock to see Senator Mabrey appear suddenly on CNN that Thursday, dark circles under his eyes, his tie slightly askew. He was speaking in front of the Capitol Building, snagged by a random reporter as he fought his way through tightened security. I looked around for Lauren, but she wasn't in the room. If I hadn't been looking at the screen, I wouldn't have identified the voice as his—it was so fiery and determined, not the mild voice of the man who'd danced with his daughters on New Year's Eve or jostled his grand-daughter on his knee.

"We must call them what they are, terrorists, because they dared to come on our soil to perpetrate this horrible act, and they deserve to be treated as terrorists," he said, in front of the flash of cameras. There were two deep creases in his forehead that I didn't recognize. "And we must not back down from this. We must hunt them down, so that they know there is no corner of the world where they are safe to hide."

The clip played on CNN frequently in those first few days, along with scenes of American flags billowing over the deci-mation of Ground Zero, and snatches of speeches by presidents and mayors and world leaders. We went to our classes and returned to the news crawl, like we'd been implanted with homing devices. We couldn't take a break from the story—we needed every detail of lives lost and lives saved, of small acts of heroism against the larger backdrop of a world in turmoil.

Even our professors had seemed shell-shocked and subdued when class resumed on Thursday, giving us grace periods on our reading, extending office hours for those who needed to talk. If they were so rattled, with their fancy degrees and years and years of adulthood, how were we supposed to make sense of it?

Lauren skipped her classes that day, hanging around the basement offices of the *Keale Courier* instead. The paper was putting out a special edition, and Lauren had been shooting the reactions of people on campus, asking how the attacks had affected them, how they were feeling. "What's the point of going to class?" she'd asked, and although I'd gone, I didn't have an answer, either.

My main source of comfort came from the Sisters, most of whom had taken Intro to Political Science last spring and had now joined me in Dr. Stenholz's hybrid political and literary theory course. Dr. Stenholz—*Miriam*, she asked us to call her—was intimidating in her slim pencil skirts and black turtleneck sweaters. A dozen gold bangles jangled from her arms, and her irises were magnified behind green-framed glasses. In our first class since the terror attacks, she abandoned her customary spot at the podium and sat with us, our desks pulled into a semicircle. "Let's just talk today," she said, fixing her unsettling gaze on each of us in turn. "What's on your mind?"

There was an awkward silence, and then we all spoke up at once, our words spilling over each other. We were scared about the state of the world. We were scared for what came next. We wondered if it were possible to have PTSD when the trauma was only being experienced second- or thirdhand.

One by one we admitted we were scared, we were nervous, we were worried.

At the end of the hour, we spilled into the stairwell, still talking. Miriam offered to continue the conversation, and so we piled into a few cars and followed her to a tiny cottage in Scofield, barely big enough for us to perch on her couch and sit knee-to-knee on the floor. She served us coffee and little chocolate cookies from a dusty tin that might have been left over from the Christmas before, and when we were still hungry, a few of the girls helped her make a giant pot of pasta topped with two jars of Prego. It took every dish in Miriam's house to feed the twelve of us.

"A toast," Miriam proclaimed, when we were all seated. She was still wearing her pencil skirt and turtleneck sweater, although she had kicked off her heels, and the seam of one stocking had ripped a small hole near one toe in a way that was endearingly human. We followed her lead and raised our glasses and coffee mugs filled with tap water. "A toast to you beautiful women. May you do great things with your compassion and intellect."

It was late by the time I got back to our dorm, but there were still clusters of girls in the common rooms, silent in the face of flashing images on the television screen. I didn't see Lauren there, and she wasn't in our room, either. I changed into my flannel pajama bottoms and attempted to do the reading I'd been neglecting all week, but my eye kept drifting to the illuminated display on my alarm clock. Eleven-thirty, twelve-fifteen.

I checked the common room again, then called the *Sentinel* office, where the phone rang and rang before Phil Guerini's voice came onto the answering machine. Lauren wasn't in the *Courier* office, and by one o'clock, when it occurred to me to check the parking lot, I didn't see her navy Saab, either. Back in our room, I discovered that her camera case was gone as well as her purse and her leather overnight bag, which was usually wedged beneath her bed next to her suitcases.

What the hell? Where could she have gone?

Lauren wasn't back on Friday morning, when I ran into Bethany in the common room at the end of our floor. She was spooning the last of her milk out of a cereal bowl, and when I asked her if she'd seen Lauren, she stopped with the spoon in midair. "Yeah, I saw her last night around six, heading to her car. I thought she was going home."

Of course. It hadn't occurred to me that Lauren might have gone back to Holmes House for some reason. But then I realized what Bethany had said. "So, she *wasn't* going home?"

Bethany shook her head. "She said she was going to New York. I told her she was going to get herself killed, but she said she just had to do something."

I grabbed Bethany's sleeve when she turned away to rinse her bowl in the sink. "She went to New York? Are you serious?"

"Yeah, I know. She's crazy. But—well, I guess I have to admire her for that." Bethany pulled herself gently free from my grasp, and I backed off, shaking.

Back in our room, I looked for any sign from Lauren—a Post-it note that had fluttered to the ground, maybe, a page ripped from my notebook, even a message I might have missed on our machine. But there was no note. There was nothing. What was she thinking? How could she not have told me what she was doing? It was chaos in New York—people were trying to get out, not *in*, not unless they were emergency personnel. What was she trying to prove, exactly?

For three days, Lauren didn't call. I was glued to the news, scanning the words on the crawl, the number of dead and missing, the short blurbs from politicians, the terror groups denying or claiming responsibility—half expecting to see her name there. I wondered if she'd bothered to tell her parents what she was doing, but this question was answered on Sunday afternoon, when Mrs. Mabrey checked in for her weekly call. Her voice was cool, and I imagined her sitting in her office at Holmes House, surrounded by photos of dignitaries and Kat's framed wedding announcement from the *New York Times*. "Oh, hello, Megan. Is Lauren available?"

Stupid Lauren. Stupid, stupid girl. Something horrible could be happening to her right now, and none of us would be able to help. I cleared my throat. "She was—just here, but she stepped out. I think she mentioned something about a photo assignment."

Mrs. Mabrey was quiet on her end, and I wondered if she knew I was lying. I'd never been that great at it—Dad said my whole face was a "tell," but I was hoping whatever weakness my facial expression held couldn't be detected over the phone.

"I can make sure she calls you," I offered. "I mean, she might not be back for quite a bit, but I'll leave her a message."

"That would be wonderful, Megan. I assume she knows my number?"

I laughed, hoping it was a joke.

Some of the Sisters and I had made plans to see a matinee in Litchfield that afternoon, but I canceled at the last minute, knowing I would spend the whole time worrying about Lauren. She was coming back, right? Instead, I paced around our room, picking things up and putting them down—the framed picture of the Mabreys out on their island, the three-by-five photo of Lizzie on our bulletin board. I looked through her closet, then her chest of drawers, touching her belongings reverently, as if she were in fact gone for good. Was that how it would work if she didn't come back? Would I have to help someone from the housing department pack up her belongings, the same as I'd done for Ariana?

Underneath my worry, an emotion competing for my attention was anger. Didn't we tell each other everything? Didn't we know each other's deepest secrets, our trust marked by solemn pinky swears? I'd told her what I had done to my father; she'd told me what happened to her first boyfriend, Marcus. At the time, with tears leaking out of her eyes, it hadn't seemed possible to me that Lauren could have left him to take all the blame for the pot, that she could have just walked away. Now I thought I could see it, though. Hadn't she left Keale without so much as a note for me, leaving me to deal with the outcome if she never returned?

But she did return, finally. It was after ten when she burst through the door, filthy and exhausted and exhilarated. She caught me in a tight hug, and I inhaled the smoke on her hair. "You will never believe it," she told me. "I have a million things to tell you, I don't even know where to start."

You could start, I thought, *with an apology. Or at least an explanation.*

She released me and went to the top drawer of her dresser, grabbing for a clean pair of underwear. She shed her clothes on the way into our bathroom, and I followed her there, sitting on the toilet and straining to hear her voice over the roar of the water pressure. Dirty rivulets spattered against the frosted plastic. Had she not showered since Thursday?

"It was amazing. I mean, it was terrible—you couldn't believe the destruction and the extent of the damage. I literally walked for miles and everything was coated in dust, windows blown out. It was like it looks on television, but so much worse. I kept running out of film, and then—it's going to take me weeks to look through all of it…"

The water came to an abrupt stop and she reached out a dripping hand. I tossed a towel in her direction and she came out wrapped in it, her tangled hair a mess, her eyes shadowed with dark circles.

"Your mom called this morning. I didn't tell her where you were, but you're going to want to call her."

"I'll do it in the morning."

I took a deep breath, trying not to let all my anger out at once. "You could have called me, you know. I had no idea where you were."

She was pulling a hairbrush vigorously through her knots, clumps of hair clinging to the brush after each stroke. "I couldn't find you before I left, and it was too much to explain in a note. But I ran into Bethany—"

"Right," I said. "She told me."

"Oh, good. I thought I would call, but it was seriously chaos. I drove as close as I could get, and then I took public trans to get down by Ground Zero. Everything was roped off for, like, a mile, but—"

"Lauren," I snapped. "I was worried. You didn't call for three days. Anything could have happened to you." She looked at me as if she were just now seeing me, and I could feel my cheeks burning. I felt like a jealous lover, angsty and embarrassed and ignored.

"Okay," she said, setting the hairbrush on the rim of the sink, where it balanced unsteadily. "You're right. But I told you—I waited around for you after your class on Thursday."

"I had dinner with the Sisters. Miriam—Dr. Stenholz—invited us to her house."

"Well, you didn't leave a note, either." She caught my eye in the mirror, and I thought how strange it was that we were looking at each other this way, with the mirror like a liaison between us.

"That's not the same thing," I said, but I was losing steam already, the anger beginning to fade. Now I was just relieved. She was home, she was fine, things were okay.

"What do you want me to say? That I'm thoughtless and selfish and a horrible friend?"

"Sure."

Lauren sighed. "All right. I'm thoughtless and selfish and a horrible friend."

I grinned. "Much better. Now, tell me everything."

She left the bathroom and I did my typical post-Lauren clean-up—a quick mopping of her wet footprints with the bathmat, a swipe of the sink with a wadded up clump of toilet paper. By the time I joined her, she had changed into a T-shirt and sweatpants, and was sitting cross-legged on her bed. Her towel was a damp puddle on the floor, and wet hair left a dark stain on her shoulders.

"I just want to get everything down before I forget," she said. A notebook was open on her lap, and she was holding one of the pens from the jar on my desk. But then, instead of writing, she told me, "You can't imagine the destruction, the terror. It's been days, and people are still looking for their missing relatives. There were literally a hundred fliers on every window. All those people missing, presumed dead."

I nodded, although I didn't really know, beyond what I'd experienced along with the rest of America while I was watching CNN.

She leaned forward, abandoning for a moment the scribbles in her notebook. "This is my best work, Megan. I can feel it. This is real, it's important, and I did it."

And then, ridiculously, I felt a stab of jealousy. I wouldn't have wanted to go, and if I'd been around when Lauren got the idea, I would have tried to stop her. It was enough to sit in front of the twenty-four-hour news, my brain racing, heart firing. But I was jealous of the sense of purpose the trip had given her, the manic energy she had that night, scribbling in her notebook long after I turned out my light. We were miles apart, I thought, no matter that Keale had thrown our lives together.

For the rest of the month, Lauren was a ghost—leaving early in the mornings and returning late at night, attending classes haphazardly, forgetting our plans. She reminded me a bit of my mom when she'd had too much caffeine and went on one of her cleaning and sorting streaks, except that Lauren didn't show much sign of slowing down. One night, after I couldn't find her in the dorms or the offices of the *Courier*, I biked downtown and met Phil Guerini at the *Sentinel*. He appeared to be packing up his desk for the night, shuffling through scraps of paper and spiral-bound reporter's notebooks.

"Ah," he said, gauging the situation before I could ask the question. "I was wondering if anyone had sent out a search party for her yet. You'd better knock before you go in."

Lauren opened the door to the darkroom. She didn't seem surprised to see me, as if we'd had plans all along to meet here. Behind her, hanging from metal clips, were dozens of black-and-white portraits—men and women of all ages and races, their faces contorted with grief or creased with worry, cheeks tear streaked or sweat stained. They were vulnerable and raw, people as I'd never seen people before.

I shivered.

Lauren said, "I'm thinking of doing some kind of collage, some tribute to the humanity in the face of a terror attack—something like that. I haven't figured it out yet."

"Lauren..." I hesitated; what I was about to say wasn't the kind of thing we said. We complimented each other, sure, but there was always an edge, a teasing underside. Mostly our friendship operated on the level of glib and funny, sarcasm and gibes and inside jokes.

"Yeah?"

"It was really brave of you. Going to New York, taking all of these…"

She wiped her hands on a stiff black apron. "Go ahead. I'm waiting for the punch line."

"There's no punch line."

"What about the giant *but*? You know, 'but maybe this isn't the sort of thing you should be wasting your life doing?'"

"There's no giant *but*. This is the exact thing you should be doing."

She broke into a grin, her teeth a white flash in the semi-darkness. "When I was out there, no one knew who I was. Except me. For the first time, I knew who I was. Is that crazy?"

I shook my head. It wasn't crazy.

It was great.

It was what I wanted, too.

Although I'd breezed through Dr. Stenholz's introductory class last spring, I was floundering in her seminar, where I could hardly form a coherent thought. In the company of the Sisters, I was content to let most of them do the talking, amazed by how insightful they were, how much better they phrased things than I could have done. When Miriam called my name, I stammered a response. I'd begun to dread her comments on my papers, which confused rather than clarified things for me. *How can we push you from summary to analysis?* she'd written once, and another time *But is this really what* you *think?*

I visited her office in the political science department several times, trying to work up the courage to knock on her door. Even her office was intimidating—tiny and book lined and intimate, the sort of small space where not much could be hidden.

Then one day she caught my eye as I passed and called out, "Megan! Do you have a minute to chat?"

I pretended to consult my watch, although my next class wasn't for two hours. "Sure."

She gestured for me to come inside. "Can I make you some tea? I'm about to have a cup myself." I nodded, and listened to the clanking of her bracelets as she readied a teapot in one tidy corner. It took me a moment to realize why she seemed different—her black heels were tucked under her desk, and she wore in their place a pair of loafers with tiny, swishing tassels.

While the water came to a boil, I worried my hands in my lap, wondering whether I would be on the receiving end of a lecture about my lackluster performance, or whether the tea was a sign of gentle pity. Maybe it would be handed to me along with a suggestion that I drop the class.

Instead, she settled in across from me, blowing across the surface of her cup. We smiled at each other for a long moment before she prompted, "Why don't you tell me something about yourself, Megan?"

"I'm—an English major. I'm from Kansas…" I shrugged, trailing off. I was about as interesting as a doormat.

She shook her head. "No, no. I don't need the vital statistics."

I hesitated, not sure what to say. "There's really nothing—"

"Right now I'm not your professor. We're just two women having a conversation over tea." Her smile was encouraging, but I glanced in the direction of the open door anyway. The hallway was quiet, the other office doors closed. Was it too late to escape, to claim I had a class? Maybe I could head to the registrar's office before it was officially too late to add or drop. Surely there was another literature course I could take, one where I could comfortably escape into the texts without facing this kind of scrutiny. She was smiling at me, like I was a curious specimen who had floated into her lab. "We're a month into the semester, and I don't know who you are."

"I'm…"

Her smile was almost pitying. "I feel the same way about your writing. I wonder if you're thinking about what I want to hear, rather than what you want to say. It's almost like you're afraid to really think."

A flush had crept up my chest, and I knew it lingered on my cheeks. "I know that I'm not doing very well—"

She waved this away, the gesture causing some tea to slosh over the rim of her cup, and she dabbed at it with a tissue. "Indulge a nosy woman. Tell me about yourself."

I glanced at the door again, but there was no getting out of this. Miriam apparently had all the time in the world. I began haltingly, telling her about my life at Keale—my classes; Lauren, who had just learned that she would be exhibiting her photos in the spring; the summer I'd spent at the admissions office, marveling at the young girls who were so smart and bright and hopeful—all smarter and brighter and more hopeful than me. It was like peeling back the layers of an onion, getting to the core. I told her about Joe Natolo, his name bringing up a near-forgotten ache, and about Ariana Kramer and the bottle of pills, about leaving Woodstock, about refusing Kurt Haschke's marriage proposal. Miriam listened, nodding; there was no judgment. I went back further, to my mom and Gerry Tallant, to my dad and his mesothelioma and the months he'd sat in his recliner. I stopped there, guarding the secret I'd only shared with Lauren.

Miriam passed me the box of tissues, and it was only then I realized I was crying.

"This is stupid," I sniffed, wiping my nose. "I'm sorry. You didn't ask for every horrible thing."

She frowned. "Why is any of this stupid?"

"Because…" I stood up, banging my knee. Miriam grabbed for my tea reflexively, steadying it before it could drench the papers on her desk. I'd taken only a sip, letting the rest grow cold. "You're not a therapist or a counselor, and I'm blabbing everything…"

Miriam waved me back to the chair, and I complied, too stunned to refuse. "You're right. I'm not a therapist, and I'm not a counselor. But I'm someone who cares. And I'm someone who recognizes potential."

I dabbed at my eyes with a fresh tissue. "So you're saying I'm like a diamond in the rough?"

She laughed. "Not so very rough."

I began stopping by Miriam's office more often, and she always waved me in, setting aside the papers she was grading or the text she was marking in the margins with her fine, exact cursive. We read through my essays, and I began to see her comments as part of a back-and-forth dialogue, one that might leave off there and resume elsewhere. When she passed back my paper about the threads of new socialistic theory, I flipped to the back. Beneath the stark B+, she'd written: "Now this sounds authentically you."

When she mentioned graduate school, a simple phrase dropped into our conversation, I laughed. Some of the Sisters referenced graduate school at every turn, like it was a foregone conclusion, the next logical move. It seemed far from logical for me. Miriam frowned. "Aren't you planning on continuing?"

I hesitated. Dad's life insurance covered four years of

Keale, and I would have to fund whatever came next. A job, I figured—not that I knew what or where.

Miriam's eyebrows rose slightly over her green frames. "Let me look into a few things."

A week later, she suggested that I look for a better job—the switchboard, she said, wasn't going to look that impressive on a CV. "What if you found a TA position? I'm teaching an introductory course in the spring."

"Really? But some of the other girls get straight A's—they would probably be better."

Miriam shook her head with the same fondness she probably gave her housecat. "Megan Mazeros. I'm not asking the other girls. I'm asking you."

I grinned.

That semester, with everything I was reading and learning, after all my long talks with Miriam, I'd finally figured out a few things about Megan Mazeros. I loved my parents, and I'd inherited their preferences like genetic traits—hamburgers and pizza, the Chiefs, the Lutheran church. And I'd been influenced by Lauren, deferring to what she liked and knew. I'd created my "Kansas" alter ego to be what she wanted me to be, rather than what I really was. Now when I told one of my wild stories and she laughed, I wondered what she would think if she knew the real me, stripped of fake boyfriends and horrible invented catastrophes. More than anything else, I wanted to be myself.

LAUREN

After our finals, we made quick trips home—me to Holmes House and Megan to Kansas, so we could return to Scofield at the beginning of January to set up for my show. *My show.* Every day, there was a moment when I woke up happy without knowing why, and then I remembered the details and let out a squeal of excitement that was drowned by my pillow. Phil Guerini had been impressed with my 9/11 portraits, and he'd talked to Dr. Mittel, and the two of them had arranged for gallery space in downtown Scofield through friends of friends. During the third week of January, the first week of spring semester classes, the space would be mine.

I tried to interest my family in the details, showing them a few of the prints I'd brought along with me, but the visit felt rushed for everyone, a quick break from our real lives. Mom had been furious ever since she learned about my going to New York—*exactly the sort of reckless behavior we've come to expect from you, Lauren*—and Dad could only take a short break from his Senate duties. At Christmas dinner, the talk was about war, the inevitability rather than the possibility. By the time the turkey carcass was dumped in the trash, Dad was out the door, stopping to kiss the top of my head like I was still a little girl.

Everything, it seemed, was changing. Lizzie was in full-blown toddler madness, tripping herself on table legs and knocking into Christmas decorations that were decidedly not baby-proof. "Where's your friend this year?" Kat huffed, trying to calm a screeching Lizzie. "I should have hired her as a babysitter."

MK was only there for a brief time, too—he was clerking for a judge in the spring and needed to get back before court resumed. There was only the faintest scar under his eye—a thin white line that disappeared into the crease of his smile. The Sophie scar, I called it.

I spent two days alone at Holmes House with Mom before Megan's flight came into Hartford. It was a relief to pick her up at the airport and make the snowy drive back to Scofield, stopping for coffee and giant, crumbly scones that we ate in the car. Megan looked at me when we passed the turnoff for Simsbury, which would have taken us to Holmes House, and I only shrugged. She chuckled into her coffee.

"What's so funny?"

"I was just thinking that I felt the same way about going home," she said.

Half of Scofield had crowded into the tiny upstairs gallery on Fifth Street for opening night, the overflow spilling into the reception space downstairs. My entire dorm was there, it seemed, along with the staff of the *Courier*, Phil Guerini and his family, and Dr. Mittel and the rest of the art department. Megan was there, of course, wearing a dress she'd borrowed from one of the Sisters for the occasion, black and tight with a back that dipped almost to her waist.

"Too much?" she'd asked, modeling it for me in our dorm room, twisting her hair into a knot on top of her head to give me the full effect. "I've never been to an art show."

"No," I'd promised. But seeing the rest of the crowd in their V-neck sweaters and boots, I thought, *Yes*.

We'd spent a full week on the installation and the final effect was stunning: faces starkly black-and-white, their eyes boring into spectators from everywhere in the room. Megan had used an old typewriter in Phil's office to write the labels—names, locations and dates. Katie, Battery Park, September 15, 2001. Jezzie, 47 Broadway, September 15, 2001. Armando, Wall Street, September 16, 2001.

Along the back wall of the gallery was our masterpiece, a ten-by-ten-foot three-dimensional collage, picture upon picture, edges overlapping. From anywhere in the room it was stunning. Individually, they were stories I remembered, people I'd stopped on the street in the midst of searching for family members, people who wanted to talk about their brushes with death, about windows blown out and inches of dust burying their furniture. Together, they told a story of resilience and survival.

It was warm in the gallery, and I was unused to being the center of attention with no other Mabreys to take the limelight. As I chatted, I could feel the flush on my cheeks, the sweat gathering in a long drip down my spine.

The compliments kept coming: *beautiful work* and *important* and *compelling*. Toward the end of the night, Dr. Mittel took me by the elbow and led me to a quiet corner, where he told me that he'd arranged for the three-dimensional collage to be housed in the upstairs hallway in the art department for the rest of the semester.

"Really?" I squeaked, looking around for Megan so I could share the news.

"You deserve this," he said, his hand heavy and warm on my arm. "Don't ever doubt that."

The crowd in the gallery had thinned, but there were still voices echoing from the stairwell although the show had officially closed half an hour ago. From the landing, I spotted Megan at the bottom of the steps, the pale skin of her bare back, a glass of wine in her hand. She was talking with someone in dark jeans, the collar of his leather jacket up to shield his neck from the cold.

I recognized him from the gallery, where he'd stood in front of one portrait in particular for a long time, until I'd come over and told him the story of Marco, the vendor who had given away hundreds of free hot dogs in the days following the attack. "That's amazing," he had said, shaking his head. "Incredible."

I'd thanked him for coming, and we'd shaken hands. Mine

were sweaty, an extension of my overheated body, and I was grateful when he didn't wipe his hands against his jeans.

Now other voices echoed through the reception area, and I couldn't hear what Megan was saying, although I caught the general tension between them. I stepped onto the stairs, feet aching in my heels, hoping Megan would spot me and both of them would turn and one or the other would say something to include me in their conversation. Instead, he reached out a hand to touch Megan's face, and she slapped it away. "All right, all right," he conceded, hands raised in defeated. A moment later he had exited out onto the street.

Megan's jaw was set, her cheeks flushed. She spotted me at the top of the stairs and said, "Oh, hey. Are we about done here?"

"Yeah. Everything okay?"

She nodded, her expression unreadable. "Can I help with anything?"

"Everything stays for tomorrow, except a bag or two..."

Megan shrugged on her flannel jacket and helped me carry a few things to the Saab, which was waiting in the lot behind the gallery. Under the lamplight, snow fell in damp, fat flakes. We shivered in the dark interior while I blasted the heater. Megan wound a scarf around her neck and angled a heating vent to blow toward her nylons.

"I can't believe how many people were there. At least a hundred, but I think probably more," I said, holding my hands up to the vents.

"Yeah, easily," Megan said.

"A lot of people were asking about buying the pictures. I mean, Dr. Mittel had mentioned the possibility, but I didn't think it through seriously. I'm not sure it seems right. And what would I charge?"

Megan shook her head, partially unwrapping the scarf from her face as the temperature rose.

"But the best part is the collage—the art department wants to display it after the show. Isn't that amazing?"

Megan smiled. "Amazing."

"Seriously, thanks for all your help. I would never have finished in time without you."

"No problem."

The windshield wipers had cut through the sludge, creating a small, circular field of vision. I backed out of the parking space and we navigated our way through the quiet streets. It was like driving through the scene in a snow globe, the flakes coming down heavily on the windshield, reducing visibility until they could be whisked away.

I glanced over at Megan, who was uncharacteristically quiet and was clearly not going to volunteer any information. "So. What was going on with that guy?"

"What guy?"

"Come on. The guy you were arguing with in the foyer."

She shook her head. "He's someone I know well enough to avoid."

I racked my brain, trying to remember if anyone fitting that description had appeared in any of Megan's escapades. He seemed like a detail she'd conveniently forgotten to include. We reached campus, and I began the process of circling the lot outside our building, trying to get close to the entrance. "Did you two go out or something?"

Megan snorted. "Or something."

I pulled into an empty spot in the fourth row and slid the gear into Park. "What happened?"

Her seat belt zipped back to the holder and she was out of the car, the door closing emphatically behind her. My heels struggled for purchase in the snow.

"Hey, wait. I'm just curious," I called.

She turned around, half her face buried behind the scarf. "If you want him, he's all yours. Just consider yourself warned."

He came back on the second night of the show and again on the third, each time with questions about specific portraits. He was waiting for me on the fourth night with a bouquet of flowers still wrapped in florist's plastic. The envelope said "Lauren," and the note inside said simply "Joe." On the fifth night we kissed in the alley behind the gallery; on the sixth night I followed his black Honda through Scofield's residential neighborhoods to his apartment above a detached garage.

I waited in the parked car, lights off, long enough to ask myself what I was doing, but not long enough to give a proper answer. I hardly knew anything about him, only that he'd been in Michigan for the last year, he was Scofield born and bred, an employee of a machine shop owned by his uncle. And of course, that he wasn't Mabrey material.

When Joe flicked on the light in his apartment, I felt like his whole life was laid out for me—a full-size mattress on the floor, sheets tangled, a table with two chairs, a couch that must have been as old as both of us combined. He reached to kiss me again, one hand on the back of my neck, and I said, "Wait."

He pulled back.

"I have to tell you something first," I said.

He held up a hand, his fingers gently touching my lips. "I have to tell you something, too. I know who you are."

My heart seized. "You do?"

"Yeah. You're Megan's roommate. We went on a couple of dates. It was nothing serious."

My heart released, like a fist opening.

"And," he added, "I know your dad is a senator, which

means you should probably not be here." He gestured around, pointing to the carpet stains, the molding ceiling tile, the mattress.

I stepped back.

"It doesn't matter to me who you are. If you want to know, I didn't vote for your dad. Nothing personal. I just don't see the point in voting." He stepped closer, cupping my chin in his thumb and forefinger.

"That's okay," I said, feeling weak, like I might crumple to the floor if he didn't kiss me, fast. "I guess you know everything about me, then."

His other hand was on my back, finding the bare skin beneath my sweater. "Not even close to everything."

Joe and I saw each other several nights a week through that spring, sometimes starting out at the Denny's in Litchfield, usually ending up at his apartment, the dusty plaid curtains drawn. After our first time, I planned to tell Megan, to lay out all my cards on the table.

It's nothing.

He's cute.

We're just having fun.

Joe insisted there had only been a flirtation between them. "Unrequited," he said.

"Doesn't that mean you're still pining for her, or that she's still pining for you?"

"Nah," he said. "Wrong word, then. I just mean, unconsummated."

I could, without too much imagination, picture the two of them together. Megan and Joe were more alike than Joe and I were. And that was partly why I didn't say anything, not at first, when I wasn't sure where it was going or how long it would last. Also, I wanted to avoid the judgment that would inevitably come, the charge that I was only slumming with Joe, that it would never be serious. For the moment, I was enjoying myself too much to admit this was true.

It was funny, when I thought about it. Mom had sent me to Keale to avoid the exact sort of man that Joe was, that Marcus might have been. For two-and-a-half years, her strategy had worked. Keale had been a safe haven for most of us girls, a refuge from the boys we'd known before and the men we would know later, the ones we would marry and have kids with, the ones who were part of our futures as surely as mortgages and carpools and summers on the Cape. Joe wasn't part of the Lauren Mabrey I had been before, and we never talked about the future, not *let's get married* or *we'll live here* or *we'll buy that*. He existed only in the present, and the present was wonderful.

Each time I drove away from Joe's apartment, blasting the air-conditioning to dry my sweaty hair, I told myself that there might not be a next time. *Impermanence*, I thought, proud as if I'd invented a new philosophy. *Happiness in the moment.* And then two days later, I'd be back on his street, climbing the rickety stairs to the apartment over the garage.

By the time I realized how permanent Joe's presence was in my life, it was too late to tell Megan. Joe and I had been together for weeks by that time, and to manage that, I'd had to invent a number of lies, claiming that I was working in the darkroom at the *Sentinel* or heading out to shoot pictures of a school board meeting. One Saturday morning, I told her I had to drive back to Holmes House for a family thing, and instead I met Joe at a roller rink two towns over. He was a horrible skater, as I suspected he would be—reckless and rough, taking lunges and leaps and crashing to the floor, then shaking himself off, mostly unscathed. Afterward, we went to a mall forty-five minutes away, since he needed a new pair of work boots. It felt funny at first to hold hands with him, like we were fully domesticated, just another couple at the mall. That night I paid cash for a cheap motel in Litchfield and we spent the entire night together, laughing every time someone used the ice machine outside our door.

There were all sorts of words to describe sex, some which you could find in a thesaurus or learn at summer camp, others mentioned slyly at Keale parties by girls I suspected were virgins. And then there was sex with Joe, the kind that went beyond language to invented vocabularies, that answered questions I had never asked.

Joe said into my ear, "I bet they can hear us in the next room."

"There's no next room," I told him. "There are no other people."

Later, I settled into the crook of his arm.

This is what it could be, I thought. This is what I could have if life was different, if I wasn't Lauren Mabrey, if Joe was someone else.

When I returned to Keale the next day, Megan was on her bed, propped up on an elbow, a textbook open in front of her.

"How did it go with the family?" she asked.

"Oh, it was fine," I answered, flopping onto my bed. I could still feel Joe's lips on my neck, his tongue tattooing circles on my skin. "Typical Mabrey melodrama."

I wished that winter could have lasted forever, but spring came in a sudden warm rush, the days hurtling closer toward summer. Joe and I spent lazy evenings with the windows open, so we could hear the sound of lawnmowers and weed whackers. When I wasn't with him, I was with Megan and the Sisters, watching the free movies projected onto the side of the Fine Arts Auditorium. Joe was my secret life, one that felt more and more like my real life.

At the beginning of April, Kat left a garbled, tearful message on our machine, and Megan and I played it a dozen times, trying to make sense of her words. The upshot of it was that my mother had a tumor in her breast. Kat had sobbed through the words *biopsy, cancer, surgery.* Megan hugged me, saying all the right things. *There are all kinds of amazing advancements in cancer treatment. It sounds like they caught it soon. She'll have the best medical care possible.* I knew all this was true, even filtered secondhand through Megan's experience with her father, but still I was racked with a horrible guilt for the dozens of ways I'd been a bad daughter.

I went back to Holmes House for a tense weekend, and early on the morning of her operation, we drove in three cars to the Yale–New Haven campus, following each other on the predawn freeway like members of a funeral procession, Dad and Mom, Kat and me. Mom handled the operation with her customary precision, arriving at the hospital with a list of questions and shoving a practical to-do list into Dad's hand in case she didn't make it through the surgery. We stayed with her in the crowded pre-op space, sidestepping nurses and machinery and IV poles. With her face free of makeup, her nails unpolished and vaguely yellow, Mom was almost unrecognizable.

We said, "It'll be okay," and she didn't answer. That was typical, though—an official *no comment.*

In the waiting room, Dad paced in his jeans and Red Sox hat, for once refusing to look at his laptop or phone. Kat called MK with periodic updates—this close to graduation, he hadn't been able to break free to join us—and left messages at work for Peter and his parents, who were watching Lizzie. I went across the street in search of coffee, and when I came back, balancing three stacked cups under my chin, I spotted Kat in the window, an unconscious hand circling low on her belly. How far along was she? Was she waiting for Mom to recover before telling anyone?

It was hours before the surgeon came out, still in blue scrubs, a mask hanging from his neck. I took notes, the way Mom would have wanted, more diligently than I'd ever taken them for any class. The tumor was encapsulated, its removal successful. Following Mom's wishes, the surgeon had performed a double mastectomy. When we were able to visit her in the recovery room, she looked ancient and weak, her eyelids fluttering, her pale hand limp in Dad's grasp. Her chest was puffy with tubes and bandages, hiding temporarily the fact that her breasts were gone.

I kissed her on the temple and stood outside in the hallway to cry. More than anything I wanted Joe to be there, to wrap his arms around me and say something soothing, even if that wasn't our typical pattern of behavior. I wanted it to be typical, I realized. Maybe, after all, I wanted to have both a present and a future tense.

Dad, Kat and I made a plan in the hallway, something we hardly knew how to do without Mom. Kat would stay in the hospital while Mom recovered, as long as Peter's parents could watch Lizzie. Dad had to be back in Washington for an important vote, but he would return on Friday morning. I had to go back to Keale—even before missing days for Mom's surgery, my grades were hovering at C's. Still, I offered to stay, to do my part.

Dad shook his head. "She's going to need you more this summer, after the chemo and radiation. We'll need you to stay with her on The Island."

"Of course," I said, nodding fast. I wish I would have

suggested it myself, the moment I learned about the cancer. "Anything."

"Actually, we should all go to The Island this summer," Dad said, looking pointedly at Kat. There was weight behind his words, as if he were making an important announcement, one that didn't require a vote or majority approval. "It would be good for her to have everyone around. And who knows? This might be the last time."

"Dad," Kat protested, "Mom's going to be—"

He raised a hand, silencing her. "I only mean, with Michael graduating this spring and Lauren next spring, who knows when we'll all be there again?"

Kat and I glanced at each other.

I hadn't really thought of it that way, but everything was changing for the Mabreys. We were splintering off the stem, veering off course. This might in fact be our last summer.

MEGAN

Miriam gave me the news that spring, unable to contain her smile—a PEW scholarship, four weeks at Harvard, all expenses paid, plus a stipend that was more than I'd earned all last summer as a campus tour guide.

I made her repeat the details three times, sure I wasn't understanding.

She passed a folded letter across her desk, and I read "Dear Ms. Stenholz, Based in part on your generous recommendation, we are thrilled to offer Megan Mazeros a position in our summer pregraduate study program."

"This is just the beginning for you," Miriam said, her eyes

brighter than normal behind her green frames. She was *crying*, I realized. She was so happy for me, she was actually crying. When I sprang out of my chair to hug her, she didn't resist.

I told anyone who would listen, from the Sisters to my professors to the cafeteria workers to my mother. *I'm going to be studying at Harvard this summer.* It didn't seem real, even when correspondence from the PEW committee began to arrive on thick, creamy letterhead.

"My little girl," Mom said, when I called to tell her the news. "Harvard! I can't even imagine. It's like a movie."

It did feel that way, like I was on the set of *Megan Goes to Cambridge*, or some documentary where a small-town girl went from waitressing at the local diner to an Ivy League school. Of course, I wasn't attending Harvard itself, but a program on its campus—a technicality that was lost on my mother.

"What about the rest of the summer?" she asked next, her enthusiasm deflating. "You'll be coming home, right? If you only need to be at Harvard for four weeks, you could spend the rest of the time with us. There's an indoor pool in the new health club, isn't there, Gerry?" In the background, I heard the sounds of *Jeopardy!*, the rise and fall of cheers from the studio audience. Gerry's muffled response might have been an answer to Mom or one of the game show questions. Lauren entered the room, tossing her backpack on the ground and plopping on my bed next to me. I gestured that I was wrapping up the conversation and she smiled, resting her head against my pillow.

"I don't know," I told Mom, thinking of Gerry's beige house and the windowless room in the tax office, not to mention the chance encounters I didn't want to have with Becky Babcock or Kurt Haschke. I pointed out the expense of airfare, the fact that I would need to buckle down in order to prepare for the seminar.

"Well, you'll have to study *some*where," Mom pointed out. "It might as well be here."

"Or maybe you and Gerry could take a vacation out here. We could even rent one of the cabins on the lake in Scofield, and I could show you around."

"But we'll be out next summer, for your graduation," Mom pointed out. "I don't know. I'll have to talk about it with Gerry."

"Yeah, ask him," I said.

When I returned the phone to its cradle, Lauren was looking at me.

I laughed. "What's up?"

Sometimes it seemed like we hardly saw each other anymore, between our classes and Lauren's job at the *Sentinel*. At least a few nights a week, she returned so late that the sound of her key in the lock woke me up. "I lost track of time," she would whisper, kicking off her shoes and her jeans and sliding half-clothed into her bed. We were too busy to make grand plans for the future, like we used to do; instead, we talked about things that were happening at that moment—the papers due or past due, the regular Keale gossip about who had done what and with whom, and how Mrs. Mabrey was faring after her latest chemo treatment.

She grinned. "What if you came with me to The Island? It's only a few hours from Boston by train."

I laughed. "Seriously? We're talking about six weeks."

"Why not? There's plenty of room."

I reached out to retrieve one of my notebooks, the pages bent backward under Lauren's thigh. "Your mom is sick, though. She's not going to want a guest hanging around for the whole summer."

Lauren considered this. "Well, if you feel bad about it, you can help me handle her. I think mostly she's going to be resting."

I stared at her, half smiling.

"What?"

"I'm just trying to figure out if you're serious."

"Why wouldn't I be serious? You came home with me for Christmas, and we all survived, didn't we?"

I shrugged. We *had* all survived, but the trip wasn't without its awkwardness—the sniping between family members, the feeling that around any corner I might intrude on someone's private moment.

"It'll be perfect," she continued. "I want to take about a million pictures, and you can bring all your books and get ready for the seminar. I promise you uninterrupted hours of study, except when we're swimming and sailing and clamming and having bonfires on the beach…"

I grimaced, thinking of my pale, out-of-shape body doing any of those things. "I'll have to buy a new swimsuit. And some decent sandals."

She nudged me, her elbow digging into my upper arm. "Those are not insurmountable odds."

"And you know for a fact that it's okay with your family?"

"Are you kidding? If they had a choice, they'd take you over me."

I had to hand it to her; Lauren drove a hard bargain. From that moment on, I was picturing myself on The Island already, no matter that I'd never been there and could only gather a few details from the snapshots in Lauren's photo album. I pictured myself with sand squishing through my toes, a lick of wind tousling my hair. I would be the perfect guest, I promised myself. The Mabreys wouldn't even know I was there, unless they needed my help.

In the end, I convinced Mom to start looking for hotels in or around Boston, for a weeklong, last-hurrah-of-summer vacation before school started. "We'll see," she said, and I knew in general what that meant. She'd said *we'll see* when I'd wanted to have my birthday party at Chuck E. Cheese's, and *we'll see* when I asked for new soccer cleats and *we'll see* when I asked if Dad's doctors might be wrong, if there was any way he might outlive his prognosis. None of those conjectures had ever become reality.

"Really see, though," I said. "We should do this."

She laughed. "We'll see."

When I wasn't studying for finals, I sorted through my closet, deciding what to pack in the giant box I would keep in Keale's long-term storage for next fall, and what to bring with me to The Island and later to Harvard. If there was any doubt that our lives were entangled, it was obvious when I tried to separate my things from Lauren's, which had spread to every corner of our room like a creeping vine—socks under my bed, shoes in my closet. Digging in her drawers, I found a shirt I'd been missing for a month. She returned one afternoon when I was agonizing over my packing decisions and flopped onto the bed with her backpack still strapped to her back.

"I'm just going to throw my swimsuits and shorts and tank tops into the car, and shove the rest into a box," she yawned. "It's very casual on The Island. You won't need much."

I stared at my clothes, most of them faded and threadbare—shorts of the athletic variety that made rare appearances at one of the treadmills in the rec center, stretched-out two-for-$10 tank tops. Somehow I suspected that the Mabreys' brand of casual would include bright sundresses and lots of linen and wedge-heel espadrilles.

"Hey," I said, tossing a pair of warm socks into the Keale box. "What are you doing later?"

She sighed. "Studying, so I don't fail my freaking art history class. I'll probably go to the library. Why?"

"Some of the Sisters are getting together for dinner one last time before we all head out. You're welcome to come."

"Thanks, but I'd better not," she said, sliding her backpack off her shoulder.

"Well, if you change your mind, I think we're trying that new Thai place."

"Cool," Lauren said. In a minute she was curled up on her side, eyes closed, and I suspected she wouldn't be doing much studying after all.

There was a twenty-minute wait at the Thai restaurant, so the Sisters and I met at Slice of Heaven, where we devoured two vegetarian pizzas and talked about our summer plans and final exams. Marley, one of the more outspoken members of our group, had written a paper about the latest Updike novel, which she dissected for us with feverish glee. Allison got up to refill her Diet Coke and came back to the table, announcing in her best imitation of Miriam, "What do we think of Updike, ladies? Mommy issues? Daddy issues? Penile penetration issues?"

A couple at the next table looked over at us, and we collapsed into giggles. I excused myself to hurry to the bathroom, my full bladder threatening public embarrassment. As usual, the paper towel dispenser was empty, and I was still wiping my wet hands on my jeans when I came out of the bathroom and found myself face-to-face with Joe Natolo.

We'd bumped into each other in January on the night of Lauren's opening at the gallery. At first, I'd thought it couldn't possibly be him, that I was seeing some kind of Joe-shaped mirage. He'd smiled when he saw me, cornering me for a chat as if nothing had ever happened between us. Shaking, I told him about that night with Ariana, my bottle of pills. He'd grimaced, offering a weak explanation. *When you didn't come down, I thought maybe you'd changed your mind, that the whole thing was a mistake.* The next week, he'd taken his friend up on the job offer in Michigan. He didn't mention that he'd missed me or that he'd thought about me—probably because he hadn't. Apparently, I'd done all the missing for both of us, scanning the coffeeshop and squinting to make out every driver of a black Honda for months afterward.

Now he was in front of me, grinning, a bookend to my semester. "Megan! Are you here for dinner?"

I gave him an icy smile. "That is what people do in pizza parlors."

He laughed. "So I've heard."

"Okay, then," I said, sidestepping him.

"So you're going to stay?" he asked.

I stared at him, not comprehending. Was he delusional? Did he expect me to slide into a booth like we'd done once before, our knees deliberately bumping under the table?

A woman came down the hallway just then, pulling a toddler-aged girl by the hand. I used this as an opportunity to back away, putting more distance between Joe and me before I turned and headed back to the table. When I glanced once more in his direction, the door to the men's room was swinging shut.

The Sisters were clearing up the last of our plates and napkins. I grabbed my denim jacket off the back of my chair, and Danielle fished her keys out of her jeans. "Riding back with me?"

I didn't turn around, not wanting to see if Joe was finished in the bathroom, if he was watching me. Danielle's Taurus was across the street, now crammed tightly between two other cars. I recognized one as Joe's black Honda, a vanilla air freshener dangling from the rearview mirror.

Danielle began the navigation for a complicated seven-point turn, craning her head to see if she was blocking traffic. "Hey—isn't that Lauren?"

I turned just in time to catch a glimpse of what was unmistakably Lauren—her dark hair brushed and glossy, hanging down to the middle of her back. Earlier, it had been up in her traditional messy ponytail. She'd changed clothes, too, and it looked like she was wearing lipstick. The last time I saw her, she'd been snoozing on her bed, an arm draped over her face to block out the light streaming through the window. The door to Slice of Heaven opened, and the woman from the hallway exited, holding her toddler with one hand and a pizza box in the other. I watched as Lauren slipped past them into the restaurant.

"Dude," Danielle said. "She blew us off, didn't she?"

"Whatever," I said, fighting down the nausea rising inside me, propelled by a tidal wave of pepperoni and Diet Coke. She'd blown me off to meet *him*. I knew it. That explained his questions—*you're here for dinner? You're going to stay?* He'd thought I was joining them.

Them.

Joe and Lauren.

★ ★ ★

The first thing I'd done after dinner, once Danielle dropped me off, was to race up the stairs, wedge a chair under the door the way I used to do back at home when I wanted absolute privacy from my parents, and dig through Lauren's stuff. At first, I found only her usual junk—books she didn't open often enough, haphazard lecture notes, more clothes on the floor of her closet than on hangers. I looked through her desk drawer, finding only odd scraps of paper with photo assignments and withdrawal receipts from the ATM. I looked through the pictures in her giant art portfolio, marveling again at her talent. None of the prints seemed new, though—the most recent additions were copies from her art show in January. Then I went for the box of prints that she kept under her bed, and I thumbed through them quickly, careful not to disturb the original order. There were dozens of pictures of buildings at Keale, of the two of us, of her family at Holmes House. And there, on the bottom, the pictures slipped into an opaque paper sleeve, was Joe— laughing, smiling, goofing.

My hands shook as I sifted through the prints: Joe at a booth in a restaurant, a plate of pancakes in front of him. Joe in a plaid shirt, sleeves rolled up to his elbows. Joe in his leather jacket and Doc Martens, standing on the riverbank. Joe on a bench at a roller rink, lacing up his skates. Joe cooking at a stovetop, spatula in hand. Joe shirtless, a swath of dark hair trailing down his chest, a sheet bunched up near his waist. In each one, he was engaging with the camera—with Lauren, behind the camera—teasing her, talking to her, encouraging her.

This was what it had come to, then. Here we were, and where we were was full of lies.

She'd been lying all semester—her busy class schedule, her hours in the darkroom, maybe even the weekend trips back to Holmes House. Had it been going on since the night of her opening in January, or even before then, the two of them planning and plotting and laughing behind my back?

I sat on my bed for the better part of an hour, trying to figure out what to do. Part of me wanted to get on my bike and pedal like mad back to Slice of Heaven, to catch them in the act of being together, to throw my realization in their faces. But of course—they already knew about each other, and I would be the one who looked foolish, the jealous roommate and jealous would-be lover, causing a scene.

In the end, I repackaged the photos of Joe and arranged everything as Lauren had left it, more or less. And then I waited.

Lauren's hair was once again in her tangled ponytail when she entered just after eleven, the lipstick rubbed—kissed?—off her lips. "Hey," she said, dropping her backpack to the floor. She hadn't been wearing it when she met Joe. Of course not— the backpack was for my benefit. It was her alibi.

I closed my notebook, which had been open on my lap for the better part of the evening, although none of the terms had registered. "I couldn't find you in the library," I said, and watched as Lauren froze, a half second of hesitation, before recovering.

"Oh, sorry. It was too noisy, and I ended up reserving a private room on the second floor." She kicked off her shoes, Lauren-style, and one of them ricocheted off the box I'd been packing earlier that day. "Why, did you need something? What's up?"

I shook my head. "Nothing. Just wanted to talk."

I watched as she undressed, pulling her shirt over her head, unhooking her bra behind her back. She squinted at her reflection in the mirror, rubbing a dab of lotion on her arms, and reached for her pajamas. There were no physical signs of Joe Natolo—no hickies, no red blotches or impressions. A crime scene tech, dusting for fingerprints or swabbing for saliva, might have found him everywhere, but he wasn't visible to me. Finally, she flopped down on the bed next to me, pulling a pillow onto her lap.

"You know what sucks?" she asked.

Being lied to? "What?"

She sighed. "All that studying, and I hardly feel like I know anything."

Lauren was asleep before me that night, apparently unashamed, so used to her lie that it no longer caused her to lose sleep—if it ever had. I seethed in my bed, watching her breathe in and out, but eventually I reasoned myself into a type of calm. I had no claim on Joe. I wasn't pining away for him; I'd moved on, and most of the time when I did think of him, it was to be embarrassed that I'd almost fallen for the first guy I'd met in Scofield, when I hadn't allowed myself to settle for Kurt Haschke in Woodstock. It didn't surprise me that Joe fell for Lauren. Any guy would go for her, given the chance. She was pretty and talented and funny; she was the kind of rich that people like Joe and me only saw from a distance. What Lauren saw in him was less clear—except that because she was a Mabrey, anything she wanted was hers for the taking.

I remembered that she'd once told me never to trust anyone in her family. At the time, I thought it was a flippant comment, unserious and self-deprecating, but now I wondered if she meant it after all. Maybe she'd even been warning me.

LAUREN

I visited Joe the night after my last final, when I really should have been packing and eating one last pan of brownies with Megan and the girls from our dorm.

Joe and I had agreed to keep it like any other night—nothing fancy, no elaborate goodbyes. Still, he surprised me with an apartment that had definitely been cleaned at some point over the last forty-eight hours. I raised an eyebrow when he produced four cartons of Chinese food and two clean plates. "I thought you said nothing fancy."

He grinned. "I even snagged us extra fortune cookies."

"And we're using a tablecloth," I pointed out. "That's a definite upgrade."

"And eating *before* sex," Joe countered. "Like perfectly civilized people."

We smiled at each other, and Joe dished the fried rice and chicken chow mein from the cartons. I handed him a set of chopsticks, and he fumbled with them gamely before retrieving two forks from the dish rack. Watching Joe with a grain of rice stuck to his chin, I felt a yawning emptiness opening up inside me, as if I were standing in front of a giant canyon and Joe was so far away that he might not have been on the other side of it at all. Later, the sex felt desperate and sweaty, each touch wrong in a way that was impossible to quantify.

Afterward, we sprawled apart, the sheets twisted between us. Joe traced my collar bone with his thumb and asked if I was sure I had to leave in the morning.

"I'm sure."

He ran a finger from the hollow of my neck down my chest, through the flat valley between my breasts.

I propped myself up with an elbow. "You'll miss me, right?"

"Absolutely. For at least a day or two." He laughed and pulled me closer, so that my head was resting beneath his, and his expression was hidden.

I wanted to ask him what happened next, if we would pick up the pieces at the end of August when I came back to Scofield. But I could hear his answer, as sure as if I'd phrased the question. *Yeah, sure. If that's what you want.* Noncommittal, unattached, impersonal, flexible. In other words, he wasn't going to fight for me, but if I showed up on his doorstep, he would open the door.

"You have my number, right?" Joe teased, and the hand resting on my stomach moved lower, in a way that signaled the end of reasonable conversation.

I stayed with him late that night, only breaking away when the television went from the late show to an infomercial to dead air. Back at Keale, I cried in my car in the parking lot, watching the shadows of girls pass in front of the dorm windows. For most of them, it was their last night on campus until the next semester, and there was a flurry of packing and binge-eating the last of the Pop-Tarts and the extra-butter microwave popcorn, all those pantry staples that would otherwise go in the trash.

I had Joe's number, but I wasn't going to call it, not from The Island, not with a horde of Mabreys passing through the house, not with Megan there, not with my mother examining the long-distance phone bill, wondering who it was I kept calling in Scofield. If he'd been an email kind of guy, we could have kept in touch that way—but Joe didn't have a computer, and he hadn't been interested in anything I'd shown him on my laptop.

Megan wasn't in our room when I went upstairs, tears wiped from my cheeks. I threw the last of my textbooks and school supplies in my storage box, extinguished the overhead light and crawled under the covers. What if I'd invited Joe to

The Island with me, instead of Megan? We could have slept together in my childhood bed, limbs never not touching. We could have waded into the surf each day, pant legs rolled to our knees. We could have suffered through dinner together, holding hands under the table and smirking at inside jokes. But of course, for more reasons than I could count, none of that would ever happen.

In the morning, Megan and I loaded the Saab for the drive to Holmes House. She chattered on about the fun I'd missed the night before—some cheesy '80s movie, a bottle of something called Purple Passion, and the fire alarm that had evacuated the building next to ours when someone burned a pan of pizza rolls.

"I heard the fire alarm," I murmured.

She laughed, her glance darting in my direction. "What's wrong with you, anyway? Missing Scofield already?" The top half of her face was hidden by an oversize pair of sunglasses with red frames. She'd worried they made her look too much like Sally Jessy Raphael, but of course they didn't. On Megan, they were adorable. She'd bought quite a few new things over the last few weeks from the Target in Litchfield; the neatly clipped tags with their sharp plastic ends had lined our wastebasket—a surprise, since Megan almost never spent anything on clothes, unless it was musty-smelling secondhand things from the Scofield thrift store.

I yawned. "Just tired."

"Yeah, I bet you couldn't wait to get out of there. I know I couldn't. I'm looking forward to seeing the ocean, getting a tan, eating lobster rolls…" She ticked the items off on her finger, as if from a list she'd memorized.

I pressed down harder on the gas pedal, and the Saab gunned forward.

★ ★ ★

We spent the night at Holmes House and repacked the car in the morning following Mom's directions. In five weeks of treatment, her hair had gone from full to papery thin to non-existent, a fact concealed by a short blond wig and carefully penciled eyebrows. She wore a tunic that floated around her body but couldn't disguise the fact that she was puffy all over from water retention, an effect of the chemo. When she gestured about which bag to load next, I noticed that her wedding ring bit into her flesh, like she was wearing a child-size trinket.

The drive from Simsbury to Yarmouth was uneventful. Mom dozed in the back seat, a scarf wrapped around her wig and tied under her chin. From the passenger seat, Megan peppered me with questions about The Island, as if we were heading to some all-inclusive resort.

"I keep picturing those tiny islands from cartoon strips, the ones with only a single palm tree," she confessed.

"It's bigger than that, but no palm trees. They're mostly evergreens, I think."

She persisted, "But *how* big are we talking? Like the size of Bermuda?"

I laughed. "I have no idea how big Bermuda is. But I'm pretty confident that The Island is bigger than what you're picturing on the cartoon and smaller than Bermuda."

She smiled. "That's not very helpful."

"Okay," I sighed. "It's probably like five acres. But—you'll see—a lot of it is rocky and steep, so it feels smaller. There's the main house, and then some cottages, a gazebo, the dock and a whole lot of trees and rocks."

Megan was quiet for a while, looking out the window. It was the sort of perfect late-spring day that promised happiness. Then she said, "I actually have no idea how big five acres is, either," and we laughed so hard that Mom stirred in the back seat, before collapsing back onto a pillow.

We were somewhere in Massachusetts by then, and I could feel the pull of it already—summer was beckoning, The Island was calling. I told Megan everything I knew, cobbled together from family stories, probably part truth and part exaggeration, but which part was which, I didn't know. On a map, it was officially named Codshead Island, although the Mabreys never called it by that name. Mom had inherited it from her parents, who had inherited it from the Holmes patriarch, that scion of steel manufacturing and what I suspected was exploited labor. According to one version of the story, he'd bought it to impress a woman who had turned down his proposal, after he'd rowed her all the way out there with a wedding ring in his pocket. In another version, he'd inherited it himself as part of a business deal or a bribe.

"My dad once won five hundred dollars in a poker game," Megan said, but my laugh felt hollow. I was missing Joe, and rushing to cover that with as many words as possible.

"When my parents married," I continued over her interruption, "they tore down the old house and built the current one." I glanced in the rearview mirror and saw that Mom was sleeping again, her mouth falling slightly open. In a lower voice, I told Megan that my parents had seen The Island as a political asset—there was enough room to wine and dine, to house guests, to throw parties. I remembered summers where we entertained all sorts of people in government and business, who'd temporarily shed their suits for polo shirts and khaki shorts. But accessibility was a definite problem—the only way to The Island was by boat or water taxi, and once you were there, you had to be able to move on foot. And this summer, with Mom sick, there weren't any plans to entertain visitors.

"Except me," Megan murmured.

"That's not what I meant. Plus, they'll probably put us to work running errands." I told her that we had some kayaks and Jet Skis stored on The Island, and that we had an old fishing boat for getting to and from the mainland. "Do you know how to operate an outboard motor?"

Megan shook her head. "I can barely go underwater without plugging my nose."

"Well, I'll show you. It's not that complicated."

It was midafternoon by the time we reached Yarmouth and found a spot in a parking garage near the wharf. Mom rallied, producing her credit card for the weekly parking rate and summoning enough energy to tip the man who lugged our bags to the boat. We sat on different benches in the empty water taxi, Mom huddled against the center beam with a shawl wrapped around her shoulders. Next to me, Megan said, "It's beautiful. It's so beautiful." And that was before we even left the wharf.

Out on the water, my nostrils stung with the scent of salt and brine, a smell that I wouldn't notice after a day or two. I brought out my camera and took the first of a thousand shots for that summer—the sky wide and blue, the water immense and endless. I shot Mom with her eyes closed, Megan with one hand on the side of the boat for balance, the other hand holding back the hair that whipped into her face.

The Island was only a few miles from the mainland, but it always felt like it was a world away, as if time were being manipulated as we crossed the water, expanding and contracting. And then it was in front of us, first a gray spot in the distance, then a towering cliff with a white house perched on top—just a single speck of civilization under a wide sky, surrounded by miles and miles of bluest blue.

Looking around, I remembered what Dad had said, back

in New Haven when Mom was coming out of the anesthesia. This might be our last summer on The Island, and we needed to make the most of it.

OCTOBER 12, 2016

LAUREN

It turned out that Mom was right after all.

Anna Kovics dropped her complaint on Wednesday, less than two days after she'd first come forward with her trembling lip and her convincing story. It was impossible to pretend it was a normal day, although I went through the motions—taking Schnauzer for his morning run, dropping off the girls at school and then sitting in front of my laptop, willing myself not to click on any more links about Senator Mabrey's sex scandal.

The trouble was that my work happened online, and it was too easy to switch to another tab, something I did almost unconsciously, so that one minute I was eliminating the creases from an old photo and the next I was replaying the attorney's statement about wishing Anna Kovics well on her road to healing.

I'd worked for various photo services over the years, including a one-hour photo booth and a national company that took school portraits. These days, I worked for Lovingly Restored, an online photo restoration business, where clients uploaded high resolution images of their damaged photos, and we turned back the clock—removing folds and water stains and sun exposures, restoring colors and contrasts. Today I flipped back and forth between a wedding picture that had been water damaged, a dark brown stain settling on top of the glossy black-and-white finish, and the unraveling story of Anna Kovics.

Based on the online backlash, Anna was a liar and a slut and a money-grubbing bitch. The trolls were out in full-force misogyny, debating everything from her breast size to her flexibility.

If Anna had wanted money, wouldn't it have been easier to show up on the doorstep of Holmes House with a demand—a figure scrawled on a piece of paper, as if she were orchestrating a bank robbery?

And if Anna's story had any merit, wouldn't that mean that there had been others, too? Another staffer, or an intern, someone young, someone relatively powerless? The internet was silent on this point. If there had been other allegations, they'd been squashed before they reached the magnitude of Anna Kovics.

Eventually, I searched again, as I'd done dozens of times before, for Megan Mazeros. She wasn't on Facebook, at least not under her own name, nor on Instagram or Twitter or LinkedIn. There were no status updates or résumés, no "Likes" on *Washington Post* articles, nothing "pinned" on Pinterest. The only hint of her existence was on the staff page for a community college in northern Massachusetts: Megan Mazeros, Academic Advisor. Even that nugget was buried nineteen pages deep in a Google search. There was no picture, and no way to know if it was the same Megan Mazeros. Maybe she wasn't a Mazeros anymore; maybe she didn't live on the east coast.

There was an email address listed on the site, however,

and I hovered the cursor over the hyperlink, wondering if I should click on it, send her a message. Are you the same Megan Mazeros who attended Keale College until 2002? Or maybe simply It's me, Lauren. But I had no idea what to say after that.

There was only one thing I really wanted to know, and it didn't seem like the sort of thing that could be asked out of the blue, fourteen years later, by someone who was now a stranger, someone who she was probably happy to forget.

But still, I wanted to know. The urge was more pressing now that Anna Kovics had dropped out of public view, now that I was beginning to question everything in my own memory. *What happened that night?*

After dinner, Brady settled into the den with the girls, and I went up to the attic with a flashlight, digging around until I found the prints I'd boxed up years ago. Each one had been labeled with a thick Sharpie, although the writing was now fading with age. Camp Watachwa, 2000. New York City, September 2001. It was like peeling back the layers of an onion—each lid I opened was another layer, pictures of Megan and me, pictures of Joe Natolo, pictures of all of us Mabreys lined up on the stairs of Holmes House in our red Christmas sweaters, our smiles newly polished and perfectly timed.

The last box was from that summer—The Island, 2002. I'd printed the pictures that fall at Keale and packed them away, the pain too fresh, salt in the wound I was trying to heal. That was the last of the boxes, because after that I was on to other things—graduating, getting pregnant with Stella, marrying Brady. Sometimes, when I looked back on it, it was amazing how quickly I'd given it up, filling my hours not with scouting out the perfect shot or developing the same negative over and over, trying to achieve the right effect, but cuddling with a fussy infant, stenciling a nursery rhyme on the wall over her crib, learning for the first time how to cook something more complicated than pasta. I switched to digital photography, later to inexpensive point-and-shoot cameras and then to the built-in lens on my iPhone. There were literally thousands of pictures of Brady and the girls on various flash drives, snapped on the fly as we walked to the park or waited in the pediatrician's office. Every now and then I pulled one up to run it through a filter, to add text and reduce red-eye and send it to Costco for printing.

Opening these boxes was like revisiting the darkroom, my nose tingling with the smell of chemicals, eyes squinting to adjust to the red glare of the safelight. I'd spent so many hours there, the door locked behind me, alone with what I'd created. How many times had I missed dinner because the hours had flown by? How many times had Megan and I gone down to the river, her bike basket containing whatever book she was reading while mine contained nothing more than the Leica in its weathered case?

I opened the box that read *THE ISLAND 2002* and spread the prints in a semicircle on the floor around me, grouping them according to subject. Faces appeared from nowhere, surprising me with their youth. It was too much, immediately. There was my mother, a scarf wrapped over her perfect bob, her body encased in wispy fabric. Kat, her belly heavy with pregnancy, looking greenish and wan on a chaise lounge. Lizzie, running in a blur of toddler motion, arms pinwheeling, golden brown curls escaping her barrettes. There was my father, dress shirt and pleated wool pants swapped for a polo and some khakis. And there was MK, fresh from law school graduation, throwing his head back and laughing. He had all of his life ahead of him.

I saved the pictures of Megan for last, unable to face them head-on. She was blindingly young and more beautiful than

I'd remembered. The camera had captured the blond curls twisted on her head in a topknot while we hiked on a rugged end of The Island, and those same curls loose on her shoulders while she sat on a bench at the picnic table, a paper plate balanced on her knee. She was uncomfortable being the subject, so half of my shots were of Megan's tongue out, eyes crossed, lips pouting in an exaggerated kiss. In the best ones, she wasn't looking at me, but out over the ocean, a churning gray in the distance, or down at a book in her lap, her brows knit with concentration. In my favorite picture, she was holding Lizzie's chubby toddler hand, and the two of them were dipping their feet into the shallows, water foaming white around their ankles.

And yet, there were so many things the pictures didn't capture—not what I was feeling that summer for Joe Natolo, a smarting ache every time I thought about him back in his apartment over the garage in Scofield. It didn't show how sick Kat really was, or how things would work out for her later, years down the road. It didn't show anything that might have been brewing between MK and Megan. The pictures had captured moments in time, but they weren't crystal balls, and they weren't capable of seeing all the trouble in the future, only days away.

There were footsteps on the rickety pull-down attic stairs, and then Brady's head was at the opening, peeking out like one of Emma's meerkats on Animal Planet. "What are you doing up here?"

"Just looking through some old pictures," I said.

Brady picked his way around the boxes, most of them labeled for winter clothes or Christmas decorations. He knelt down next to me, reaching for a photo of my parents in their Adirondack chairs on the deck. "It's hard to remember they were this young."

I nudged him with an elbow. "That was only six months before we were together."

"I'll never understand how time works." He put the photo down and picked up one of Megan sitting on the railing of the gazebo, a tanned leg dangling down on the ocean side. "Who's this?"

"My roommate," I said, my voice catching.

"Oh, right. Megan." He picked up another from the stack, and another, all those young Megans flashing before me. Young and beautiful and stupid, too. He stared longer at a picture of MK shirtless, balancing in the fishing boat.

"He's hardly changed," I said, nodding to the photo. "Of course, you've known him forever, too. What was he like at Reardon?"

Brady laughed. "You were there."

"Right, but six years younger. The first time Mom dropped us off together, he made me promise I wouldn't tell anyone that we were related."

"Sounds like your brother."

"But you were friends back then, right?"

Brady hesitated, choosing his words. "Not *friends*, per se. But we were in the same class. He was more…"

"More what?"

"More everything. More confident. More outgoing. He always had at least one girlfriend, and you know how it is. There were always stories, rumors."

"Rumors?"

Brady ran a hand through his hair. "I mean, we were teenagers. It was just—"

"Do not say 'locker room talk,'" I warned.

He gave me a sheepish smile. "None of it was true, I'm sure. Everyone made up stories. No one wanted to be known as a virgin. That would have been the kiss of death at Reardon."

I began stacking the photos, lining up the corners this way and that. Maybe this winter, after we were back from our vacation, I would go through the boxes and weed out the ones that didn't mean so much anymore. There was no point in keeping them if they just sat around gathering dust. "What rumors?" I repeated.

Brady ran a hand through his hair, and some of the curly ends stayed upright, like little flags. "I haven't thought about this in years."

I waited, watching him.

"It was probably nothing. Just— I had this roommate one semester, Steven, and he said he walked in on your brother and some girl after a dance—"

I waved a hand to indicate he could skip the details.

"Well, Steven said it didn't seem like she was enjoying herself too much."

I fitted the lid back onto the box and got to my feet. "What are you saying? He raped her?" My voice rose with the last question, and I clapped a hand over my own mouth, thinking of the girls downstairs, the little pitchers with big ears and social media accounts.

"I'm not saying anything. It was just a story, and I never even heard who the girl was. So it was probably just..." He shook his head. "Shit. At the time, I didn't think much of it. But now I'm a dad with these two adorable girls..."

The indignation was stinging. "You never told me."

"I'm not saying it's true."

"But you never said anything."

Brady was incredulous. "What did you want me to say? Hey, Lauren, there was this rumor at Reardon that your brother might have raped a girl. Do you want to talk about it?"

"No," I said, stunned by the words. "No, I—"

"You see? I'm sorry, but there was no way I could have that conversation."

I pushed past him, heading for the stairs.

"Where are you going?" Brady asked, right behind me.

"Anna Kovics," I whispered. "It's true."

Downstairs, I hurried through the house. The girls were still in the den; they turned toward me with stunned faces as I passed.

"Mommy?" Emma called.

My laptop was on the kitchen island, the browser still open to a recipe for taco soup. With shaking hands, I typed in the name of the community college in Massachusetts, navigating my way again to the staff contacts. There she was: Megan Mazeros. I copied the email address and opened my Gmail account. I would do it this time. I would send the message. I would ask the question and I would accept the answer, whatever it was.

But there was no need to email Megan Mazeros. There, in my inbox, her name was staring back at me.

SUMMER
2002
MEGAN

I'd been hearing about it for so long, The Island had taken on mythical proportions in my imagination, fueled by the family photos I'd seen scattered around Holmes House with younger versions of Katherine and Michael and Lauren on sailboats, orange life vests strapped around their skinny chests, and younger versions of Senator and Mrs. Mabrey, their arms around each other like newlyweds, a gray sea in the background, foamy whiteheads kicked up in the surf.

I felt like calling everyone I knew back in Woodstock and mentioning, casually, where I was spending the summer. *With my friend, the senator's daughter. That's right, on a private island off the coast of Maine.* At the beginning of the summer, that excitement overshadowed everything else—all Lauren's lies, all the hurt that had been bubbling inside me since that night when I'd found her photos. To be in the presence of the Mabreys' generosity, on the receiving end of clean linens and plates of tiny cucumber sandwiches and handmade pastries, was enough to let me push all that hurt to the side. When Lauren and I sat side by side in the den at night, sharing the same blanket, watching one of the gazillion Disney movies her family had stored in the towering white cabinets that lined the room, I wondered if it really mattered at all. What was a lie or two between friends?

And then a moment later, I'd remember the way my mom always said that dealing with things right away was better than putting them on the back burner, where things had a way of simmering away, forgotten, until they suddenly boiled over.

Lauren and I, in one way or another, were headed toward a giant explosion.

For the first few weeks, it was like floating through a dream. We slept in late each morning, waking to whatever breakfast the cook, Jordana, had left for us: freshly squeezed orange juice, grapefruit halves, yogurt, scones, covered platters of bacon and eggs. Then Lauren and I would wander down to the beach together for a morning swim, the water so brisk and cold, our legs went instantly numb. Afterward, we might shower or not; the day didn't require much of us. There was lunch and a nap and halfhearted studying for me and sometimes a trip back to Yarmouth, with Lauren operating the outboard motor like my chauffeur.

On those days, it felt like everything was fine between us, that there was no Joe and there were no lies, just ice cream on the pier and shopping in the overpriced boutiques along the water. Lauren always bought something—visors or sunglasses or tank tops with touristy slogans—more out of idleness than anything else, since she didn't seem to need them, and most of her purchases only piled up on her dresser in plastic shopping bags.

Other times, the silence stretched deep between us, an immeasurable gulf. Lauren's room on the second floor was sunny and lined with shoulder-high wainscoting, the knotty pine floors covered here and there with colorful rugs. She slept on a queen-size bed next to a window that faced the Atlantic, toward thousands of miles of nothing and then an entirely different continent. I had the daybed tucked under a sloping alcove, the ceiling so close to my head, I might have been in a top bunk. At night, with each of us in our beds and only the striped rug and the piles of Lauren's discarded clothing between us, it felt like we should have something real to say to each other—*I've been seeing someone*, she might say, or *I know about you and Joe*, I might say, but mostly we joked and laughed until Lauren stopped responding to my comments and I knew she was asleep. Then I snapped on the bedside lamp and read late into the night.

I was presumably on The Island to help take care of Mrs. Mabrey, but it was clear from the first day that Mrs. Mabrey intended to take care of herself. She seemed in every way weaker than she had been the previous winter at Holmes House, although she went about business as usual—phone calls and emails in the morning; reading on the deck each afternoon, shielded by a giant umbrella. Lauren and I checked on her regularly, bringing water or tea, fetching something from another part of the house or delivering the mail that came each afternoon on the water taxi. But mostly Mrs. Mabrey waved us off, seeming annoyed by the attention. Any resemblance to my dad's illness was only fleeting: Mrs. Mabrey wasn't confined to a dingy, low-ceilinged living room, the gloom only mitigated by the canned laughter from a television in the corner. She had ocean breezes and catered meals, a view that changed from minute to minute, as if an artist were wielding a giant paintbrush on the horizon. A nurse came from Yarmouth every few days to check on her, noting vital statistics and asking intrusive questions Mrs. Mabrey wouldn't answer if anyone else was in the room.

"I'm fine, thank you," she said, as if on cue when I hovered in the doorway, one of the texts for my seminar tucked under my arm. "Go—read, do whatever it is you need to do."

Other times she might say crisply, "Send Jordana in," as if whatever she wanted was a task too important to be entrusted to me. Feeling sheepish, I would interrupt Jordana in the middle of chopping vegetables or marinating chicken, and she would wipe her hands on the apron tied around her waist and regard me with a silent fury.

"I'm so sorry," I would say. "She asked for you specifically. Otherwise of course I would—"

Lauren laughed when I told her that I felt bad about the extra work for Jordana. "Why should you feel bad? She's just doing her job."

"I'm not used to it," I admitted. "I feel guilty." Up to this point in my life, the only people I knew who had household help were characters in Jane Austen novels.

"Well, don't," Lauren ordered, giving me one of her bone-shaking shoulder knocks. "Just relax a bit, okay? This is your vacation, too."

In the second week of June, the rest of the Mabreys began to arrive. Kat, five months pregnant and noticeably sluggish, came when Lizzie's preschool finished for the summer. Dark circles ringed her eyes like bruises, and other than her rounded belly, she was pin thin, arms and legs emerging like sticks from her babydoll dresses. The nausea caught her suddenly, morning and afternoon, and she was never more than a few feet from a bucket, just in case. "I didn't have it this bad the first time," she moaned. "After nine weeks, I could eat anything. But now…"

We began to refer to the south deck, where Kat and Mrs.

Mabrey lounged silently side by side, magazines unopened on their laps, as the Sick Bay.

"Look at them," Lauren said, gesturing through the open window. "This whole place is practically an infirmary."

"Invalid Island," I said, relishing the alliteration.

"Yes! Invalid Island. That's exactly what this is."

Since Kat clearly wasn't up to the task, and Jordana's hands were full, I offered to watch Lizzie in the mornings. This was a more difficult task than it had been at Holmes House, since The Island had a series of walkways and steps leading from one deck to another, and the entire east side faced treacherous, tumbledown cliffs. Only the west side of The Island had an actual beach, twenty yards or so of sand ringed with sharp shells in the morning along the rack line. The boat was docked there, tethered to the end of a somewhat rickety pier with Lauren's expertly tied knots. We spent our mornings there, collecting shells and strange severed crustacean limbs, occasionally splashing with Lizzie in the cold shallow water while her arms were held aloft by giant pink floaties. "Watch me, watch me!" she shrieked, stamping her feet in the gentle waves. We burned and peeled and developed dark, sun-kissed tans. Lauren documented it all, the shutter on her Leica clicking away.

"I should pay you for your help," Kat said more than once, but I always shrugged this off. At least, in one small way, I was earning my keep.

Time moved so slowly on The Island, where the day might hold only a single, meaningful task, that it was surprising to realize that I'd already been there for three weeks, then a month, then five weeks. Every day I woke up to sunlight streaming through the window in Lauren's room was one less day of paradise. Lauren, of course, would stay until the end of summer, living out the same blissfully uncomplicated hours, day after day, week after week. There was no reason to think she wouldn't be back here summer after summer, taking work vacations, bringing her children one day, continuing traditions like Saturday night crab feeds and motoring to shore in search of ice cream on the hottest afternoons.

Sometimes, I had to remind myself of my place—the guest who would be heading out soon and not returning, the girl from Nowheresville, Kansas, who had once looked forward to a weeklong vacation on a lake so small, we could see inside the windows of the cabins on the other side. Sometimes, I had to remind myself that I didn't have a claim to anything on The Island, not the house, not the shady spot in the gazebo where I often retreated with my books, not the edge of the pier where I liked to sit with my toes skimming the surface of the water. I was only a guest in this life, an actor pulled in for a bit role. I was supporting actress to the golden girl, the one who sometimes spent the entire day in her bathing suit, a sarong tied low on her hips, her wet hair drying in crunchy waves. By being born at the right time and to the right people, she belonged to this place, and this place belonged to her.

At Keale, I'd noticed Lauren's looks in an offhand, taken-for-granted kind of way—she was attractive enough in her jeans and ponytails, even with the thick cream she slathered on her face after a shower. But here, she was beautiful. There was no other word for it. She was beautiful when she started a fire, cupping her hands over the weak flame and blowing it to life. She was beautiful in the boat, one hand controlling the motor, seaspray stinging her face. She was beautiful when she fell asleep in the lounge chair, the edges of her sarong fluttering in a light breeze.

I could see why Joe had pursued her after that night in the gallery, when he had been so quick to discard me. Lauren had everything, but most of all she had the knowledge that no matter what, her life was going to turn out okay. She had more than a safety net from a life insurance policy; she was protected from things turning out wrong. I needed this summer program at Harvard to propel myself forward, but Lauren didn't need anyone or anything to validate her existence. She didn't need a poor, funny Midwest sidekick or a boyfriend who worked in a machine shop, but those were things she could easily have.

Sometimes at night, we snuck a bottle of wine down to the beach and split it between us, the alcohol making her silly and wild, and making me serious and contemplative, lost in dark thoughts. I wondered if we would still be friends five years into the future, or ten, or fifteen, if we would bump into each other at a Keale reunion and spend the night laughing over some long-ago memory, each of us getting the important details wrong. Or would we stay in touch, living in the same city, talking on the phone every day, meeting for lunches where she would tell me about her latest vacation, the most recent accomplishments of her famous family. Even in the unwritten future, I still imagined myself as the tagalong friend, with nothing of my own to contribute.

Once, in her silliness, she laughed so hard she pissed herself, then laughed even harder at the dark stain spreading down her shorts. Megan Mazeros of Woodstock, Kansas, would never have lived this down; she would rather have died of shame. Lauren Mabrey, who had everything she could ever want, waded into the ocean and emerged, pronouncing herself clean.

"Nothing that can't be fixed." She grinned, and I smiled back, but inside I was wondering if there wasn't a part of me—a small, bitter, jealous, horrible part—that didn't like Lauren Mabrey at all.

LAUREN

I meant to tell Megan about Joe—I really did. Every day presented dozens of opportunities, and every night ended with us chatting in the darkened shell of my bedroom, the moon hanging like a pendant outside the window. Somehow, the moment never seemed exactly right, or maybe the moments were right, but something about me was all wrong.

And then all of a sudden it was the end of June and the beginning of Megan's last week before leaving for Cambridge. Following tradition, everyone began arriving on The Island, as if summoned by some sort of magnetic pull—first Dad and MK, then Peter, then some of Mom's cousins with their kids.

Megan had overheard Mom refer to them as the "Brewster Holmeses," a phrase that fascinated her. "Will the Brewster-Holmeses be joining us for dinner?" she asked in a bad imitation of a British accent, something she must have picked up from PBS.

"Their last names is Holmes, and they're from Brewster," I explained, but that wasn't enough to stop her.

"The Brewster-Holmeses are in for a treat," she remarked when she overheard my mother discussing the weekend menu with Jordana. And another time: "Will the Brewster-Holmeses be able to land their jet on The Island, do you think?"

It was best, maybe, to ignore her.

We took the boat to meet Dad and MK in Yarmouth, and it wasn't until I spotted them waiting on the wharf that I realized how good it would be to have other people around. As much as I loved Megan, it had begun to feel claustrophobic with her in my bedroom, with her damp towels already looped over the rack before I got out of the shower. Together, we'd watched enough TV and told enough stories and worked enough jigsaw puzzles on the circular table in the den, and it was time for something new.

Megan half stood, waving, and on the wharf, MK raised a hand in acknowledgment. Dad was on his phone, briefcase clenched in one hand like he was on his way to the Capitol. Between them were two small suitcases. I killed the engine and the boat drifted over shallow water toward them.

"Ahoy, there," MK called, reaching out with a skiff to pull us the rest of the way.

I caught the end of Dad's conversation, something about not making any promises, about having others to consult before he could make a decision. Then he snapped his phone shut and looked from me to Megan. "Well, if it isn't my girls."

I stood, angling my cheek for a kiss. "Hey, Dad."

MK handed one bag down to Megan, then the other, before taking an uneasy step onto the boat.

"How are things?" he asked.

I shrugged. "Things are things."

He settled onto the bench next to Megan. "Haven't you had enough of the Mabreys?"

She smiled. "It's been torture."

He gave a sharp, snorting laugh. "I'll bet."

Dad said, "Good to see you again, Megan," and leaned over to give her a casual one-armed hug before settling down across from her. In his suit and wingtips, he looked comically out of place. With the luggage in one end and me in the other, the three of them were crammed in the middle, legs angled to the side to avoid smashing knees.

"Ready?" I called, and yanked the cord to start the engine. Over my shoulder, I caught snatches of their conversation, shouted over the motor and splash. Dad was asking Megan

something about her seminar and her responses were enthusiastic. Of course—anything to do with Harvard impressed
him. They were still talking when we approached The Island.
I cut the engine, and we coasted toward the pier. Kat and
Lizzie were on the beach, and Lizzie jumped up and down in
the surf, calling to us in her incomprehensible toddler lingo.

"If it had been possible," Dad was saying, "I would have
stayed in school forever, racking up degrees."

Megan's laugh carried across the water. "I know what you
mean. I'm thinking of grad school next fall—"

I brought the boat to an unsteady stop along the dock and
didn't feel too bad when it caught everyone slightly off balance. Dad exited first, extending a hand back to Megan.

MK grinned at me. "What about you, Lolo? Would you
want to stay in school forever, too?"

"Fuck off." I gave him a push, and he grabbed my forearms
for balance, grinning.

"That's my girl."

MK took the boat back in the afternoon to fetch Peter,
who had arrived just in time for our crab and lobster feast.
There was a happy chaos around the table now that we were
all here, and even Mom rallied, holding court about plans
for the weekend—a family photo on the morning of the
Fourth, the specific meals we would eat at specific times, the
arrangements for the Brewster Holmeses. Jordana had made
two giant pitchers of sangria, and we each vied for pieces of
the wine-sodden fruit, spearing them with forks until Mom
informed us that we were behaving like barbarians. Somehow MK and Megan began sparring again over the value of
being an English major, with Peter chiming in that finance
trumped anything the humanities had to offer.

"Excuse me," I said.

"Now, now," Dad interrupted, as if he were stepping into the middle of the ring, ordering us back to our corners. He'd changed out of his suit, and his arms were pale in a short-sleeved shirt. "I'm proud of all of you." He winked at Megan and nodded at Peter. "Even the ones I had nothing to do with."

We settled onto couches in the living room afterward, the humid air displaced by the rotating blades of the overhead fan. It was too warm, we were too full and the night itself felt restless. MK opened bottles of beer and passed them around; Kat and Peter tucked Lizzie in for the night and only Peter returned. The conversation waxed and waned, ranging from Mom's health—*Fine*, she insisted, although not very convincingly—to the weather in Washington to MK studying for the bar exam, and somehow always circling back to Megan's upcoming seminar. I kept waiting to hear my own name on someone's lips—*And Lauren, how is the photography coming? How were your classes? Have you picked a project for your senior exhibit?* I wished then that I'd stayed with Joe in Scofield, even if he hadn't extended the offer. Joe cared. I was important to him.

Dad's phone rang in his pants pocket, the sound startling us momentarily out of our stupor. "Hold on," he said. "Let me get where I have some decent reception."

We watched him as he wandered out onto the deck, slapping away the night's bugs with one hand.

"So, did I hear you say this was a PEW scholarship?" Peter asked, turning to Megan. "That's a pretty big deal, isn't it?"

She beamed. "Yeah. My professor wrote me a recommendation. I didn't even know what it was all about until—"

I clapped my hands together, sick of it all. "Let's play a game or something. What about Pictionary? Don't we have that whiteboard in the office?"

"Pictionary?" MK groaned. "What are we, ten years old?"

"There are some games in the cupboard under the stairs," Mom said. She'd wrapped herself in a blanket, but still seemed chilled, although the rest of us were covered in a sheen of sweat.

We all looked in the direction of the stairs, but it took too much effort to move.

From outside, somewhere on the pathway around the house, Dad's voice cut through the dark. "You tell that lying piece of shit that we're not going that way. I'm not going to have my hand forced…" A minute later he was back, cell phone in hand.

"I thought you were taking a break from work," Mom commented drily.

"You're right. No more calls tonight." He settled onto the couch next to Megan. "So tell me more about this program," he said, stretching out his legs on the ottoman in front of him. "It's pregraduate. What does that mean as far as credits are concerned?"

"Oh, for God's sake," I said. "Isn't there anything else to talk about?"

Megan looked at me, stung.

"Someone needs her happy juice," MK said.

I glared at him and took a long slug of beer, spilling some down my chin.

He laughed. "Classy."

"Will you please fuck the fuck off?"

Mom sat up, the blanket falling from her shoulders. "We do not talk like that in this house."

My *sorry* was an automatic reflex, as if she'd whacked me on the knee with a mallet.

"What's the matter, anyway?" MK asked, trying to control

his glee. "I mean, you're not jealous, are you? It's just a PEW scholarship. It's just Harvard. No big deal."

From her spot on the couch, I could feel Megan watching me. Dad, ever the peacemaker, asked, "Can't we just have a nice evening here?"

"Yes. Yes, you can." I stood up, banging my leg against the table. Some of the magazines fell to the floor.

"Where are you going?" Megan demanded. I caught the note of alarm in her voice: *don't leave me here.*

I waved my hand in the direction of the beach. "Taking a little walk. I'll be back."

"Don't worry. She just needs a time-out," MK said, and I heard their laughter behind me.

I unlatched the gate that had so far managed to keep Lizzie from tumbling down the back steps. On my way to the beach, I finished the rest of the beer in three great gulps. Was I jealous of Megan? Of course not. But it would have been nice to be noticed by my own family for once.

The water was dark, purple shot through with black, the waves rolling forward, tugging back. In the distance, the lights in Yarmouth glittered. I settled onto the end of the pier, dipping my toes into the water. It was cooler down here than it had been in the house, and the night's breeze dried the sweat on the back of my T-shirt.

Suddenly, footsteps thudded along the dock and MK was behind me. "You forgot this," he said, holding out an open bottle of cabernet like a peace offering. The liquid sloshed in the half-full bottle.

I laughed despite myself. "You are such an ass."

He sank down next to me, the wooden planks shifting under his weight. "Maybe. But you're the one who's acting like a three-year-old."

I took a sip of wine, and then MK took one, and we passed

the bottle back and forth like we used to do when we were kids, back when getting caught would have had actual consequences.

"How's life after law school?" I asked.

He shrugged. "All they have me doing is studying for the bar, so it feels like I'm still in law school."

"And then what, you conquer the world?"

"All in good time, little sister. All in good time."

I reached for the bottle again and felt MK's hand on my lower back a half second before a push sent me off the edge. The water was waist high and frigid, a shock to the system. "Jerk! What was that for?" I sputtered, thrusting my arms toward him. "Help me up."

"Seriously? You think I'm going to fall for that?"

In retaliation, I yanked the hems of his shorts and he fell into the water with a splash that soaked the rest of me. The bottle of cabernet came with him, filling with salt water and bobbing silently away. I swung at him, and he caught my arm, the two of us play fighting until he took me by the shoulders, dunking me all the way under. I stayed there for a moment, long enough to locate his crotch with my knee. When I came up he was wincing, hands cupped beneath the water.

"Fuck, it's cold," MK said, his teeth chattering. "Let's get out of here."

"You didn't happen to bring any dry towels, did you?"

We waded closer to the shore and stumbled onto the beach, dripping and shivering. "Maybe Megan can bring us some towels," I said, and together we bellowed, "Me-gan! Meeeeeee-gan!"

There was no answer. Between us and the house, the trees waved silently in the breeze. I twisted the fabric of my T-shirt, sending a stream of water trickling onto the beach.

Next to me, MK had stripped down to his boxers, his wet clothes bundled in his arms. "What's her deal, anyway?"

I laughed. "What do you mean?"

"I mean, why is she here?"

"I invited her, you moron. We're friends."

"Right…"

I shoved him harder than I meant to, knocking him off balance. "What, are you upset that she's not interested in you?"

He grinned. "Who says she's not interested in me?"

I remembered, as I hadn't in a long time, their sloppy New Year's Eve kiss. "Seriously, don't be such a pig for once."

MK smirked. "I'll try, but I'm not making any promises."

I started for the footpath, hurrying against the cold. "Can't you just pretend to be a normal human?"

From behind me came the unmistakable sound of MK beating on his chest. "Me man. Me no have friends. Me have conquests."

The house was quiet when I entered, dripping water all the way upstairs. There was a light in the living room, and I caught a snatch of low conversation as I passed—my parents, having a heart-to-heart. In the upstairs bathroom, I left my clothes in a heap and grabbed a clean bath sheet, wrapping it around my body.

Megan was already in bed, but the reading light was still on and a book was open in front of her. Her smile was hesitant, and I felt every inch the bitch I had been earlier, when I'd left her with my family. Megan was completely right to be proud of her scholarship. She had every right to be happy.

I hovered over the bed until she moved her legs out of the way, giving me room to sit down.

"You went swimming?"

Dad put a hand on my shoulder. "I've already called the hospital. An ambulance is going to meet them on shore. And your mom will call as soon as they know anything."

"What about Lizzie?" Megan asked.

Dad glanced at her. "She's sleeping. Maybe when she wakes up…"

"Yeah, of course. I'll watch her," she said.

Even though it was too late, I hurried down the pathway to the beach, with Megan close behind me. Halfway there, we heard the motor sputtering, then the familiar catch. At the steps leading down to the beach, I stopped, spotting them out on the water, sliding away from us. Peter was at the motor, and Mom and Kat were on the bench seat, a blanket draped over Kat's bony shoulders. Her moan floated back to us like the call of a lonely sea animal, until the boat was too far away, and the sound was absorbed by the water.

MEGAN

Peter and Mrs. Mabrey took turns waiting with Kat in the hospital, and the rest of us stayed behind, getting updates by phone. Lizzie became my sole responsibility, and somehow that felt right, as if all along I'd been hired to be her au pair, making sure her teeth were brushed and her hair combed. Kat was released two days later, with the promise that she would be on full bed rest. After the fourth, Peter would take her back to Connecticut.

Kat's return to the house coincided with the arrival of the Brewster-Holmeses, who had been forgotten in the general craziness of the previous days. They spilled out of their fancy chartered boat with American flag T-shirts and inflatable inner tubes, instantly overwhelming The Island's relative quiet. There were five of them—Mrs. Mabrey's first cousin Patrick, his wife, Sue, their ten-year-old twins, Eric and Patrick Jr., and seven-year-old Annabelle. They were sleeping in the guest cottages, but during the day they spread out in the main house, occupying every lounge chair, sofa and bathroom. Wet towels and swimsuits dripped from surfaces; it was impossible to enter the front door without kicking a pile of flip-flops out of the way.

"We should have a picnic lunch," Sue Holmes suggested at eleven-thirty, when breakfast dishes had finally been cleared away. "All of us, down on the beach. There are too many of us in here, and the kids are going crazy."

Jordana flung up her hands in exasperation.

"I'll help get it together," Sue said, sensing that she'd thrown the domestic world into chaos. "Now, where do you think I can find a picnic basket?"

"Can we go out on the boat after lunch?" one of the twins asked, prompting a dash for swim trunks and towels and sunblock.

I asked Lauren if she would watch Lizzie while I stayed behind.

She raised one of her perfect eyebrows, product of a waxing last week in Yarmouth. "You're not coming?"

I shook my head. "Just feeling a little tired."

It was a relief to have them gone, the house quiet without kids shrieking or balls being tossed. But it was just as much of a relief to have a break from Lauren. We hadn't talked since her casual announcement the other night. There had been the chaos of Kat's condition and then the arrival of the Brewster-Holmeses, but there was also the fact that I was feeling restless, ready to wash my hands of all of them.

I helped myself to a leftover breakfast scone and escaped to the small room under the stairs that served as the Mabreys' home office on The Island. With the door closed, I felt the instant relief that came from quiet, from escaping constant noises and needs. I'd been emailing my mother every few days since I arrived, and she'd replied, the gist of her message hidden in long newsy bits that made me miss her with a sudden, twisting ache. Woodstock was hot. Mom had gone shopping for new patio furniture but hadn't seen anything she liked. Gerry was hoping I could pick up a Harvard sweatshirt for him, and he would pay me back when they saw me at the end of the summer.

This was normal, regular life.

I dashed off a quick reply, hesitating before I hit Send. Mom had friends, women she'd known since high school or even earlier, who she still saw regularly in town. They planned semiannual trips to the casino together; they met once a month for Margarita Mondays at the Mexican restaurant just outside of Woodstock. I knew Mom would be good for friendship advice, but it seemed too much to go into here, too difficult to provide the wording and tone and context needed for an email. Besides, I could imagine her reply, the sort of simple logic that was nonetheless compelling. *Sometimes people just grow apart. Maybe that's for the best.*

They came back from the beach in the late afternoon, leaving a trail of toys and towels from the front porch through to the foyer, Jordana's freshly mopped floor sprinkled with sand. I was sitting on a couch in the living room with a book on my lap and a highlighter clenched between my teeth.

Michael put a hand on my forehead. He smelled like sun and sweat. "Feeling better?"

"I'm fine," I said. "Where's everyone else?"

Lauren yawned. "Dad's helping Uncle Patrick return the cruiser. He only rented it for the day." She plopped down next to me, leaning against my shoulder. Her wet hair was braided and tied with one of Lizzie's chunky elastics. "God, I'm tired. Think I'll take a nap." I expected her to head upstairs, but instead she pulled the quilt from the back of the couch and curled up next to me, her head heavy on my shoulder.

We ate dinner on the back deck, the only place that could seat twelve comfortably, with Lizzie perched at one end in her high chair. I picked listlessly at my food, wondering if I was in fact coming down with something or if it was a general malaise, brought on by heat and exhaustion.

"Tonight's fireworks night, isn't it?" asked one of the twins, the one with the flat mole by his ear. This was apparently the only way to distinguish them, except that I'd already forgotten whether it was Eric or Patrick Jr. who had the mole.

"Tomorrow," Mrs. Mabrey corrected. "They do a big thing in Yarmouth, and we have front row seats from our beach."

"What about the ones we brought?" Annabelle whined.

Sue rolled her eyes. "Patrick stopped at a roadside stand and spent hundreds of dollars on these stupid fireworks. He's basically turned our children into pyromaniacs. I promised that we could do some down by the beach, where they won't start anything on fire."

Mrs. Mabrey smiled tightly, annoyed to have the schedule disrupted.

"It'll be nice to do our own fireworks," Senator Mabrey said, his words carrying all the weight of a judicial pronouncement. "We haven't done that in years, not since Lauren was little."

Just after sunset, we traipsed down to the beach with lawn chairs and towels and a case of beer and a box of long-reach oven matches. The Brewster-Holmeses—I couldn't *not* think of them that way—lugged boxes of fireworks onto the beach, and Michael shone a flashlight while Eric and Patrick sorted the fireworks into piles, by category. Annabelle tried to help and was rebuffed at every turn; she ended up claiming the sparklers for herself and Lizzie. Peter lit them one by one, and the girls went into a wild sparkler frenzy, dancing in and out of the water, like fiery amphibian creatures. Lizzie charged toward me, demanding that I appreciate the whirls and sparks.

"Okay, okay," I laughed, brushing off a spark that landed on my bare leg. "Why don't you write something in the air, like your name?"

She grinned, making indecipherable swirling marks in the air that might have been the letters of her name or nothing at all. "Do you think Mommy can see?"

Mrs. Mabrey and Kat had decided to stay and watch from the back deck of the main house. The space between the house and the beach was thick with foliage, but they would have been able to see little bursts of sparkler light and the ambient glow of fireworks.

"Mmm, maybe," I said, and Lizzie ran off again, back toward the water.

We settled onto the beach in a line, waiting for the show—Peter and Mr. Mabrey and Patrick and Sue, empty bottles of Sam Adams sticking out of the sand like little flags marking their territory. I lowered myself onto a beach towel a few yards away and did the math in my head. Thirty-six more hours, and I would be on my way to Cambridge. Lauren would get me to Yarmouth, and a bus would take me the rest of the way. I was both nervous for the experience—would I be even half as smart or qualified as the other students in the program?— and excited for a break from the Mabreys, from smiling and being polite and navigating their social rules.

Lauren had brought her camera, and was documenting

the scene with the diligence of a forensic analyst. Later, she could tuck the prints into an album to prove how wonderful they all were, how wonderful and happy. She laughed at something Lizzie said, and I remembered her coming into the bedroom the other night, suddenly determined to unburden herself to me. *I'm sleeping with Joe.* Not an explanation—just a statement of fact. Also: *I know I should have told you earlier.* Not an apology, not an acknowledgment of the lies she must have told night after night, about having to work in the darkroom or study in the library. She hadn't apologized for all the times she'd blown me off, for putting sex ahead of friendship, for the ultimate betrayal of Joe being someone I had cared about. Immediately after her confession, she'd seemed lighter to me, no longer burdened by the weight of what she knew. Her conscience was clear, and everything was supposed to be fine between us. Her perfect world could resume.

"Who needs another one?" Senator Mabrey asked, holding out a bottle. "Megan?"

"Sure." I took fast sips, reveling in my bitterness. Near the water's edge, Lauren was teasing reactions out of Annabelle and Lizzie, who were hamming for the camera.

"All right," Michael called. "Let's get this show on the road!"

Three fireworks had been set up on a plank, and one of the twins struck a long oven match, tapping it briefly to the fuses and jumping back.

"Don't go burning your fingers off!" Sue called, her voice shrill.

These weren't serious fireworks, like they'd been in Woodstock. Most of the things my family had experimented with fell into the category of "illegal explosive devices," to which the law enforcement in Woodstock had turned a blind eye. My dad liked things that he could tamper with in the garage, things that shot into the air with huge booming sounds. The Brewster-Holmeses' fireworks were relatively tame, with short whistling sounds and flashes of impressive color. I watched as Lauren moved silently around the beach, camera held steady with both hands, getting too close to the explosion at times and backing hastily away. Some of the fireworks that were designed to spin fizzled out in the sand, and there was much discussion about whether they could be lit on the end of the pier, with Sue vehemently stating no and eventually being overruled.

Michael came over and nudged me with his foot. "Can you get some more beer?"

I glanced around, annoyed that this task was falling to me. "Are we already out?"

"We've got some serious heavyweights in this group," he said, offering a hand to pull me to my feet. "In a few minutes, I bet they'll be restless."

I brushed loose grains of sand off my legs. "No problem. Be right back."

The Island was eerie at night, something I only noticed when I was by myself. Footpaths cut through the trees, heading in a rambling way to the main house, to the cottages, to the beach, to the gazebo, to benches placed here and there. In our early weeks on The Island, when it had only been Mrs. Mabrey, Lauren and me, I'd been scared to go too far from the main house on my own, especially after sunset. Lauren had teased me about it—*what do you think is going to happen?* I'd laughed at myself, too, figuring I'd seen too many horror movies at the dollar theater in Woodstock. But now that there were so many people here, their voices carrying through the night over the hisses and booms of the fireworks, I felt more secure. I wasn't likely to go toppling off the side of a cliff, and nothing was likely to jump out and get me.

So I didn't even turn around when I heard footsteps behind me, the soles of tennis shoes slapping against the flagstones.

Then Michael was there next to me, out of breath.

"Really," I said. "I've got this. A couple more six packs should do it."

"Figured I'd keep you company," he said.

"Weren't you helping with the fireworks?"

"Peter's got it under control."

We took a few steps in silence, and then I felt his hand on my lower back, the touch light, like a form of chivalry, as if he were escorting me up the path. What was this? I walked faster, moving out of his reach. I remembered that New Year's Eve back at Holmes House, the unwelcome kiss I'd been unable to dodge.

"Hey," I said, when his hand found me again, lower this time, his palm cupping my ass in my denim cutoffs. I whirled around. "Yeah, I don't think so."

"Sure you do," he said. There was a strange smile on his face, an expression I hadn't seen on him since that night in the basement, when I'd sidestepped his obvious hard-on. What was it he'd said then? Something about bragging rights, something I owed him.

"Really, I'm flattered, but no. Okay? No." I reached out and gave his shoulder a let's-be-friends, no-hard-feelings kind of pat, and I turned around, hoping that had done the trick.

I hadn't gone far when one of Michael's arms went around my neck and his other hand clamped down over my mouth. I yelled, a muffled sound that didn't go anywhere. We were maybe halfway between the beach, with its crack and sizzle of fireworks, and the house, a towering behemoth lurking behind a canopy of trees. I remembered Mrs. Mabrey and Katherine watching fireworks from the deck. Would they be able to hear me if I yelled?

With Michael's hand against my mouth, I screamed again, writhing in his grasp. He lost hold for a moment and I bit down on his finger, tearing the skin with my teeth. This was a joke, wasn't it? Like when he and Lauren tussled, grabbing hair and going for the nuts. He was going to let me go and we were going to laugh, and he was going to make some comment about me overreacting.

Then he hooked his other arm around my middle, a fist pressing into my ribs. This wasn't a joke. There was no punch line. There was only Michael and the darkness, an island with few places to run, the scattered members of his family.

"You're not going to scream again, and you're not going to bite me," Michael said into my ear. "Do you understand what I'm saying? You're not going to pretend this is something you haven't wanted all along."

I felt helpless and sick, the night's dinner rising on a tide of nausea. What was better—to resist or to fight? Which would give me the best chance of getting away?

"What's it going to be, Megs?" My nickname felt dirty and unfamiliar in his voice.

I nodded, wide-eyed, and he took the hand from my mouth.

"That's better," he said, and the smile was there again, grim and unpleasant, as if this was somehow a bitter necessity, something he was bound to see through to the end.

I darted out of his reach, seeing my chance, and made it a few stumbling steps before he grabbed me again, his arm tight on my elbow. "Please," I whispered. "I don't want this."

He propelled me forward, his knees knocking into mine. I glanced around wildly, trying to gauge how I could break away, where I could run. One of Michael's hands was on the back of my neck now, my hair twisting there with each movement. He jerked me to the left, to a side path that led away from the house, toward the gazebo where I'd spent so many hours this summer, glancing between my textbook and the constant, drifting waves. At its northern end, the gazebo was perched over a steep drop through dense foliage and jutting rocks. I dragged my feet and we floundered, moving forward in a herky-jerky dance.

"Let me go," I begged. "I won't tell anyone. I'll just leave and—"

His hand clapped over my mouth again.

If someone had come upon us at that moment, I wondered what they would see. Two drunken people playing a rough game? Two lovers, engaged in a wild embrace? At what point would it look like a struggle? He pushed me into the gazebo, bending my body like we were ballroom dancers, and my body let me down, succumbing to choreography I hadn't remembered learning. I imagined myself describing him to the police: six-two, broad-shouldered. He probably had sixty pounds on me, a weight I calculated as he lowered his body onto mine. But of course, he wasn't a stranger. I knew his fucking name. I knew him.

With my free hand, I clawed at his chest, trying to pry his hand from my mouth. I punched at him, hitting his back and side. I made a fist and swung it, hoping to connect with his crotch as he unzipped his shorts.

"Stop fighting," he hissed. "You know you want this."

There was a second when he let go of my mouth, twisting both arms behind me and securing them with one hand. In that second, before his hand could silence me, I let out a scream louder than I'd ever screamed before. Not a word, not language. I couldn't form *help* or *stop*; this was a primal sound, the cry of one animal being attacked by another.

It didn't take long, start to finish. The floorboards of the gazebo were rough, and pine needles bit into the back of my thighs. I tried to keep my legs together, to attack with my feet and knees and arms. I scratched his face; he bruised my elbow, slamming it onto the deck so hard I literally saw stars, tiny sunbursts in the black landscape of my closed eyes. He pulled down my shorts and ripped off my underwear. He was inside me, saying "I knew you'd like this, I knew you'd like this" in rhythm with his thrusts.

I don't know why I stopped screaming. Maybe, at some level, I didn't want anyone to find us—not when I was naked from the waist down, crying and helpless, unable to protect myself. The shame was starting, the deep-down burn that went beyond scratches and bruises and things that could scab and heal. I'd been here before, that last night with Kurt Haschke, although I hadn't said no then, hadn't screamed or fought, hadn't feared whatever came next.

Sometimes, when I thought about it later, I wondered how I hadn't had a better sense of who Michael was and what he was capable of doing. Over the years I would replay every moment, looking for the time when I must have sent the wrong signal, encouraged when I didn't mean to encourage. Was it on the boat, when our legs had been pressed against each other, knee to hip? Had I been too sexy in my black one-piece, my shorts too short, the V of my T-shirt too low? Had I given off a scent, a pheromone only he was attuned to, like a dog to a high-pitched whistle? Only that afternoon, he'd pressed his warm palm to my cool forehead, asking how I felt. Now his fingernails dug half moons into my skin, his breath quickened.

I thought about what it meant that he wasn't using a condom, that I wasn't on the pill.

I thought every horrible thing a person could think.

Michael said, "Fuck, someone's coming." Just like that, he was off me, zipping up. I scuttled back like a crab, struggling into my shorts, which were still hanging off one ankle. I felt around on my hands and knees for my underwear.

We heard Mr. Mabrey before he came into sight. He was talking into his phone, head bent, strides purposeful. In one hand he held three empty bottles, the glass clinking as he passed. Was he wondering what was taking me so long, why I hadn't returned with a new case of beer? Had they even noticed I was gone, and Michael, too?

I didn't call out, didn't try to get Mr. Mabrey's attention. It was too late; it was done now.

Michael tucked in his shirt, straightened the collar and brushed pine needles from his arms. He smoothed his hands through his thick hair, as if he were completing his regular grooming ritual in front of a mirror.

I wiped my hands on the hem of my shirt, then wiped the tears from my eyes with my dirty palms. *You're the same person you were ten minutes ago*, I promised myself. *This doesn't change who you are.*

Michael took a few steps out of the gazebo, looking in either direction down the footpath before turning back to me. I froze, my eyes darting around for a weapon. If he came closer, I would scream. I would kill him, even if I had to do it with my bare hands. Was he going to get rid of the evidence— strangle me or hit me with a rock or toss me over the edge of the gazebo, watching my body tumble down the side of the cliff? Would he follow me, chase me if I ran?

But Michael only said, "You call me if you ever need anything." It was dark in the shadow of the gazebo, and I couldn't see his face, couldn't read anger or regret or satisfaction there. A sob came up my throat, and I bit it back.

There was a loud boom from the beach, followed by a fizzing sound, like the sky was opening a giant bottle of soda. I wrapped my arms around my knees, and Michael disappeared down the path, heading back to the beach.

LAUREN

The fireworks were winding down by the time I finished a second roll of film and dug around in my bag for another, coming up empty-handed. I'd captured close-ups of sparks and bursts of fireworks, and now I was thinking of other angles—on my stomach on the beach, aiming upward? What if I went out on the boat and shot from there, catching the reflection of light on the water? If I hurried, I had time to grab a fresh roll or two from my bedroom before they finished.

"Hey," I called, spotting the white of MK's T-shirt as he came down the path. "Where have you been? The natives are getting restless."

MK's face was red, and he was breathing hard.

"Don't tell me we're out of beer," I said.

He gave me a funny, hesitant smile and looked over his shoulder, to where the path disappeared around a bend. "Promise you won't be mad."

"Why would I be mad? What did you do?"

"It just happened," he said, palms up, like he was trying to explain a shattered vase. "We didn't plan it or anything."

I jerked my head, scanning as far as I could see into the foliage. "You did not. You fucking did not."

He grinned.

I pushed him on the chest, and he stepped back, laughing. "What the hell were you thinking?"

He raised his hands, trying to distance himself from me,

from what he'd done. From what *they* had done. "It's not my fault! She's single, I'm single, she's been flirting with me all week...look, don't make it into a big deal. It wasn't that great."

"You asshole," I spat. "She's my friend. Is nothing safe around here? Is everything that moves fair game?"

"Don't say anything," he said, grabbing my shoulder. "I promised I wouldn't tell you."

"I wish you hadn't!" I shoved him again. "You are such a— I don't even know the word. How could you do this to me?"

He did manage to look at least a little bit contrite. "I know, I feel bad already. Look, I promise, it was a onetime thing. But we're adults. We can handle it. Nothing has to change."

"Bastard," I said, my mind reeling. "Of course it changes everything."

"Oh, come on," he said, flicking the end of my braid so it whipped over my shoulder. And then he had the gall—the fucking gall—to whistle as he disappeared down the path, back to the beach.

MEGAN

I don't know how I made it into the house, or how I made it up the stairs, or how I was suddenly sitting on the closed toilet seat in the bathroom next to the room I shared with Lauren. I was shivering, rocking back and forth, trying to form thoughts. *Get out of here. Call the police.* I didn't have a cell phone, but there was a landline in the office. Could I call 911 from there? Would the police come out from the mainland? Was The Island even in their jurisdiction, or was it somehow outside geographical boundaries? I couldn't imagine police arriving here, docking at the pier, shining flashlights up the path, searching the gazebo for evidence—would there be evidence, other than scattered pine needles, the swirls of dirt and dust that had been trampled by our feet?

I tried to think. The evidence was on me, inside me. *Go to the hospital.* After what had happened with Kat earlier in the week, I knew there was a hospital in Yarmouth. There someone could do an examination and contact the police for me. This much I knew from watching endless *Law & Order* marathons with my dad, a million years ago. Someone would swab for evidence and that would trigger an investigation, and then I would...

Okay, think. I could call my mom. Even if she dropped everything to come, it would be a full day or more before she arrived. I could call one of the Sisters, although I didn't know their home addresses or if their parents even had listed numbers. And there was Miriam, five hours away in Scofield. If I could get her home number, she would do something, I was sure of it. She would take me back with her, feed me and hold me while I cried. But then I would miss the start of my seminar at Harvard—unless she could smooth that over for me, make some phone calls.

Just get off The Island, then. Get off the fucking island.

Was I safe with Michael nearby? Was he done with me or waiting outside the door for another opportunity to catch me off guard, drag me down the hallway to his bedroom, stuff a pillowcase in my mouth and tie me to his bed with the sheets? No—he wouldn't. Yes—he might.

Someone was going to have to take me to the hospital, or at least get me off The Island. I would have to tell Lauren. I would have to just come out with it: *your brother raped me.* That was the right word. It was the word I would have to tell the police. I would have to tell her everything, too—how he came up behind me, how he'd forced me to the ground, how he'd pulled down my shorts...

For the moment, I had to wait. Lauren was still down at the beach. Michael was probably there, too, helping to shoot off the last of the fireworks. For the moment, I was safe, then. For the moment, I could think.

Someone knocked on the door, a soft rap of the knuckles. I watched as the knob turned. *Michael.* He had come back for me, and I hadn't even had the good sense to lock the door.

"Stop," I sobbed, but the door opened anyway.

It was Mrs. Mabrey, a blanket from one of the downstairs couches draped over her shoulders. "I thought I heard someone come in," she said, and we stared at each other. She looked slightly off center, and I realized she was wearing a wig, a bit askew on her scalp. Of course it was a wig—she must have lost her hair with the chemo and radiation, but this whole summer, not one of the Mabreys had mentioned it.

I could see my reflection in the mirror over the sink, so I knew that my face was smudged with dirt and streaked with tears, and that my right arm was red at the elbow, where Michael had slammed it into the wood planks. My arms and legs were scratched, and a few pine needles were still attached to my filthy shirt and shorts. Semen had dried on my thighs in a sticky trail.

Here was my chance to get help. *Talk to a responsible adult.* Wasn't that what I'd been taught, all the way back in elementary school, in those lessons about "stranger danger"? I needed to say something. I had to ask for help. I whispered, "I was outside by the gazebo... I was walking back..." It wasn't the way I should have started; it wasn't the way that made sense because where I was and what I'd been doing weren't the important part of this story.

I didn't want to have to say it. I wanted her to see me and

understand what had happened to me. I wanted a surrogate mother who would put her arms around me and promise that it would be okay.

But Mrs. Mabrey's face was expressionless. "We may have our faults as a family," she said, the words coming out dry and raspy, as if from a voice that hadn't been heard in a long time. Her gaze moved from the scratches on my arms up to my face. "But in the end, we always support each other." She pulled the door closed in a way that felt final and definite, like screwing the lid on a jar, or slamming shut the pages of a book, or telling me that no one would ever believe what I had to say.

LAUREN

I was shaking when I reached the house, furious with both of them. Megan was my guest, my friend. Didn't that mean something? Wasn't she obligated to act like a guest, to follow the basic courtesies and expectations that came along with being a guest? At the top of that list was "don't sleep with my brother"—right? It was one of those obvious things that didn't need to be spelled out to any decent human being.

And Michael. *God.* He was such a pig. If she had the working parts, he was interested. Apparently, he had no moral quandaries, either. She was *my* friend, *my* roommate, but there were unwritten rules for siblings, too. There were just as many *thou shalt not*s.

From the den, I heard my mother's voice. "Who's there? Michael?"

I almost laughed then, realizing the full effect of what

they'd done. Imagine if my mother knew. Dad was another story—he would shake his head and say he was disappointed and that would be the end of it. Mother would—what? Make Megan pack her bags and dump her on the wharf in Yarmouth in the middle of the night? Forbid her from ever contacting anyone in the family again? Megan might have been my roommate, but this would solidify the fact that she wasn't Mabrey material, not at all. Forget Keale, forget the program at Harvard. There were a million other ways she didn't measure up.

My mother was lying on the couch, staring up at the ceiling. Her wig was tilted at a strange angle, exposing part of her scalp.

"Where's Megan?" I demanded.

Mom didn't look at me. "Upstairs."

Something didn't feel right. Did she already know about Michael and Megan? Had she sniffed them out, the way she'd always sniffed out the trouble I got myself into?

"What's going on?" I asked. "Are you okay?"

"What do you mean?"

I took a step closer, and she screwed her eyes shut, like a child pretending to be asleep. "Why are you acting so weird?"

The screen door slapped behind me, and I turned around to see Aunt Sue dragging Annabelle by the hand. Annabelle's shorts were wet at the crotch, and her cheeks were tear stained. "Someone had herself a little accident," Aunt Sue said, and the two of them disappeared into the downstairs bathroom, the soles of Annabelle's shoes squeaking on the hardwood.

Mom ignored them, still staring up at the ceiling fan, practically catatonic.

I stormed upstairs and found Megan sitting on her bed, arms wrapped around her body, rocking back and forth. She stopped to look up at me. "Lauren—" she began, and then she seemed stuck, as if there was no way to continue. That was fine with me; I wasn't interested in her version of the story. I didn't want my brother to be an anecdote for her future stories. *This one guy, this one time.* I didn't want to know the particulars, the whats and the hows. I was going for the bigger question.

"Just tell me. Why did you do it?"

She blinked, surprised. I noticed then how dirty she was, as if she had been rolling around in the bushes. Which was probably what had happened, one of the specific details I didn't want to know.

I unwound the strap from my neck, set my camera carefully on top of the dresser and closed the door. It was too late to go back to the beach; the fireworks were done by now, and I didn't trust myself not to scream at MK in front of everyone. "I know what happened, okay? I ran into my brother, and he told me everything."

"He told you everything?" Her question came slowly, as if she were sounding out the words.

I shook my head. "I guess not. He spared me the salacious details, which I'm just fine not knowing, thank you very much."

Megan bent forward at the waist, head over her knees.

"You're not going to tell me why you did it? I trusted you." She didn't say anything.

I began undressing, stepping out of my shorts and T-shirt, sliding off the bathing suit I'd been wearing since before breakfast. My pajamas had disappeared into the day's laundry, so I chose a pair of too-warm flannels and a tank top. I heard movement from Megan, and when I turned around, she had her duffel bag out, the zipper gaping open.

"What are you going to do?" I demanded. "Cut and run a day early?"

She didn't answer.

"I don't blame *him*," I snarled. "I mean, you are female and you are alive and you did cross his field of vision. I just can't believe you fell for it. Jesus. He's my freaking brother." I shuddered from a brief vision of the two of them together, MK's lips pressed against Megan's.

"You blame me," she said, like a robot programmed for repetition.

I rolled my eyes. "God, Megan."

She opened her dresser and pulled a clean shirt and shorts from the top of two neatly folded piles. As she changed, she turned her back to me—surprising modesty, I thought grimly, for someone who didn't have qualms about sleeping with my brother when his family was literally within ear-shot. She wasn't even wearing underwear, I realized, turn-ing away in disgust.

"Can I use this?" she asked a moment later, holding up a plastic bag that had been sitting on top of my dresser for weeks. It held a trinket I'd bought in one of the stores by the wharf, a sand globe with purple lettering that read Maine 2002. "Just the bag," she clarified.

I shrugged, watching as she wadded up her dirty clothes and placed them in the bag. She tied the ends and shoved the plastic bag into her duffel, then began transferring the rest of her clothes. She seemed remarkably calm for someone who had just upset the whole order of our friendship.

"How long have you been planning this?"

She whirled around. "What?"

"I know that you kissed him that New Year's Eve."

Her eyes were wide. I'd surprised her, for once. "How did you know that?"

I laughed. "I was there, remember? I was the one who invited you to stay with my family—just like this time."

"You were sleeping."

I shook my head. "I woke up in time for the main event, I guess."

"Then you know that *he* kissed *me*. It's an important distinction."

I shrugged. "You were both flirting. You could have stopped it."

Again, a blank stare. Then she turned her back to me, removed her books from the shelf next to her bed and placed them inside her duffel bag, sliding them into the gaps left by her clothing. All summer she'd handled those books so reverently, highlighting lines in clean yellow streaks, making precise notations in the margins with the fine point of her mechanical pencil. She was packing for her trip to Harvard, of course. That had been coming all along, the expiration date looming on our summer together. But doing it tonight, in front of me, made the act feel more final.

The bag packed, she heaved it off the bed and onto the floor. Finally, she turned to me again. "I think it would be a good idea if I left in the morning."

"Seriously? That's dumb. Everyone's expecting you to be here tomorrow." Tomorrow was the Fourth of July and all our festivities, the real hurrah of the summer. Maybe tomorrow, she would see what she had done wrong. Maybe tomorrow, I'd realize that I'd blown things out of proportion.

She sat on the edge of the bed, looking at me. "Did he tell anyone else?"

I rolled my eyes. "I very much doubt it. My parents wouldn't exactly be thrilled." Then I remembered Mom downstairs, the strange way she was staring at the ceiling.

What did she know? "Seriously. You're staying at my house. On a tiny island. Did you think no one would ever find out?"

She didn't answer. She was sitting stiffly on her bed, hands on her knees. I felt bad for her, almost. If it hadn't been my brother, I would have sat next to her and hugged her and told her that we all make mistakes. But Megan hadn't considered my feelings, had she? She'd hardly even talked to me over the last few days, ever since I told her—

"Wait," I blurted. "Is this because of Joe?"

She straightened like a puppet controlled by an invisible string. "Is *what* because of Joe?"

My head spun. I'd told her that I was sleeping with Joe, her ex-whatever, and just a few days later, she slept with my brother. It was a twisted kind of payback. At the time, her reaction had seemed too strange, so un-Megan-like, so reserved and nonchalant. But now it all made sense. Should I have seen that coming? I felt uneasy now, sick to my stomach. "Did he really mean that much to you? You never mentioned his name to me, not once."

Megan's hand was on her knee, her fingers tracing a thin red line that ran up and over her kneecap and coming away, faintly pink with blood. "Well, then," she said. "I guess we must be even now."

And then her hand reached over for the bedside lamp, plunging the alcove into darkness. The mattress creaked for a moment as she settled into it, and the room was quiet.

Bitch, I thought, still fuming when I slipped between my cool sheets a moment later. It was earlier than I normally went to bed, but I didn't want to go downstairs and run into MK or deal with my sugar-hyped cousins. It was best to let the exhaustion take me, to close my eyes and be done with this day. Only that morning, Uncle Patrick and Aunt Sue and the kids had arrived, and Kat had been discharged from the hospital. Already those events seemed distant, etched into the long-ago past. In the present were Megan and MK, and tomorrow the nuclear fallout, the half-life of what they'd done.

Maybe I wouldn't fight her if she wanted to leave a day early. Maybe, I thought, the reflection of the moon playing across my closed eyelids, it was best to just let her go.

The first scream came just after midnight, waking the whole house. There was no doubt this time that it was Katherine. A moment later, Lizzie was screaming, too, a high-pitched, relentless *Mom-my! Mom-my!* that stung my ears. I met Peter in the hallway, still wearing the clothes he'd worn down at the beach for fireworks. He rushed past with a handful of towels, barking "Call the hospital" in my direction.

"What do you mean?" I asked, following him toward their bedroom. Annabelle and Lizzie were both awake, crying in the doorway. "Peter, what's happening?"

Mom and Dad were at Kat's bedside, trying to reason with her. I caught snatches of their conversation around the girls' sobbing. *We have to get you out of here. You need to see a doctor.*

But the worst was Kat herself, repeating in a controlled voice, "It's just a little blood. I'm not having a miscarriage. It's just a little blood. Just a little blood."

"Okay, we're going to get you downstairs," Peter said. He and Dad made a sling out of their arms and hoisted Kat, with much grunting and swearing, down the stairs.

Mom came into the hallway, clutching the formerly white bathroom towels now stained dark with blood. She dropped them into a heap on the floor. "We're going back to the hospital. You and Megan need to look after the girls while we take care of this."

I nodded numbly and held out my arms for Lizzie, who stopped midshriek, her mouth open, too stunned for sound. I held out a hand for Annabelle. "Let's go get your mom."

"I don't know where my shoes are," she whined.

"That's okay. You don't need shoes for this."

MK came in, shirtless, running a hand through his hair. I could hardly look at him. "What's going on?"

Mom said, "Kat's having a miscarriage," and pushed past him, her nightgown trailing on the stairs.

Lizzie screeched in my arms, and I turned her away from the faint impressions of bloody footprints in the hallway. Where was Megan? She would be able to handle this better than I could. Balancing Lizzie on one hip, I peeked into our bedroom, wondering if Megan had somehow slept through the chaos. Her bed seemed to be empty. Not just empty, I realized, flipping on the light—the sheets were tucked in, the comforter folded back, the pillows neatly stacked. The duffel bag she'd been packing earlier was gone.

Shit.

I bumped into MK and Annabelle in the hallway and took the stairs carefully, Lizzie still in my arms. MK and Annabelle followed with heavy, lumbering steps.

We should have heard the motor by now, the sound splitting the night. Instead, Peter came racing back up the pathway.

"What's going on?" I called.

"The boat's gone," he panted, passing us at a breathless pace. "I'm calling the police, the water taxis, the Coast Guard, anyone I can get on the phone."

"The boat's gone," I repeated. "And so is Megan."

I turned to MK, and his face was pale, realization dawning. For once, he had the decency to look ashamed.

MEGAN

In some ways, those minutes on the boat, floating out into the darkness between The Island and Yarmouth, were the worst moments of my life—worse than my father dying, even worse than those moments in the gazebo with Michael, when I was already promising myself I would survive.

I couldn't make the same promise to myself now. After the house was finally quiet, I'd lugged my duffel bag down the stairs, out the door and down the footpath, loading it with a mighty heave into the Mabrey's fishing boat. Too late, I realized that the bottom of the boat was filled with a few inches of sludge from the day's excursions, and no one had bothered to tip it over. Well, *shit*. Wherever I was going, I would arrive with damp clothes and ruined books.

Behind me, The Island's quiet was ominous, the sound of waves and wind indistinguishable from each other. *Get out of here, get out of here now.* I untied the knots, freeing the boat from the pier, and pushed off with an oar. For a dizzy moment, the boat spun, directionless, while I steadied it. I knew the motor would be too loud; it would split the night and wake everyone back at the house. I would have to row, at least until I was far enough away to risk the noise.

I struggled to get both of the oars in place, eventually finding a shaky rhythm. Sweat dripped into my eyes. My arms were instantly tired. If I'd known I was going to have to row alone in the middle of the night on the Atlantic Ocean, I would have taken a different PE class than beginning jazz dance. What if I never made it to shore? What if the motor didn't work, or the boat took on water, or a giant wave came over the side, washing me into the ocean?

These were good questions, and I focused on them, stroke

by stroke. The next one—what was I going to do when I got to shore?—was harder to answer. But I didn't doubt that I'd done the right thing. I couldn't stay on The Island one more night, not under the same roof as Lauren's scorn and Mrs. Mabrey's indifference, to say nothing of the threat that was Michael, sleeping just down the hall.

Something bumped against the side of the boat, and as a reflex, I leaned over, seeing nothing but the lapping of the water, not even my own face reflected darkly back to me.

I didn't allow myself to turn around until The Island was far behind me, ringed by its exterior lights. It was beautiful and fantastical, a dream and a prison. From this distance, the house itself was solid and massive, like a natural element, formed over time, impermeable and everlasting. I thought about everyone back there, sleeping in their beds—Mr. and Mrs. Mabrey, Kat and Peter and sweet, spoiled Lizzie; the horror show that was Michael; the Brewster-Holmeses in their cabins; and Lauren, the loss that would hurt the most. Lauren who had been so kind and funny and clueless; Lauren who was now my enemy.

Here was where it ended, here in the middle of nowhere, in the middle of our lies.

There would be no more Lauren and Megan.

I pulled the cord to start the engine, but nothing happened. *Deep breath.* I remembered how easily Lauren had done it, how she'd said, "Hold on, hot stuff," when I picked that moment to crawl over a bench to get closer to the stern. How did she make it look so effortless? Because she'd done it her whole life. Because everything was easy for her. I pulled again, too slow and too weak. *Damn.* What the hell was I doing? It was freezing, and I was alone, wearing tennis shoes weighted down with seawater. At this moment, no one on earth knew where I was, and no one was waiting for me to arrive on the mainland. I couldn't tell how much time had passed since I left The Island—ten minutes? Half an hour? Longer?

Then I remembered Dad's long-ago lesson in our front yard and gave the cord another yank, this one quick and decisive. *Like a lawnmower.* The boat shot through the water, nearly knocking me off balance.

I was aiming for the lights of Yarmouth; beyond that, it didn't matter. The Mabreys would find their boat or they wouldn't. Jordana would probably be the one to notice it was missing; by the time everyone gathered for breakfast, it would be clear that I was gone, too. The boat would be an inconvenience for them—they would have to call the water taxi and figure out something once they got to Yarmouth, but at that moment I didn't particularly care about inconveniencing the Mabreys.

For once, I was going to care about me.

I almost sobbed with relief when I could make out the landmarks I recognized—the restaurant at the end of the wharf, with its gaudy lobster outlined in blinking red lights, the ferry building with its slanted roof. I tried to slow like I'd seen Lauren do countless times over that summer, but I cut the engine too late, misjudging the landing and crashing hard into the side of another boat tethered to the wharf. The noise was loud enough that I figured someone would come running, but the only movement was the water churning against the sides of boats, jostling them gently against their moorings. I hadn't paid close attention to the knots Lauren made when she secured the boat, so I tied the same simple loop twice, my fingers fumbling in the dark. It would do. It would have to do. I reached for my soggy duffel bag, nearly losing my balance as I threw it over my shoulder.

And then, for the first time since I'd dried my tears in the upstairs bathroom, I allowed myself to cry, just a little.

★ ★ ★

Somewhere between The Island and Yarmouth, I'd made a decision without knowing I was making one. I wasn't going to the hospital, and I wasn't going to the police. To do either one was to put myself squarely in the path of the Mabreys for the foreseeable future, and possibly for the rest of my life. Michael would deny any accusation I made, and the wagons would circle. It had already happened—Mrs. Mabrey must have known, and she'd turned away. Lauren hadn't even questioned her brother's version of events. She'd already framed me as the jealous slut, bent on getting revenge. If I told the truth, I would be reminded, over and over, that I was a no one from nowhere, that the Mabreys had the kind of power that could buy justice, that could shape truth.

I remembered Lauren's story, the dark secret of her boyfriend who had ended up dead in a prison yard. The pot had been found in Lauren's backpack, but she'd never been charged. Even with the evidence right there, she'd walked free. It would be the same with Michael. The semen that was still crusted between my legs only proved we'd had sex, a story he'd already told. Somehow, I would be the bad girl, the ungrateful houseguest, the horny roommate, the girl who was plotting to bring down a modern-day Camelot.

And then there was me—all the lies I'd told, but the truths, too. Maybe Lauren was right now unburdening herself in front of her family, telling them what I was really like, a fiction cobbled together from my foolish bravado. *Oh, please. She's had a lot of boyfriends.* Maybe she would even offer up my darkest truth, the pillow I'd pressed over my father's face and held there, willing myself not to feel anything, until he was gone. *Do you know she actually killed her father?* This was all the evidence they needed, wasn't it? Megan Mazeros couldn't be trusted, not even as a character witness for her own character.

No, I wouldn't put myself through that. I would do anything not to see the Mabreys again, even if it meant staying silent about Michael's crime.

We'd passed the bus station on the way into Yarmouth six weeks ago, but it looked different at night, buses lined up silently next to their platforms, casting giant rectangular shadows in the moonlight. It was after two-thirty, according to the clock over the locked gate. The station opened at five-thirty, and there were buses to Portland every forty-five minutes, beginning at six-fifteen. That was nearly four hours from now. My elbow throbbed and the cut on my knee stung, but more pressing was my general exhaustion and the niggling edge of panic. Would the Mabreys report their boat missing, sending someone from the Yarmouth police department out to find me wandering through the streets? Would one of the Mabreys themselves locate me before I could get on a bus and on my way to safety, away from them?

I left my duffel bag on the bench outside the bus station and crossed the street to an ATM, drawing curious looks from a man in a pickup truck that rattled slowly past. The town stretched in front of me, its streets deserted, gutters littered with food wrappers and tourist debris. I withdrew my daily limit, two hundred and fifty dollars in crisp twenties and a ten. Thirty-eight dollars would get me a bus ticket to Boston, but what would I do when I arrived there, a day earlier than scheduled and on a federal holiday?

Back at the bus station, I lay down on a bench, using my duffel bag as a lumpy, soggy pillow. I'd been awake for nearly twenty hours, during which time I'd survived a rape by my best friend's brother, rowed several miles through the Atlantic and lugged a heavy duffel bag through half of Yarmouth. I had a horrible moment of déjà vu when a car turned into the empty parking lot, remembering how I'd met Joe Natolo at the bus station in Scofield. I'd thought I had it bad then. Now I was alone again, in much worse shape, with fewer options.

The car—navy with white lettering on the side—stopped in front of me. *A-1 TAXI, PORTLAND*. The driver, an older man with a trim white beard, called through the open window, "You heading somewhere?"

I sat up. "Can you take me to Boston?"

He whistled. "That's a couple of hours. Maybe less at this time of night."

"How much?"

"Hundred and fifty," he said.

I nodded.

He left the taxi idling while he loaded my bag into the trunk. I climbed into the back seat, numb and relieved. I noted the identification badge pinned to the dashboard: Jim Perkins. We navigated Yarmouth's dark streets, its slowly blinking traffic lights, its credit unions and crab shacks.

"You got an address in Boston?" he asked, just as I was drifting off.

"Cambridge," I said. "Harvard."

Jim whistled, studying me in the rearview mirror. It occurred to me that he was the age my dad would have been, with the same kind eyes. "Harvard. Not bad."

I unbuckled my seat belt and curled up across the back seat, staring out at the purple-black sky. I would have to call someone when I got to Boston, but none of the options looked any better than they had a few hours ago.

Despite all logic, I wanted to talk to Lauren. Since I left Kansas, she'd been the hearer of all my thoughts, the holder of all my secrets, but she was the last person I could talk to now.

Would she be worried about me in the morning, the same

as I'd felt when she went to New York? Somehow, I didn't think so.

Once, Lauren had told me that the Mabreys would pay two million dollars to keep their scandals out of the media, and I'd laughed, thinking it was a strange kind of joke, political humor that I just didn't get. Now the number seemed very specific, a calculation of risks versus benefits. How much was their son's future worth to them? I tried to imagine myself cornering Senator and Mrs. Mabrey, presenting them with evidence and demanding a specific amount of money. No—it probably didn't happen like that at all. These things undoubtedly involved lawyers and mediation, a piece of paper pushed back and forth across a table, the dollar amount being negotiated, like the purchase of a used car.

What was the going rate for my body? I was twenty-one, with larger breasts than I needed, hips like a bell curve, a scar on my forearm from where I'd scalded myself with hot coffee at the Woodstock Diner, a dimple that only showed when I really, really smiled. What was all of that worth? Or would the calculation relate to time, in seconds rounded to minutes, from the moment Michael's hand had groped my ass, to the moment I'd been on my back, staring up at the peeling paint of the ceiling of the gazebo? More likely any calculation would take into account our futures, our relative worth. Whatever amount I was offered would represent only a fragment of Michael's potential future—lawyer, politician, bearer of the family name.

I must have slept at some point, because I woke to Jim asking a question. I ran a tongue along my teeth, grimy and unbrushed. My throat was dry—the last thing I'd had to drink was a Sam Adams on the beach during the fireworks. It took a full minute for me to remember why I was sore—my arms bruised, legs aching.

Michael Mabrey, the gazebo.

I sat up, blinking. The sky was a lighter shade of purple now, buildings visible out the window. "Sorry, what?"

"We're in Cambridge, coming up on Harvard Square. Is there anywhere particular you want me to drop you? I mean— pretty much everything is closed at this time of day."

I asked if there was a coffee shop nearby, and Jim circled for a few blocks before finding a bakery where a woman was setting out chairs on the sidewalk. I counted off one hundred and fifty dollars, but Jim handed fifty back to me. "Do me a favor," he said, shoving the bills into his pocket. "Call your parents, would you? It's a holiday. I bet they'd love to hear from you."

I spent the morning drinking strong coffee and eating day-old bagels at the bakery, trying to figure out what came next. Most of Cambridge seemed to be closed for the Fourth, and traffic outside the window was light, only a few pedestrians passing the storefront in jogging shorts, their dogs panting at their sides. I felt safer the farther I was from the Mabreys, until it occurred to me that they knew I would be here. They'd asked incessant questions about my program, and I'd obliged with what I was studying, where I was staying, what my daily schedule looked like. It wouldn't take more than a phone call to the program administration to track me down.

I asked the woman behind the bakery counter about hotels in the area, and I watched her unsubtle gaze take me in—the matted hair, the bruises on my arms, the duffel bag that contained, for all practical purposes, everything I owned. "There is a place," she said, and drew me a map on a rectangular napkin.

"The Algonquin," I said, reading the name.

"Yeah, it's not too fancy or anything, but..." Her eyes lingered on my wrist, where a bruise was forming. Michael had held me there, pinning my arms over my head. "Listen, if you don't mind my asking—"

I snatched the napkin from the counter, my elbow smarting from the motion. "That's perfect, thanks."

The Algonquin was better than I expected, although after a summer on The Island, my standards had been greatly inflated. I paid sixty-eight dollars for a room on the fourth floor. The pillows were lumpy and stained beneath their cases, but the bedding was clean. I tried to pick up the remote control that operated the tiny television in one corner, but it was anchored to the nightstand. The door had a lock with a deadbolt, but just in case, I wedged the room's only chair beneath the knob, then settled fully clothed onto the bed and sank into a relieved sleep.

When I woke, it was dark, and I was surrounded by gunfire. No, not gunfire—fireworks. I peeked out the window and saw an explosion high in the sky, out over distant water.

Back on The Island, the Mabreys were probably watching the fireworks from Yarmouth, the adults lined up in the sand on the beach, the kids splashing in the water. Lauren would be there with her camera. Michael would be there, maybe chuckling to himself over how easy I'd been, how he hadn't even had to break a sweat. Mrs. Mabrey would be grateful that I was gone.

Forget about them.

Forget everything.

I found the bathroom down the hall, showered without any soap, and dried myself on a scratchy towel that may or may not have been clean. It was late when I ventured out into Cambridge, clutching my money and identification inside the front pocket of my jeans, not trusting the security of the Algonquin. More people were outside now, drinking in bars, wandering the sidewalks and lingering in the square. I bought a slice of pizza from a vendor and then went back for another, washing it down with a warm can of Coke. Following street signs, I wandered the perimeter of the university. It was massive, much larger than I expected, the gates imposing and immense. Students milled past in groups, laughing and talking. Someone yelled the word *entropy!* and was answered by a call of "Long live entropy!" from a nearby group. I was the same age as they were and dressed roughly the same, but I wasn't one of them. They were brimming with confidence as if they knew their place in the world, and this was it.

That would be me tomorrow. Anytime between noon and four, I would gather my belongings from the Algonquin and walk down Massachusetts Avenue to the campus, where I would find Boylston Hall and complete my registration. I'd read the letter from the PEW committee often enough to have memorized the important details—registration until four, room assignments, meeting with program organizers in the dorm, dinner, opening lecture and mixer. Tomorrow, I would be one of those students, talking about literary theory, name-dropping Foucault and Derrida. I would put Lauren and Michael and the whole mess of the Mabreys behind me, and I would do it on my own.

I decided to cut through one of the parks near campus, trying to avoid being jostled on the crowded sidewalks. Cambridge was drunkenly celebrating. I moved forward, still clutching my half-full Coke, trying to embrace the feeling of being one of them, someone who belonged. Every noise had me on alert—the random crackle and pop of fireworks, the occasional sound of glass breaking as a bottle hit the ground or went clanging into one of the giant metal trash bins. *You're okay*, I told myself. *This is okay. This is all normal.*

I didn't hear the man until he was nearly on me, his footsteps hitting the earth with solid thumps. I whirled around, terrified, bracing myself for whatever might be coming—an arm around my neck, my knees knocked from under me. He was about ten feet away, close enough that with a determined lunge he could reach me. Under the shadow of his baseball cap, only his mouth was visible, his breath coming hard.

"Get the fuck away!" I screamed. The only weapon I had was the Coke can, and I lobbed it in his direction, the liquid arcing over the grass, the can coming to rest by his feet.

The man stopped, and I saw him for what he was: a runner in a tank top and spandex shorts, white sneakers. A key hung from a cord around his neck. "What the hell? Are you crazy?" He took a few steps to the side and then continued his run, muttering "bitch" as he passed me.

I was back in the Algonquin ten minutes later, the chair wedged under the doorknob, sitting with my back to the exterior wall, arms wrapped around my chest, sobbing.

I woke to someone pounding on the hotel door, the knob rattling. I grabbed one of my tennis shoes for protection. "What do you want?"

The voice that answered was female and gruff. "It's after eleven. You're supposed to be checked out. You've got five minutes before we come in."

I moved the chair and opened the door. The woman was about my mother's age, dark hair twisted into a messy knot on top of her head. She wore a heavy utility apron with her name, Krystine, written in permanent marker on the pocket.

"Check out time was eleven," she repeated more slowly. And then she looked at me, her expression softening. "Are you okay?"

Krystine let me shower and gather my things, and when I headed past the desk in the front lobby half an hour later, she nodded at me silently and didn't demand any extra payment. I struggled down the sidewalk again with my duffel bag, heading in the direction of the university. I made it as far as the entrance to Boylston Hall, where a sign indicated REGISTRATION FOR PEW SCHOLARS.

There was a bench across from the hall, and I sat on it, collecting myself. I didn't have to register until four, and that was still hours away. Occasionally, students went in the building in groups of one or two, exiting with maroon folders. These were my peers in the program, the other promising young scholars of tomorrow. They looked healthy and happy, ready to discuss philosophy and culture and literature. They didn't look damaged or frightened or insecure. They didn't have bruises in the shape of fingerprints on their forearms, or look like they'd spent the night cycling from one nightmare to another. They looked normal, like I used to be.

At four o'clock, I left the square and returned to the hotel.

I stayed in the Algonquin for the next five weeks, paying day to day. I kept my head down when I passed men in the hallway and, back in my room, I wedged the chair beneath the doorknob, my low-tech security system. Most of the time I slept, and in the evenings I tuned in to one of three television stations, finding the comedies unfunny and the dramas unrealistic. Once a day, I ventured out for food, usually passing near campus with my plastic bags of half sandwiches and potato chips and soda. Although school was out for the summer, there were all kinds of special programs and groups on campus, and I watched the students curiously, like they were visitors from another planet. What were they reading? What were they learning? What was it like to sleep through the night? What was it like to be that happy?

The night I was supposed to register for my seminar, I'd

found a payphone near the hotel and called information for the phone number of Miriam Stenholz. She answered on the third ring and seemed thrilled to hear from me. "Tell me all about everything," she'd said, and I hesitated before launching into the story I'd rehearsed that afternoon while I watched students enter and exit Boylston Hall.

Something happened, I explained, trying to sound sad and resigned, which wasn't that difficult in my current situation. There had been a family emergency, and I would be heading back to Kansas for the rest of the summer.

"For the rest of the summer?" she repeated. "You don't think you could return to the seminar at all, only a little late? I could make some phone calls on your behalf..."

"It's not the sort of thing that will be better in a week," I told her. "And I should probably go, because things are just... I mean, it's pretty bad."

I could read the disappointment in her silence. She was probably thinking it had been a mistake to recommend me for the seminar when any of the Sisters would have been just as good and more reliable, too. Finally, she asked, "Will you call me later, when you have an update?"

I promised that I would, knowing I probably wouldn't. Maybe when I was back at Keale in the fall, I would tell her everything, all the things I could hardly acknowledge to myself, everything that began and ended with the Mabreys.

In the public library, I created a new email account and wrote to Mom every few days, long, newsy accounts of the seminar I wasn't attending. Good for you, kiddo, she wrote back sometimes. And then: Your dad would be so proud. She signed her emails always XOXO, Mom.

What kind of horrible person lied to her own mother?

I called Lauren three times at the number on The Island— once at lunch and twice around dinner. Mrs. Mabrey had answered each time, and the silence around her was deep, her words echoing as if she were standing in an empty space. Where was everyone else?

On the first two calls, I hung up without saying anything. The third time, I cleared my throat and asked to speak with Lauren. I was going to tell her what had happened—just give her the information and back away. There was a silence on the other end of the line, and I tried again. "Is Lauren there?" My heart was pounding—of course Mrs. Mabrey would recognize my voice.

Her response was icy, and I had the feeling that she knew it was me the other times, too—maybe she'd only been waiting for me to speak. "Don't call here again," she said, her voice sharp and authoritative. "Do you understand? You'll regret it if you do."

I dropped the phone and ran back to the hotel, as if I could outrun all the hatred I'd heard in her voice. *Your son raped me*, I thought, nearly falling over my own feet. *He raped me, and you let him get away with it.*

They were all a bunch of monsters—Michael and his mother, and the rest of them by extension, and that included Lauren, too, for sneering at me that night, for suggesting that I was a slut who just couldn't control herself, that I was only jealous of her.

And because they were monsters, they could get away with anything.

In the middle of August, when the seminar I wasn't attending came to an end, I took a bus from Cambridge to Westport, a little town in southern Massachusetts. Mom and Gerry met me there in a rented Ford Taurus and we spent a week in a cottage overlooking Buzzards Bay. It was unimpressive after The Island's endless amenities, although Mom pronounced it "paradise" at every turn.

Gerry wore the Harvard sweatshirt I'd bought him from a street vendor in Cambridge, and Mom beamed at me, proud by association. "Did you ever think, back when you were waiting tables at the diner, that your life would turn out like this?" she asked, squeezing me in a tight hug.

I almost told her everything then; it had been exhausting to maintain the lie all week, to be yet another fake version of Megan Mazeros. If only Gerry hadn't been there—but that was a lie, too. My shame was rooted more deeply, already part of who I was.

They hugged me goodbye at the bus station that weekend, and I promised Mom that I would call when I was settled in at Keale. Then I sat for a long time on a bench while travelers hurried around me, listening to departure calls.

There was no way I could room with Lauren again—I knew that. I needed to talk to the housing department to figure out new arrangements. Was it possible that Lauren had already done this? But even the thought of running into Lauren—bumping into her in class, in the library or on one of the footpaths—made me break out in a cold sweat. How would I make it there a full year without breaking down, without screaming at her that her brother was a rapist, without letting my shame spill out at every moment? I was scheduled to take a full load of classes, but I hadn't even been able to contemplate taking a single seminar at Harvard. Most days, I'd slept for at least twelve hours and zoned out in front of the television for another three or four, and still I felt unbearably tired.

No, I couldn't go back to Keale. I couldn't brush off everything that happened that summer and sit in class and pretend I was the same person I'd been before. That night, I took the last bus back to Cambridge, and in the morning, I called Keale from the phone booth outside the Algonquin.

It would be months before I told the truth—or at least, a part of it—to my mother.

When I did, she railed at me over the phone. "Are you crazy? You've got three years under your belt. You're so close. And all that money spent..."

"I might finish someday," I said, vaguely, not believing it myself.

"At least come home, then," Mom pleaded, as if Woodstock, Kansas, still fit that description. "There's always a place for you here."

"Mom," I said, fingering the coils of the phone cord. "I'm sorry, but no."

By that time, I had moved out of the Algonquin and into an apartment I shared with three other girls, all waitresses and part-time students. It hadn't been hard to find a job or slip back into the routine of restaurant life. I spent my afternoons and evenings at The Sea Shack in a white shirt and black pants and thick-soled shoes, tucking my tips into the money belt I wore clipped around the inside of my waistband, an old trick I'd learned at the Woodstock Diner. The shifts kept me so busy that I hardly had time to think at all.

Still, sometimes when I was bussing tables or taking orders, I would catch a glimpse of someone who reminded me of Lauren—glossy dark hair, a confident set to her shoulders, an unabashed laugh. Other times, I froze when I thought I saw the back of Michael's head at the bar, and it would all come back—the hand on my neck, how easily he'd pushed me onto my back, the pine needles pressing into my skin—and I would step outside the service entrance, taking a few deep breaths.

That's all behind you, I promised myself.

None of the them can ever hurt you again.

LAUREN

The day after Megan left, when everything was still in chaos on The Island, a Coast Guard official found our fishing boat floating in the bay, not far from Yarmouth. Save for a few inches of water, it was empty. There was no sign of Megan or any of her belongings.

"She must have tied a sloppy knot," Uncle Patrick decided—everyone else was in Yarmouth with Kat by then, and it was only his family, Lizzie and me left on The Island. "It probably just floated loose."

It made sense—Megan wouldn't have known how to tether the boat properly. If she'd left it and made her way to Cambridge, she was probably right now settling in with her roommates and attending her first seminar. On the other hand, since she hadn't left so much as a note, and she hadn't called, there was no way to know if she'd made it at all. I had nightmares, those first nights after she left, thinking of Megan sinking to the bottom of the Atlantic, her curls fanned out from her head like seaweed. But when I woke, I was angry again, stung by her absence, the fragments of my family she'd left behind.

That horrible night, down at the pier, Mom had taken me by the shoulders and given me a bone-rattling shake. At the end of the pier, Kat was curled on her side, one bare foot dangling close to the water, waiting for the police cruiser that would take her to the hospital in Yarmouth. "Where did Megan go?" Mom had demanded. "What's she going to do?"

And all I could manage was that I figured she'd gone to Harvard a day ahead of schedule because she wanted to get away from The Island. She'd been packing; she'd been upset. The words from our fight rang in my ears. Well—not *our* fight, exactly. Megan had just listened; I'd done all the talking. But there was no way I was going to have this blamed on me. "Ask Michael," I spluttered. "He's the one—"

Mom had reared back her hand like she was going to slap me, but her hand whizzed emptily to the side of my face. Still, it stung—a phantom slap. So Mom knew about Megan and MK, or she suspected. Either way, it was unfair that I should bear the brunt of what they'd done.

"Ask him," I repeated, darting out of her reach. "Ask your golden boy what he did."

I whirled around, looking for him, but MK wasn't down on the beach with the rest of us. Even when the cruiser arrived and Kat was hooked up to some monitors and whisked away with Dad and Mom and Peter, he didn't make an appearance. Later, walking back to the house with Lizzie in my arms, tears dried on her cheeks and hair, I spotted him sitting on the railing of the gazebo, looking out over the cliff at the water.

It had been the plan all along for him to leave on the seventh, but still, it felt like a cowardly move. It was easy for him to set into motion a chain of events and then disappear, leaving the rest of us to pick up the pieces. We had stayed away from each other except for mealtimes, although it was difficult to tell who was avoiding whom, or if it was in fact a mutual evasion. On the day he left, I called my goodbye from the deck, not looking up when I heard the motor start and not relaxing until the hum faded into the day, lost in the sound of waves and seagulls.

Kat spent a week in the hospital—first recovering from the miscarriage, then some internal bleeding from the D&C and an infection that was slow to heal. She refused to go back to The Island, insisting it was the cause of all her problems. If she'd just stayed home in Connecticut, after all, if she'd just been able to relax without all the chaos, her baby would be alive.

"It wasn't The Island's fault," Peter fumed on his last night with the rest of us, Kat and Lizzie's bags packed and waiting at the door to be lugged down to the pier. He glared at me from across the dinner table. "It was your friend, that bitch. If she hadn't taken the boat, this would have all been different."

I didn't say anything because there were no words that would bring back their baby. The morning after everything had happened, I'd seen Jordana haul Kat's bloody sheets and towels to the burn barrel, and by afternoon she'd scrubbed down the hallway and stairs, erasing smears of blood from the hardwood. There had been too much blood, even before they discovered the boat was gone. No, Megan hadn't caused Kat's miscarriage, but she had managed to drive a wedge firmly between the Mabreys.

"You," Peter continued, pointing a finger at me. His face was unshaven and there were deep hollows under his eyes. "You should track her down. She should pay for this, somehow. At the least, she should be arrested for theft."

Dad cleared his throat. "The boat was found."

"That doesn't change the fact that it was stolen in the first place," Peter huffed.

"She's at Harvard," I reminded them. "I don't think she's hiding or anything."

Mom looked around the table, taking in each of us—Peter, Lizzie drowsing in her high chair, Dad, me. "We will do no such thing," she announced. "None of us will contact that girl. Is that understood?"

I started to object. *That girl.* That girl who had spent half the summer asking Mom if she wanted more tea or a blanket or something to eat. That girl who I had shared everything with, who I was rooming with again in the fall.

Dad said, "Sounds reasonable," with a nod at me.

I didn't protest, but inside I scoffed. My parents could make all the official pronouncements they wanted, but there was no way they could enforce them. Of course I would talk to Megan again. But as the days passed, the silence between us grew deeper and more profound. It was the longest we had had gone without talking, or emailing or calling, in almost three years.

By the middle of July, it was just Dad and Mom and me on The Island, three people who had never spent any significant amount of time with each other. Dad was on his laptop or cell phone, and the conversations I overheard dealt with the budget and staffing and subcommittee business. Still, I was sad when he left, since it would be only Mom and me for the rest of the summer, moving politely around each other on an island that seemed to be haunted by the ghosts of our family members.

Without Megan, I missed Joe more sharply than I had the rest of the summer. I wanted him there in the mornings when I woke up, realizing I would have to face the day alone. I wanted him when I sat on the end of the pier, the loneliness in the air like a crushing weight on my chest. If I couldn't talk to Megan, at least I could talk to Joe. Maybe I could explain to him all the things I wanted to explain to her.

Finally, I did call him, holding my breath while the phone rang once, twice, three times.

"Hello," he said, and he was so Joe, so himself, I almost cried in relief. I imagined him in his apartment, yesterday's dishes crusty in the sink, the mattress still dented with the shape of his body.

"It's Lauren," I said.

"Oh, hey. Are you back already?"

Tears stung in my eyes. "No—I'm still out here. I was wondering—" The words I'd rehearsed so many times dried in my throat. "Why don't you come out here? Just for a few days?"

"Come to Maine? Isn't your family there?"

"No. It's only my mom and me."

"I mean…" The pause told me everything I needed to know. "You know I'm working, right? I'm on the schedule for the week, so I can't just…"

"Forget it," I said quickly. "It was a stupid idea."

He didn't disagree. "But you're coming back soon anyway. School starts in August, doesn't it?"

"Right. Never mind. I'll see you then."

"Okay, yeah," he said. I waited for him to ask me why I had called, what was wrong, but instead he offered up the information that Scofield was hot, that he was going camping over the weekend, that he wasn't getting as many hours at the shop as he wanted. I hung up feeling lonelier than before.

One day during our lunchtime, the phone rang, and Mom picked up the extension in the den. She shook her head when I asked who was calling—a hang-up then, a wrong number. Not many people had the number of our landline, not since Dad's election when numerous steps had been taken to protect our privacy. There was another phone call later that evening, dismissed just as quickly by Mom when I looked up from the catalog I'd been browsing, lazily dog-earing pages. The following night, the phone call came when we were eating dinner, a bounty carefully prepared by Jordana even though it was just for Mom and me, and neither of us had our full appetites. Mom took the phone into the other room, and I heard her say something before she returned, placing the receiver into its holder with a decisive click.

Was it Joe—did he have our number? My heart thudded. Later, after Mom went upstairs, I picked up the receiver and dialed ⋆69. The phone rang and rang, the sound echoing distant and tinny in my ear. Eventually, there was a click and a man, not Joe, said, "Yeah."

I explained that someone had called me earlier from his number.

He laughed. "Lady, this is a pay phone. Coulda been anyone. Now can you get off the line so I can make my call?"

"Hold on," I pleaded. "Where are you? Where's the pay phone?"

"Ah," he said. "Let's see. Church and Brattle. Cambridge, Mass." There was a click, then a silent moment, and a dial tone.

Cambridge, Massachusetts. So Megan was alive and well—just as I figured.

And eventually, she would have to talk to me.

OCTOBER 15–17, 2016

MEGAN

An attorney, Rachel Hogan, arrived at our house on Saturday morning with a briefcase full of papers to sign. She and I sat at the kitchen table while Bobby paced the room, interjecting questions. Later, a media consultant arrived—Rosie Spiers, looking young enough to still be in college. It would be Rosie's job to notify the major news outlets by eight Monday morning, and the press conference would be live at ten.

Bobby went shopping with me at the mall on Saturday night for almost the first time in all the years we'd been together. Everything in my closet had been deemed wrong for the purpose—my work uniform was inevitably a pair of black or gray pants and a brightly colored cardigan, paired with my faithful Dansko clogs. Rosie advised me to look for a gray suit, a feminine but conservative blouse, low heels.

Bobby said, "That looks good," each time I opened the dressing room door, doubt writ large across his smile.

Eventually, I found a suit that didn't require tailoring and a lavender blouse with iridescent polka dots. In the dressing room mirror, I looked like I was heading into an interview.

"That's cute," Bobby said, pointing to the blouse. "You could wear that to work anytime."

But I knew I would never wear it again.

Rachel had asked me to prepare my family and closest friends for what was about to happen. "If they don't already know, that is," she said, and I shook my head. In fourteen years, I'd told exactly two people, Miriam and Bobby. But on Monday morning, the entire news-watching world would know.

I made the phone calls on Sunday: first to my mom, who bawled and asked too many questions and said she knew something was wrong with me that summer; next to the wives and girlfriends of Bobby's closest friends, the women who had become my closest friends by default. Finally, I sent a carefully worded email to the counseling department at Northern Essex. Together, Bobby and I wrote a Facebook announcement, which he would post at the same time my statement went live on television. There was no point in avoiding the truth now since the questions were bound to come flooding in. *Wasn't that your girlfriend I saw on TV?*

Finally, I logged on to Bobby's Facebook account one last time and looked up the contact information for Lauren (Mabrey) Leavitt, and I sent her a two-sentence email.

Your brother raped me on July 3, 2002. Tomorrow, I'm going to tell the truth.

I signed it simply Megan.

We drove into Hartford on Sunday night and had dinner in the hotel with Rachel and Rosie, and I tried not to think about how expensive this was going to be when it was all said and done. Bobby assured me that it didn't matter, but he ordered the chicken and not the steak.

Sleep was elusive that night, although we had the luxury of a king bed and thousand-thread-count sheets. I couldn't stop thinking about the Mabreys, and how they would react to the press conference. I wondered how long it would take Lauren to assemble a list of lies and misdeeds, so the process of discrediting me could begin. Not too long, I figured. I'd certainly provided her with enough ammunition. Or would she believe me, the email triggering her memories from that night on The Island? When the alarm went off at five, I was still awake, exhausted from my mental marathon.

Bobby went down to the lobby for coffee when a short, bustling woman arranged by Rosie arrived to do my hair and makeup.

"I don't want to overdo it," I warned her. "I don't usually wear a lot of makeup."

She consulted her notes. "Confident and trustworthy," she read and pointed at the dark circles under my eyes. "That means we've gotta take care of those."

In the end, I was grateful to put myself in the hands of a professional, someone who could sweep away the years with a few strokes of the brush. Rachel and Rosie met us in the lobby at nine, and we climbed into the back seat of a town car. Behind the hair sprayed to stiffness and the layers of foundation, the real Megan Mazeros was a quivering mess.

By 9:30 we were in place, waiting behind the scenes as the press swarmed into the building. I'd rehearsed my statement so many times, I could have said it during the sleep I wasn't getting.

"It's not too late to back out, if you want," Bobby told me at one point while I paced the room nervously.

I stared at him. Of course it was too late. "I'm doing this."

He smiled. "Good."

Miriam entered with a fresh cup of coffee and held my hand while Bobby read the headlines off social media.

"The *Huffington Post* has picked it up," he said. "They're reporting that another woman has come forward in the Michael Mabrey case."

Miriam squeezed my hand, one of her oversize rings digging into my flesh. She looked the same as she'd looked eleven years ago when she'd delivered my belongings from Keale, when we'd sat side by side on a park bench and I'd told her the entire story, every horrible second of it. Over the years, she'd urged me to come forward, a gentle insistence that I'd been only too eager to ignore. Now she stared at me from behind her magenta frames, nodding encouragement.

Bobby frowned, still staring at his phone. "Some hack site is reporting this as political maneuvering. Well, never mind them. The *Globe* is all over it. They're saying it's suspicious that Anna Kovics has disappeared so completely from the media."

I took a sip of coffee, my mouth suddenly dry.

"They're also saying that his career is over, this close to the election. Absentee voting starts this week." Bobby stopped scrolling and slid his phone into his pocket. "You've got this, kiddo. Boot this guy back to where he came from."

I gave him a shaky smile. Michael Mabrey came from Simsbury, Connecticut, from generations of money and privilege. He came from a family that would defend him, no matter what. A team of lawyers was probably preparing his defense right now, drafting generic statements designed to praise him and slam me. Once I opened my mouth, I would be fair game.

At 9:50, I checked myself one last time in the mirror, giving my lipstick a quick touch-up. Miriam straightened the shoulders of my jacket, and Bobby gave me a careful hug, not wanting to ruin the effect.

"I'm so proud of you," she said.

"I'll be right there in the back of the room," Bobby told me. "If it gets to be too much, it's okay for you to stop. I'm right there, I'll come rushing forward. I'll fight my way through the crowd if I have to."

I swallowed back a lump of tears. "My knight in shining armor."

He smiled. "Okay, I'll take that."

The room was full; I could hear the commotion inside, the bubble of voices. It was just as loud when the door opened, although the energy focused, flashbulbs popping. I followed Rachel onto the raised platform, planting my feet where she had planted hers, as though I were tracking her in the snow. She read from her statement, and I didn't hear anything but the words echoing in my own head. In my hands, I clutched a single piece of paper.

I looked out at the room to where I knew Bobby would be standing, and he was looking back at me, nodding. Maybe I would say yes, finally, when all of this was done. There were dozens of people in the room, behind cameras and on their phones, and all of them were looking at me. And then the door opened, and a woman entered, moving through the clump of cameramen by the door. I would have known her anywhere, anytime. She was still tall and slender, her hair pulled back in a ponytail, a shoulder bag hanging on her arm.

It was Lauren.

She had come.

2002 AND AFTER

LAUREN

Megan didn't call again, even though I hung around the house for the next few weeks, barely venturing beyond the back deck, and my emails to her Keale address went unanswered. She would contact me by the end of July or the beginning of August, whenever her seminar was finished, whenever she was ready to start planning for the fall, I figured. But eventually the summer wound down, Mom and I packed up the house, made our way to Yarmouth and then on to Simsbury. Four days before classes were scheduled to start, I repacked the Saab and drove to Scofield, rehearsing in my mind how my reunion with Megan would go. Tears, accusations, screaming. Or would it be explanations, laughs, forgiveness?

We were supposed to share an on-campus apartment with four other girls, but by the day before the semester started, she still hadn't arrived. I kept telling myself that the next time the door opened it would be her, lugging that tired duffel bag, spilling some horrible travel tale, but it never happened. Classes started; our senior year began and Megan still wasn't there. I waited in a long line at the housing department and eventually explained to a woman in an ill-fitting sweater that my roommate hadn't arrived, and I didn't know what I was supposed to do.

She typed some information into a database on her computer and said, "Oh. Megan Mazeros. That's right. There's a note here that she contacted us last week about her deposit. It looks like she's not coming back this year."

I leaned forward, nearly toppling my chair. "She's not coming back? At all?"

"I don't know about that, but it does say she won't be here this fall." She made a few more clicks, smiling absently at her computer screen. "It's a good thing you're here, then. We have a number of returning students on the waiting list for housing, and if there's an empty spot in your apartment—"

I stood up. "No, no way. You're not giving me a new roommate."

The woman looked surprised, two warm round dots appearing on the apples of her cheeks. "It's the school's policy to charge extra for a single room, you know."

"I don't care how much it costs." I seethed. "Add it to my bill, then. But you're not giving me a different roommate." This, at least, my parents would understand.

Over the next week, I tracked down everyone Megan knew—some of the Sisters had graduated last spring, but the ones who were still on campus had the same story. All they knew was that Megan was spending the summer with me before heading to her Harvard seminar. No one had heard from her since May, and they were equally shocked that she hadn't come back.

"Shouldn't you know where she is?" one of them demanded. "Didn't she spend the summer with you?"

Of course I didn't say anything about Megan and Michael or our fight or the boat she'd stolen. It seemed more and more ridiculous every time I thought about it. Three years of friendship, and it was all gone in a night.

I even tried Dr. Miriam Stenholz in the political science department, the tiny, intimidating woman who had taken Megan under her wing last spring and gotten her into the program at Harvard. After our initial introduction, Dr. Stenholz cleared off a cluttered chair in her office and insisted on making me a cup of tea.

She sat across from me, squeezing the tea bag with her spoon, dark swirls staining the water. "It's very strange that Megan didn't contact you. Why do you think that is?"

I shook my head, shifting the warm mug from hand to hand without bringing it to my lips. I hated even the smell of chamomile tea. "I haven't seen her since the beginning of July, before she left for her seminar at Harvard. I don't know what happened after that."

Dr. Stenholz stared at me, lowering her cup to her desk. "But she didn't go to the seminar, of course. There was a family emergency. She told me she went directly from her time with your family back to Kansas."

I chewed my lip, thinking this through. Megan hadn't mentioned anything about her family that last night we were together. I was sure of it. If there had been an emergency, she would have told me.

"She was so disappointed, of course, poor thing. After being so excited to receive the scholarship and all those hours of studying..." Dr. Stenholz shook her head. "I can't think why she didn't tell you."

I could think of a few reasons. "Do you think she's still there? In Kansas?"

Dr. Stenholz's brows pinched together. "I suppose she must be. I've emailed her multiple times—she was supposed to TA for my fall class, but I had to find someone else. When you get in touch with her, will you let her know I would love to hear from her?"

I nodded, setting the untouched tea on the edge of her desk. My next class started in half an hour, but instead I blew it off to get in my car and go for a drive, slowing as I passed all the places I'd been with Megan, as if she might somehow be there, waiting for me. Had there really been a family emergency? But why wouldn't she have called or emailed or dropped me a note—anything? And if she had gone back to Kansas, who had called the house on The Island from a pay-phone in Cambridge?

I was dealing with another disappearance that fall, too— Joe Natolo was gone. I'd called him my first night back in Scofield, hoping to put the awkwardness of our summer conversation behind us and pick up the pieces again. Maybe he would want to grab a bite and catch up and help me unravel the mystery of Megan. And sure—I would have happily gone back to his place, stripped off my shirt and shorts, and slid into the sheets that probably hadn't been changed since I left in the spring. But instead of hearing his voice on the other end of the line, I'd received a tri-tone alert and an accompanying message by a mechanical woman: *The number you are trying to reach is no longer in service.* I dropped everything, rushed out to the Saab and drove into Scofield, laughing at my frenzy. There was some obvious, uncomplicated explanation, because that's how Joe was—obvious and uncomplicated. I'd probably dialed the wrong phone number in my hurry, or Joe had forgotten to pay his phone bill that month. When I knocked on the door to his apartment, he would say, "Hey, there," and I'd fall into his arms and tell him the whole terrible story of Megan and that summer and wait for our conversation to become kissing, for day to blend into night and night to blend into day.

But Joe's car wasn't in his usual spot, and new curtains, white with royal blue fleurs-de-lis, hung in his windows. There was a flowerpot on the windowsill, the dangling limbs of a fern reaching out to the sun. No one answered when I knocked on his door, so I descended the steps and rang the bell on the detached house. A friendly, frosted blonde woman opened the door, an apron tied around her hips.

"Joe Natolo," I said, unable to form a sentence, the name itself a question.

She smiled at me, shaking her head. "I'm sorry, dear, he moved out a few weeks ago."

As she began to shut the door, I blurted, "I'm sorry, I don't know if this is inappropriate or something, but do you know where he's moved to? I need to see him."

She shook her head, her eyes kind. "He mentioned something about a job in Minnesota. No, Michigan. I think it was Michigan."

Minnesota. Michigan. I was going to be sick, right here on the front porch of Joe's landlord. Former landlord. "Did he leave a forwarding address? I mean, for his mail and things?"

She frowned. "I don't know that he ever got mail here. But that would be something to check with the post office, I think."

I checked with the post office, and I checked with the machine shop where Joe had worked, and I tracked down leads for a Cathy Natolo, the mother I'd never met, like I was some kind of private investigator. She lived in the Philly area, Joe had told me, but 411 didn't have a number listed for a Cathy or Catherine Natolo anywhere in the vicinity. I called Michigan information and found forty-seven Natolo surnames, eight beginning with a J. I called the first five, and then I stopped. What was the point? Joe Natolo knew exactly where *I* was. He could have reached me through the switchboard at Keale at any time. I wouldn't have been particularly difficult to locate, if he was interested in trying.

That fall, as I stumbled through my classes and returned each night to my unshared bedroom, it was impossible not to imagine the two of them together somehow—Megan and Joe, the missing pieces of my life. I missed Megan's openmouthed snores, her infectious laugh, her crazy stories. I missed those nights with Joe, the two of us wearing only our underwear, eating Pasta Roni straight from the pot. They'd both disappeared as surely as if they'd been plucked by an alien hand reaching down from a hovering spaceship. And if I allowed myself, even jokingly, to entertain that possibility, how much more likely was it that they were simply somewhere together, their connection reestablished, their bond forged over stories of me?

More and more, I thought back to my last night with Megan, wondering how it could have been different. Maybe if I hadn't let her out of my sight, she never would have wandered off with my brother. Maybe if I'd actually let her tell me about it, I would have understood the *why* beyond the *how* and the *what*. Maybe I would have forgiven her by now, and we would be back in our twin beds at Keale, gossiping about our suitemates and getting sloppy drunk once in a while and telling each other our best and worst truths and lies.

I didn't even take pictures that fall, except for the odd digital snapshot for the *Sentinel*. Instead, I spent hundreds of hours in Phil Guerini's darkroom, developing the pictures I'd taken over the summer—Lizzie in her sunflower-print dress with her tiny saltwater sandals, Mom and Kat in side-by-side lounge chairs, the wide brims of their hats shielding their faces. Dad and Michael standing next to each other on the pier, silhouetted against the sunset. Michael and Peter helping the boys light fireworks. Lizzie and Annabelle waving the burning ends of sparklers in the air. A shot of Dad and Uncle Patrick and Aunt Sue, all sitting on the sand, empty beer bottles stationed around them. Ten feet to the side was Megan, her knees drawn to her chest, her chin resting on her knees. This was right before she'd left the beach, then, right before she and Michael had wandered off together. Once they were developed, I boxed up the prints and wedged them into a dusty spot under my bed.

I wanted to forget everything that had happened—the summer of Mom in her wig with her painted-on eyebrows, the summer of Kat's miscarriage, the summer of Megan and Michael, the summer I'd lost everything.

After Christmas, Mom and I went back to Washington with Dad to visit with MK and his new girlfriend, Rebekah, a Georgetown graduate. They were both working for one of the top law firms in the city. Mom said that Rebekah had all the marks of a politician's wife, which was the highest praise she could offer. She looked like a female version of MK—tall with thick dark hair that was often slicked back into a low ponytail or chignon. I never saw her that winter without three-inch heels, even when we walked through snow and on icy sidewalks.

On my last night in town, I went with MK and Rebekah to a Georgetown alumni party. When Rebekah excused herself to the bathroom, MK told me that she was the real deal. "This is it for me," he swore. "No more dicking around."

"Oh, by the way," I said. "Megan sends her love."

I was satisfied when he nearly spat out his drink.

Twenty minutes later, I was bored and on my way to drinking too much from the punch bowl when I saw Braden Leavitt smiling at me from across the room. I raised a hand to wave, and he began making his way toward me.

It was one of those funny moments in life where time slowed down, where things became sharp and clear. Still, if Joe Natolo had walked into the room right then, I would have fallen into his arms and demanded to know where he'd been and escaped with him two minutes later to kiss in the stairwell. But Joe was gone, and Braden was there, and I had the feeling that my life was about to go in a completely new direction.

"Lolo Mabrey," Braden said, taking my hand and holding it to his lips, like he was some kind of courtier, and I was some kind of lady. I gave him a clumsy curtsy.

"Lauren," I reminded him.

"I know." He smiled. "That's not the kind of thing a person can forget."

Brady came to Scofield for Valentine's Day and took me out to dinner at a new Chinese place in town, and we ended up back in my unshared room, moving quietly so we didn't alert my suitemates to his presence. I visited him in Washington over spring break and he took me to too many Smithsonians and the jazz club where we'd first reconnected. Most nights we talked on the phone, long, lazy conversations that started nowhere and went nowhere and left us wanting more. In the past, I would have spent those nights in the darkroom, the smell of chemicals sharp and familiar. Or I would have spent those hours with Megan, the two of us telling stories or listening to music or doing nothing at all. Or I would have spent them with Joe, knowing that we were operating on borrowed time. It was different with Brady—he was levelheaded and mature, smart and compassionate. He was studying immigration law; he cared about the things my family professed to care about but didn't unless it was an election year and a sound bite was needed.

"You're so funny," he said once, when I'd told him a story about the Mabreys, one of the pieces of my life I was carefully doling out, one by one, trying not to scare him away. "So funny and so different."

I laughed. "I'm trying to figure out if that's a good thing, being different."

"How could it be anything other than a good thing? You're just being you."

I was already pregnant when I graduated that spring, although you couldn't tell in my oversize black gown, whipped side to side in the wind of a storm that was just about to blow through Scofield, sending the whole commencement crowd running for cover.

But there was no hiding it from anyone at the end of the summer when I married Braden Leavitt in a little chapel on Georgetown's campus with only our immediate families present. Mom had a hard time smiling; it wasn't the wedding she would have planned for me. There was no dress shopping, and since my feet were swollen, I wore a pair of white Converse tennis shoes with the laces out.

Stella was born when we were still in DC, and Emma when we moved to Rhode Island a few years later. Brady's job meant long hours, at best average pay and a sense of satisfaction that more than made up for it. Before long, our lives were so crazy and so full that I hardly thought about Megan Mazeros at all.

MEGAN

The full impact of what I'd done didn't hit me until that spring, when I should have been graduating from Keale, when I should have made definite plans about my future. I wondered if Lauren had graduated, if she'd figured out what came next in her life, or if she'd let her mother do that for her.

I didn't call Miriam again until that summer, a full year after I'd promised to keep her updated.

"Oh, my God," she said. It felt horrible to hear the relief in her voice. "I was so worried."

"I'm sorry for everything," I whispered, holding back the tears that threatened to come.

"I don't understand why you need to be sorry for anything. Do you want to come back? I can make some phone calls, and we can get you enrolled for the fall. I've been here long enough that they won't refuse me anything." This was probably true.

"No," I said quickly. "I just need a bit of a favor." I told her about the boxes I'd left in Keale storage, full of books and winter clothes and the mementoes I'd kept from my childhood.

"Of course. Do you want me to bring them to you?"

"No," I said too quickly. I couldn't imagine Miriam in my cramped apartment, teeming with roommates, every surface littered with our junk. "Maybe you could just keep the boxes for me for a while? Like, in your garage or something, if that's not too much trouble?"

"Yes, but I'm happy to—"

"Thank you," I whispered, hanging up the phone before she could undermine my resolve with her generosity. I fought the urge to call her back and unload everything—the rape, the fight with Lauren, my frantic trip back to the mainland, the job where I earned just enough in tips to break even.

But I wasn't going to complain, because this was what I had chosen. This was my life now.

Sometimes, at parties where I'd had too much to drink from the keg or the punch bowl, I told stories about Lauren. I changed her name and didn't mention the political connection, but the rest was true: the monthly clothes allowance that would have paid my rent, the estate in Connecticut, the private island off the coast of Maine.

"Get out of here," someone would say. "A private island? Who the hell has their own island?"

And I would laugh along with them, like it was the funniest thing in the world, these silly rich people and their silly rich lives.

Eventually, I ordered my transcripts from Keale and a few years later, I finished my courses at a state school, attending class during the day and waitressing at night. I met Bobby on one of those nights, when he came in with a group of fourteen for a birthday party, and I flirted with him in the same family-safe way I flirted with men, women and children alike. That was part of the schtick of being a waitress, the difference between a lousy tip and a decent one, between just making rent and having something left over at the end of the month. As a rule, I didn't pay attention to men in the restaurant. It was a rare week when one of them didn't leave me a note on a receipt or a business card that I promptly crumpled and tossed into the trash.

When I saw him a few weeks later at a gas station, filling his Toyota across from my crumbling Cabriolet, he said, "Hey! You're that waitress."

I raised an eyebrow. "Lucky guess."

"No, from the lobster place. Remember my family? Aunt Harriet turned ninety-three. You sang her 'Happy Birthday.'" He was wearing a Red Sox cap, and he took it off, gesturing to his hair, as if that might make him more recognizable. "I wasn't wearing a hat that night."

I smiled. "Now that you mention it, I do remember Aunt Harriet."

He was watching me, and the gas was pumping slow, and I thought we might be stuck smiling at each other for a very long, very awkward time, until he blurted, "Do you like Shakespeare?"

"Do I like Shakespeare?" I repeated. "That's a nonsequitur."

"Smart and pretty," he said, and I blushed.

I said, "I mean, he's not on my top-ten list. But yeah, I like Shakespeare." The gas nozzle clicked, and I transferred it from my car to the holder, wondering if I could leave before my interest in other white, male, dead authors could be probed.

He leaned against the gas pump. "That wasn't the best way to ask what I wanted to ask. What I meant to say was I'm Bobby. Short for Robert, but Bobby has basically stuck, even though it might be ridiculous for someone who is thirty-one. Which I am."

I nodded, moving slowly backward toward the driver's door.

He was talking faster, trying to outpace me. "And you probably know there's a Shakespeare in the Park thing going on this Saturday. I think it's *Much Ado about Nothing*. Something light, you know. A comedy. Guy gets the girl, girl gets the guy."

"Right," I said, opening the door to my Cabriolet.

"So a big group of us are going, and it would be great if you came, too. I mean, I think it would be great. Obviously we don't know each other that well…"

"Obviously." I couldn't stop myself from grinning. "Well, maybe I'll bump into you there."

"Wait! I mean, it'll be a madhouse. There will be people milling around everywhere. I couldn't risk your not finding me. So if you decide to come, and no pressure, whatever you want, I'll be at the wine stand by the entrance half an hour before the show starts. If you don't come, it's cool. If you do come, that would be even better." He tapped the top of the gas pump twice, as if signaling an end to his soliloquy.

"Thanks, I'll think about it." I gave him a short wave and stepped into my car. There was an embarrassing beat while the starter choked and before the engine finally came to life, but then I was pulling away, and in the rearview mirror I saw that Bobby no-last-name had a hand raised, like a goodbye or maybe a benediction.

I went—and not quite on a whim. I worked Saturdays, every Saturday, year in and year out, because the parties were bigger and the tips were higher, and that was how it went in the restaurant business. But I found someone to cover for me, and I met Bobby at the wine tent, because I figured, what the hell? I was twenty-seven years old, and I thought the ugliness was all in my rearview mirror. Other than a drunken kiss here and there on New Year's Eve, I'd kept my distance from men ever since Michael Mabrey.

Bobby and I dated and broke up and dated and broke up and then we finally moved in together. He asked me to marry him three times, until I asked him not to ask me anymore. "This is good," I said, gesturing around the little house we rented, a ten-minute walk from the Merrimack River. The ratio of books to people was extremely skewed, but there was enough room to breathe. "Maybe it's even better this way."

He said he couldn't promise never to ask me again.

I said I wasn't going anywhere.

Gerry and Mom came out to visit every summer, and we flew there every other year for Christmas or Thanksgiving, alternating with Bobby's family in Boston. It was fairly uncomplicated, and the visits always seemed too short.

I had given Bobby pieces of my life over the years, like little offerings, the most I had to give at any moment. I told him about my dad dying, and how I'd left Kansas and, later, how I'd left Keale, leaving out most of the specifics. He wasn't an incredibly curious guy; what I told him was always enough to satisfy him at that moment.

"I'm just not that complicated," I always said, shrugging.

He professed to love that about me, my sweatshirts and jeans and Converse, the curls that sprang out from my ponytail at the end of the day.

But of course, inside I was as tangled as a root ball.

I went back to school for my master's degree in counseling and ended up in a course about sexual assault. I learned all the things to say to victims, all the things not to say. It was a strangely clinical way to learn about everything I had been feeling for more than a decade, and stranger still to use the techniques to counsel myself.

Before too long, I could recognize them on sight, the young women and sometimes young men who came into my office. What they wanted to talk about was always something else at first—trouble with registration, struggles with a particular course that was holding them back. I answered questions, directed them to the appropriate avenues. And then sometimes I asked, "Was there anything else? I've been told I'm a good listener. In fact—" I would lower my voice, glance to the office door that gaped open a few inches "—I'm actually paid to listen."

Sometimes, it came out right then. The abusive boyfriend

who had left a trail of finger-shaped bruises up both arms. The controlling partner who demanded that she be home by five o'clock sharp, which meant that night classes were out of the question. The suspicious boyfriend or girlfriend who demanded a response to a text within two minutes. Sometimes, it stayed locked inside them, the pain lingering in smiles that never reached their eyes.

I learned a new vocabulary—*survivor*, not *victim*. I had been, for a very long time, a victim. In a way, that was easier. I got to wallow in the details, to feel sorry for myself, to keep my mouth shut. Being a survivor required a different level of courage.

I was at work in 2013 on the day Lauren's father died, a fact I received from the NPR station that played like white noise in the background of my office. According to the report, he'd passed away suddenly—a heart attack, only hours after addressing Congress. For the next week, I was a news junkie, Googling for an obituary and tributes, reading through the entries in an online guest book. "Senator Mabrey worked tirelessly for our country." "Blessings to his family." I watched clips of his funeral on the news and then, later, found a longer video on YouTube, posted by one of his constituents. Michael Mabrey had delivered the eulogy from the pulpit of First Congregational Church in Simsbury, and I watched with my fist in my mouth, remembering how I'd attended church there with Lauren's family, sitting next to her in a pew in my corduroy skirt and scuffed boots. Michael talked about how wonderful his father had been, a provider, an honorable person, someone who fulfilled his promises, someone who cared about the citizens of our country.

"Sounds like a political speech," Bobby commented, listening from the other side of the room with a stack of essays spread out on the table in front of him.

I nodded, not able to speak.

In the audience of mourners, I saw them all lined up in a pew—Mrs. Mabrey with her cropped hair, a black veil partially shielding her face. Kat and Peter and a grown-up Lizzie, gangly, with a brush of acne on her chin. There were two girls with them, twins, their features decidedly Asian. Then Michael and his wife, Rebekah, tall and dark-haired, with their lookalike boys in matching dark suits and ties. And Lauren, always lovely Lauren, with her husband and two girls, sweet in their navy dresses. A united family, a united front.

Imagine if I had said something that night on The Island.

Imagine if I had tried to unravel one of those threads.

A month later, I read that Michael had been appointed to fill his father's congressional seat until the end of the term in 2016. Just like that, the man who had raped me was a senator of the United States of America. Inside, I raged and seethed, forming long internal monologues about political cronyism and nepotism, but the real problem, of course, was that Michael Mabrey was a rapist, and he would never have to pay for what he did to me.

The nightmares had started again after that, the ones where he came up behind me. The location kept changing, though— sometimes it was in the parking lot of the grocery store, other times I heard footsteps behind me in a deserted stairwell. I carried my pepper spray like a talisman; I took a one-unit self-defense course on campus so many times that I was asked if I was available to coteach in the future.

Maybe now would be a good time, Miriam had written me when Michael Mabrey took office. She was retired by then, and the postcards she sent me were from places so exotic I could hardly imagine them. This one was from Bali, where she said she wouldn't mind staying for the rest of her life, wrapped in a sarong.

But I'd held on to my secret longer; I'd been waiting and waiting for the girl I was to catch up with the woman I'd become, for the two sides of me to become one brave and whole person.

OCTOBER 17, 2016

LAUREN

In theory, the drive to Holmes House should have taken only half an hour from downtown Hartford, but I got caught in a snarl of traffic leaving the city, and the highway in front of me became a sea of red taillights. After the press conference, Megan had been hustled off the stage before I could talk to her, but her words rang in my head as I drove, my jaw set.

On the night of July 3, 2002, Michael Mabrey came up behind me...

He forced me off the path and into the gazebo, where he held me down and raped me.

It had been so easy, so uncomplicated and undemanding, to believe that it was consensual sex. It was easier to be offended and angry than horrified, and easier to place blame wrongly than deal with the fallout from assigning it correctly.

I didn't think I could come forward. Who would have believed me? Not even her best friend.

It took me fourteen years to do it, and the truth is, I might never have done it without the bravery of Anna Kovics. But enough is enough. Now it's time to hold Michael Mabrey accountable for what he's done.

Traffic eased, and I pressed harder on the gas. Megan had told the truth, at the cost of her privacy, at the cost of her reputation. It was time for me to be just as brave.

I half expected to find Michael's navy BMW in front of Holmes House, but the driveway was empty. I looked up at Mom's bedroom window on the second floor as if the curtain was pulled back and her pale face was waiting to encounter mine.

Hildy answered the door, covering her surprise well. She'd always seemed ageless, but today her movements seemed slow and stiff. Had she been watching the press conference? She gestured for me to stay in the foyer, as if I hadn't grown up in this house, as if I weren't somehow a member of the family. "I believe your mother is resting this morning. Would you like me to check in on her for you?"

"I'll check for myself, if that's okay," I said, sidestepping Hildy before she could stop me. I took the steps of the giant curved staircase two at a time and burst into the master suite without knocking.

Mom was on her bed, propped into a sitting position by a half-dozen pillows. She'd given up on the wigs with her new diagnosis, and her eyebrows hadn't been applied for the day. The face she turned to me was naked and unformed as a child's. She held a remote control in her hand, and I followed her gaze to see Megan's face on the screen.

"You knew," I said, abandoning the preamble. "You knew what happened that night. You've known it all along."

Mom didn't deny this. Until then, I didn't realize that I'd been hoping for at least a shred of the usual pretense that held things together for our family. Instead, she cleared her throat. "It's always been about family, Lauren. That was the bigger picture I couldn't get you to see."

"The bigger picture," I repeated.

"You were always living in the moment. You could never see past the end of your own nose."

"Were there others? Interns, girlfriends—" I remembered what Brady had told me about the girl at Reardon, and then with shocking clarity, I remembered MK at the end of our stay in DC, the black eye, the gouge of a fingernail on his cheekbone. What was her name again? Sophia? Sophie?

Mom raised a weak hand, which settled back onto her bedding. "So naive," she continued, as if I hadn't spoken. "What it's taken to hold this family together over the years…"

I remembered the baggie of pot that had been found in my backpack, and the way I'd walked away. Had she done that for MK, too, smoothing over the complaints by producing a checkbook, time and again, girl after girl? My laugh was brittle. "Good thing the Holmeses made a fortune in steel, right?" And then, knowing in my marrow that it was true, I added, "Megan won't take any of your money. That's the problem, isn't it? You finally met someone who can't be bought."

Mom's eyes were hard, the lids narrowed. "Why are you here?"

"Because I'm done," I said. Once the words were out, my body felt lighter, like I'd shed an invisible weight. I *was* done, no matter what came next—more accusations, an investigation, a trial. Fourteen years ago, I'd chosen the wrong side.

How much of what happened had been my responsibility? What might I have seen coming? What if I hadn't stayed on the beach when I saw Megan leaving, winding her way through the trees and back to the house? What if I'd listened to her afterward, up in my bedroom, when she sat hugging her knees? I wasn't sure how Mom rationalized her actions, but I was going to have to face mine.

"You're done," Mom repeated, the scorn rising from her

body. She took a deep breath, no doubt ready to plunge into all the ways that was inadvisable, all the ways I would come to regret my separation from the Mabreys.

But this time, I didn't give her the chance. I was out the door, nearly knocking over Hildy in the hallway, and down the steps, and then gunning the engine down the driveway. I was miles down the road before my heart settled back into a normal rhythm.

It had taken me too long, but I was finally going to be free.

EPILOGUE
FEBRUARY 2017
MEGAN

In just a few months, everything changed.

After I came forward, another girl did, too—Lindsey Anderson, twenty-two, a senior at Eastern Connecticut State University who had interviewed Michael for a project on public policy. After dinner with some members of his staff, he offered her a ride to the train station, but instead of dropping her off, he'd reached his hand up her skirt. She fought him off, but at the time, she didn't dare to come forward. "I thought it would look like I wanted it," she said later on an interview on CNN. She wasn't emotional like me; she was matter-of-fact and tough as anything. "I got into his car willingly. I put myself in that position," she said. "But he needs to pay for what he did." There were others, I knew, watching silently with their fists over their mouths, but between Anna and Lindsey and me, it was enough.

Michael Mabrey didn't just withdraw from the race—he resigned his position immediately. There was a statement about seeking counseling and spending time with his family; not an admission, but not *not* an admission, either, as Bobby pointed out. Lindsey had followed through with her threat to press charges, and Michael was awaiting a trial that promised to be delayed with dozens of motions.

Online, he was routinely vilified, his smug expression the fodder for a meme. There were some who believed he was the victim, though, helpless in the face of V-neck sweaters and hems that ended above the knee. There were rules for victims, and those were impossible to shed. I followed the story for a few days before deciding I would be a happier person if never searched for his name again.

All in all, the scandal was only a blip on the national radar. There was a new president and a new congress, and half the country wasn't speaking to the other half, and no one seemed sure what to believe anymore. For all but a few of us, Michael Mabrey was easily forgotten.

Lauren and I had emailed a few times after the press conference, and we agreed to meet for coffee in Norwood, the midpoint of northern Massachusetts and southern Rhode Island, as far as Google Maps was concerned. What with the light traffic of a Saturday and the fact that in my nervousness I'd budgeted way too much time, I was the first to arrive. I staked out a seat near a window looking out onto the street, and from there I caught sight of Lauren behind the wheel of a gray SUV, circling the block twice before pulling into an empty spot, ten minutes late. Maybe she was having second thoughts, too.

On the sidewalk she spotted me through the window and stopped, then gave a little wave of recognition. It was so strange to see her, even though we'd arranged the meeting, and there was nothing unexpected about her presence. In the years since I'd left Keale, I'd had visions of us bumping into each other at a shopping mall or a movie theater, the sort of chance meeting that would unnerve us at the moment and potentially jolt us back into each other's lives. Now we said polite hellos, awkward as two Craigslist strangers. Lauren shrugged out of her coat, and we went to the counter, where she ordered a complicated drink that took a small army of baristas a comically long time to make. I ordered the house blend, one cream and one sugar. And then we were finally sitting across from each other, calmly sipping our coffee, and the entire thing seemed too contrived. The moment stretched to its breaking point, and we both spoke at the same time.

"I'm so glad that—"

"Thank you for—"

We laughed.

"You first," I insisted.

"I'm so glad that you sent me that email. I know that it must have been—well, no. I'm not going to claim that I know anything about what you've been feeling. I'm just glad you sent me that email." She lifted the mug and took a small sip, a thin ridge of foam lingering on her upper lip. I fought the urge to do something—toss her a napkin, the way that I would have if we were eating a meal in the Commons, or at least lick my own lip to mirror what needed to be done. But we weren't those girls anymore, and I did nothing.

I said, "And I'm glad you came to the press conference. That was brave. If the roles were reversed, I don't know if I could have done it."

"Yes, you do," Lauren said. "You were always more brave than I was." Her eyes had gone bluer than normal, and I saw that she was fighting tears. "There's no way that my saying sorry at this point will mean anything. But I am sorry. Every day I think about what I said to you that night, and I wish I could go back. I wish I could change so many things."

She was right. An apology couldn't erase what had happened, and more apologies wouldn't make up for the deficit.

But there was no point in putting tally marks in columns anymore, calculating who owed whom and how much. Lauren hadn't been the one to attack me; that was an apology that would never come. All I could say, fighting the lump in my own throat, was a whispered thank-you.

She played with a napkin, crumbling it in her hand. "How are you doing? Since...everything."

I smiled. "Better." My colleagues had been fantastic; I received the occasional handwritten notes from students saying I had given them courage. In many ways, coming forward had been like opening up a part of me that had been off-limits for years—Bobby and I were closer, my mom and I now talked several times a week. I'd driven back to Scofield to visit Miriam on a long weekend, and we'd talked and cried and drunk wine and laughed. I had so many things to say, not only the sad stories, but the happy ones, too, the memories that had been accidentally boxed up together. I took her advice to see a counselor, finally, and the nightmares were less frequent—still there, but now they served as a reminder of what had been, and who I had been, and what I'd survived.

I turned the question to Lauren, worrying my own napkin to shreds. "How are you doing? I can't imagine, with your family..."

"Yeah, well..." Lauren's smile was flat, the corners turned down. "I only know what you know. Rebekah took the boys to live with her parents in New York. From what I understand, my brother is staying at Holmes House now. I—" She stopped, considered her words, and finished, "I've had to let them go."

I touched her hand, just for a second, a fleeting gesture. Once she'd leaned across the table and kissed me on the mouth just to make a point. But now her hand, with its chewed cuticles and thin silver wedding band, wasn't familiar to me in any way. I wouldn't have recognized it in a lineup of hands, wouldn't have known hers from my next door neighbor's.

"I need to apologize for something, too," I admitted. "When we met—I don't know why anymore, but I think it had something to do with insecurity and a whole lot of other bullshit—I told you some lies."

Lauren's face was a mask. The bit of white foam had dried on her upper lip, like a toothpaste stain.

"I exaggerated certain things—like how poor my family was, and how many boyfriends I'd had. It all seems like excuses now, I know. But I wanted to be someone else, someone different from the boring girl I really was. I thought somehow it would make me..." I thought about saying *cool*, but the word seemed so lame, inadequate to everything I'd felt about myself then.

"Cool?" Lauren suggested.

I laughed. "Yeah. But it was stupid. It was wrong."

"I have a confession, too," she said. "Brady had a conference in Kansas City a few years ago, and I flew out there with him. One day when he had meetings, I rented a car and drove to Woodstock."

I gaped at her. "Seriously?"

"I wanted to see where you were from. And—I don't know—I thought maybe you'd gone back there, after that summer. Anyway, I did some digging online, and I went to your old address. It wasn't in a trailer park like you said. It was just this little yellow house."

I closed my eyes. "And it wasn't on a dirt road. And it didn't have a giant satellite dish in the front yard."

"Or a chain-link fence," Lauren added. "You know what, actually? It was kind of a cute town. I went to the diner where you used to work and ordered a piece of pie."

"I hope it was the apple."

She smiled. "What else?"

I thought about all the implications of my lies, the outward ripple effects of tossing a stone into a pond. In so many ways, I'd hurt myself—I'd made myself a person who couldn't be believed. "You must have hated me. You must have thought you never knew me at all."

"Maybe a little bit. But then, I made my mistakes, too," she pointed out.

I sat back. "What ever happened to Joe Natolo?"

She shook her head. "He moved to Michigan, I think. He wasn't a bad guy, but practically speaking..."

I finished her thought. "It wouldn't have worked."

"I wonder if he still lives over someone's garage," she mused.

"I wonder if he still picks up girls at bus stops. Or art galleries."

For the first time, Lauren's smile looked like the old Lauren's smile. "Touché."

I took a fresh napkin from the dispenser and leaned across the table to wipe the last trace of foam from her lip.

It felt good to laugh. After a while, we refilled our coffees and split a scone the size of my hand. I asked about her husband and kids, and she asked about Bobby. I told her that we'd recently adopted a cat from an animal shelter, a tiny, scruffy, fierce thing that had already shredded one of our lampshades. A cat wasn't a ring, but it was its own kind of promise. I asked about her photography, and she shrugged.

"I loved it, but...I don't know. Some things you just move on from."

"Are you kidding? I figured you'd have your own studio by now, or some kind of fancy business where you charged thousands of dollars for portrait sittings."

She laughed. "I wasn't that good."

"Yeah, you were. You were really talented. Still are, I bet."

"Well...maybe someday, when the girls are older..."

"Definitely," I said. "You should."

She drained the last of her coffee. "I have about a million pictures of you in some boxes in my attic. Maybe I'll send them to you. Or I could bring them for next time."

"Yeah," I agreed. *Next time.* "That would be nice."

When it was time to say goodbye, we reached for each other awkwardly, our shoulders bumping, our arms unsure.

I told Lauren that I needed to use the bathroom before I got back on the road, but for a long moment, I stood at the window, watching her get into her car, adjust the sun visor, reverse onto the street and head out, back to her other life, the one that didn't intersect in any way with mine.

A lump rose suddenly in my throat, and I swallowed it down.

I didn't know if Lauren and I would ever see each other again, although I'd learned that just about anything was possible in life. Things were always changing and always moving on, and who we were at one moment wasn't necessarily the person we would be forever.

But at least we were being our true selves—no matter how messy and imperfect and complex.

And that had to be a good thing.

★ ★ ★ ★ ★

AUTHOR'S NOTE

I took some liberties with locations in this book. There is no Woodstock, Kansas, for example—although hat tip to Nancy Patrino Russo for suggesting the name. (At least there isn't a town by that name anymore; it's now listed as one of Kansas's ghost towns, with the post office closing in the 1800s.) There's no Scofield, Connecticut, and no Keale College, either, although there are towns like Scofield and schools like Keale throughout the United States. And if you travel to Yarmouth, Maine, you'll find lots of picturesque coastal vistas, including some of the thousands of islands off the state's shore, but Codshead Island exists only in this book.

ACKNOWLEDGMENTS

My mother always described each of her children as coming into the world in different (and sometimes very dramatic) ways. I have very little experience with children, but I can vouch for the fact that this is how writers feel about their books.

For the most part, I kept my head down when I was writing *Here We Lie*, holding the subject matter close and deflecting questions until it was well on its way. Sometimes, I've learned, when you set out to write one book, another idea keeps demanding to be heard. That happened with this story, which underwent various iterations in my mind and on paper before becoming the book you are holding in your hands. *Here We Lie* is a small part of a much larger conversation, and I'm humbled to submit my piece.

And just like raising a child (last time I'll use that analogy, I promise), it took a small village to bring this book to life. The team at Park Row Books deserves my gratitude, especially Michelle Meade for her support and my editor, Liz Stein, for her wise (and so patient!) eye. Quinn Banting designed this amazing cover, and Heather Martin curbed my obsession with hyphens. I'm also grateful to those in marketing and publicity, especially Emer Flounders, who work tirelessly to promote authors and their books. Thanks, too, to the good people at Trident Media Group: Melissa Flashman believed in this book from day one, and Sarah Phair helped me cross the finish line.

I'm indebted to the Go Deep writers, especially Shanyn Vitti Avila, Yvonne Sanchez, Debbie Soro and Tim Buchanan, among others. It does my heart good to listen, share and laugh with you.

Beth Slattery and Kelly Jones selflessly read drafts of this novel and provided much-needed nudges in the right direction. Thanks also to Leah Dashe, Beth Boon and Sara Viss for wise insight and hand-holding. For his videography skills and general friendship, I'm grateful to Rob Brittain, who may or may not have moved out of state just to avoid me randomly showing up on his doorstep. For general listening and commiseration, thanks to the trivia crew at P. Wexford's and the Del Monte Avenue Feature Film Freaks.

Every day, my students at the University of California, Merced, challenge me and make me a better teacher and human being. And—dare I say it?—they keep me young. Writing this book made me reminisce about my own experiences at Dordt College—so naive! So hopeful! I'm grateful to the roommates I had along the way: Sarah Bliss Bakker, Sarah Mosser, Stephanie Brown, Charity Lopez Heerema, Jodie Zwart, Jolene Van Dyke, Lisa Smit, Heidi Bakker and Melissa Phaneuf Lucania. We're pretty much scattered around North America at this point, but I'd give anything to have us all together again.

And thank you, always, to my dear EGs. This last year—and the writing of this book—has cemented in me the belief in friendship and in each other. I'm a better person in every way for knowing all of you—Cameron Burton, Alisha Wilks-Vasche, Jenna Valponi, Whitney Fanjul, Laura Ochoa-Wilbur, Nichole Meyer, Amie Carter, Michelle Charpentier and Mary Swier.

Much love and appreciation goes to my Treick and De-Board relations near and far. Three cheers for sisters and sisters-in-law—Debbie Miller, Beth Boon, Sara Viss, Heather DeBoard-Ayala and Christina DeBoard Young.

There are many others who I'm probably forgetting—it's known around these parts as *book brain*—but with all my heart, I need to thank Will DeBoard. He always believes in me, even when I don't believe in myself. Best, he makes me laugh—something I might forget to do otherwise.

ABOUT THE AUTHOR

Paula Treick DeBoard is the author of *The Mourning Hours*, *The Fragile World* and *The Drowning Girls*. She is a lecturer in writing at the University of California, Merced, and lives in Northern California with her husband, Will, and their four-legged brood.

HERE
WE
LIE

PAULA TREICK DeBOARD

Reader's Guide

PARK
ROW
BOOKS

1. In the beginning of the book, Megan finds herself in an agonizing situation with her father, who is suffering with the advanced stages of mesothelioma. Why does she agree to do what she does? How do you feel about her decision? Is it understandable under the circumstances?

2. At one point in the book, Lauren compares the way her mother talks about Mabreys to the Mafia family in *The Godfather*. What drives the Mabreys? Are they right in assuming that their wealth makes them a target? Does their behavior seem consistent with that of other powerful families?

3. Megan tells Lauren a series of lies about her childhood and upbringing when they first meet. Why do you think she does this? What is she hoping to accomplish, and does she succeed? In what ways do Megan's lies come back to haunt her? Is there such a thing as a harmless lie?

4. After the incident on Megan's last night on The Island, why doesn't she immediately tell Lauren the truth about what happened to her? Do you agree with her decision

not to come forward to authorities? Why does she leave The Island, and what prompts her decision not to return to Keale at the end of the summer?

5. This book deals with a fictional situation that unfortunately is all too real for many women who experience sexual assault. Do we hold our famous figures (politicians, celebrities, etc.) to a different standard when it comes to these types of crimes? Are Megan's feelings of powerlessness understandable?

6. Megan observes that society prefers its victims a certain way—innocent, sympathetic, uncomplicated. Do you think these observations are true? If so, where are these beliefs learned? How can they be challenged? What might encourage more women to come forward in these types of situations?

7. After everything that has happened between the two, do you think Megan and Lauren can ever resume a friendship, or move forward with a new, changed relationship? How difficult is it to forgive a friend who has lied or wronged you, and to trust that person again?

The novel deals with female friendship, sexual assault and political scandal. Why did you decide to bring these three elements together to form the narrative? What was your inspiration for this story?

I've learned that with most of the things I write, the end product isn't what I initially envisioned. Somewhere over the course of writing the first draft of this book and letting the characters really speak to me, the story that I planned changed. I initially envisioned these two very different girls as college roommates driven apart and reunited years later, but the idea of a sexually charged political scandal only came to me later. I'm an avid news watcher and an obsessive news reader, and some of what I was watching and reading sneaked into my story as I was going. The more I wrote about Lauren and Megan, the more some of this story line felt natural and even necessary for me to write.

The relationship between Megan and Lauren is complicated and intense. They love each other but they also get frustrated, jealous and angry with each other. Can you speak to their dynamics? Did you draw on your own female friendships?

I've dedicated this book to my sisters and my female friends, who have blessed my life in immeasurable ways. As I grow older, I value these relationships more than ever, which is not to say that friendship can't be full of complexities. Megan and Lauren are young, and due to the events of the book, their relationship doesn't get the chance to grow and change, and they don't get to experience each other at different stages of life. Thankfully, my friends and I are over the drama stages— mostly we cheer each other on and comfort each other when things don't go well, and find new ways to make each other laugh.

Here We Lie is told in alternating first-person perspectives and moves between the past and present. Why did you choose to narrate the story this way?

I thought it was very important for each of the main characters to have a voice in the story. I liked that Megan and Lauren came from such different backgrounds and as a result saw the world in such different ways. In my early drafts, I focused on the years they were in college, and later it was fun to craft their lives fourteen years down the road. They did get to have a mini college reunion, only not under the best of circumstances. I wanted the time gap to represent the ways that our words and actions have consequences, sometimes resulting in years of hurt and resentment.

The book is set in a private all-girls college in New England. Why did you choose to do this? Have you personally experienced this type of setting? What did you draw upon to create this world?

I attended a private liberal arts school in Iowa—not an all-girls school, but one that at times did feel secluded from the rest of the world. Keale is mostly a product of my imagination, but it's an imagination formed by reading and watching and listening, and I hope the result is a place that feels authentic.

It wasn't until I was in college, on my own and more than a thousand miles from my family, that I really began to think for myself and learn who I was and what I was capable of doing. I wanted Megan and Lauren to have these realizations, too, although they came to them in somewhat different and more challenging ways. I can also vouch for the fact that the friends you meet in college can be your friends for life, even when you live in different countries and communicate via social media. That's how it is with my good friend Sarah. We went "potluck" as roommates our freshman year, lived together for four years without managing to kill each other and still keep in touch.

Lauren feels like an outsider in her family and is deeply against following the traditional Mabrey path. What did you seek to explore through Lauren's attitude and disregard for her family's ideals and values?

In my mind, Lauren just wanted a "regular" family. Most of the time in this book, she's blind to the privileges that come with wealth and connections, and she just wishes she could have a life where she doesn't have to live up to the expectations of others. It might not be easy to have sympathy for a character like Lauren when there are so many people struggling against very real challenges, but she represents what it's like to grow up in a politically charged pressure cooker. Ultimately, she's rejecting not just her family but being inauthentic; ironically, that's part of what draws her to people like Megan and Joe.

It's revealed early in the story that Megan feels she is responsible for helping her father die, and this weighs heavily on her mind. Where did this idea come from? Do you know anyone who has had to live with such a secret?

I've known many family members and friends whose lives have been affected by cancer, and I struggle with the idea of a medical system that prolongs life beyond what might be natural and at great cost to patients and their loved ones.

While I was writing the first chapter about Megan and her father, I found myself wrapped up in their situation. Megan wrestles with a terrible sort of moral complexity there, and ultimately, that's a burden that stays with her over the years. I haven't experienced a situation like this myself, and don't know of others who have—but I do know that we all carry secrets and burdens, and those do have a way of sticking with us and shaping the people we become.